MASTER

EVERNIGHT PUBLISHING ®

www.evernightpublishing.com

Copyright© 2021

Sam Crescent

Editor: Karyn White

Cover Art: Sour Cherry Designs

Jacket Design: Jay Aheer

ISBN: 978-0-3695-0310-7

MASTER

DEDICATION

To all of my amazing readers for coming on this journey with me, and for their constant support and love for The Skulls and Chaos Bleeds. Writing this series gives me immense pleasure, and even though I never know what to expect, I find each new book a challenge in itself.

Thank you to Karyn White for her constant patience, and her love/ hate relationship with each character. Also, a big thank you to Evernight Publishing, and Stacey Adderley for giving The Skulls and Chaos Bleeds a home. Without every single one of you, I wouldn't be writing this dedication.

Thank you all so, so much.

Chaos Bleeds, 8

Sam Crescent

Copyright © 2016

Prologue

Piston County

Spider couldn't open his eyes. He was so damn tired, and he was in pain. He hated pain, unless he was the one inflicting it.

Paris!

Celia!

Fuck, he'd taken them. Master had taken them, and someone called Sir. What the fuck was going on? He didn't know what to believe anymore, or what to make sense of. He was all over the place, and he didn't know what was right or wrong.

They had taken them.

Opening his eyes, he groaned at the bright light.

"Shit, he's coming, too."

Was that Devil?

Where the fuck was he?

He should be helping Celia and Paris. Someone

had to help them. Master was going to kill them. He couldn't live with himself if anything happened to them.

Spider couldn't die. His mission was to stay alive. Death was not an option, not today. Opening his eyes, he became aware of the pain once again, and the need to fight. He had to fight. Sitting around on his ass was not what he had in mind for the rest of the day.

Get up.

Get the fuck up.

"Spider, can you hear me?"

Everything came to life, and he gasped, choking on something lodged down his throat.

He couldn't breathe.

Fuck, the pain.

Grasping the tube down his throat, he started to tug, and suddenly nurses and doctors were around him.

I need to live. Got to live. Got to save Paris and her sister.

"If he fucking dies, I'm coming for all of you," Devil said.

Spider took note of the hospital room, his brothers, and his brother's old ladies. Fuck, he was tired. He needed to get out of here. This was wasting time. The longer Master had them, the worse it was going to be.

"Fuck, Spider, calm down," Butler said.

He recognized all of his brothers, but he couldn't speak. The nurses pinned him down as they took the tube from his throat. The moment he could breathe, he gasped out.

"Gotta go."

His voice was hoarse, and he tried to move. Everything fucking hurt!

"We can't let you leave."

"No, I've got to go. He needs to know I'm alive."

"Spider, it's all good, we're here," Devil said.

"He's taken them." Tears filled his eyes, and it only served to make Spider angry. Never in his life had he ever cried in front of his Chaos Bleeds brothers. Crying wasn't something he did. "I've got to save them. He took them because of us."

"Get out!" Devil issued the order.

"This is my hos—"

"I'm the one paying for the fucking treatment. Get out," Devil said.

Spider held his chest, and waited as the nurses and doctor left the room. Every second counted, and he didn't know how long he'd been out of it.

"What the fuck is going on?"

"Master and Sir, they've taken them. They've taken Paris and Celia, and I've got to win them back."

"How?" Devil asked.

Spider winced, becoming aware of the pain in his shoulder and in his thigh. Why hadn't he put up more of a fight? Fuck, he was in a lot of pain.

"I've got to play his game."

"This is fucking horseshit," Pussy said. "We don't jump to someone else's tune. It's not who we are."

"He's going to kill them. Celia, she's not like us or Paris. She's sick, and has the mental capacity of a child, Devil. I promised Paris I'd help her, that I'd look after her. I can't fail."

"What game?" Devil asked.

"I have to stay alive. I have to keep on breathing."

"You died."

Spider shook his head. "I'm alive right now."

"According to the ambulance crew, they had to shock your heart. It stopped."

"I don't care, Devil. I'm alive, and we need to make them safe. Please. I have never begged for anything in my life. I'm begging now. My loyalty to the club has always been absolute."

"I'm not questioning your loyalty."

"Please, I can't live without her." Spider didn't know what he felt for Paris, only that he cared about her. "They're going to get hurt if we don't save them."

"We've got to call in The Skulls," Devil said. "We can't hold it off any longer."

"Do it. We need to end this fucker once and for all."

****

Paris tried not to show how damn scared she was. Being left alone to care for her sister, stripping her clothes off, even working for the biker club, Chaos Bleeds had not been as scary as this. She'd gladly get naked for a roomful of men rather than be with this … man.

"I have to say there is something beautiful about a woman strung up, at my mercy," Master said. "You know your sister has gone back to your friends. The boyfriend in the biker club. It's a pity he actually lived. I was going to have so much fun hurting her. I wonder if she'd scream, or if she would be too damn stupid to know I was hurting her. It'd make for a great scientific study."

Paris closed her eyes, trying not to be afraid as he spoke about Celia like that. This man was a monster. There was nothing good about him, nor was there anything good about the man who worked for him. Both of them were vile and needed to be put down.

"I thought you'd be a lot more talkative. We're alone, and your sister is safe."

"You took her," Paris said.

"Ah, she speaks now."

"You took her, and you're the reason my sister

stopped being safe. You." Her arms hurt from being in the same position for so long. She was tired, fed up, and part of her wanted to give up. She couldn't though, not yet. Celia needed her.

"I wonder how much Spider is willing to do to get you. Do you think he'll take care of your sister? Personally, I'd put her out of her misery, and kill the bitch."

"Stop." His cruelty knew no bounds.

"No, I don't want to stop." He climbed out of his chair and moved toward her. She couldn't help but tense up. Every time he came near her, he always caused her pain. She didn't want any more pain. He gripped the back of her head, and tugged until she followed his hand, crying out. He held onto her jaw. "No whore tells me what to do. You see, Paris, you may be pretty to look at, but I'm the one who calls the shots, not you. Your role is to be quiet, and to give what a man needs. You're nothing more than a bunch of holes for me to use. Your mouth, your cunt, your ass, are only good for one thing and that is being filled." She gasped as he tugged her hair so tight she thought he was pulling it out of its socket. "Your ass is mine. I wonder how much I can break you before I give you back to Spider."

The moment Paris started screaming, she thought she'd never stop. Master was determined to ruin her, and she truly believed he'd succeed.

Chapter One

Right after Gash

"What the fuck?" Stink looked around the chaos of The Skulls compound, and he couldn't believe what he was seeing. There was blood, carnage, and death around him.

"Fuck, fuck," Adam said, holding onto his leg.

Tugging his belt, Stink quickly wrapped it around the top of Adam's leg. "Keep pressure on it."

"As if I wasn't fucking doing that already, bastard. Fuck! Andrew got this one down."

Stink tried to cut out the child's screams, focusing on Adam before he moved onto the next one. "You good?"

"Yeah, help everyone else."

"I've called medics," Pussy said.

He looked toward the Chaos Bleeds member, and saw Pussy's old lady, Sasha in his lap, out cold. Blood was coming from her head, and her dog was whining.

"She can't fucking die on me."

Rushing toward him, Stink placed his fingers against her neck, feeling the faint cold. "What else happened?"

Pussy held onto her shoulder, and blood soaked between his fingers. "She got shot, and I fucking reacted, and I didn't cushion her fucking head. She hit the ground hard."

"Keep her still, Pussy. The ambulance is on the way."

Moving on, Stink's heart was racing as he looked around the main compound. He couldn't see Sandy anywhere. The moment the bullets started firing, he'd taken Eva down as he'd been near Tiny's old lady at the time. Where was *his* woman? He couldn't lose her, not now. They were just starting to make a go of it.

"Simon!" Devil's scream of his son's name had Stink turning around to witness the leader of the Chaos Bleeds lifting his son in his arms. There was no sign of life in Simon's body, and right next to him, Tiny lifted Tabitha.

"No!" Eva ran toward her daughter, and Stink watched helplessly as two of the children were held tightly against their parents. Neither Simon nor Tabitha showed signs of life.

"I'm not going to wait for a fucking ambulance," Tiny said, rushing toward the car with Devil following close behind.

Lexie and Eva were both waving at them, sobbing. Miles wrapped his arms around his mother, as Lexie's kids did the same with her. Everywhere he looked, there was pain, fear, violence.

"Ah!" Angel screamed, panting, trying to close her legs. Lash was by her side. "I can't hold on, Lash."

Suddenly, Stink took a deep breath as he caught sight of Sandy lowering herself before Angel. "We've got this, Angel. We've done it with Anthony, and we're going to keep on practicing, aren't we?" She took some deep breaths, and Stink turned away.

His woman wouldn't appreciate being taken from her work, and there was so much to do.

Twisted grunted as he lifted up Judi. Ripper got to his feet, rushing toward the house. There were babies inside, and Stink made to follow but stopped as he caught sight of Millie, the toy shop owner who Baker was besotted with.

"I've got to stop the bleeding," she said, sobbing as she did.

Stepping close, Stink saw that Nash was there as

well.

On the floor, covered in blood was Happy, the brother who'd joined them from the Nomads in the hope of settling down. He was a brother who'd not spent all that much time at the clubhouse, but his loyalty had known no bounds.

Baker came forward and hugged Millie, trying to stop her from attending to Happy. No matter what she did, Happy was gone. A bullet to the head had taken him, along with several more to the chest.

"No! I've got to help him." She kept trying, but it was no use.

With no other choice, Baker wrapped his arms around her, and pulled her away using sheer force. Millie screamed and tried to kick out, begging for them to save him.

"He's gone, Millie," Stink said, reaching out and pushing his eyelids down. "He's dead."

Millie ceased her struggles and fell to her knees. Tears fell from her eyes. "What happened?" she asked.

"It's okay," Baker said.

"No, it's not okay."

Getting to his feet, he put a hand on Nash's arm.

"I don't need your support," Nash said.

"What?" Stink asked.

"Sophia was inside. She was safe." Nash looked up at him with tears in his eyes.

"Help! Help!"

Stink looked up toward the broken window Ripper leaned out. "Sophia's been shot! We need some help up here."

He didn't need asking twice and rushed inside at the same time. Charging upstairs, he heard the sound of steps behind him, and he hurried into the nursery, finding Ripper pressing on Sophia's chest.

"She's losing blood, man. I don't know what the fuck to do."

Sophia's eyes were watering, and she was gasping for breath. This was not a situation he could handle. He'd been part of Sandy's many labor classes that she'd given him in case he was alone with one of the pregnant old ladies. Rushing downstairs, and outside, he traded places with Sandy. "You're needed upstairs. Sophia can't breathe. I think you need to relieve the pressure in her lung."

Kneeling down on the floor, he looked at Angel, seeing the pain clearly on her face. She was holding her shit together, and he respected her for that, also considering the fact she was heavily pregnant.

"We okay?"

She nodded. "I'm fine, but it's not okay."

"I know."

"People are dying."

"No, they're not. We're injured, but we're fine," Lash said.

Stink shook his head. "We're not all fine."

"What?"

"Happy that I know of, he's gone. Bullet to the head. Tabitha and Simon are on their way to the hospital. Pussy's old lady, Sasha, she's not waking up. Take a look around, Lash, it's not okay."

Stink didn't know what to say or what to do.

"Go, Lash, your club needs you. They need you now more than ever."

"I'm not leaving you."

"I'm fine. Go!" Angel gave him a look, which had Lash gritting his teeth.

"Anthony." Lash grabbed his son, and held his arms. "You stay with your mother, you hear? Do whatever she needs, and come find me if anything happens."

"Yes, Dad."

"It's okay. Take deep breaths," Stink said, showing her what he meant by deep breaths.

"It hurts."

"I know. The ambulance is coming."

****

Staring around the compound, Lash looked at his fallen brothers, each one a part of The Skulls. Fort Wills was The Skulls' home. There were members of the club elsewhere, in Nomad or different towns, but this was where it all started, where it all began, and now, it looked like it was going to be where they all ended.

Happy was dead. Adam, their only British member, was injured, not to mention everyone else.

Pushing his panic down, Lash allowed the anger that had been dormant inside him for so long start to pull up to the surface. Angel, she calmed the monster within him, and little by little the attacks on his club had been rocking his very core. Andrew—Master, Gash's brother, whatever you wanted to fucking call him—had gone too far.

This was his club, and he was determined to fucking protect it.

In the distance he heard the sirens, and he started to work his way through the crap. Each step he took, his anger built. Picking Adam up, he placed him by his woman, who was nearest the parking lot entrance. She was going on the first ambulance out, along with Pussy and Sasha.

"What the fuck, man? How can you fucking lift me?" Adam asked.

Lash didn't say a word, and kept on moving.

"I can't move her," Pussy said.

"Fine, I've got to help the others. We'll get her

taken care of, Pussy, I promise."

"How can I help?" Killer asked.

"Where are Kelsey and Markus?" Lash asked.

"They're fine. They were in the fucking pantry for more food. They're fine. They're helping Sophia upstairs."

Lash froze. "Sophia?"

"Sandy's with her. She's been hit bad."

Fuck, his brother wouldn't be able to handle anything if something happened to Sophia.

Rushing toward the house, he saw Nash was carrying his woman downstairs with Sandy holding something against her rib cage.

"We need to get to the hospital now," Sandy said.

"Ambulance is outside."

Lash was back, and he put Sophia, Nash, Pussy, and Sasha into one ambulance. In the next went his wife, followed by Adam.

For the next hour, Lash helped his club and Chaos Bleeds sort through the damage that had been left in Master's wake. From the Chaos Bleeds crew, Curse and Mia had both had to go to the hospital. The bullet had grazed Curse's knee and impaled Mia's thigh. Jessica, Snake's old lady, had a gunshot wound to her arm. Phoebe, Vincent's woman, had to go to the hospital as well with her injuries. The ambulance crew kept coming and going. The Chaos Bleeds two prospects, Bob and Wild, were fine.

The Skulls didn't fare much better. Murphy was hurt, and Tate rounded up the kids that weren't injured. She had Anthony, her Simon, Rachel, Miles, Daisy, and Darcy. Sally was hurt, as well as Lacey. Whizz assisted both to the hospital.

Fighter had to go to the hospital, along with Blaine, Zero, and Alex. Sunshine had gone into labor, and had also gone to the hospital.

It was killing Lash to still be at the clubhouse and not with his wife, in the hospital. This was his job, his responsibility, and Angel would be pissed at him if he put her first.

He took hold of his son's hand, and together they walked back inside.

"All the babies are okay," Ripper said. "Judi's helping Kelsey to help them rest."

Lash nodded. "We've got to clean this place up and head to the hospital."

"There's no way we can leave anyone behind. That's our club Prez, Lash, and his son is not going to die today." Ripper talked about Devil, the Prez of the Chaos Bleeds.

"We'll clean up, and round everyone up to head to the hospital." Crouching down, he cupped Anthony's face. "I need you to be a big boy now for me, Anthony."

"I will."

"Help Tate for me before she loses control and starts screaming."

"Everyone has been screaming."

"I know, son, I know." Lash pulled Anthony toward him. He had his mother's beautiful blue eyes. Just looking at him, made him think of the love he possessed for Angel. That love kept him strong. This was his life, and he'd pulled Angel into this life. He had to be stronger than ever before.

Lash watched as Anthony walked across the yard toward Tate. The woman was a crazy bitch, always causing shit, but when the club needed her, she was there without question. Right now, Tate was pulling her shit together and helping with the kids, so he didn't go ordering her around.

Spider came toward him, holding onto his

crutches. "There's a club whore dead behind the bar you'd set up."

"We'll handle it. The cops are going to be here soon."

"It was Master, wasn't it?" Spider asked.

"We all know it was him, but we can't go ratting him out. There's no way we can tell anyone about this shit."

"Did you ever know Gash's brother?"

Lash sighed, turning toward the Chaos Bleeds member. From what Devil had told him, Spider's woman was missing, taken by Master. Her sister was handed back to them, but no word on his woman. They all knew if they didn't get to her soon, her days would be numbered. Master wasn't going to show mercy or kindness.

"I remember Andrew, yes."

"Didn't you have a thought to kill him? Take him out, stop all this bad shit from happening?"

"It was a long time ago. I wasn't even a prospect back then. I was a fucking kid. The club made a mistake in letting Andrew get away, and we're going to solve it."

"How? How are we going to solve it? He's taking us out one by one."

"I know you're hurting—"

"You don't know shit. All the fucking Skulls know to do is sit around twiddling their bastard thumbs."

Lash reacted. Grabbing Spider's jacket, he threw him up against the nearest wall. "You think I'm sitting here twiddling my thumbs? We fucked up years ago letting that monster loose, but no club has a rule of in or dead policy. Andrew didn't make it to be a fucking Skull, he was gone, end of story. You want to start going for blame, you're the one who brought him back to us. This is our problem!"

"Enough," Gash said, coming to stand beside him. "This is what Andrew does. He ruins people. Gets inside their heads and fucks them over without even trying. This is what you want?"

Lash shook his head, followed by Spider. "No."

"Then stop fighting each other. We've got to fight the fucker who put us here," Gash said. "He's fucked us over, I get that, but don't let him win, not now."

"He won today!" Spider said. "Every day that passes and I don't have my woman, he continues to win."

"We're going to get her back."

"When? How much longer?" Spider asked. "I promised I'd protect her, and he's hurting her. This very second he's hurting her, breaking her down until what remains? Nothing."

"You don't know that."

"We all know that!"

Lash waited for Gash to hand him back his crutches before releasing him. Tears were in Spider's eyes. "He's going to be hurting her, every chance he gets. This is what he does. We can't pretend otherwise, so don't try. That's exactly what he's doing. We don't have a clue how to stop him."

"We will," Gash said.

"Until then, Paris is being hurt, and we've got to deal with all the shit he's going to throw at us. People are dying, and we've got to wait?"

"There's nothing else we can do right now. We'll get him, Spider, and you'll be there with all of us, ready to kill the fucker, got me?" Lash asked.

Spider sighed.

It didn't matter how many times they talked, none of them were going to get what they wanted, not today, not tomorrow—there was no limit to the trouble that surrounded them.

****

Sandy was exhausted, and once again the hospital was full of The Skulls and Chaos Bleeds. They really needed to stop doing this, coming to the hospital. It was more of a home than the clubhouse was. She didn't know if she should be happy about that. The hospital had welcomed her back with open arms like always. She'd wanted to take a break from being a doctor, but being with The Skulls, it made it impossible to have a break from saving a life. Being a doctor that took a break was impossible. Every other week they seemed to be in some kind of trouble.

She was already in scrubs with her black hair pulled up into a band. Ever since Lacey had joined the club, she'd brought with her the enjoyment of experimenting with dyeing their hair. Even Angel had changed her hair color, much to Lash's annoyance.

Sophia was stable, and had been operated on to repair the damage to her lung. The bullet had gone through, deflating her lung. Operating on her friends was starting to take its toll. Sophia was her friend. All of the old ladies were her friends. This was so fucking hard, and she didn't want to keep going through it. This was the life she wanted, though. The Skulls were her family, and she would stand by them for the rest of her life.

Rubbing the back of her neck, she made her way into the main waiting room, which was covered with Skulls and Chaos Bleeds members. This had hit the club hard, and she was struggling to hold it together.

Gash was there, and he seemed to have taken the lead for The Skulls. Lash was with his woman, and so was Tiny. Alex was in surgery. Out of the corner of her eye, she spotted Stink getting to his feet. Ripper had also come forward as the guy for Chaos Bleeds.

"Sophia's stable right now. I'm going to go and

check on everyone, and I'll bring you updates."

"Does Lash know?" Gash asked.

"No. I'm going to go and tell him. Everyone is at different places within the hospital. I'm doing my best, but like everything, it takes time." She smiled at each of them, taking a breath, and stepping away. "I'll be back with more information."

She moved toward the door, and Stink stopped her. "How are you doing?"

This was what made it hard for her to turn Stink down. He was always concerned about her. She'd never known a guy be so totally caring about her. Her life had been about being the pussy of the club. She'd fucked many guys in her time, and at nearly forty years old, she truly didn't know if she was settling down kind of woman. Stink never looked at any other woman. She couldn't even be sure if he'd been with another woman since he'd taken her in. He didn't care about the past, and he only ever saw the future. How could she not love a guy like that? Stink was one of a kind. Most of the time he seemed to be overlooked by so many, but that wasn't true.

A few years ago she had stopped being club pussy, but Tiny hadn't kicked her out. She was as much part of the club as anyone else.

Her loyalty had been shown many times over the years, and she loved all of the club. They were her friends. They were her family.

"I'm doing okay." She took another deep breath, trying to prove that she was more than fine.

"You don't have to pretend for me, Sandy. This is me."

"I'm trying not to fall apart right now. Crying won't help."

"I know. I know." He went to hug her, but she

shook her head, taking a step back, holding onto the door. She really couldn't handle it right now as she struggled to hold it all in.

"I can't right now, and if you let me, I'm not going to stop. I've got to stay strong right now, and I won't be strong if you hold me."

Stink nodded. "I'll be here."

She forced a smile, and left him alone, going through the door. Next stop for her was the children's ward. Out of all the places to go the children's ward was the worst. One of the things she hated about being a doctor was death. When it came to children, death was even worse. They'd not had the chance to live, and for Sandy it had always been hard to say goodbye to young patients. Many a night she had gone home in floods of tears, wondering why the hell she'd become a doctor in the first place. Simon and Tabitha, they were two sweet children that hadn't been given the real chance to live. Sally was also there as well. She was still considered a child even though she'd been through her own kind of hell. Sally had been adopted by Lacey and Whizz, who couldn't have any children of their own. Sandy really felt for Lacey. For all of Lacey's faults, there was one thing Sandy couldn't fault her on and that was her ability to mother.

Outside the door, Sandy washed her hands in the anti-bacterial solution, and entered. She nodded at the nurses and staff as she passed them by. No one stopped her.

"The Skulls and Chaos Bleeds kids, where are they?" she asked, stopping at the main desk in the room.

"Over there," the nurse said.

Sandy made her way down the far corridor and saw the large room that was big enough to fit two patients. On one bed lay Simon, on the other, Tabitha.

Eva and Tiny sat by the bed of Tabitha holding her hand. Devil and Lexie were next to Simon. They knew they didn't have to worry about their other babies. It was why being part of The Skulls and Chaos Bleeds was so good. There was always someone willing to help. They were all a family at the core.

"What's going on?" Sandy asked.

They all turned to her.

Tubes were hooked up to both children, and Sandy found herself collapsing against the doorframe. "Fuck!" This was not a sight she ever wanted to see. Simon and Tabitha, they were good kids. Their affection for each other was truly startling, and at times, Sandy found herself wishing she'd had that growing up. Then she'd look toward Stink, and she'd see it in his eyes.

"Simon stood in front of Tabitha, took a bullet, but it went straight through," Devil said.

"They were both hit with the same bullet?" Sandy asked.

"Yeah. Fuck, Tiny, these are our kids. I've got a man who is at the end of his fucking patience. Spider is losing his shit. This shit can't be happening for much longer. Andrew, he's got to go, and we've got to hit him hard. This is just a distraction. He's keeping us busy."

Tiny nodded. "We're going to pay him back. Andrew is going to know what real pain is like."

Sandy entered the room and picked up Simon's chart. She forced herself to keep on going, to keep on moving. The only way they survived was to keep on moving forward. She read through the transcripts seeing that he'd been in surgery to repair the damage the bullet had caused. There was also a note of a concussion, and Simon needed to be checked on every few hours. She did the same to Tabitha, seeing the young girl had the same problem. Staring at the two kids, Sandy wondered what it was that connected them. From when they were kids, they'd gravitated to each other, always by each other's sides whenever they had the chance. Even during the fight between Devil and Tiny, the two kids had found ways of contacting each other. Their determination rivaled most marriages.

Ever since they were babies, there had been this hold that gripped the two. Everyone saw it, but no one understood it. It was just there. Tabitha and Simon were convinced they were going to be together, married, and she'd even heard them both planning it. No matter how many times their parents thought this would go away with age, it never did. If anything, the connection between the two had only gotten stronger. She had to wonder what it would be like for them when they reached their teenage years.

"They're stable," Sandy said, letting out a breath.

"What's going on?" Tiny asked.

"Sophia's stable at the moment, but she got shot, and it pierced her lung."

"How is that possible?" Lexie asked. "She was checking on the kids."

"The bullet hit the window, and got her," Sandy said. "There's, um, there's a lot of our people in the hospital. I'm going to go and check on them. I'll be back soon."

"How is everyone?" Devil asked.

"They're down in the waiting room. It hasn't been a good day today." She did her best to smile, but once again, she couldn't find a reason to. Today was not a good day. "Happy died," she said, looking at Tiny. "We had a lot of loss today."

Before the tears threatened to take over, she left the room and held her stomach as she made her way toward the older section of the children's ward. Standing at the window she saw Sally lying in a bed with Whizz and Lacey on either side of her. Lacey had been injured with a grazed arm, so a few stitches, and she'd been discharged. Sandy knew it wouldn't take Lacey long to be by Sally's side.

"You've got to go see Daisy," Sally said.

"Daisy will be taken care of. She knows we love her," Lacey said.

"She's younger than me. Please, just, for me, go see her," Sally said. "She must be frightened, and I can't stand the thought of her being frightened. Please."

"I'll stay with her," Sandy said, entering the room.

"Are you sure?" Whizz asked.

"I'm sure. Please, Daisy's younger than me. I get it. I'd be with her myself, but I can't leave."

Whizz and Lacey both left the room, and Sally released a sigh.

They turned back at the door. Sally smiled at them, and Sandy took a seat. "What's going on?"

"They're so worried about me, and I'm not used to having someone worry about me. It gets a little overwhelming at times. Kind of scary."

"Don't be scared. They love you. What happened?" Sandy asked.

Sally removed the blanket, showing off her bandaged leg. "Bullet went straight through my thigh, just above my knee. I can't feel it right now. I heard the doctor say that it shattered my knee or something. I don't know, I was a little out of it. I'll have one hell of a scar though. Makes wearing skirts trouble." Sally forced a laugh.

"You look scared. What's up?"

"I heard them talking, and they repaired my knee as best as they can." Sally looked down at her thigh.

"They could take my leg. I mean, I could have imagined the whole thing, but I see the way they looked at me. I don't think I was imagining much."

"What?"

Sandy grabbed the file and read through the damage that had been reported around her knee. Sally kept on talking, and Sandy listened as she read.

"It's bad, isn't it?"

"Sally?"

"Just, please tell me I heard it right. They could take my knee, but it's a last resort, right?"

Sandy sighed. "It's a last resort, but, Sally, you could be in pain for the rest of your life."

"I don't want to lose my leg. Please make sure they don't take it. I like my leg."

"Honey."

Sally shook her head, tears spilling from her eyes. "I can't do this. I can't have no leg, and I can't—I'm not strong enough to survive that!"

"You're strong enough."

"I'm not. I'm really not. I can't do this, Sandy."

Sandy got to her feet and pulled Sally into a hug. Just as she was about to speak, there was a knock on the door, and then Steven entered. "Is this a bad time? I just wanted to check in."

Holding her hand up to stop, Sandy shook her head. "No, it's not a bad time. I've got to go check on the others. Everything will be all right, I promise." She pressed a kiss to Sally's head, and left Steven to deal with that.

Coward!

There was a reason she had never had kids, and one of those reasons was how helpless she had just felt.

Chapter Two

Stink sat in the waiting room chair, sipping his coffee as he listened to Miles read. There was a selection of toys, and all of the kids were sitting in the circle the clubs had created, playing. It was moments like these that Stink wondered why the clubs had gone their separate ways. They had always gotten along beforehand. Then something stupid had been said, by Tiny no less, and everything had fallen apart. He hoped nothing like that happened again. They were much better as friends than as enemies. Stink didn't even want to think about them being enemies.

"I heard you and the good doctor have a thing going on?" Sinner asked. He was a Chaos Bleeds member.

"You heard right."

"She's a hot piece of ass."

"I'm not going to hurt you in front of the kids, or while we're in the hospital, but you continue to talk shit about my girl, and I *will* hurt you." Stink wasn't afraid of a fight. He'd proven himself over the years.

"I heard she was a club whore."

"Again, I won't forget your shit. Be careful."

Sinner held his hands up. "Just thought I'd use this time to talk, seeing as we're going to be here a while."

"Are you an asshole on purpose?"

"Nope, that is my job," Dick said, taking a seat beside him.

"Am I just the unlucky one today?" Stink asked.

"Nope, you're the only one not looking freaked out," Martha said, coming to sit on Dick's knee.

Stink was freaked out, but over the years of being part of The Skulls, he'd come to see that reacting on his feelings never helped anyone. "What's that got to do with anything?"

"Look around you, everyone is freaked," Sinner said. "Even I'm finding it fucking hard. Kids are hurting, our women, and our men are all in pain."

"We're in the safest place for them. Now, I'm listening to Miles read, so I'd appreciate it if you didn't interrupt him."

Stink leaned forward, but Sinner, Dick, and Martha stayed with them. Hours passed until Sandy finally came toward them, and she actually had a chart in front of her.

Gash got to his feet as did Ripper.

"Everyone is doing okay at the moment," she said. "I've got a list of everything that is going on. First, Sunshine gave birth to a little girl. Alex should be waking up soon. He got a bullet to the thigh that they had to remove. The anesthetic should be wearing off soon. He'll be grouchy, but that is his personality, so yay.

"Phoebe is doing okay. Her vitals are good, but she had a bullet to the shoulder. Murphy and Fighter are doing okay. Each had a gunshot wound to the stomach. The damage has been repaired, but they need to be checked to make sure there are no leaks with the repair job."

Tate sighed in relief, bending down to hug her Simon. "Thank God."

Sandy nodded, going back to her list. "Blaine will be out tomorrow after they've ran some tests. The bullet took his ear, but the doctors are hopeful of no permanent damage. Curse is fine, only a few stitches needed. However, Mia lost a lot of blood, and needed a transfusion. She's doing okay but needs to have an eye kept on her."

Each person she spoke about left Stink more

relieved. They had lost a couple of people, but it seemed they were mostly injured.

"Sally," Sandy said, and stopped, licking her lips. He saw how hard this was for her. "She's, um, they may have to amputate from her knee down. The bullet caused too much damage. They have repaired as much as they could in an attempt to keep her leg, but it's not looking good. The risk of infection is too high."

"Fuck," Gash said.

"Yeah, she's not handling that well."

Lacey and Whizz leaned against each other, and he saw Daisy between them. "We'll go to her, take Daisy with us."

Stink watched as Anthony rushed over and hugged Daisy tightly to him.

The Skulls kids were fucking weird.

"Steven is with her now, but you're going to need for her to go through with this."

"What about Simon and Tabitha?" Ripper asked.

"They were both shot and have suffered concussions. We're waiting for them to wake up."

"Sasha? What's going on with her?" Brianna asked.

Once again Sandy looked sick. "She lost a lot of blood, and ... she's not waking up."

"Is she dead?" Death asked.

"No, she's not dead, and she's also not brain dead. Her mind is showing activity, but she should have woken up by now. The doctor who treated her head wound before believes there may be an underlying condition. We're running tests to make sure."

"If anything happens to her, Pussy won't be the same. It'll kill him," Death said.

"Keep an eye on her."

"What about Angel?" Gash asked.

"She's having contractions, and the doctors are trying to ease them without inducing labor." Angel still had another six weeks to go before she gave birth. "That's it for now."

Many of them may not have died, but they had lost a great deal. He couldn't imagine being in Sally's position right now.

Stink moved forward, taking hold of Sandy's hand, and leading her away from all of the questions. She didn't need this now.

He walked into the bathroom, he shut and locked the door.

"Breathe, it's okay. You're okay. It's just us."

"It's not okay. I'm not okay. I can't give them all the answers they need. I can't save them."

"I know. It's not your job, okay? All you have to do is take care of them, help them, that's it. You're not God, nor are you a miracle worker."

Pulling her to him, Stink held her tightly before she finally let go. As a doctor she had the training to keep all the fear and all the panic at bay. Once that was over, only a shell remained, and he was determined to break through that shell she'd created. He was not going to allow Sandy to be forgotten.

"The bullets, Stink, they've hurt our friends, our family. I want to kill him."

"We will."

"Sally's going to lose her leg, and she's going to need to practice with a prosthetic. She's only just getting her life back, and already part of it is being taken away. Tabitha and Simon, what if something goes wrong? Sasha, she's blind, and she's not waking up. They believe there is pressure building on her brain. There's so much that can go wrong, and I can't fix everything."

He pulled away, cupping her face. "Look at me."

Her eyes were full of tears, and seeing them was breaking him apart. "I can't help them."

"You're not God, Sandy. You're not God. You don't control who lives and who dies. You're Sandy. You're a doctor who helps. You're helping."

She nodded.

"No one can do what you can do. You're strong."

Sandy shook her head. "No, I'm not. I'm weak."

Stink slammed his lips down on hers. It was not the appropriate time, and probably not the response she was looking for, but it was all he had. Those moments of the bullets firing had nearly killed him. He hadn't been near Sandy. He'd been near Eva, and so had taken her down just before Tiny reached them.

"I thought I'd lost you," Stink said. "I was scared one of those bullets had taken you away from me." He let his own tears show.

"I'm not good enough for you, Stink."

"You are, and I'm going to prove it to you." He wiped away her tears. "You're one of the strongest women I know."

She forced a laugh. "I'm not. I know a lot of stronger women who have faced a hell of a lot more than I have. I'm not strong at all. I couldn't survive the loss of a child. Angel and Charlotte have been through that. Fuck, Lacey can't even have kids. They're strong women, Stink, not me. I just fuck."

He pressed his hand against her chest. "You have faced more horrors within these four walls than any of The Skulls and Chaos Bleeds combined. You keep your shit together, and you don't fail. That, to me, is strong. You're a strong woman, and together, we're going to help our club, our family to make it whole."

"I want to kill him, Stink. I want to plunge a knife into his cold chest, and watch him bleed. I want him to beg, and only feel pain as I hurt him some more." She'd been staring off somewhere past his shoulder. "I took a vow to do no harm to anyone, and yet I want to murder, and I intend to enjoy it when it happens."

"I'll make sure your vow is never broken." He kissed her lips. Sandy was a good woman. No matter what Andrew did, Sandy wouldn't be able to take his life. There were two clubs, though, that were planning on it. Between the two of them, Andrew was going down. They were together now, fighting against him. They would win. "Are you okay?"

"I'm fine."

"Don't lie to me."

"I'm not going to be fine right away, Stink. You know that better than anyone."

He kissed her temple. "Don't try to hide this from me. The club, we'll get through it together."

"He's not going to stop though. This is just the beginning."

"It's the beginning, and we're going to fight. He caught us unawares, but none of us are going to make that mistake again."

She opened her mouth to speak, and then closed it again. "What?"

"Andrew attacks anyone. Men, women, children, there is no end."

"You're afraid?"

"Aren't you?"

Stink nodded. "I am. Andrew is a deranged bastard, but we've got Gash."

She licked her lips, and shook her head. "Even with him, Gash didn't know this was going to happen. Gash is not deranged. He's vicious, two different things. We don't know what he's doing to do next, and it scares me."

"I'm not going to let anything happen to you."

"I don't care what happens to me. It's everyone else, including you." Sandy stared at his chest, and she ran her hand across the lapel of his leather jacket. "I can't lose you, not now."

"I'll be careful."

"Promise?"

"Yes. I love you, Sandy." He'd been in love with this woman since the first moment he saw her. At the time he'd been enjoying club pussy, and had refused to sleep with her. Sandy had never tried to garner his attention, or his affection, but she'd gotten it without even trying. He loved her. She was part of his life, and he was never going to let her go.

She never told him that she loved him, but he could wait.

Sandy was skittish. Push too hard, and she'd run.

Stink had waited a long time, so a few more months, even years wouldn't matter. He wasn't going anywhere, and neither was she.

****

The words were on the tip of her tongue, yet Sandy couldn't say them. It wasn't because she didn't feel them, because she did. She loved Stink. He'd become her whole world, and she found herself seeking him for comfort. At night, she lay in bed and wondered if he was thinking of her.

Her whole life had been about finding pleasure, not caring where it came from. She never needed sweet words, chocolates, flowers, or a steady relationship. In The Skulls, she'd found friends, loved ones, a family.

Being with Stink the past few years, she had found herself yearning for something she believed at one time she'd never need. She'd witnessed so many relationships fail through cheating or death. Being a doctor, she'd seen many people become inconsolable at the thought of being alone, without their loved one.

Even in The Skulls, she saw the rare kind of love that was only supposed to happen fleetingly, or at least so the good books say. Angel and Lash, their love was so strong, so powerful that it made her envious of what they shared. The moment Angel walked into a room, Lash searched for her. He couldn't go long without touching or kissing her, the slight caresses carrying a huge meaning of his love as he did. It was hard not to wish for something like that.

She could go on with each couple, even Tate and Murphy. That woman was a first class bitch, and yet she'd seen the way Tate melted when Murphy was near. For the right man, Tate's bitchiness ceased to exist. Sandy hadn't believed it, and even questioned Murphy. He'd simply told her that no one knew the real Tate, the one he loved.

Leaving the bathroom, Sandy felt better, whole, like she could handle anything that was thrown at her.

"Where was Celia?" Sandy asked.

The young sister had been put in their care after Andrew dumped her. Paris, the older sister, and the one Spider was trying to hunt, was still missing. Celia wasn't a problem. She missed her sister, but she'd accepted them and their care.

"She's back home with Millie and Baker. They're taking care of her, and keeping an eye on the clubhouse."

"I'm going to go do my rounds. I'll see you back at the clubhouse?"

"None of us are going to leave until Devil and Lash come down. We've got to regroup, and be strong."

"We can't leave them in the hospital alone," Sandy said. "It's too easy to get to them."

"Exactly. The Skulls and Chaos Bleeds will be

here until everyone has been discharged. Including me, I'll be here for you."

She nodded. "Thank you."

"Go on. Go save some lives."

Sandy turned, and left the two clubs to wait as she made her way back into the hospital. The first ward she got to was the emergency room where Jessica, Snake's old lady, was bandaged up.

"How are you doing?"

"Wishing I could fucking help. I didn't put myself through school and train to be a nurse to get fucking shot and be useless. I should be helping, only now, I can't help. Best I can do is assist, and with the medication they've given me, I can't do that."

"You sound a little pissed," Sandy said.

"I *am* pissed. I've been shot. I'm not exactly happy about that." Jessica blew out a breath. "I'm so fucking angry right now. My arm hurts, and I'm going to have to have some kind of shot. I'm pissed off. Not to mention that some fucker thinks he can just shoot at us."

Sandy chuckled. "You're fighting, then?"

"Aren't you? I know I am. I'm not going to take shit from anyone. Especially not a fucked up guy, and not from *him*."

Jessica stared down at her arm, and Sandy saw the pain in her eyes.

"I completely forgot. You were taken by Andrew, Master."

"Yeah, I was taken by him, and he left me there to die. He's now shot at me. It may not have been him pulling the trigger, but it was him that ordered the kill. I want him dead. I don't want any other woman to go through what I've gone through."

"He has a woman right now."

"I know. We've got to get her back. He tries to

break minds, and in doing that, he breaks bodies, and tries to shatter our souls. No one can survive something like that. No one."

"Jessica!" Snake rounded the curtain and grabbed her. Sandy watched as he claimed her lips, kissing her deeply. "I couldn't fucking find you."

"Why didn't you ask Sandy?"

"I couldn't find *her*. I've been looking all over this fucking hospital."

"I'm sorry. I should have known to come find you. I apologize."

Snake wasn't interested in hearing her apology, and seeing as she was no longer needed, Sandy left them alone.

Rubbing her temple, she started to make her rounds, going to Sophia's room. Jessica was going to be discharged and was no longer at risk. Providing she rested, her arm was going to be fine.

Nash was sitting beside his woman, who still hadn't woken up.

"What's going on?" Sandy asked, seeing the doctor filling in the form. Doctor Berman was one of the best surgeons in Fort Wills.

"Nothing. We've repaired the damage, but Sophia stopped breathing twice during surgery. Now we have to wait for any possible brain damage that could occur."

"What do you think the chances of her not recovering? She has two kids, Berman."

"Sandy, I respect you, and even though I don't agree with your decision to step down from your position here, you know I can't answer that."

She did, but it would have been nice to hear some kind of hope, and told him so.

"Why don't you retake your position here?" Berman asked.

"I'm not ready to return."

"You're a gifted doctor, a fantastic woman. Tell me what more would it take to get you to return."

Sandy smiled. "I think that is the most compliments you've ever given me."

"Well, let's just say your replacements are proving less than savory. You were dependable, even at the end of a day. Also, my wife misses hearing about you."

She chuckled.

"She wants to know if you've met a nice young man yet?"

"You can tell her that I have. I'm even thinking of settling down."

"What about coming back here? The place hasn't been the same without you."

"I don't know. I'd have to think about it."

"Think about it." Berman patted her arm. "With regards to the young woman, hope and pray."

Letting out a sigh, she entered Sophia's room.

"Don't worry, I heard everything. I know the risks. I know what could happen to Sophia. She could end up brain dead, and my wife could be nothing more than a memory."

Out of all of the club brothers Nash had struggled with addiction, and gone down a road that had almost cost him his life, and his position within the club. Lash had saved him. Lash and Sophia had both helped to turn his life around.

"There's nothing anyone can do."

"She'll come back to me. Sophia won't leave me," Nash said.

Moving toward him, she placed a hand on his shoulder. "We've just got to wait."

"Yep, that is what we've got to do. Wait, and

she'll be back."

Sandy stayed with him for several minutes before she moved on to the next person. There were so many people to see. It was so hard, going through the motions, and not breaking down in the face of her best friends hurting. Sasha lay in her bed, and Pussy was there, by her side.

"How is she?"

"She's still breathing," Pussy said. "I'm a stupid fucker. I shouldn't have pushed her that hard. When the shooting started, I saw a bullet hit her. She panicked because she couldn't fucking see." He held onto Sasha's hand. "She couldn't see, and she nearly fucking died. I shouldn't have shoved her to the floor. I heard it smack the fucking concrete. Fuck!"

Sandy couldn't do anything.

"We were talking about having kids. You know, once all of this shit is over with Master—or Andrew—fuck." Pussy stopped, pausing as he pressed his head against her hand, gathering his thoughts. "Sasha wants kids, but she's terrified, scared. She can't see, and she doesn't think it will make her a good mother."

"Do you want kids?"

"I want to have whatever Sasha wants. She doesn't want to have kids that she can't care for herself. I've had to fight for her. Devil considered her a liability to the club, a risk. I fucking love her. I don't care if she can't see or not. I'd leave the club before I got rid of her."

"She knows this."

"I just want her to know I love her, and I'll do anything for—"

The machine beside Sasha started beeping, and her body tensed up.

Sandy reacted, pressing the emergency button,

and moving Pussy out of the room. There was no time to explain. She hated the fact she was scaring him, but there was nothing else she could do. This required immediate attention. The doctor rushed inside and started to check her vitals.

"We've got to relieve the pressure in her head. Get me set up for an emergency procedure."

Sandy went straight ahead, and did as he asked, prepping the room. There was no time to take her to theater.

Pussy stood at the window, pressing his hand to the glass. She couldn't allow him to see what was about to happen, and lowered the blinds. Then she called Stink to come get him.

The day was not over yet, and it was killing each and every one of them.

Chapter Three

The days had all melded into one, and Paris didn't know where she was, or what was going to happen next. She closed her eyes for sleep to come, and she dreamed. The peace of her dreams was the only thing that kept her sane.

"What are you doing? Spider asked.

"I'm dancing." She was standing on a beach, sand between her toes. Beside Spider sat Celia, who was happily building sandcastles. Spider had kept his promise to protect them.

"I can see you're dancing, and you look so beautiful doing it."

"Yeah, she's beautiful all right, but she's not yours." She turned in time to see Andrew approaching. Her body tightened, and she stared down at her thigh to see the brand that he'd marked her with. It was red, swollen, and it looked infected.

Suddenly, he was there, wrapping his fingers around her neck, choking her. "She stopped belonging to you when you failed her. Paris is mine now."

Cold water washed over her, making Paris gasp as she came out of her dreams.

"We couldn't have you sleeping right now. There's time to sleep, and then there is time to be awake," Andrew said. "It's time to be awake, sweetie."

Ever since she had learned his name, she had stopped thinking of him as Master. He wasn't *her* Master.

"Sir, what are you doing?" Russell asked.

There were two of them now. Sir and Master, or Russell and Andrew. Only Russell referred to Andrew as Sir and Master as he was the one in charge, whereas Russell was just a minion.

"Well, we wait. I have to say I'm curious about Angel the most. I don't know why." Andrew stared at her. She didn't have a clue what he was talking about. "It's a shame you're a newbie. What I really need is a woman or a man who is in the club, knowing everything. Eva, Angel, Sophia, even Kelsey could give me what I want." He reached out, gripping her hair, and tugged her up to her feet. There was not a single bone that didn't feel pain. Her arms were mottled with different shades of bruising. Paris didn't know how much longer she was going to last under his abuse. Little by little he was killing her, destroying her, but she held on. The memory of Spider helped her to keep on fighting.

"You really think he's going to come and save you?" Andrew asked.

"He will."

Andrew slapped her across the face. "No one is going to save you until I say so." He spat in her face, and dropped her, before landing a blow to her stomach. She curled into a ball, humiliated.

"Was that necessary?" Russell asked.

"Are you becoming soft, my little prodigy? If you are, I can find your replacement quite easily."

Russell sighed. "If you want to play with her for any length of time, you need her to recover. How many women do you need to go through to understand this?"

Andrew nodded. "You're right. He's given you a reprieve for now."

She curled into a ball and lay in the corner where he had put her. Paris didn't have the strength to run away, and no longer needed shackles. He only fed her enough to keep her alive. Any energy she had was wasted in screaming. She tried not to scream, but she failed.

Would she ever see her sister again?

Would the pain ever cease?

She had to wonder about Spider. Was he looking for her? Did he even care that she was gone? Paris hated the fact she'd kept him at a distance, always afraid to let him in. She didn't want to risk trusting in someone else, especially when people always let her down.

She hated this life.

"So, what is going on then?" Andrew asked.

Glancing up at the wall filled with screens, she squinted, catching sight of the hospital.

"I'm into the hospital feeds," Lola said.

Lola was a woman that Andrew had picked up a few days ago. From what Paris had been able to understand, Lola was some kind of computer genius, and was young, only eighteen years old. Andrew had taken her off the streets and proceeded to beat and rape her until Lola had agreed to do what he wanted.

"No one knows we're tapped into this?" he asked.

"No. We're secure."

Andrew placed his hand on Lola's shoulder, and the girl tensed up.

"Relax, Lola. Do what I want, and I won't touch you." He gripped her face, making Lola cry out. "Betray me, and I'll make every day of your life a living hell. I'll even pass you around to my friends, and provided they keep you breathing, they can do whatever they want to you."

Lola sobbed. "I won't betray you."

"Good girl. This will teach you to hack into government sites, Lola. You'd be surprised how many people want your many talents."

Andrew finally released Lola, and the young woman looked like hell. She was just as bruised as Paris, only Lola had broken. Paris wasn't broken yet, and she was going to find a way to get them both out of here.

"So, this is the hospital," Andrew said.

"Yes. These are all the cameras in the Fort Wills hospital. The waiting room—"

"Is full of Skulls and Chaos Bleeds. Fantastic. Show me different areas."

Lola tapped on the screens, and different parts of the hospital appeared.

"Show me the maternity ward."

"You're still planning on going after Angel and Lash?"

"Lash has a bit of a reputation. He loves Angel more than anything. Rumor is, they reckon he'll be a ticking time bomb if anything was to happen to Angel. The thing about hospitals is anyone can get in there. I was thinking of introducing myself. My brother likes her, and I want to get to know the woman who everyone seems to love."

"In a hospital covered by men who know what you look like. Whizz got your picture. He knows what you look like."

"That may be so, but it doesn't mean that everyone knows me. I can get in and out undetected. It's very easy to do."

"You're asking to be killed."

"You're such a buzz kill. Gash thinks he knows what I'm going to do next. Let's see if he knows who I'm after next."

Whizz was the computer genius at The Skulls. If Paris could get a message to him, he might be able to help them. She had to get through to Lola, and somehow convince her that The Skulls and Chaos Bleeds would save them. It was worth a try. Anything was better than this.

****

Night had fallen, and Spider pacing up and down

using the crutches he'd been given since he'd gotten out of the hospital. His leg was bandaged up, and the rage was building inside him.

He needed to get his leg better to get to Paris. There were nights when he fell asleep that he imagined her screaming for him to come and save her. Each time, he failed, and she was there covered in blood, blaming him, hating him.

"How are you holding up?" Stink asked.

"Part of my club is in the hospital, my woman is still missing, and my leg is pissing me off." Spider turned to look at him. "How do you think I'm holding up?"

Stink held his hands up. "You've turned into a pussy."

Spider paused. "What the fuck you say?"

"Oh, I'm sorry. You see, I thought you were part of the Chaos Bleeds crew, but right now, I'm seeing a fucking wimp." Stink folded his arms, and Spider was aware of both crews standing around them.

"What the fuck is going on here?" Ripper asked.

"I'm tired of pussy-footing around this asshole. We've all got problems, and I know his woman is in trouble. We're working on finding her. Instead of helping us right here, right now, he's moaning like a little bitch."

"She could be dead!"

"She's not dead. You guaranteed that by staying alive. What we know is that Andrew is unpredictable, but he hasn't lied to us yet. Have fucking hope. I know it's a long shot, but hope and fighting is what is going to get us through this."

"He won."

"*Today*, he won. Today we underestimated him, but one day soon, we'll get him back. We will make him pay for what he has done."

"As much as it grieves me to say this, he's right,

Spider," Ripper said.

He knew they were all right.

"What the fuck is going on here?" Devil asked.

Spider looked past Stink to see his Prez near the reception desk. Beside him stood Tiny and Lash.

"They're giving me shit that I deserve," Spider said.

"You finally getting your head out of your ass?" Devil asked.

"Yeah, but it would have been nice if my own club had done it rather than a Skull."

"We couldn't do that, you've been a damn girl for the past week," Snake said, coming out of another door with his arm across Jessica's shoulders. The woman was bandaged up, and she looked pale.

"I'm sorry. You're right. I've been letting fear guide me, and I won't do that. I need to save Paris, and the only way to do that is to fight, so that's what I'm going to do. I'm going to fight."

"Good."

"Any news on Simon and Tabitha?" Tate asked. She rushed to her father and threw herself into his arms. Tiny caught her easily and held her tightly.

"They're still asleep, but that is good news. The doctor believes their bodies have dealt with a trauma, and they need the rest."

"Get your fucking hands off me!" Pussy was pulled out of the doors by three security men. "That is my fucking wife, and you can't keep me from her. Sasha! Sasha!"

Devil rushed toward his man, grabbing his arm. None of them wanted to get arrested, not with what was happening. They all had to stay together, having strength in numbers. "What's going on?"

"She's fucking dying, man. She's got pressure in

her skull. Sasha could fucking die. She can't die."

"Where's Sandy?" Stink asked.

"I don't know. She kicked me out of the room, dropped the blind so I couldn't see. My woman could fucking die, and I'm not ready. I'm not ready to say goodbye to her."

Spider watched as Pussy broke down.

They had all taken turns to look after Sasha. She was blind, and they had come to see that everything within the clubhouse needed to stay in a certain way. If a table was moved an inch out of place, it could harm her. Spider had even caught her before she landed on the floor.

Sasha was one of them, and had been from the moment Pussy claimed her. The very thought of her no longer being with them cut Spider to the core.

"We're here, we're all here," Devil said. "Today, Andrew won. There's no denying that. He won, and we lost." Devil looked around at each one of them. "Fighting each other is what he wants. I don't want to give him that. It's easy to point fingers. I could even point a few, but I'm not going to. The Skulls and Chaos Bleeds, we've had our problems, and we'll continue to have them. We're different, but we're the same when it comes to our battles. We fight together, to the death, and we don't do it alone."

Lash nodded. "We need to regroup, to think about what is going to happen next. We can't do this here, but we also can't leave the hospital." He turned to Gash. "What would be his next move?"

"He'll hit us when we're down. Andrew will come to the hospital. It'll be within the next twenty-four hours. He'll come," Gash said.

"You're sure?"

"Yeah, it's what he'll do. Andrew is going for the

shock factor. He'll strike at the one we least expect."

"Then we put men on them. No one is left alone. Do you hear me?" Lash said.

"We keep a vigil, here and at the club," Devil said.

"We need to stick together now," Tiny said, speaking up. "I'm not in charge anymore, but Lash wants me to help."

"This is what we need to do together," Lash said.

It felt good to have the clubs back together again. Spider had missed The Skulls, and coming to Fort Wills. It wasn't right, Devil and Tiny being at each other's throats.

"I need to get back to Sasha. I can't be here."

"We'll go together, Devil said.

"Where's Whizz?" Lash asked.

"You haven't heard?" Gash asked.

"Heard what?"

"Sally's going to lose her leg, from the knee down."

Spider watched as Lash showed no sign of emotion, nothing. It was all in his eyes, and if you didn't know him, you wouldn't detect it.

"I'll go and see him and Sally."

The brother was angry, clearly consumed by his grief, but no one would know.

He watched as Lash left through the door, and Spider returned his attention toward Pussy. The brother was swearing all kinds of vengeance.

They had already lost too many. None of them wanted to lose another one.

****

Rounding the corner, Lash pressed his head against the wall and took several deep breaths. He tried to control his growing temper, but nothing had prepared him for that, nothing. Sally was going to lose her leg. Tabitha in the hospital, the rain of bullets. He hadn't been prepared for any of it, and even now, he wasn't.

"Fuck!" He screamed the word at the top of his voice and hit the brick wall, exerting all of his rage against the wall.

Over and over, he slammed his fist against the wall, relishing the pain.

"Enough!" Tiny grabbed his arms and pressed him against the wall. "What the fuck are you doing?"

"Dealing."

"This is not how a leader deals, Lash."

"Sally's about to lose her fucking leg, Tiny. She's been part of the club two minutes, and she's going to be changed forever."

"And she'll have the club by her side, taking care of her. We're not going to make her do this alone. None of us are. She has all of us. Remember that."

"He's winning."

Tiny shook his head. "He won't win this war."

"Look around you."

"I am looking around me, Lash. What I see is a bunch of men and women who are ready to take this fucker down. He wants to go to war, let him. He's building our army for us."

"Our women are not an army."

"No? I've seen Angel with that gun. Give her a chance, and I bet she'd take him out. We're going to have to bury Skulls and Chaos Bleeds crew. You tell me what you'd do?"

Lash stared past his shoulder and saw the nurses and doctors were looking at him. He didn't give a shit what they were staring at.

"I'd get them to fight," Lash said.

"Exactly. We're only half a club without our

women. They're ours to protect, and we can protect them by making them able to fight for themselves as well."

"I've got to go see Sally."

Tiny nodded. "You're doing good, Lash."

Lash snorted. "I'm not doing good. I'm falling a-fucking-part."

"No, you're not. You're dealing well. We've just been attacked. They will fall to you."

"I'd say hitting a wall is a much better way to cope," Devil said. "I've been known to go on a killing spree of all the people who've pissed me off. I've even been tempted to take out the postal lady for taking a long time to deliver a Christmas present to Lex."

Lash laughed. He couldn't help it.

"You were given this club for a reason, son," Devil said. "I may not have agreed with it at the time. Tiny can still ride, and even if he is a little slow at times, he still can run this club. I see why he did it."

"Thanks!" Sarcasm was laced in Lash's voice.

"You're welcome."

"Will you be passing Chaos Bleeds over?"

"Fuck no. That's my club, and my men look up to me, want me for direction. Simon will get my club, and I'm teaching him the rules by which he needs to abide. He'll be one hell of a leader. Especially if his love of that girl is anything to go by."

"Your son is not marrying my Tab. She's staying a virgin all of her life."

Devil snorted. "We'll see. This was a good chat. You're doing good, kid. Love the club, adore and fuck your woman, respect your men, and you'll have their loyalty. Nothing pisses me off more than a weak fucker who bullies." Devil shook his head. "That's not me."

Lash watched as Devil walked off in the direction of the children's ward.

"He's right. You're doing good."

Doing good was what he was going to have settle for. There was nothing else right now that he could do.

****

They were going to take her leg. The damage was too great, and if they didn't take it, infection, pain, and maybe even death would be her future. She'd die with her damn leg. Sally stared down at the bandage around her knee that went from mid-calf, up past her knee, to her thigh.

Lacey and Whizz, or Mom and Dad, which she liked to call them, were trying to find out if there was anything they could do. They didn't know the pain was getting worse, and had been ever since she got out of surgery.

"You'll still be beautiful," Daisy said.

She smiled at the little girl who'd recently become her sister. Daisy was so sweet, so nice, and she tried to make everyone smile.

"Oh, Daisy, what did I do to deserve you?" Sally cupped Daisy's face, trying not to show her pain as the little girl bounced on the bed.

"I think you should get off there," Steven said, rounding the bed and picking up the little girl. Daisy squealed as Steven started to tickle her.

She rushed out of the room, going to take Whizz's hand, and sticking her tongue out.

"They'll figure something out for you, Sally."

Glancing down at her leg, Sally felt tears rush to the surface. The last few months had been the best of her life. She loved Lacey and Whizz. They had given her a family.

"Daisy's right, you know."

"Right about what?"

"You're beautiful."

Sally looked at the man whom she'd had a crush on since the first moment she met him. Of course, she'd denied it when she heard him being told the truth. It was embarrassing, having a crush on a guy who didn't even notice you. "Don't pity me."

"You've been through a lot, Sally."

"Yeah, a leg, it's not the first thing I've lost."

He sat down, and she wished he'd leave her alone. Steven had never shown her any attention. He'd always been nice to her, but that didn't mean anything, did it? The last thing she wanted was pity because of her situation.

"I'm really sorry," he said.

Staring at him, she frowned. "What?"

"I didn't protect you."

"It's not your job to protect me."

"I don't consider it a job."

"You're confusing me."

"When you say it's not the first thing you've lost, what did you mean?"

Her cheeks heated, and she pushed herself up the bed, trying to get comfortable. The pain medication had long since worn off, and deep down, she just knew she was going to have to lose her leg. There was no other way for her to fight the pain. "I don't want to talk about it."

"Well, I do."

"We don't always get what we want."

He took hold of her hand, locking their fingers together. "Tell me."

For several minutes she hesitated. "I was in foster care for most of my life, Steven. I was passed from one home to the other, and not everyone is … nice without cause. Sometimes they wanted something in return for being nice."

"You were a young girl, an innocent."

"That niceness came at a price. It didn't last, though. Nothing ever lasts. If you think for a second that I'm some sweet, innocent girl that needs saving, you're wrong. I'm not innocent, and I haven't been for a long time. That's all I'm going to say about it."

"I'm not going anywhere," he said, holding her hand.

Damn it!

Tears sprang to her eyes as she stared down at his hand holding her. Why did she have to be attracted to this man? Why couldn't it be someone else? She seemed older than her actual years. She'd been told that a time or two, much older than sixteen.

"I'm going to lose my leg."

"I'll be with you, helping you."

"I like my legs."

"I know." He leaned forward, and kissed her head. It had to be one of the sweetest touches she'd ever experienced.

Chapter Four

Sandy was exhausted by the time she made it down to the main reception later that night. So much had happened. Her head was pounding, her feet numb from being on them all day. Several of the guys were there, and others had left to take the kids back.

Within the past five hours, Simon and Tabitha had woken from their comas. When their parents tried to separate them, different rooms, both had caused a hell of a lot of problems. They were now staying in the same room, providing each other with the means of recovering. Devil and Tiny were taking turns guarding the door.

Everyone else had been bandaged up, treated, and either told to stay in for observation, or discharged. Curse had been discharged, but Mia had to stay in. Sunshine had to stay, and so had Alex. Both had been to visit their girl though. She was a beautiful baby. The only person who hadn't shown any progress was Sasha. After the pressure had been relieved on her brain, they had bandaged her up, performed some MRI scans, and checked to see if there was any more damage. Nothing showed.

They now had to wait to see if she'd wake up with any problems. Moments like these, Sandy hated her job, the not knowing was worse.

Stink stood up the moment he saw her, and made his way toward her. "You look ready to drop."

"I am."

"I've got a car outside. I'll take us to get something to eat, and then back to the clubhouse."

"What about security?" she asked.

"We've got a system in place. The guys are going to take it in turns to be at the hospital. We'll protect everyone."

"What about protecting yourself?" she asked.

"I can handle myself. You don't need to worry about me." He kissed her head and took her hand. She said her goodbyes and promised to be back the next morning.

"I don't want anything to happen to you," she said.

"I won't let it."

He helped her into the car, and she strapped herself in.

Stink climbed behind the wheel, and they were on the road, heading toward a fast food joint. She ached all over, and she stretched her neck in an attempt to relieve the pressure.

Moaning, she cricked her neck from side to side.

"I heard Sasha's surgery went well."

"Yeah. She didn't code out, and we were able to relieve the pressure in time. I saw the signs, and we got there fast."

"Do you think she'll ever wake up?"

"It's hard to tell with cases dealing with the brain. On the one hand, I don't like to say no. On the other, you have to be prepared. Everyone is different. I heard the doctor speaking with her old doctor back in Piston County. There was no evidence or reason for her to remain blind after her fall. Each person reacts a different way to the same surgery."

"If she doesn't wake up, we've lost Pussy."

"Yeah, we have. It was hard for me to drop those blinds so he didn't see. I couldn't let him. Witnessing someone drilling into a brain of a loved one, it messes with your head. I couldn't handle it if it was you."

He took hold of her hand.

When he started doing that she used to find it really annoying, and hated the intimacy of the touch.

Now, she loved it. It calmed her, let her know he was there no matter what.

"You did the right thing. Don't blame yourself. You didn't make her blind, and you didn't fire that gun."

"Stink, there's a chance she might not wake up."

"And there's a chance she will. Have a little faith."

"It's really hard to do that with everything going on."

He squeezed her hand. "You've got me."

She smiled. "You know, I never thought I'd find comfort in a man telling me that I had him, but with you, I do." She leaned over and rested her head on his shoulder. "I don't want anything to happen to you."

"I'll be careful."

Sandy knew they'd gone over this, but with everything going on, she felt like her life was going over and over in the same cycle. "Will it ever end?"

"The club having enemies?"

"Yeah."

"I don't know, baby. Maybe we'll stop having shit like Master, The Darkness, and stuff. That's what I hope for."

She sighed. "It's just hard. So many people are getting hurt."

"What's going to happen with Sally?"

"Her leg from just above her knee is going to have to be removed. It's the left leg. She'll get a prosthetic, and spend a great deal of time in physiotherapy. Also, she'll need to see a therapist to help deal with her loss of a limb. It's going to be tough for her. She's only sixteen."

"She's got the whole club around her. We'll be there with her."

She mumbled her agreement. He felt so

comforting, even with her head on his shoulder. This was what Stink did to her. He made her feel.

"Do you know what surprised me?" she asked.

"Nope."

"Steven. He was there by her side, even when the doctor gave the news, and Sally broke down. I mean, she only accepted Whizz, Lacey, and Daisy's affection, but Steven was there. I think there could be something between them."

"Nah, not Steven."

"Seriously. Tomorrow, go and see for yourself." She pulled away. "He has feelings for her."

"He's nearly thirty, and she's a kid."

"No, it's not those kinds of feelings. Well, he may care about her, but it's not like that. It's not gross. It's sweet. Steven wouldn't act on it anyway." Now she wished she hadn't said anything. Steven wasn't the kind of guy to prey on vulnerable people.

Stink chuckled. "It would teach him right, you know. I believe you. I don't know why I doubt you with these things. You've been right about everything else."

"You bet your ass I have."

"Steven is such a whore. He fucks his way through so many women."

She held her finger up. "So you haven't noticed he hasn't been around a lot of women lately? See, I told you."

"Just because—"

"Don't even try to fight this. He's got a thing for Sally, and I think it's going to be kind of sweet. If I was Sally, I'd make him work for it. Steven has always been cocky, always had ladies chasing after him. There are times he even expects it."

Stink glanced over at her. "You sure know how to make a man work for it."

They pulled up into the parking lot of the fast food joint.

"Why didn't you fuck me?" she asked.

"What?"

"I've been with a lot of the club men, Stink. I was a club whore, and to most, I still am. You had a chance to have me. Why didn't you take it?"

She'd never behaved like a slut in the club. Even though any guy could have her, she'd never actually given in to the stereotype of being fucked one after the other. Some of the women who came and went over the years would climb on the table, and one after the other, the men would bang the fuck out of them. Of course, they'd wear a condom. Since most of the guys had settled down, it had been different, calmer. Sandy had never wanted that. She didn't mind showing off a little, putting on a show, but it had to be one on one.

"You were always so beautiful, even when you were younger. You came to the club when you were what, twenty-six?"

"Yeah."

She'd been doing an internship at the hospital, working long hours. Sandy's dream of being a doctor had stopped her from forming any close connections. She'd loved saving lives, and when she needed to blow off steam, the club had been available to her. Sure, the guys at first hadn't exactly been very open with her back then. She'd been young, taking sex, and leaving. Over time, and possibly a million stitches, she'd slowly earned their trust to the point where they were now. She was part of The Skulls. They were a part of her, a part she'd never want to lose.

"I remember seeing you, so young, so fresh, yet you weren't like anyone else. There was real passion in your eyes. When you had to stitch up Lash when he was a kid before he joined the club, everyone kept their eye on you."

She remembered that. Lash was about sixteen years old, and he'd cut his side on some broken glass because he'd broke into one of the warehouses to fuck some random girl. Nash had carried his ass to the clubhouse, and Sandy had been there, getting fucked by one of the brothers. It was so long ago that she didn't even remember who it was. Tiny had wanted to take him to the hospital, but seeing as the damage was the result of a break-in at the club's own factory, Tiny hadn't wanted to draw any attention.

Sandy had heard the argument, and had stopped what she was doing, putting herself together, and gone to assist Lash. She'd checked over his cut, and seen it was just surface. With the whole of The Skulls watching them, Sandy had kept her composure, and stitched Lash up. She had pushed aside her club whore status, taking on her role as a doctor.

After that, she'd become part of them.

"What does that have to do with it?"

"I knew in that moment that you were going to be something more to me than a quick fuck. You were already working your way in here." He tapped his head. "I wasn't ready to try to claim you, and you weren't ready."

"You're ready now?"

"I've been ready for a couple of years, Sandy. Are you?"

****

The one thing Stink always tried to avoid was putting Sandy in a position that made her uncomfortable. She liked her space, and to be able to come and go as she pleased. He was more than happy to provide her that.

His love for her would never die. Stink had

known that. He loved her for the woman she was, not what he wanted. She was so strong, intelligent, and gentle. The doctor inside her didn't know any other way.

Turning off the ignition, they made their way toward the diner. He was in the mood for some meatballs. Angel was one of the best cooks in the clubhouse, and she wouldn't be cooking tonight. Tate was okay, but he feared she would more than likely spit in the food she was cooking.

They took a seat, and like always Sandy grabbed the menu and started to peruse the offerings. She liked to try new things, and if she didn't like what she had, she always ate half of his. It was one of the reasons he always ordered a larger portion for himself. The biggest problem was if she ordered what she liked, he was left with a large portion. He had to visit the gym a few times to drop a few pounds.

"Oh, they have a garden burger."

"You tried that three months ago. You didn't like it." She'd spat it back out, looking green.

"Oh, right, it had way too much cilantro in it." She wrinkled her nose. "What about … the chicken parmesan? No, I've had that. Meatballs?"

"I'm going to have that."

"Meatloaf? I haven't had that in a while. It's nice and comforting. What do you think?"

"I'm having meatballs, so pick whatever you want."

"Oh, this is so hard."

"Can I help you?" the waitress asked.

"Yeah, spaghetti and meatballs for me, coffee, large, black, no sugar." Stink sat back and looked toward Sandy.

She bit her lip, looking through the menu again. "I'll take the buffalo wings, house special burger, chili cheese fries, and a double helping of apple pie with whipped cream and ice cream. Strawberry milkshake as well, thank you."

The waitress left them alone, and Stink stared at his woman. "Wow."

"Working, it makes me really hungry, and I haven't eaten all day. I'm starved. Angel usually knows what to cook for me." She sighed. "We can't have it all our own way."

She ran her fingers along the edge of the table.

"You didn't answer my question."

"I know. You were getting ready to leave, and being hungry and all, this isn't the kind of conversation you want to have on an empty stomach."

He ran his finger across his lip, staring at her. Stink would never get bored of simply staring at her. She was a beautiful woman, vibrant and full of life.

"I know you're ready to give us a chance, so that's not my question."

"I get the difference, Stink. You want to know if I'm ready to finally settle down, have a relationship with you."

His heart started to pound as he stared at her.

For Sandy, it was a huge step.

"Yes, I am. I am ready for you, and for us to be something."

He reached across the table, taking hold of her hand. Until that moment he didn't realize how worried he was about her answer.

She chuckled. "Looking a bit scared there, mister."

"Just a little. I haven't even gotten you naked yet."

"Like I've told you before, you can get me naked any time you want." Sandy shrugged. "I'm ready."

Stink stared down at her hand, seeing how steady it was. There were times he'd touch her, and she'd be shaking.

Sandy had had to deal with a lot when it came to the club.

"Tell me why you became a doctor."

"Really? That's what you want to talk about? I just told you we can fuck, and nothing?"

"I've waited all this time, what's a few more hours, days, weeks, months? I want more than a simple screw."

"Okay. Being a doctor. It's the usual, I wanted to help people. My family..." She paused, and he noticed her eyes suddenly fill with tears, which only created more questions to him.

"If it's too hard—"

"It's fine. I want to talk about it. I lost my family a long time ago. My mother was killed from septicemia. The doctor misdiagnosed her condition, and she was in pain for hours up until she finally died. She died in my father's arms."

"Wow," he said. Sandy didn't talk about her family. He couldn't even recall her recounting a single memory. He always figured she was too embarrassed, or there was no family to tell.

"It was a long time ago. I was, um, I was eleven. I remember not knowing that there had been a fuck-up until later on. I did some research and learned the doctor had a gambling problem." She laughed, but it wasn't humorous. It was forced, and near hysterical. "He was more interested in putting on his next bet than he was to listen to my mother. I remember thinking if someone was there who really cared, she'd still be alive."

"What about your dad?"

She laughed. "My parents had one of those

relationships that was similar to Angel and Lash. They really connected. Their entire lives were about each other, and I got to witness that. I was part of it." She tucked some hair behind her ear. "After Mom died, he couldn't cope. He couldn't handle being alone. There was no other woman for him. In the early months after her death, he'd spend all night crying, and at work, he just couldn't function." She paused, licking her lips. "One night, he, er, he took a drink of whiskey, and then another. It started to numb his pain. He didn't have to think about my mom or what he'd lost, nothing."

"He became an alcoholic?"

"You got it. The beer took him, but he wasn't a mean person. He tried to hide it, and it wasn't like he became a slob." She chuckled. "The beer actually made him a good parent. He stopped driving, and he started taking the bus to work. He never drank excessively, just enough to make him able. If that makes sense. People would talk about it, but he never put anyone at risk. Not even me. I was hurt once. I climbed a tree to look at a bird that had nested. I didn't hold on well enough, and I fell. Broke my leg in two places." She chuckled. "After that, he did try to stay sober. We had to wait for the ambulance, you see, and he had to fill in paperwork. I think it scared him a little."

"Where is your dad now?" Stink asked.

"Um, going to get some groceries, he was run over by a guy having a heart attack." Sandy shook her head. "It was just after my eighteenth birthday."

"You became a doctor to help people."

"To make sure no one else ever felt loss, or knew pain like I have. If I was there, then I knew that every person who came into my care would be protected. I wouldn't fail them." Sandy stared down at the table. "Life sucks sometimes."

"You've been on your own since then?"

"Pretty much. My dad was well off, so I've never really had to worry about money, or security. I've been really lucky that way. Others, not so much."

"You'll always have me."

She smiled. "It makes me a lucky woman to have you in my life."

He didn't let go of her hand, offering her the support and love she needed by that one simple touch.

"I've never told anyone that before."

"Never?"

"No, never. It's in the past, and I don't want anyone's pity." She let out a breath. "Wow, it's a lifetime ago."

"Your parents would be proud of you."

"Really?"

"Yeah, look what you've achieved."

"I'm not married, and I don't have any kids."

"There's more to life than marriage and kids."

"Do you want them?" she asked.

"Only if you do. All I want is you, Sandy—kids, no kids, I don't care."

"You really are a great guy, and you really shouldn't have a name called Stink."

He laughed. "I like it. It beats Norman."

"I know. No wonder you were happy with your name."

"I'm screwed either way."

"Ha ha."

Their food arrived, and Stink was happy. With all the shit going on, he'd found his happiness with Sandy.

Once the waitress left, he dove into his food, relishing the taste of the juicy meatballs and tomato garlic sauce. Twirling the spaghetti around his fork, he took a large bite while also watching Sandy devour her food. She wasn't kidding.

He grabbed a chili cheese fry, taking a bite.

"Good, isn't it?"

"Yeah, it really is."

"I don't know if I'd want kids someday. Maybe, maybe not. I'm getting older. Should I really be having kids?"

"I think you should do whatever makes you feel happy."

"Being with you, it makes me happy."

****

The following morning Angel woke up and smiled over at her husband. Lash was asleep with his arms folded. She had offered to move up, and to give him room, but he wouldn't take it. He was always taking care of her, loving her.

"You're awake," he said.

"Yeah, only for a few minutes. You don't have to worry about getting up."

"Don't be silly. I want to." He yawned and stretched out.

"Where's Anthony?" she asked.

"Tate. She took care of the kids last night with the men. Some of us stayed."

"Like who?" Angel was curious to know what was going on. She hated being kept out of the loop on stuff like this. Lash was the President of The Skulls now, and so, to her, that meant she had to play her part. Eva had been by Tiny's side through it all. Angel was determined to be a good old lady to her man.

Lash blew out a breath. "Don't worry about it."

"Seriously? I'm sitting here, and I'm worried about it because you're not telling me the truth. Just tell me the truth, Lash."

"Tabitha and Simon are fine. They woke up, but

65

they need to be kept under observation."

She nodded. Even though she wanted to shed a tear, she couldn't. Crying wouldn't solve anything. Being strong, and offering support would help. Simon and Tabitha were both good kids, sweethearts. No one should ever harm a child. The very thought Andrew could, angered her. There was no way that sadistic man was related to Gash. She couldn't believe it. Gash was so damn nice.

"Alex is a father. Sunshine gave birth to a beautiful baby girl. You'll get to see her today, if you'd like."

"Of course I'd love to." Angel smiled, so happy for the lovely couple.

He went through everyone who had been injured. Knowing people she loved and cared about from both The Skulls and Chaos Bleeds were hurt annoyed her. She wanted to hurt Andrew for what he'd done. The club was her family. They were uncles, aunties, guardians, everything to her son and her husband. When Lash was away from her, she knew without a doubt that he was being taken care of.

That was what separated The Skulls from many other MCs. They cared, period.

Suddenly he stopped, and the sadness in his eyes was so easy to see. "What is it?" she asked.

"Sasha, Pussy's woman, the blind one."

"I know. She's so sweet, and loving. I also know she worries about him all the time." Angel had spoken to Sasha an hour before the attack. The other woman was so worried that her blindness was taking something away from Pussy. It wasn't. Pussy loved Sasha. All Angel saw was the love that he had for her.

"I don't know how to say this."

"What?"

"Sasha got shot, and hit her head. There was … swelling, and they had to perform emergency surgery to relieve the pressure."

"She's okay, right?"

Lash rubbed at his eyes, and all the happiness she'd had a moment ago was gone.

"There's a chance she might not wake up."

"But there's a chance she might?"

"Yes, it could go either way."

"Then we've got to show Pussy support during this time. We can't fail him." Tears filled her eyes, and she tried to wipe them away.

"I don't want you getting upset."

"I can't help it. Sasha is a good person, and I'm tired of bad stuff happening to good people." Running fingers through her hair, she shoved the blanket from her, and got to her feet.

"What are you doing?"

"I'm getting out of this blasted bed. I'm fine, Lash. It was just Braxton Hicks, and they're taking more precautions because of who you are. I'm going to go see our friends, our family."

"Angel—"|

"Don't Angel me. This is what is going to happen. Now, I can walk, or you can push me, but either way, I'm going to go see them."

He stepped toward her, placing a hand on her stomach. "I'll take you." Lash pushed the hair out of her face, and she smiled up at him.

"Thank you. I must look awful." She hadn't brushed her hair, nor did she feel sexy. Her stomach was like a large ball between them.

"You're the most beautiful woman in the world."

"You always know what to say."

"That's because you're mine."

Her stomach fluttered at his declaration. She loved him so much.

"Let me grab the chair." He kissed her head, and she closed her eyes, loving the feel of him around her.

Seconds later he came back, and she was sitting on the chair being escorted out. "Where would you like to go first?"

"To anyone. I want to see everything, Lash."

****

Sally couldn't sleep. She stared down at her leg that was currently bandaged up. The pain was only getting worse, and she was sweating worse than anything, the moisture pouring off her. There was no way she could continue to hide the pain. She'd never felt anything like it, the burning.

She needed to call the doctor, but if she did it would mean only one thing: she'd have to lose her leg.

Glancing across the room she saw Steven had fallen asleep. For most of the night she had watched him, hoping the pain in her leg would lessen.

Lacey and Whizz had left at her request. Even though she was in the hospital, she didn't want Daisy to be without a parent. They didn't want to leave her, but she made them. This was not the time for Daisy to be stuck in the hospital. Daisy was just a baby really, and she needed the love and support of both of them. Sally wasn't selfish, and she knew that they cared for her. Not once did she ever question their love for her. They'd given her a home when no one else would, and a family.

A sudden shot of pain rushed through her body, and she whimpered, gripping her thigh.

The noise woke Steven up as he got to his feet coming toward her.

"What is it? What's wrong?"

There was no way that she could handle the pain.

It hurt too much, and the pain was getting worse. She didn't know how she was going to survive the rest of the night with this kind of pain. She had to face the inevitable.

"It hurts." She sucked her lips in trying to keep the pain at bay. Nothing was happening. Gasping out, she felt the tears spilling down her cheeks, and it was all too much.

"I'm getting a nurse."

"No. They'll take my leg."

"Then let them take your damn leg. You could die, Sally."

"I don't care. I don't want them to take my leg."

He shook his head. "That's not your decision." He left the room, and Sally screamed. Seconds later the doctor rushed in.

"What's going on?" he asked. "Talk to me, Sally."

"It hurts."

"How long were you able to sleep?"

"I haven't."

He removed the bandage, and Sally knew something wasn't right.

"We've got to operate now."

"I'll get her parents."

She was starting to feel dizzy. Leaning over the bed, Sally vomited and saw stars.

The last thing she heard was Steven calling her name.

Chapter Five

Stink stared down at Sandy as she slept. They had come to the clubhouse last night, and the moment she'd lain down, she'd been out. He pushed some of her hair out of the way, and relished the numbness in his arm. This was what it was all about. Falling asleep beside the woman he loved after taking her out to dinner.

Time passed, he didn't know how much, and she opened her eyes, smiling up at him.

"Hey," she said. "Were you watching me sleep?"

"Maybe."

"That's not creepy at all."

He chuckled. "Maybe a little creepy."

"What time is it?"

Glancing over at the alarm clock he saw it was a little past six, and told her so.

"Ugh, I better get up. I want to go and check on everyone. You know Berman asked me when I was going to take my old job back."

"What did you say?"

"I didn't really say anything. I don't know if I want to go back to that."

"You don't?"

She stretched, yawning. "You don't think I do?"

"I don't know what to think, baby. Being a doctor is part of you, and last night I saw why you love it."

"It's so hard, and it hurts. Being a doctor comes with knowing that people are going to die. I can't save everyone."

Stink locked his fingers with hers, holding her close. "You're scared that you're going to lose some of the club?"

"Aren't you? We've already lost people, and this last attack, we lost our own."

The police were going to head to the hospital today to interview the rest of them. Stink was going to be there to give his statement.

"I'm not a fan of death. You train for this. Do you miss it?"

She sighed. "Sometimes. Yesterday I was able to just help, and to know what to do."

"You spent a great deal of your life training for this moment. Don't let anyone ruin that for you."

"I won't." She smiled. "I like this."

"One day we'll fuck," he said.

"I was going to fuck you last night."

"You were too busy snoring. Don't worry. I wouldn't know if you had bad breath or anything."

"I can fart and you won't know."

"I can't smell, but I'm not deaf."

She slapped his arm.

Her cell phone started to ring, and Stink reached across her, grabbing it. He didn't recognize the number.

"Hello." The smile that was on Sandy's lips disappeared as she listened to whoever was on the phone. "I'll be right in."

She snapped the phone closed and jumped to her feet.

"What is it?"

"Sally. Her knee has shown signs of an infection. They have to remove it now or she'll die. He already fears septicemia. I'm needed. I've got to go."

Stink got out of bed and pulled on his jeans but didn't button them up. He followed her into the bathroom, taking a piss after her, and washing his hands then brushing his teeth. Within ten minutes they were downstairs, and out of the door.

Neither of them stopped to give a heads-up to anyone. Stink would come back and let everyone know what was going on.

Climbing in his car, he turned over the ignition, and together they made their way out of the clubhouse parking lot.

"I can't believe everything that has happened."

"Don't worry about anything. We'll all be there for her."

Stink got her to the hospital in record time. He promised to bring her lunch, and watched as she disappeared inside. Whizz and Lacey were pulling into the parking lot, and Stink got out.

Lacey was carrying Daisy.

"Is she going to be all right?" Stink asked.

"I can't stay. She needs me." Lacey rushed toward the door.

"You can't take Daisy," Whizz said.

Stink held his hands out quickly as Lacey dumped Daisy on his lap. "Love you, darling." She kissed the young girl and left.

Daisy smiled at him. "I can go down."

"It's okay." He wasn't used to having kids dumped into his arms, unless they needed a diaper change. The brothers seemed to enjoy watching him change a shitty diaper without heaving. He'd lost his sense of smell a long time ago. Cleaning toilets, changing diapers, doing other gross shit didn't affect him. It was awesome that he couldn't smell anything bad, but it also meant he couldn't smell anything good. He went through life not knowing smells, not understanding what people were feeling.

Angel's food tasted sort of good to him, but he didn't get that loving smell that others got nor an overwhelming sense of taste either. He'd watched the men and women practically salivating just for a taste of Angel's food from smell alone.

"Did you drop Sandy off?" Whizz asked.

"Yeah, the moment she got the call."

"We should have stayed with her last night. She insisted we take Daisy home."

"I don't mind sleepovers. Sally needs to get better," Daisy said.

"I know, princess." Whizz took Daisy from him, hugging her close. "Do you know anything?"

"It's an infection that means they have to take the leg."

"Yeah, it's what we heard. Fucker needs to be brought down."

"Do you know anything?"

Whizz sighed. "I wish I did."

"Nothing?"

"I've got to go back to Andrew, and I need Gash for that. I was just starting to access his life when we got this attack."

"Seriously? You're going back to when he wasn't a problem."

"Hey! Listen, the Andrew he is now, I can't trace him. He's got security at all angles. I go back, I follow up to this point, and I can get to him. I've got to go back in order to get to now. Got it?"

"It actually makes sense."

"Of course it makes sense. I'm not some amateur." Whizz looked toward the hospital. "I've got to get in there."

"Do you want me to take her?" Stink asked.

"Would you mind?"

"I don't mind. We can do this, can't we, kid?"

Daisy nodded then kissed Whizz's cheek. "Kiss Sally."

Stink took hold of her and watched as Whizz rushed into the hospital. With Andrew having them rushing around chasing their own asses, they weren't focusing on him. This was going to end badly, and Stink needed to get someone else to see the danger that surrounded them.

"What would you like to do today?" Stink asked, placing her into his car. He already had a car seat so that he could take care of everyone.

She shrugged. "Whatever you want."

He climbed behind the wheel, and they drove back to the clubhouse. When he walked in he saw all the kids and several of the brothers at the table. Tate was serving up some burnt bacon, and the toast was black as well.

"What is this?" he asked, putting Daisy down. He watched as she took the empty seat beside Anthony.

"I attempted pancakes. I'm not very good. Angel is clearly the talented one."

"Clearly."

"So what's going on?"

"I need to go and see Murphy today. Can you watch the kids while I do?" Tate asked. "Jessica has offered to help as well. She can't do a lot seeing as her arm is bandaged."

"I'm here as well," Martha said, holding her hand up. "I can help."

"Good. We're going to need all the help we can get." Tate left the table, and Stink watched as someone rushed toward the trash to put in the bacon. Shaking his head, he couldn't help but chuckle. Everyone went still as Tate came back in. "We're also putting together a care package for Pussy. He hasn't left Sasha's side, and we're going to try and offer our support."

"Okay."

Stink took a seat at the table and rubbed at his temples. "At lunch I'm going to the hospital."

"That's fine. Tomorrow we need to drop the kids off in school."

"What about the Chaos kids?" he asked.

"Simon is in school, but he's at the hospital. Elizabeth is in her first year, and has work to complete at home. Lexie took care of it," Tate said.

It was the first time he'd seen Tate completely in control, and not being a bitch. He didn't know if he liked or recognized this person. They needed to keep her stressed more often.

"I'm here to help as well," Prue said, speaking up. "Zero can't do much as he's been shot in the butt."

The kids started laughing.

Stink cleared his throat and glared at them. "That's Uncle Zero you're laughing at. It's not nice to laugh at other people, and I don't want to hear any more rudeness, understood?"

The kids went back to eating, and Stink took a drink of coffee. He thought he heard a kid mumble, "but it's funny." He couldn't be sure though.

"How is everything?" Dick asked. He was sitting opposite his woman, Martha.

"I'm fine. I'll be happier when I can get this shit handled."

"Andrew has really fucked with us this time, hasn't he?" Dick asked. It was more of a rhetorical question.

"How is Spider handling everything?" Martha asked.

"He's still at the hospital keeping a vigil. It's breaking him apart. I've never seen the brother look so lost," Dick said.

"We'll find her. We don't have a choice." They'd either find her alive or dead. Stink hoped for the former rather than the latter.

MASTER

****

Angel had been around the whole of the hospital, and now she was at Sasha's door. Lash hadn't left her side. She'd spent a great deal of time with Simon and Tabitha. Tiny, Eva, Lexie, and Devil all looked so damn happy that she hadn't wanted to leave. Sunshine and Alex were happy as well. There was happiness, and then there was sadness. Sally was still in surgery, and Sasha still hadn't woken up.

The door to Sasha's room was open, and she saw Pussy sitting on the chair beside the bed. He held onto Sasha's hand, and he was talking.

"Do you remember that time I took you on the picnic, and we were near the field outside of the library? You asked me to describe how beautiful everything was. It was summer so all the flowers were in bloom. The grass seemed greener than any other time I'd seen it. I'd never known such beauty. The truth was, I only cared about looking at you. I didn't know if there were daisies or daffodils. There could have been two people fucking right next to us, and I wouldn't care. You're my world, Sasha." He paused, and tears filled Angel's eyes. "I can't live without you. There was a time I promised myself I'd never fall in love, but you destroyed that, Sasha. I love you, and I need you. This being asleep is nonsense. Please, wake up, I'm begging you." Once again he stopped. "Who else is going to listen to me in the shower, or tell me if I'm burning something? I love you, Sasha, and you promised me forever. This is not forever, not even part of a lifetime. I expect you to stick by your promise and give me forever."

Lash cleared his throat, and Pussy looked back.

Angel wiped away her tears as Lash pushed her into the room. "I wanted to come and see you."

"It's fine. Honestly, the more people, the better.

The doctor said talking to her might help. I'm just trying to wake her up. I have to say it's tempting to shake her." Pussy tried for a joke, but Angel saw how much it was cutting him up.

Staring at the bed, Angel saw the bandage wrapped around her head, and her heart went out to Pussy, and to Sasha. They were so happy, and they'd found each other. She knew that Sasha was nervous about her blindness, and felt like she put a lot of pressure on Pussy. Angel saw that Pussy didn't care about the stress. He loved his woman more than anything, and would do anything for her.

"I'm so sorry."

"Don't worry about it." Pussy took his seat. "It's not like I can do anything about it. Just keep on talking to her, and hope she wakes up soon."

"We'll get the bastard who did this."

"I know, and when we do, I want my shot at him. I want to fuck him up."

"We'll all get our chance. I promise."

"It can't come soon enough. All this waiting, it's just making me hungry, Lash, hungry for revenge." The way Pussy looked, Angel was pleased she wasn't Andrew. There was going to come a point when this all turned on him, and when it did, he'd regret every single decision he'd made.

She was oddly not afraid of him. A man like that, he was the worst kind of monster, and like all monsters, they needed to be put down, and that was exactly what The Skulls and Chaos Bleeds were going to do, put him down.

She hated thinking this way, but he deserved it. Angel had tried to find something decent in Andrew, and there was nothing.

Angel stayed with Pussy and Sasha for a good

hour. Pussy kept on talking, and only when it was time for her to see her own doctor did she leave. She promised to see Sasha and Pussy again.

Once inside her room again, she climbed onto the bed with Lash's help.

"You need to go and check on everyone," she said.

"I'm not leaving you."

"I'm fine. Whatever the doctor was worried about, you don't have to worry about me."

"Angel—"

She held her finger up, stopping him. "I love you, and I know you care. I love you, too. The club, they need to come first right now."

"You—"

Shaking her head, she pressed her lips against his. "The club was hit, Lash. We were all hit, and as their leader, you need to deal with this. It's not going to fall on Tiny. You also shouldn't be letting Tiny deal with this. You're the leader."

"You and Anthony, and our baby…"

"Are fine. I've got them, and when I get out of here today, I'll deal with Anthony. We're a team, Lash. A team that relies on each other. If you fail now, you don't have the right to call yourself a leader."

He nodded.

"Your brother needs you."

"Sophia's stable."

"I don't care. He still needs you."

The doctor came in then.

"Go, and help him, help the club," she said, kissing him.

Lash kissed her back with a passion that surprised her.

"Hello, and how are we feeling today?" the

doctor asked.

Angel returned her gaze to the doctor and frowned. He was sweating, and he looked really nervous, not exactly comforting for a doctor.

"Are you okay, Dr. Peters?"

She had never seen him sweating or looking so panicked. The sight of him alarmed her. This wasn't normal.

"Yeah, everything is okay."

He grabbed her file, and she noted that his hands were shaking.

Dr. Peters was a good doctor, and she had seen him a few times during her last and recent pregnancy. He'd also been the one to assign her to a psych ward after her breakdown from her miscarriage.

This man before her was not what she was used to.

"There has, um, been some problems with some of your tests, and they haven't come back normally. I have a doctor I need to consult, and I'll just go get him."

The hair on Angel's arms stood on end, and she quickly reached into her drawer, and grabbed the blade that Lash had given her. Ever since she had started training with Gash, and Lash had taken over, he'd been showing her ways of protecting herself. Whenever she was in doubt, they had advised her to trust her instincts, and that was what she was doing right now.

Staring at the door, she watched as a man entered.

She had never seen him before, but he was vaguely familiar. His hair was dark, and his eyes the same. Angel placed her hand beneath the blanket as she looked at him.

"Where's Dr. Peters?"

"He's busy, but don't worry. I'm here, and I've been looking through your tests." He turned closing the door.

Angel's heart started to pound, and the baby within her started to kick. "I want Dr. Peters back."

This was not what she wanted.

Flicking the blade open, Angel stared at the man, and really looked at him. He was vaguely familiar, and there would only ever be one reason for that. He was related to someone.

"Hello, Andrew," she said.

"Well, I have to say I didn't think they'd tell you about me." He grabbed a chair and took a seat, watching her.

"They didn't."

"So tell me, how does a woman like you end up with a bastard like Lash?" he asked.

"None of your business."

Her heart was racing, but she wasn't going to give him the satisfaction of showing that she was afraid.

"Fighting talk, I like it."

"What do you want?"

"I came to see you."

"Where's Paris?" she asked.

"Ah, Spider's woman. She's healing. You should be relieved actually. I decided to come and see you rather than take her for another time."

"You're a sick man." This man disgusted her. She hated him, and for Angel, that was a hard emotion to think about.

Andrew chuckled. "I'm just a boy in a man's body." He got up, and she quickly moved away, holding her arm away from her so that he wouldn't see it. "I like playing games."

"Let Paris go. Be the good man."

He stood, cupping his face as if he was debating it. "Nah, I don't think so." He lunged at her, and using all the training that Lash had shown her, she plunged the knife into his shoulder, screaming as she did so. Andrew pushed her against the wall, wrapping his hands around her neck. "I wonder what Lash will think of you when I'm done."

Even as he started to squeeze the life out of her, she gripped the blade and twisted it, making him scream.

Suddenly, there was a loud crash, and she looked just as Tate was slamming a chair against Andrew's back. Pulling the knife from his shoulder, Angel struck him again.

Neither of them were a match. Andrew slammed his fist against Tate's face, knocking her to the floor, then slammed Angel against the wall.

Angel cried out, cupping her stomach as the pain jolted her entire body.

The screams had alerted staff, and Andrew rushed out. Seconds later, Devil, Lash, and Tiny rushed down. She screamed that it was Andrew, and they went after him.

Suddenly, her water broke, and she was calling for help.

****

Sandy sat in the waiting room with Stink. A lot had happened within a day. Sally had lost her leg, Sasha still hadn't woken, and Sophia was still in stable but critical condition. Angel had also given birth to a little girl, Chloe. They were waiting for Lash to come and see them. They were all aware of what had happened, Andrew's visit to the hospital which had put them all on edge.

Stink held her hand, and she gripped his as well. She had to. She was totally shaken by what had happened.

Minutes passed, and finally Lash and Devil came

through the doors. Most of the club was here, and they all stood up.

"As you all know, Andrew came to the hospital today. He found a way in, and it would seem that Dr. Peters committed suicide in his office later this afternoon." Lash ran a hand down his face. "Whizz, he knew when I left. He's watching us, and he's watching this hospital."

"You don't know that."

"The fucker was able to get in and out. He got to Peters. Someone who is a computer genius is helping him. Trust me."

"You want me to go and see?" Whizz asked.

"Yes. I want to know who is helping him, where from, and exactly what he did today."

"Got it." Whizz stood, leaving, and heading toward the security room.

Sandy looked around the room, and she saw the anger, the fear, and the determination to beat this fucker.

"We're hurting," Lash said. "I get that. We're all hurting."

"What exactly do you want to us to do?" Dick asked. "Do you want us to sit on our asses, and wait for the next attack?"

"We don't," Devil said.

"Look, I know our people, and our women, our kids are in here. If Andrew is watching the hospital, we can't talk about it here," Stink said, speaking up. "We need to talk." Stink stood up, staring at Lash, both men communicating together.

"Agreed. Round everyone up. We will do this in two shifts. I don't want any of our own at the hospital. I'm not going to risk it."

"Good for you, I'm here." Everyone turned as Ned Walker entered the room, flanked by at least ten other men, fighters.

"What the fuck?" Tiny asked.

"My little girl called me. Told me what was going on, and I'm here, and look who I brought along for the ride." Ned pointed behind him, and Sandy smiled as she caught sight of Butch. He was the brother who had betrayed the club and made amends but had been sent to Vegas to help The Skulls' association there.

"Butch," Lash said.

"Miss me?" He was embraced as The Skulls and Chaos Bleeds hugged and slapped him on the back. It had been a long time since she'd seen him.

"Did you know about this?" Sandy asked.

"No. I didn't have a clue they were coming."

"Daddy," Eva said, rushing toward her father.

Ned opened his arms and held onto his daughter. "I came as soon as you called."

"I know, and thank you so much for coming. Really, thank you."

Sandy felt tears spring to her eyes as she watched the reunion between father and daughter. That was something she was never going to experience. Her family was dead. "I came with some reinforcements," Ned said.

"I can see that."

"Now, you guys need to go and do whatever the fuck it is that MCs do. I'm here, and so are my boys."

"Hey, Gavin," Eva said.

The large man beside Ned greeted her, as did many of the other fighters. Sandy hadn't seen so much bulk and muscle in one place. Mix the fighters in with the MCs, and it was a large bed of amazing. Damn, would they allow her to get some baby oil?

This was not the time to have her mind in the gutter. She needed to step away from the gutter, and focus on everything else.

Sandy watched as the men arranged to go off and have their meeting. She stayed in her seat.

Minutes later, Stink came toward her. "You're going again, aren't you?"

"I don't have a lot of choice. We need to deal with this fucker."

She stood, tucking her hair behind her ear. "They probably need me around here, so I'll do that."

He reached out, gripping her hips. "Talk to me."

"It's nothing. I'm just worried."

"Ned and his fighters will be here. He's the only one I trust with you, and with our women. Lash knows what he's doing."

"It's not about that. He came into the hospital, and got past us all. Angel almost died, and Tate's got a whopping big black eye to prove it. I'm asking you to be safe, for me, please." She cupped his face, running her thumbs across his cheeks.

"I'm not used to you being worried about me. I kind of like it, and I think I should do it more often."

"What? Have me worried about you?"

"Yeah, I like it. You should be worried about me." He leaned in close and claimed her lips. "I love you."

Kissing him back, Sandy smiled. "I love you, too. Be careful."

She watched him disappear, and folded her arms around her waist.

"It's okay, Sandy. We'll take care of you," Ned said, placing his arm across her shoulders.

She sighed. "Do you really think we've got a chance?" Ned was the kind of guy who gave it to her straight. He didn't sugarcoat anything. Everything he said and did was for a reason. Eva was one hell of a woman from being brought up with him.

"Andrew, the evil one we all know as Master?"

"You're in a chipper mood."

"Nothing like a visit to my daughter and grandkids to make me feel alive." Ned chuckled. "What you've got to remember, Andrew is just a man. He was once an addict, and his anger has been pushed into pursuing revenge against the club. We know who he is. Master was faceless. We didn't know him. He could have been anyone. Now, we know who he is, what he's capable of, and now we can handle him and anything else he throws at us." Ned pointed toward the doors where both clubs had just exited. "Don't forget, he's hit us all hard coming after the clubs. What he doesn't realize is both Skulls and Chaos Bleeds feed on this. They will hunt him down, they will destroy him, and they're going to make him wish he was never fucking born."

Sandy rested her head on his shoulder. "I knew there was a reason why I loved you."

"Honey, if I was ten years younger that man wouldn't stand a chance."

"I bet you still put the ladies in their place, even now."

"I have been known to try." Ned winked at her. "Now, I've been told a young girl has just lost a leg. That's got to be tough."

"Yeah."

"Come on, Sandy, show me to our wounded so that I can give them a pep talk."

****

Paris stayed curled up in a ball as Andrew threw another chair against the wall. Russell stood away from the mess, arms folded, clearly waiting for whatever his boss was going to do.

"Fucking, whoring, bitch!" The words were yelled out.

"Are you going to calm down so I can have a look, or are you going to cause more damage?"

"I need stitches." Andrew sat down on the chair. "All women, they're fucking cunts. They're only good for one thing and that is having a dick rammed inside them."

"What did you expect? You went into the hospital, and that Peters guy pretty much gave the game away. Angel was already tensed and ready. You were too fucking blind to see it." Russell peeled the shirt away from the wound, which looked ugly. "We're going to need to get the doctor."

"Then call someone." Andrew rubbed his temple. "I fucked up."

"You think?" Russell shook his head. "This is not going to be an easy fix. Why didn't you fuck over Sophia, or the one in the coma? Angel's a fucking old lady, and clearly a fighter."

"My information was wrong."

Paris looked over at Lola. The young woman had a black eye and mottled bruises along her body.

It wouldn't be long before they were thrown into the cells down in the basement. She wanted that to happen.

"Before we get the doctor here, what do you want me to do about these two?" Russell asked.

"Get them out of my sight before I fucking murder them," Andrew said.

One by one, they were grabbed and dragged into their cells. It was freezing in the basement, and it was hard to form a coherent thought.

"Hey," Paris said.

"We're not allowed to talk. I don't want to get in trouble," Lola said. "I don't know why I care anymore. Death would be easier."

"Are you still in high school?"

"Not anymore. I'm locked in a basement, waiting for the man who tortured me to let me go. That's stupid, right? Waiting to be let go? It's like dangling a bone in front of a dog. I'm never being let go. I'm going to die here."

Paris shook her head. "He let my sister go." She had to think that Celia was okay. Spider would take care of her. She was sure of it.

"Lucky sister."

"If you could, would you be able to send a message out?"

"Theoretically, yes, of course I could. It would depend on if someone was able to interpret it, and to also know that it was a call for help. With technology you can do most things." Lola shook her head. "I shouldn't even be talking to you."

"Lola, listen to me. The guy I know, he's with an MC club. The one that has been in the hospital." She crawled toward the cages, hoping to get closer to the other girl.

"You want me to send a message to the Master's enemy?"

"I want you to send a message to my friends. If you don't, we're not going to get out of here. Look at me." There was not a spot on her that wasn't covered in bruises. "He's going to kill me, and then he's going to move on to you. He's going to hurt us."

Lola had tears spilling from her eyes. "I'm so scared."

"I know, I know. Chaos Bleeds are friends with The Skulls. If you can get a message to one of them, we could get out. When they brought you here, did you see where they were going?"

Slowly, Lola nodded her head.

"You did, that's good. That is great. Who have they been wanting you to watch?"

"A guy named Whizz."

"Send it to him." Paris started to tell her the message, and she hoped to God that they two clubs were smart enough to find it.

Chapter Six

Three days later

After the fuck up three days ago, life was returning to normal, or as much normal as two clubs being together could handle. Stink took Sandy to work so that she could help with the brothers. Sasha still hadn't come around yet, but Sophia was showing a marked improvement. She was still hooked up to machines and being carefully monitored. Those with shots to the arms, shoulders, and legs, had been sent home. Stomach shots were being forced to stay at the hospital.

They still hadn't gone any further in their relationship, but Sandy made sure to kiss him now every time she saw him, and every time she left. She wasn't going to have not kissing him as a regret, she'd told him.

Standing outside near his bike, Stink drank his coffee and stared at the clubhouse. So much had happened in the last few years. There had been a lot of death, a lot of loss, but also a lot of love.

"What's going on?" Butch asked, coming to stand beside him.

Holding his hand out, he shook Butch's, and pulled him in for a hug. "I've missed your fucking ugly face."

"Yeah, Vegas is not the same."

"Do you miss us?" Stink asked.

"Yeah, I do. I never thought I'd say that. Michael misses his dad as well." Michael was the result of a one night stand between Cheryl and Alex. Butch claimed Cheryl as his own, but after his betrayal in helping another club, he'd been sent to Vegas, taking both Cheryl and Michael with him. "It's good to be back."

"I'm sorry it's not under better circumstances."

"I don't care about the circumstances. Once I heard that there had been a mass shootout at the club, no one was keeping me back. I fucked up, but you guys are still my family. I'll help where I can. Did I hear right? This is all on Gash's brother."

"Yeah, shit went down before Gash went to prison. Both of them prospected for the club. Gash got in, Andrew got the boot."

"So this is Andrew's way of getting revenge."

"That, and we also took out the seller of the women he branded and tortured," Stink said. "Brianna and Jessica both have his brand. There was a club whore as well, Lydia, I think."

"That shit is fucked up, even by our standards." Butch shook his head.

"So, what has been happening in Vegas?"

"Lot of fights, lot of training, and deals. I work closely with Ned, helping him organize shit. It's not the same as being in an MC."

"You ever thought of starting a Vegas Skulls?" Stink asked.

"I'm not the kind that can be a leader."

"It's just a thought."

"A good one, but still a thought."

Since Ned Walker had come with his fighters in tow, they had been able to collect themselves. Whizz had been able to locate the feeds from the hospital, and discovered someone had left a trace after being tapped into them. Andrew was watching them, but Whizz had said that he must have someone doing the work for him. It was amateur hacker stuff but someone who was damn good at it as well. The kind that got people noticed.

The fact Whizz was able to do anything was huge. Sally wasn't taking her operation well at all. She was still in the hospital, and the only person who could talk to her was Daisy. Steven, Lacey, Whizz, Lash, all of them had gone to see her, and not once had she shown any sign of actually responding. The moment Daisy was there, she tried her hardest to comfort the little girl.

Simon and Tabitha would be leaving at the end of the week. The doctors were keeping them for tests and further monitoring.

"This place looks amazing," Butch said.

"What did Cheryl think of you coming here alone?" Stink sipped his coffee.

"She knew what was happening. I don't keep secrets from her. I learned my lesson with all of you. Anyway, tell me what the fuck is going on with you and the hot little doctor?"

"Sandy? We're a couple."

"Seriously? For real this time, and not just pretend."

"She's all mine." Stink couldn't wipe the smile off his face. It was damn good to finally say that Sandy belonged to him.

Before either of them could say anything, Lash's car pulled into the parking lot. Stink placed his cup on the wall behind him and approached the car. Angel was back from the hospital. The baby was fine, more than fine, and so was Mommy.

She climbed out of the car, and grabbed the baby seat from the back. "We're home for now."

With the threat of Andrew, they were all on lockdown.

Those still in the hospital were being protected.

Spider came out of the clubhouse. Celia was in the play area on the swing. They had all taken to the young woman who had the mind of a child. She was beautiful, but they all cared for her wellbeing. Since they had her back, she'd been getting more upset, screaming for Paris, for her sister. Stink didn't know what to do to help the brother. Every day Spider was getting stronger, but his rage was getting harder.

Angel came toward them, holding her baby. Stink smiled down at the little girl, Chloe. She was sleeping peacefully. Anthony was at school, along with the rest of the kids. "Do we have any leads?" she asked.

He spotted the black eye and cut lip that Andrew had given her. Tate's wasn't much better either, and Murphy was desperate to fuck over Master, one way or the other. Stink didn't know who was more pissed, Tate or Murphy.

"No leads, nothing new."

They were all waiting for Whizz. Between his visits to Sally, and working, he wasn't finding anything solid yet, but they all knew it was only a matter of time. It had to be. They were all counting on him, everyone.

Angel nodded.

"You're okay," Gash said, coming toward her. Stink watched as Angel was embraced by Gash. Lash tapped him on the arm, and telling him that was enough.

"It's okay, Lash," Angel said. "Hey, Charlotte."

"I'm so pleased you're okay, and you have a new addition to your family. She looks so cute."

Everyone came out of the clubhouse to greet Angel, staring at the baby, and it was while they were all doing that Stink made his escape, jumping on the back of his bike, and heading toward the hospital.

Kids, he'd have them if Sandy wanted them. Throughout his life, he'd never wanted to be held down by them, but every time he thought of Sandy pregnant, swollen with his kids, he got rock hard.

Seriously rock hard.

Parking his bike, he headed into the hospital in time to see Sandy placing down a file. She looked tired, exhausted, and in that moment, very fuckable. She turned, and the moment she saw him, the smile that played across her face melted his heart.

"Stink, what are you doing here?" she asked.

"It's nearly lunchtime, or as close as you can get. Come on, I want to take you for a ride. Get away for a little bit."

She stared down at herself. "I'm a mess."

"You look perfect, and don't let anyone tell you different." He reached out, taking her hands, and pulled her close. "Come on. We need to get away from all of this."

They left the hospital, and he straddled his bike, handing her the helmet.

"Seriously, you're going to make me wear this?"

"Andrew is still out there, and until we know where he is, what he has planned, you're putting that on. I'm not having your brains smashed because I wasn't thinking straight."

She gave him a pointed look, but didn't argue, which he was pleased about.

"Excellent," he said, when she placed the helmet right over her head. "You're the sexiest woman I've ever seen."

"Bite me, Stink."

"One of these days, baby, I'm going to do just that."

He rode out of the parking lot of the hospital, and Sandy wrapped her arms around his waist, holding on to him tightly. His cock pressed against the front of jeans, wanting inside her.

Focus, fucking focus.

This was not the time for sex.

Riding out of town, he went toward the mall. The ride took a little over thirty minutes but having Sandy

93

pressed against his back was more than fine with him. He loved the feel of her pussy pressed against him. Soon, he would he fucking her, and claiming her properly. Until then, he was more than happy with having her any way that he could get her.

He pulled up into the bike space in the underground parking facility of the mall. Sandy climbed off first, handing him back the helmet. "Why are we here?"

"We're here to forget about all the troubles that are going on."

"Do you really think that is right? With everything that has happened, they need us to be ready."

He pressed a finger to her lips, silencing her.

"No, no more work or talking about what is going on." He kissed her lips, smiling at her.

"I don't know."

"Do you trust me?"

"Of course."

"Then trust me. We need this, and each of the men at the club is going to be doing exactly the same thing with their women."

"I'm your woman?"

"My old lady."

Once again the smile on her face melted his heart. "I never thought I'd be happy to hear those three words."

"Get used to it. I may even get you inked just so you know who has claimed you."

"I'll never forget."

Taking hold of her hand, they made their way toward the main food court. Pulling her in front of him, he wrapped his arms around her waist, kissing her neck.

"I feel like a young school kid with her boyfriend."

He chuckled. "Be prepared for more of where that

came from."

They got some burgers and fries, heading toward the main seating area. Finding a little quiet place for them to have some peace, he sat opposite her.

"This is great," she said. "Really, it is."

Taking a bite of his burger, he watched as she dove into her own food. He adored watching her eat, and with Sandy, he saw what his other brothers saw with their own women. Watching her eat actually made him horny.

****

Sandy put all of her troubles out of her mind and focused on Stink in front of her. "This is good, I mean, really good."

"I know."

"Ego?"

"Nope. I've been to the mall a few times, and I love it here."

"Is it safe?"

"For now. Andrew is injured, and I've told you to trust me, and to not worry. I've got this, baby."

"I know. I know." She smiled at him.

"I also want to head out to my house to check on it, make sure I didn't leave water boiling or anything."

Sandy laughed. "You wouldn't do something like that."

"And why wouldn't I?"

She stared down at her food before returning her gaze to his. "Because you're a safe guy like that."

"Exactly, and you should…"

"Trust you."

"I've got this, Sandy. I've got you, and we're going to make it safe."

She nodded. "You're right. So, let's talk about something else. What are your plans for after all of this?"

she asked.

He took a large bite of his burger, and she watched him. This was what she found herself doing most times, watching him, observing, loving.

"It depends on you," he said.

"It does? How?"

"How do you like Vegas?"

"It's … okay."

Stink nodded. She didn't understand why he suddenly looked nervous.

"What's going on?" she asked.

"There's something I want to ask you, and it's really important that I do."

"All right, go for it."

"Sandy, I love you. I mean, I really love you. You're my life, and I don't see me being anywhere but with you." He didn't get down on one knee. Stink slid a velvet box toward her.

"What is this?"

"It's what I've been wanting to give you for some time. I bought it a couple of years back."

"You've been meaning to propose to me for a few years?"

"Yep. I've always been waiting for the right time. It's no pressure at all, Sandy."

"No pressure? You're proposing?" Her heart was racing, and tears filled her eyes. Staring across at the man who had not only protected her, but who had shown her what it truly meant to be loved, she couldn't believe it.

"Yes."

"We haven't even had sex."

"I know. I should probably take you out for a test drive, right?"

She giggled. "Yes."

Stink took the ring out of the box, and slid it onto

her finger. "When all of this is over, I want to take you to Vegas, and then I want to take you wherever you want to go in the world."

"Really?" This was why she had fallen in love with Stink. He was such a charmer, a caring man, and she loved him with all of her heart.

"Yes, really."

"What if you don't like fucking me?" she asked.

"You just can't get your head out of the gutter."

"Stink, I'm forty years old. I know a relationship lasts a lot longer if there's something keeping it together. Most of the time that something is sex."

"Well, I'd say that we're going to be the ones to keep it together. You, me, and us. This is what is going to be keeping it together."

She stared down at the ring, shocked and delighted with his proposal. "I love you, Stink."

They finished eating their food before they looked through several of the shops. Stink had eyes for no one else but her, which she found to be a heady combination. There were some scantily clad women trying to get his attention, but he didn't give them the time of day.

The time away from the hospital was a delight. In the past three days Sandy had loved and hated her job as a doctor. Seeing Sophia's health returning, Sally's depression, followed by Sasha's stillness, it had slowly started to tear her apart.

If Stink hadn't taken her away from it all—she really didn't know what she'd have done if it wasn't for him. He completed her. In the early years of spending time with him, she didn't really think much of him.

Stink was very silent. He spent most of his time watching rather than doing anything else, which was a strange combination to have. The club adored him as did she. She couldn't imagine a life without him. He'd slowly gotten underneath her skin, and forced her to look at him.

After she bought some fresh clothes to replace the ones that had been damaged in the gun attack, they were back on his bike heading toward his home.

He lived thirty minutes from the clubhouse, close to Lash and Angel, Tiny and Eva. It was his own space, a three-bedroom house with a backyard that also had a pool. Stink enjoyed life's luxuries, which was another surprise about him. She thought he'd be a slob at home. It hadn't been the case. Also with his lack of smell, she could enjoy smelly cheeses, garlic, and every kind of food delight imaginable. He never complained.

That is because he loves you.

She climbed off his bike first, pulling the helmet off her head, and taking a deep breath. "I really hate wearing a helmet. Can't you get me to wear something else?"

"We kill Andrew, you get to ride without a helmet."

"Do you really think that is possible?"

"To kill him?" Stink asked.

"Yeah, he's been pretty invincible."

"He's a guy, not some devil in disguise. We'll find him. Whizz just needs to do his thing."

"It's hard for him to do when he's worrying about his kid," Sandy said.

"Once again we're talking about stuff that I don't want you to worry about." He entered their home, stopping her to kiss her head. "Stop worrying."

"Doesn't it concern you that he was able to take two women? Paris and Celia."

"First, we've got Celia back. Second, we're going to take Paris back. Third, no one was watching them.

They were an easy target. We're not going to let that happen."

"Just once I think I'd like a life without drama, without worrying if I'm going to get my face blown off, or if I'm going to watch my friends get blown apart." He cupped her face and pressed a kiss to her lips.

Sandy loved the feel of his lips against hers. Wrapping her arms around his neck, she pushed him back just a little, kicking the door closed as she did. Her pussy grew slick, and need took over.

For a long time she had been holding back these feelings for him, but she didn't want to hold back anymore.

"Sandy?"

"I want you to fuck me, Stink."

"What? Not now!"

She stepped back and tugged her shirt from her scrubs. "Now." Wriggling out of her bottoms, she stood before him in a lace bra and panties, desperate for his touch. Stepping up to him, she ran her hands beneath his jacket, against his chest. "Please. I want you."

He stroked his thumb across her cheek.

"Are you sure about this?"

"This is what I'm sure about. You, us, this, it's what I want." Leaving one hand against his heart, she glided the other one down, cupping his cock. He was rock hard, and she smiled. "You can't tell me you don't want me."

Suddenly, he turned her so that her back was against the wall. "I never said I didn't want you. I've done everything in my power to make you feel comfortable with me."

"I do, and now it's time for you to take what you want." She pushed his jacket off, yanking up his shirt. "Take me. Make me yours, and only yours."

He sank his fingers into her hair, claiming her lips in a kiss so searing, Sandy knew she'd never be the same again. The whole of his touch, the feel of him against her was only serving to drive her crazy. Nothing else could do.

Tugging at his belt, she unbuttoned his jeans, sliding them down as he tore her bra and panties from her body. "I'll buy you some more of them."

Sinking to her knees, she took his jeans down to the floor, waiting as he kicked out of his shoes, and pushed everything aside. Taking his cock out of his boxer briefs, she covered the tip with her mouth, enjoying the taste of his pre-cum as it covered her tongue. Swallowing it down, she licked down the large vein that pulsed at the side.

"Fuck, baby, your mouth is like fucking heaven," he said.

He ran his fingers through her hair, and Sandy glanced up his body, watching as he stared right back at her.

"I have dreamed of this moment, of your beautiful lips wrapped around my dick."

"Is it as good as you thought it would be?" she asked, releasing him long enough.

"It's better." He groaned as she took him to the back of her mouth, swallowing him down. Stink was certainly blessed with a nice fat cock. For the first time in ages, Sandy wanted to fuck. She wanted to be naked, and have hot, sweaty, no holds barred sex.

He wrapped her hair around his fist, holding onto her head as he started to slowly thrust into her mouth.

Keeping her gaze on him, she took as much of him as she could, fighting past the gag reflex. Sliding a hand between her thighs, she started to play with her pussy. Her cream made it easy for her to slide between the moist folds, teasing her clit.

"You're touching your little cunt, aren't you, baby?"

She hummed her answer, watching as he gritted his teeth.

"You're going to be the death of me."

Pulling off his cock, she flicked the tip, and smiled at him. "It would be one hell of a way to go."

Stink stepped away from her, and she couldn't help but pout. He rid himself of the boxer briefs, and sank to the floor. Sandy released a little squeal as he opened her thighs. His hand slapped hers away.

"If anyone is going to be playing with this pussy, it's going to be me." His fingers stroked between her cunt, and he groaned. "So you like to keep it nice and bare."

"I don't like anything to get in the way." She always waxed between her thighs.

"Lie back, baby. I'm about to make you feel a whole lot better."

Sandy lay back, opening her thighs. She reached down and spread the lips of her pussy. "Does this make it easier for you?"

"Oh, fuck," he said. Two fingers slid inside her, and she moaned.

"Feels so good. I wish it was your dick."

"Baby, you're going to get my dick. No need to worry about that. I'm going to give it all to you."

He leaned down, and Sandy cried out as his tongue slid across her clit. Stink sucked her nub hard, using his teeth to create that bite of pain she loved so much. It had been a couple of years since she'd been with a man, and a lot longer since she had one go down on her. Stink's tongue was utterly wicked, and he took her over.

He flicked over her clit, moving down to fuck inside her. Each time his tongue fucked inside her, he removed his fingers.

"You're so damn wet. Have you been torturing us both with this wait?"

"Please, Stink, fuck me already. I can't take much more."

"You're going to take more, and fucking love it."

Stink more than made up for lost time as he brought her to a screaming orgasm with the use of his tongue. He didn't stop there. Stink wouldn't let it be over, and he flipped her onto her knees, drawing his fingers up against her asshole.

He used the lubrication from her pussy to get her ass nice and ready. As he slid his fingers inside her ass, Sandy gasped at the sudden invasion. Stink had two fingers, working in her ass, stretching her out. With his other hand, he continued to finger her pussy, teasing her clit.

"I want another orgasm out of you, Sandy, before I take this to the bedroom. You're going to give me what I want."

When had Stink become so dominant? He was like a whole other man, one she hadn't seen before. He had her on her knees, vulnerable to him.

"Do you want me, baby?"

"Yes."

"You want my cock in your pretty little cunt?"

"Yes." She screamed the word, needing him desperately. Throughout the whole of her life she'd never been this excited, nor this full.

Stink teased her ass, her clit, and her pussy. The fingers on her clit would move down and fuck inside her. He matched the pace of the fingers inside her ass.

"If you want my cock, sweet Sandy, you're going

to have to give me another orgasm. I want to hear you scream my name, and only when you have, will I give you what you want."

Chapter Seven

Sandy's tight pussy was like a fucking glove as it squeezed his fingers. Stink wished he could smell her heady fragrance. The scent he wanted wasn't the divine smell of food. No, it was the scent of her pussy he wanted more than anything.

"Oh, God, it feels so good."

"That's not God, baby, that's all me. I'm giving it to you, no one else." He started to finger-fuck her ass. Stink had never known a woman to be so aroused. Sandy's pussy was fucking dripping, and his instincts had been completely right about her. She wanted a man who took charge, who didn't take shit. Pushing three fingers inside her weeping pussy, he used his thumb to press against her swollen clit. "You want to be fucked so bad, don't you, baby?"

"Yes, I want you. I need you."

"You're going to get me, baby, and when you've had me, there's not going to be any other man for you. Once I put that ring on your finger, you belong to me."

"Yes, yes, please," Sandy said, begging.

"I could get used to you begging me. Your sweet sounds echoing around the room as I fuck you."

He relentlessly stroked over her clit, feeling her cunt tighten around his fingers. A second orgasm started to build, and his cock felt like it was about to explode.

"Oh fuck, Stink!" She yelled his name as she splintered apart. Pulling out of her pussy, he kept his fingers on her clit, and aligned his cock to her pussy. He was so hard, he didn't even need to feed his cock inside her cunt. Stink had opened her up and got her wet enough that he only needed to fuck within her.

The heat of her surrounded him, and mid-orgasm, her muscles tightened around him harder than anything he'd ever felt.

Cursing, he kept fucking her ass with his fingers, knowing by the end of the day he was going to claim her ass all to himself.

He slammed inside her, going to the hilt.

Only when she couldn't take it anymore, did he released her clit and grip her hip. Pounding inside her, he gave her it all, and didn't wait for her to beg for more. There, in the entrance hall of their house, he fucked her hard, giving her all of him.

She pushed back against him, taking more of him.

"I'm not going to last, baby. Years of using my hand was nowhere near good enough, and I want your pretty pussy." He hadn't put on a condom, nor was Sandy protected. Stink had been so impatient to get inside her, he hadn't thought about protection.

Fucking her harder, he gritted his teeth, and within minutes of the first thrust he was coming hard and deep. In the last second, he pulled out, and beat his cum onto the curve of her butt and base of her back, his seed running across in thick, copious streams. Sweat dripped from him, and the pleasure was so intense it made him lightheaded. "Fuck! Fuck! Fuck!"

He panted, eased back, and released her ass.

Sandy knelt up, and he banded an arm around her waist, kissing her shoulder. She rested her head against his chest. The cum he'd just decorated her back with was now pressed against his pelvis as she rested against him.

"That was amazing," she said.

"Good."

"No, I mean it. It was better than I imagined."

"Ah, so you admit that you've imagined me, babe." He kissed her shoulder again, chuckling as feeling started to return to all of his limbs.

"You know I've thought about you. I've done

nothing else but think of you. And you know what?"

"What?" he asked.

"Now that I know how good you are, you've got no excuse. That performance I expect every time."

Stink chuckled. "Sandy, that performance was nowhere near my best."

"It wasn't?"

"Nope. That was the past couple of years of beating off into my hand."

"No. You had to have been with someone, anyone."

"Who would I fuck? Who would I want to fuck? I told you, for a long time it has always been you. I haven't been with another woman. Here is your competition." He held his hand up, and she gasped, turning to stare at him.

"Really?"

"Baby, I'm not a liar, and I wouldn't dream of starting now. What I said is the truth, all of it. You, me, this, it was going to happen." He leaned in kissing her.

"I think we need to take a shower. We smell like sex."

He sighed. "It's a smell I'm never going to know."

Sandy laughed, really laughed. She stood up and held her hand out.

"I've got your cream over my fingers."

"So? It came from me. Besides, I'm a doctor. I hate to say it, but I've had a great deal worse."

This time, he laughed. Taking hold of her hand, he got to his feet, banded his arms around her as he followed her upstairs toward the bathroom. Pinching her butt, he loved the way she giggled as he did. The sounds she made were absolutely magic, and he wanted to keep her like that for the rest of their lives.

Wrapping an arm around her waist, he hauled her up, and dumped her in the shower, following her in, and locking the door.

"What are you doing? Stink, what?" She released a squeal as he turned on the water, spraying the two of them with cold.

Laughing, he held her tight against his body even as she fought to get away.

"You mean bastard!"

Reaching out for the soap, he rubbed his hands in it, dropping it to the floor before he placed his hands all over her body.

She continued to fight him, but he was just as determined to have her coming apart in his arms.

"Stink, stop."

"Sh, the water is warming up now. You've got nothing to worry about."

They were both laughing, and Sandy sank into his arms. "I want you again." She reached her arm behind his neck, turning a little so that he could claim her lush lips. "Just out of curiosity, have you imagined me in the shower?"

"Sandy, I've imagined you every single way that I can get you. It doesn't stop for me." Washing his hand of the soap, he slipped his fingers between her thighs. "What about you? Have you imagined me?"

"I've touched myself plenty of times, and imagined it was you." She started to thrust her hips onto his hand. He finger-fucked her several times before drawing them up, and teasing over her swollen clit.

Pressing her against the wall, he watched as she placed her hand against the wall, the glint from the diamond engagement ring, catching his eye. Soon, she was going to belong to him. It turned him on even more. Sandy belonged to him.

"I love you," he said, biting her shoulder.

"I love you, too."

He kept teasing her pussy even as his cock demanded attention. Focusing on her, he felt how wet she grew. Her body responded to each touch, each flick, driving him crazy for more of her.

She let go of the wall and reached around to grab his cock. "I don't think it's fair that you get to play, and I don't."

"Baby, my dick belongs to you, always. Take it whenever you fucking want it." He growled the words against her ear. Pinching her clit, he roughly fucked into her, once again using his thumb.

"If that's the case, I want your cum, Stink." She was out of his arms in a flash and stood before him. Her hand gripped his cock, and in the next second her mouth had covered the tip.

"Fuck!"

"You say that a lot." She released him long enough to speak before taking him back into her mouth. Sandy didn't hold back. She took what she wanted, and he fucking loved it.

This time, he held onto the wall for safety as Sandy tortured him with the pleasure of her mouth. She sucked the tip, sliding her tongue down the vein along the side, going further down to suck one of his balls into her mouth, then coming back up to take his cock.

With the hand not wrapped around his dick, she cupped his balls, playing with them.

He moaned as she scored her teeth down the whole length.

Stink watched her pink lips spread wide, forced to take all of his length, relishing the feel. In and out, he thrust, feeling her throat working to swallow him down. Every time he beat off didn't even begin to compare to this moment with her. Every single moment was by far better than anything he ever imagined, and he'd done a lot of that while waiting for her to be ready.

"You want to swallow my spunk, baby?"

She hummed her answer.

"You've kept me waiting a long time for this."

Her hands moved to his ass, sinking her nails into the flesh. "Do you think I should let you have it?"

She nodded, moaning as he fucked her mouth.

Stink wasn't going to last much longer. Thrusting into her mouth, he watched her take him. There was no way he could look away, even if he wanted to.

"Are you ready?"

Another hum.

"Good, because this is all for you." He groaned out as the first wave of his orgasm spilled out, landing in her mouth. Her mouth worked, swallowing him down. The sight was fucking beautiful.

Sandy milked him of every single drop until he had no choice but to pull out of her precious mouth. Turning the shower off, he picked her up, carrying her through to his bedroom.

"Stink, what's going on?"

He didn't answer her. Dumping her on the bed, he followed her down, spreading her legs and settling between them. Opening the lips of her bare sex, he swiped his tongue from the entrance of her cunt all the way to her clit. Circling the swollen bud, he repeated the same action, over and over again. She cried out his name, thrusting her pussy onto his face. He really wished he could smell her. Instead, he had to relish in the subtle tastes he got from her pussy, and bask in it.

"Fuck, Stink, yeah, just like that … oh, so good."

Listening to her pleasure was a heady thing. Sucking her clit hard, he used his fingers to drive inside her.

Her pussy quivered, squeezing his digits, and he loved it.

"Oh, God … too soon…"

She came screaming his name, filling the air with her sounds. He loved every second of it, and he didn't stop until she reached a second orgasm, and collapsed on the bed, begging some more.

Crawling up the bed, he licked his lips.

"Where the fuck have you been hiding?" she asked.

He chuckled. "Sandy, baby, I've been right here. You just haven't seen it."

"Well, now, you better be prepared to be owned. I'm not letting you, or your magical tongue get away. Not now, not ever."

"It's about fucking time."

****

Sandy stared at the ceiling, and she was in heaven. They hadn't gone back to the clubhouse, and had spent all afternoon fucking. Stink had gone down to the kitchen to make them both something to eat. Her pussy was sore, as was her ass. He hadn't fucked her there yet, but it was only a matter of time before he did. She wanted it. Sandy wanted it all with Stink, and staring up at the ceiling, she could only question herself. What the fuck had she been doing with her life? Being with Stink, she couldn't think of any reason as to why she'd kept him at arms' length. She'd never been particularly good with relationships, and it wasn't something she actually thought she was good at, far from it. Still, it was her own cowardice that kept her away. She saw that now. Her parents had such a loving relationship, and she saw firsthand what happened when you tore two lovers apart. She never wanted to be controlled by someone else. The

MC life was so fragile and dangerous, and she didn't want to risk it. Now, she saw the risks, and she wanted to revel in the time she had with Stink. To live a life of no regrets.

He'd been there for her, offering her love and comfort for a long time, but she'd never taken him up on his offer. Why?

She didn't know.

There was no answer for her as to why she would do what she did. She was a complete and total idiot.

Holding her hand up, she stared at the simple yet beautiful engagement ring. She never thought she'd get married to any of the bikers she fucked. Marriage was supposed to never happen for her, or be with a guy that was a fellow doctor. A boring marriage where she didn't have to worry about a thing.

Stink is better than any other man.

He was sweet, charming, loving, loyal, a hard ass—everything that she could think of when it came to Stink, only made her love him more. Her lips tingled from his passionate kisses. Her whole body was on fire with the memory of him.

"You're not having second thoughts are you?" Stink asked.

She sat up, watching as he came into the bedroom. He held a large tray, and her stomach growled.

"I should have stopped fucking you earlier to feed you."

"If you had, I wouldn't be talking to you," she said, teasing him.

"Come on then, second thoughts?"

"None. I don't have any second thoughts. I'm wondering why I waited so long for you." She reached over the tray, and cupped his cheek. "Why did I wait?"

"I was always curious about that myself. Let me

know what you come up with."

"For a doctor, I'm stupid."

Stink shook his head. "You weren't ready."

"Why didn't you make me?"

"What? Rape you? Sandy, I'm a lot of things but a rapist isn't one of them. When we got to this, it was going to be because the two of us wanted it more than anything. I love you. I can wait. I'm a patient man."

"I'm not patient. I've never been a patient person. Life is hard, and it's unfair. Nothing good ever comes to those who wait patiently. Life is fucking brutal."

He covered her hand with his own. "It is brutal, and it's hard. There are times I hate it as well. The past few years with The Skulls have been the most trying. I've witnessed love, passion, betrayal, redemption, and family. Lash found Angel for a debt of her father. Their love, it has been something I have witnessed, and I didn't even think it was possible for that man to fall in love."

Sandy chuckled.

Out of every single relationship that had developed in The Skulls' clubhouse, Lash and Angel's was the kind people read about or watched. They were the most unlikely of couples, and yet they were, at times, the strongest. One couldn't live without the other, and vice versa.

"The Skulls, though, we're a family. Every foe that has come our way, we have defeated because that is who we are. It's what we do, and we'll always do it. Always together, always as a family. It's why I was patient all these years for you, Sandy. Even if you wanted to wait to get married, I'd wait for you."

"I don't want to wait. I want us to go to Vegas, now."

Stink sighed. "Now?"

"Yes, we can get Ned to organize it, or we can get

Alex. I want to belong to you. Andrew is here, and we're fighting him. If something bad happens, I don't want to live a life of regret, and I don't want you to live that kind of life either."

Stink kissed her lips. "I'll make some calls."

She nodded.

"First, you've got to eat, and I'm watching you." He pointed at his eyes, and then at her.

"I'm eating, boss man." She took a bite of her sandwich, and watched as he grabbed out his cell phone and started to make some calls. Sandy watched him, admiring the hardness of his body. The way he commanded attention.

She tuned out what he was saying as the happiness consumed her. This was what she'd been fighting all these years. She was angry with herself for making them both wait.

After a couple more calls, Stink hung up.

"Get dressed."

"What?"

"We can head out on Alex's private jet. If we get to his place within the hour, we can be in Vegas tonight. He's already got the casino ready to receive us, and he's organized a chapel to do the ceremony. We're not going to have any friends, but we're going to have each other."

Sandy got off the bed and started rushing around, putting on clothes. Her heart was racing, and she was so excited. After all this time she was finally going to get married.

Within five minutes they were on the road, heading toward Alex and Sunshine's reclusive house that was several miles outside of Fort Wills. In that moment, Sandy had to wonder why the fuck Alex lived so far away. It was far enough away from the clubhouse for privacy. The more she thought about it, the more she understood.

No one could barge into Alex's place uninvited, whereas at their house, or at the clubhouse, anyone could barge in. Also, Alex's place offered a great deal of security. Stink typed in the code in the security gate, and he drove down the long path toward the house. They got there to see three men waiting to escort them.

Stink got out of the car, and rounded it toward her. She held his hand, her heart racing as they got into the helicopter. Once they were secured, Stink held her hand again. "Are you ready for this?" he asked.

"Ready as I'll ever be."

****

Lash rubbed at his temples as he stared at the abundance of computer screens that Whizz had set up. He'd never seen so many screens before. The entire basement was now lined with them, and he was sure there had to be fifty different screens. With how fast Whizz was typing, it was causing Lash a headache. He never understood computers, and he still didn't. What was the point in them when you could talk to someone? Yeah, he was going to be the generation that went to the cashier rather than do it all by himself in the supermarket. Angel loved those little machines, scanning everything before putting it into her bag.

Someone walking downstairs had Lash turning around to see Tiny. "I've just had news from Alex. Stink and Sandy are on their way to Vegas to get married."

"Good for them. It's about time Stink got what he wanted. He's been chasing after that woman for so long. I'm surprised he didn't change his mind, and date someone else."

"Amen to that. I was thinking of starting a poll or something. How long will it take Stink and Sandy to get together," Whizz said.

"It has taken them some time, I'll grant you that," Tiny said. "What's happening with all the glowing screens? We about to have a zombie invasion or something?"

"This is technology, Tiny. You know, the advancement of robots, our future, and soon they won't even need us to procreate," Whizz said.

"I hope not. I love getting my dick wet," Lash said. He thought of his woman upstairs, caring for their new baby. Chloe, another kid in the mix. Anthony seems besotted with her, which was a huge relief. In private, away from anyone seeing, Lash had been reading books on siblings and rivalry. He'd never experienced it with Nash. Hell, just recently he'd even talked to Nash about it. He didn't want Anthony and Chloe at each other's throats, or to fear for either kid. There was no way there would be a favorite in his family. Besides, if his kids wanted to start on the whole favorites, they'd fucking lose. His favorite was Angel, his woman.

"I'd fight machines for the right to fuck," Tiny said.

"You know Miles and Tabitha, and Luke," Lash said.

"I think so. They're my kids."

"And Tate as well. Do they fight? Not get along? Or anything?" Lash looked toward Tiny, his mentor, his ex-Prez, and most importantly, his father. Tiny had taken them in when his own parents were killed. Tiny had been more of a father to him than anyone else. Tate was like a sister to him, an annoying, bitchy sister who pissed him off all the time.

"Luke's just been born. He's a baby, Lash. Miles and Tabitha get along great. To be honest, Tabitha spent more time fighting with Devil's Simon than anyone else."

"And now they're totally in love," Whizz said.

"Shut up," Tiny said, glaring at Whizz.

"You have to admit they are perfect for each other. There's nothing else to say about it." Whizz held his hands up. "Perfect little couple. Possibly bring two MCs together."

"Seriously, Whizz, enough. They're kids. They don't know what love is. No one knows what love is at that age. They care more about chocolate and candy."

Lash truly believed Tiny was deluded, but that was going to have to be something he figured out himself.

"What's going on?" Tiny asked.

"Whizz, I'll let you answer that."

"Okay, so I was delving into Andrew's past, and at the moment, I've got that computer over there looking for all possible leads. It's pretty much starting at his life's history, coming into present day. Instead of me staring at a screen that is only scanning, I've decided to go ahead, and do this."

"What is this?"

"Simple. The clubhouse is surrounded with security. I'm accessing the security footage, and using face recognition software to discover who attacked us. On the one part of the scale, I'm using Andrew's history to discover everything we need to know about him to this day. For the present, I'm going to find out the fuckers who thought they could take out The Skulls. We're going to get even for Happy."

"Yeah, I reached out to The Skulls' Nomad division, and they're not happy. They want justice," Lash said.

Every MC that Lash knew had a Nomad division. It was a selection of men who wore the MC, but didn't stick to the clubhouse. So "The Skulls: Nomad" was seen on the uniform. That was where Adam, Twisted, and Happy came from. The Nomads all knew each other, and occasionally came to the clubhouse to stay. They didn't settle down. They rode hard, partied hard, and never got caught up in this kind of shit.

"How much justice?" Tiny asked.

"Ten of them are coming home, Tiny. They want blood, and they're not going to settle until they get it. Happy had a lot of friends."

"The dude was named Happy. People like being around happy people. It's a fact."

Lash shook his head, laughing.

"Come on, you all know it's true."

"True or not, we've got to get a handle on this shit," Tiny said.

"Ned is handling the hospital watch. We're regrouping, and our people will be out."

"What about Nash? How is he holding up?"

Lash paused. "Nash isn't leaving Sophia's side until she's guaranteed to come out of the hospital safe and well."

Tiny nodded. "I get that."

"Pussy, he's not left Sasha's side, and the brother is starting to smell. Real bad."

Whizz sighed. "Andrew hit us hard. I'll give him that."

"Yeah, he hit us hard, and we're going to hit them back," Lash said.

"Angel hurt him, right?" Tiny asked.

"Yeah. She stuck the knife I got her, right into his shoulder, why?"

"'Cause I'm thinking we keep on hitting him," Tiny said.

Lash smiled. "Why do you think I'm down here? Whizz gives me an address, and we round up some boys,

117

and we take them out."

"Got it," Whizz said.

Turning toward the computer screen, Lash saw six men. Their faces came up holding arrest photos.

"So, it looks like Andrew paid three million for the hit on the clubhouse."

"It would take a lot of cash to get a two-bit gang to our clubhouse," Lash said. "Get me their information, Whizz. I'm going to round up the guys."

Pulling out his cell phone, he put a call through to the hospital, requesting to speak to Nash.

"What is it, Lash?"

"What if I can guarantee you a chance of fucking over the men that shot at Sophia?"

"A chance?"

"Whizz found out the guys that shot at us. Took a measly three mil to pop us."

"Are we going?" Nash asked.

"Grab our guns, brother, we're going on a search party."

****

Sally stared down at her bandaged knee. There was nothing covering the rest of her leg. It was completely covering her knee, like a head cap, over her knee. Tears fell down her cheeks as she stared at her lost limb.

"Hey, sweetheart."

She looked up to see Ned Walker. He was Eva's father, and for some strange reason had considered himself the club's grandad.

Wiping away the tears, Sally stared at him, not knowing what to say.

"You're not a very trusting little thing, are you?"

"I'm not little."

"No. You've been through your own idea of

hell."

"Where's Steven?" she asked. He hadn't left her side once since her leg was taken. Wow, it had been a little over three days now. He didn't stay for long.

"From what I can gather, the club has information on the shit that happened to you. They're going to go and deal with it like real men."

"So you're forced to babysit me."

"Are you telling me you consider yourself a baby, or do you think of yourself as a woman?" Ned took a seat beside her.

"A woman."

"No, I'm not here to babysit. I'm here to help."

"I don't need any help."

"So those tears that were dancing down your face are not a problem?" he asked.

"They're none of your business, not really."

Ned sighed. "You remind me a little of Eva when she was younger. She's my little girl. My only girl." He patted her hand. "I killed her crackwhore of a mother, and I've been raising her alone ever since.

"Why are you telling me this?" she asked, tensing. If he was telling her this, did that mean he was going to kill her as well? She hoped not.

"Afraid of dying?"

She nodded.

"I bet you didn't for a second believe that was possible after the hell you've been through." Ned eased back in the chair, staring at her. "It's a relief to know you're not going to do anything stupid."

"I'm not going to kill myself if that's what you're worried about."

"I don't know. From what that boy has been telling me, it's a fear of his that you're going to do something stupid."

Even as she tried to fight them, the tears kept on coming.

"You've got to let them out, honey."

"No, I don't. I don't want to cry anymore. It doesn't solve anything."

Ned sat on the bed and placed his arm around her shoulders. "It looks bad now, but in a few years, it won't look so bad."

He rubbed her arm, and the comfort he offered her was her undoing. "I've lost my leg." She sobbed each word out, gasping for breath.

"I know."

"I can't have it back, and I want it back." She wrapped her arms around his waist, and held onto his strength as she finally let go. No one needed her to be strong. In that moment, she understood why everyone looked toward Ned for guidance, for love, and for support. He offered it without any expectation of getting anything back. Ned was simply a rock, and they were not.

He patted her back. "You know, in this day and age I've been told they do wonders with prosthetics."

She nodded.

"When Eva started dating Tiny, I wanted to kill the bastard. No one was good enough for my little girl, and to be honest, they're still not good enough. At first, I wanted her to have a fighter because it meant she'd be closer to home. I'd keep an eye on the little bastard in case he tried any funny business. So her falling for an MC guy … I wasn't happy. I even contemplated putting a hit out on Tiny."

"What changed?"

"I saw the way Tiny was with her. Even though the club life is dangerous, The Skulls, they have your back. They're a family first, not later."

"Why are you telling me this?"

"So you see the truth. Your leg is gone, and you're going to need the love and support of a family. Whizz and Lacey come with The Skulls. They're your family, and for the rest of your life, you're going to be loved, and protected."

"You shouldn't have been a fighter. I'm thinking you should have been a poet," she said, chuckling.

"Nah, you haven't seen me fighting, honey. Then you'd see that even with good words, I'll always be a brute."

****

Simon looked across the hospital room and saw Tabitha struggling to sleep. She was whimpering, crying out, and it hurt him to see. Climbing out of his bed, he gathered up his equipment when the large guy Gavin came into the room. He was a friend of Ned's, and had been ordered to take care of them.

His mom had to go home, as had his father.

He wasn't stupid. Simon knew the threat that had put them in the hospital was still out there.

"Get back to sleep, little man."

"My girl is hurting, and you're not going to stop me." He climbed off the bed, ignoring the pain. Simon had made a promise to Tabitha. As long as he was alive, he would do everything to make her safe. Bad dreams included, and he wasn't about to break his promise. Even if his father threatened to stop him calling her, he wasn't going to stop. Gavin took a step closer, and Simon held his hand up. "I will scream if you come any closer. I'll make sure the nurses don't let you near me."

"Look, you little shit—"

Stepping up to the large man, Simon glared. "Finish that, I dare you. My father is Devil, President of the Chaos Bleeds MC. I am going to follow in his footsteps. That club will be mine one day, and I will not forget about this. I will hunt you down, and hurt you, in ways you can't even imagine. My girl is hurting, and I promised to help her. I'm not going to break that promise."

He'd listened to his father command the same voice. Simon had spent hours practicing so that he could be exactly like him. Devil was respected and feared. Simon intended to make sure he was the same.

Gavin kept on staring.

"I'm going to lie down with her. That's all."

Stepping away from the man, Simon made sure not to turn his back. It was one of the first warnings his father had given him.

"Fuck this. Little shit…" Gavin kept on muttering as he left the hospital room. Wheeling his medication, Simon placed it opposite Tabitha's, and climbed into bed with her. The movement woke her up, and she gasped staring at him.

"Simon?"

"Yeah, it's me. You were having a bad dream."

"I just want them to go away. All the dreams go away." She lay down, and before her head rested on the pillow, he gathered her up in his arms. She rested her head on his arm, and he stared down at her.

He didn't know what it was about this girl, but Simon couldn't stop thinking about her. Love. That's what it was, love. He loved her more than anything. She called to him in ways he didn't even know was possible.

"I'm here now. Dreams won't hurt you."

"Do you have bad dreams?"

"I dream about you."

"You know Miles has a girlfriend. Her name's Bertie, and she goes to our school. I don't like her."

"You're my girlfriend."

She giggled. "Yeah, I am. Mom says I'm too young to have a boyfriend."

"What do you say?"

"I don't care. You've always been mine." Her eyes started to droop. "Don't go."

"Never."

Simon held her as she fell back to sleep, falling himself. This was how he wanted the rest of his life. To fall asleep with Tabitha in his arms.

Chapter Eight

Stink carried his wife across the threshold of the hotel suite, the honeymoon suite that Alex had reserved for them. Sandy giggled as he placed her on her feet.

"Was I getting a little too heavy for you there, sport?" she asked.

"Not at all, but I'm ringing." He closed the door, at the same time pulling out his cell phone. "What's up?" Stink asked.

"So, Whizz did his computer nerd thing, and found the gang that took the hit out on us," Lash said.

"No shit?"

"Lucky for you, we got them, and they're at the warehouse. I don't know how long you're going to be on your honeymoon, but if you want some payback, then you better get your ass here. Nash is going mental on them. Not to mention the others."

"Is Pussy there?"

Lash paused. "No. He didn't want to miss Sasha in case she woke up. If she's disoriented, it could scare her."

"Okay. I'm going to enjoy my honeymoon. I'll be back tomorrow."

"Have fun, brother."

"Always." He hung up.

"Do we need to go back?" Sandy asked. She looked worried.

"The group that took the hit, the boys have got them back at the warehouse in Fort Wills. The boys are showing their frustration."

"Don't you want to go back?"

He closed the distance between them, wrapping an arm around her waist. "Why would I want to do that?"

"They hurt the club."

"I know. You see, I can quit my honeymoon with you right now, to go and beat the shit out of a bunch of guys that deserve it. Or I can let the guys get pummeled by those that have been wronged by them. I've got you, and I just married you. One night is what we're going to have. We can deal with the rest when we get back home."

"One night?"

"Well, it's one night of many." He fingered the collar of her shirt. They were both wearing the clothes they had flown in. Neither of them had wanted to waste the time to change.

"So, wife of mine, I think it's time you took your clothes off, and show me what belongs to me now."

"Is that right?"

"Yeah. You see, I haven't explored every single inch of you, and I think I'm going to have to start at the top and work my way down. We're married now, so you're going to look very different."

"How different?"

"Like you belong to me."

He gripped the lapels of her shirt and tore it down the center. Buttons sprang everywhere.

In response, Sandy groaned. "I love it when you go all tough on me."

"Baby, I haven't even started." He tugged the shirt from her body. Pulling the blade out of his pants, he opened the knife, and sliced the straps of her bra, watching it fall away.

She sighed. "I'm blown away."

"Don't worry. I've got a few more tricks up my sleeve."

Closing the knife, he pocked it. Kicking off his boots, he removed his clothing while watching Sandy. She still wore a pair of his briefs, which seemed to swallow her up. When she made to cross her arms over her breasts, he shook his head. "Don't cover yourself up. I want to see all of you."

She lowered her arms, and he watched her.

Once he was standing before her naked, he wrapped his fingers around his cock, running up and down the length.

"I just want to fill you with my cum," he said. He moved toward her, circling her. "I want to lay you down on the bed, pound inside your pretty cunt, and after I've filled you, I want to watch it fall from between your pussy lips." He touched her stomach, and she gasped. "Do you like the sound of that?"

"Yes."

"Tell me I can do that, Sandy. Tell me I can fill your pretty cunt with cum."

"Yes, you can."

Picking her up in his arms, he carried her toward the large bed. Placing her on the edge, he sank down to his knees, and took the boxer briefs off her. Next came the sneakers, and he knelt on the floor.

"Show me your pussy," he said.

She leaned back and opened the lips of her sex, revealing her creamy clit and cunt. He wanted to taste her. Pushing her back, he flicked his tongue over her clit, sucking the bud into his mouth, and using his teeth to create a small burst of pain. She cried out, and he eased the pain out by licking her pussy.

Moving down, he thrust his tongue inside her, fucking her pussy. He used his fingers to tease her clit when he wasn't using his mouth. He didn't stop, making her take every single spark of pain and pleasure.

"Please, Stink, I can't take anymore."

Hearing her beg was sweet music to him. When she was at the pinnacle, and he had her poised, ready to go over the edge, he stopped. Getting to his feet, he moved her up the bed. Settling between her spread thighs, he gripped his cock, and sank deep inside her. "This time, as man and wife, I'm going to be inside you when you come. I'm going to feel every little quiver."

He fucked inside her hard, going to the hilt. Stink didn't stay there. He pulled out so only the tip remained in. "Finger yourself, baby. I want you to come all over my cock, and only when you have will I give you my spunk."

She teased her clit, and he groaned at the pleasure of having her surround him.

"Yes, fuck, yes," she said.

Stink pounded inside her, feeling her cunt tighten around him. The pleasure was out of this world, indescribable, and perfect. "That's it, baby, come for me. Come all over my cock."

"I'm so close."

Leaning down, he took one of her nipples into his mouth, sucking on the hard bud. Sliding his tongue across her chest, he did the same to the other one. She was so sensitive, so needy that she came apart, screaming his name.

Stink thrust within her, going deeper. He took hold of her hands, pressing them on either side of her head as she stared into her eyes.

"You're mine."

"Yes."

He fucked her harder than ever before, and this time when he came, he stayed within her, each pulse, flooding her womb with his cum. She didn't push him away.

Kissing her lips, he held his weight above her, staring into her eyes.

"Don't you want to watch?" she asked.

He chuckled. "You do like getting a little dirty."

"Not just a little. I like getting dirty a whole lot of the time." She cupped his cheek. "Don't you?"

Pulling out of her pussy, Stink stared down at her cunt watching his cum slowly leave, trailing to her ass, and dripping onto the bed.

Only when he'd looked his fill did he lie beside her. Taking hold of her hand, he kissed the finger where he'd placed the ring. "I love you, Sandy."

"I love you, too. More than you'd know."

****

Later that night, or at least early morning, Sandy watched as Stink moved out of the shower, coming back into the bedroom. His body was covered in a layer of water, the moisture dripping down his body, over his ink, and muscles. She wanted to lick every inch of his body. She also caught sight of the ring they had purchased at the chapel.

When they got home, she intended to find the perfect ring for him.

"I can feel you eye-fucking me all the way over here."

"Really? You can feel that, can you?" She put down the chocolate she was eating, and walked toward him. Sandy wasn't wearing any clothes, and with Stink, he gave her all the confidence she needed. Years ago, she had always been on a diet to look slim. Even working long hours as a doctor, it had concerned her. For the first time in her life she was more than comfortable being a size sixteen. The curves she'd once detested were now something that she loved. Since being in the club, Sandy had grown comfortable within her own skin, and with that, she'd found her love of food. The time away from the hospital, she'd put on weight, and she loved her fuller body. She loved her big tits, and rounded stomach, and fat ass. All the time she saw death, the thinness combined with the fear and regret. She didn't want that.

She touched his arm and slowly circled his body, so that where she was looking, he felt the touch.

"*Now* do you feel?"

"It's hard not to. I feel like little electric shocks are going off in my body."

"Good. That's exactly the way I want you to feel."

She tugged the towel from his hands and threw it to the floor. His cock was already rock hard, and she sank to her knees, licking the tip.

"I've been thinking about you," she said.

"Yeah?"

"Oh yes, and you haven't lived out all of your promises."

"I haven't?" he asked.

She sucked on the head of his cock, bobbing her head up and down before pulling away.

"You've neglected my ass." She pouted up at him.

"Baby, I'm always about saving the best 'til last."

She licked the pre-cum that was leaking out of the tip, moaning as she did. Stink was incredibly erotic. She couldn't recall a time when her heart was pounding, and her pussy on fire for what was about to happen next. Stink took it to the next level, and beyond.

"I'm ready for you," she said.

He took her hand and helped her to her feet. Stink wrapped his arms around her, and slowly eased her back toward the bed. He took possession of her mouth, kissing her with a passion that took her breath away.

Stink eased her down on the bed until she was lying flat with her legs hanging off the bed. His hands cupped her tits, stroking one nipple before stroking over to the second. He did this, going back and forth, and working her up to a fever pitch. Her pussy was so wet that she felt her cream leaking down the crack of her ass.

He kissed down her body, sucking on each nipple before caressing down her stomach. When he took her clit into his mouth, she gasped, shocked that he would go down on her still. His fingers fucked into her pussy, sliding more of their lubrication to her ass. Stink eased his cock inside her, making her moan as he filled her up.

"You're so damn tight," he said, releasing a little growl. She couldn't look away from him, even as he pulled out, and told her to grip her thighs.

Stink stared at her ass, stroking his fingers over the puckered hole. "Are you sure about this?"

"Yes." She'd had anal sex plenty of times and knew she enjoyed it.

With Stink, she wanted to share everything with him. Her body, her heart, her soul, everything.

The tip of his cock pressed against her ass, and she pushed out, helping him fight that tight ring of muscles.

He groaned as the tip of him eased inside.

"It may have been a while," she said.

Stink kept his hand on his dick, and slowly began to fuck in the remaining inches of his length. When he was all inside, Stink paused. "You've got it all now, baby."

"I belong to you now. No part of me will know another man. I'm yours. Only yours."

He eased out of her ass only to slide in once again. She gasped, and her ass tightened around him. Reaching down, she stroked through her pussy, staring into Stink's eyes as he looked back at her.

"You're going to be the death of me."

"I'd rather die like this, loving you, than any

other way." Sandy didn't hide her feelings anymore. She embraced them. The love Stink had started building inside her, had only gotten stronger. She loved him, wanted to be with him, and knew it would never stop.

He fucked her ass, and she stared into his eyes, loving the whole of them. No more hiding, no more fighting.

"Fuck my ass, baby," she said.

They were not two school kids. They were married, mature, and ready to fight the world together.

Sandy looked forward to the future.

Fuck you, Andrew.

You're going down.

****

"I need you, Sasha. Come back to me."

Her head was really hurting her, like the worst headache in the world.

"I know the doctors said you weren't going to wake up, but I want you to prove them wrong. Come on, Sash, give me something, anything."

Her hand was being squeezed.

What was going on? Something was stuck down her throat. Moving her head from side to side, she heard distant beeping.

"She's waking up! Doctor! Doctor, get your fucking ass in here."

Was that Pussy? He sounded distressed, panicked. Had she fallen down again and hurt herself? She was doing that a lot lately. To be honest, she was kind of scared of how often she was bumping into things.

Suddenly, Sasha recalled the banging, the shooting, the pain. Pussy rushing toward her, crashing her to the floor, and then ... nothing. There was a whole blur of nothing. There was gunfire, and they had been at The Skulls' clubhouse.

They had an enemy … who was it?

Master.

No, he had a name.

Andrew.

So much death and carnage.

Opening her eyes, she saw the white ceiling. Blinking her eyes, Sasha frowned. No, that couldn't be right. She opened her eyes once again, and there was the white ceiling.

"Sasha, can you hear me?" the doctor asked, shining a light into her eyes, and making her blind.

She saw stars.

"Wait? She blinked at the light," Pussy said. "She never blinks at lights, never."

Her man was here.

Opening her eyes once again she turned toward his voice, and saw one of the handsomest men she had ever seen.

She could see.

Her eyes were working.

Sasha panicked, and screamed.

Chapter Nine

The following morning, Stink woke up to Sandy curled in his arms. She looked so beautiful sleeping peacefully. His wife. There was no way he was letting her go. She'd had her chance to walk away, and she didn't take it. Now, he was going to prove to her that she had been missing out on some of the best things in life.

It was only a little after seven. He'd been fucking her until four in the morning, and she had passed out from all the sex. Stink had only needed a few hours sleep. Years of taking quick powernaps had meant he rarely had a full night's sleep.

His cell phone started ringing, and he reached behind him, hoping to catch it before Sandy woke up.

"Stink," he said, failing as Sandy opened her eyes, stretching out, and yawning.

"It's Lash. The gang that we took out last night used to run coke deals for Gonzalez. They went under the radar, and have since been working for Andrew."

"How does one go from coke deals to hits?"

"Three mil upfront, with the promise of another three mil when the job is done."

"Six? That's a lot of money."

"A lot of money, and Whizz is working on Andrew's funds right now. We're going to be having church today. We've got to discuss some shit. Can you get home?" Lash asked.

"Yeah, we're heading home today anyway."

"There's going to be nothing left for you. Nash has some anger management issues. I should get him to look at that."

Stink chuckled. "They went after his girl, I can understand their anger." He watched as Sandy sat up, stretching out her muscles. Her hips had fingerprint bruises from him. He rather liked seeing his marks on her body.

"I didn't hold him back. You might want to tell Sandy that Sasha is awake, and get this—she can fucking see."

"What?"

"Yeah, she looked at Pussy and screamed even with the tube in her mouth. I heard it was scary as fuck."

"I'll tell her."

"See you soon, brother."

Stink hung up.

"What's going on?" Sandy asked, turning to look at him.

"Sasha can finally see."

"Seriously?"

"Yeah." He laughed. "Wow, she can see. I bet it scared the shit out of her seeing what she married."

"Don't be mean. The doctor always said that the brain affects everyone differently. Sasha just handled it a little differently."

Stink nodded. "Well, she can see."

"What's going on?"

"Whizz has got some information. The guys that attacked us, the club are handling them."

"We've got to be heading back?"

Stink reached out, cupping her cheek. "We put Andrew in the ground, you and me, we'll go for a real honeymoon, no excuses."

"I'd like that. I've been thinking about going back to the hospital for a little time."

"Have you missed it?"

"Yeah, I have. I love the club, and I don't want that to change. I'll always be with them."

"You took your break, and now it's time to go back."

"That's how I'm feeling," she said, resting her cheek against his palm. "We got married."

"We got married." They both smiled, and Stink let out a breath. "No regrets?"

"None." She kissed his palm. "Why would I have regrets? This is what I want."

"You're not going to wait for a man who can smell."

"Why? I can break wind and you won't complain."

He laughed.

The smile dropped from her face. "We've got to go back. Our little bubble is about to break."

"Yeah, for a short time."

He kissed her lips, and pulled away. "Let's get going."

****

"They have taken them," Russell said.

"I know!" Andrew placed his hand over his shoulder. That fucking whore, Angel, had really gotten him good. He hadn't anticipated her being prepared for him. *Fuck!* Now the fucking bastards had taken out the little gang who'd taken three mil to do the hit.

"Also, it looks like some of their Nomad Chapter are coming to town."

This was not what he had planned.

"What would you like me to do?"

"I want to get inside that fucking clubhouse, and I want to kill the bitch who thought she could put a knife inside me."

Russell sighed. "Andrew, you ever thought of just letting this go?"

"Letting it go!" He spat each word out, turning to glare at Russell. "They fucking started this." They had taken the man who supplied his toys, and they had called to him. Andre had been prepared to take Jessica, but then The Skulls had gotten involved. As far as he was concerned, this was payback.

Gash had turned his back on him, and he'd taken out his revenge by putting him in prison. Now they were back, and he was pissed.

"You're losing."

He spun around to face Russell. "Excuse me?"

"The Skulls have a history of taking a hit, and coming back harder than ever."

"I have killed some of their men and women. I've taken limbs, and I've wounded them. I have one of their women at my fucking disposal. How the fuck am I losing?" He advanced on Russell, slamming him against the wall. "Tell me, Russell, how am I losing?"

"You're not, Sir."

"All I did was anticipate them reacting a different way." Andrew did have plans for the gang to attack again. With his own injury, he hadn't acted swiftly enough. Angel, he was going to fucking murder that bitch. "Bring me the whores," he said.

He'd get what he wanted one way or the other.

****

Three hours later

She was going to die. Paris stared up from the floor where she was bleeding. One of her eyes was swollen shut, and her body ached in places she didn't even think was possible. She had offered enough of a distraction for Lola, though. Providing the other woman did what she asked, there was a chance they could get out of this mess.

Whatever had angered Andrew, it hadn't put him in the mood to fuck, which she was thankful for.

Please, Lola, please send it.

"What do you want me to do?" Lola asked.

"I want you to get The Skulls' and Chaos Bleeds' attention. I want their eyes on me, and their women as well."

"I don't know—"

"Figure it out, otherwise it's going to be you there."

****

Stink was fucking tired. He had dropped Sandy off at the hospital, and made his way straight to the warehouse. Their bikes were parked outside, and the two clubs were standing in the main gym, which they had used for training many times. They really needed to do something with this warehouse. The old tumble down building that had once housed the Savage Brothers MC was being turned into a gym for the locals.

"I hear congratulations are in order," Devil said, coming to stand next to him.

He held his hand up that the gold ring was on. "You heard right."

"Fuck, man, I never thought you and Sandy would tie the knot. Must be something in the air."

"What do you mean?"

"Simon today told me he wanted to marry Tabitha before we head home. Kid's got it bad, like really bad." Devil shook his head. "I don't even want to think about what I've got to do with his ass when he's grown up."

"He'll be a teenager and moving onto other girls."

"Yeah, that's what Tiny thinks. I doubt it."

"Why?"

"There's just something about my son. He's stubborn, but when it comes to Tab, he's different. Even I see it."

"Maybe a Skulls Bleeds one day." Stink chuckled.

"Not happening. We're friends, but the clubs will never be bound together."

"Is it something you forbid?"

"Fuck yeah. I worked hard making my club what is it. Settling down in Piston County was not a decision I took lightly."

"What happened?"

"What do you think fucking happened? I saw Lexie, and that was it. I was gone for everyone, and every fucking thing. That woman will be the death of me, I'm sure of it."

There was a smile playing on his lips that told Stink, he loved every second of it. "Would you give it up?"

"No. I wouldn't." He snorted. "When I was younger, I truly believed relationships were for pussies. There was not one woman who could keep this man down. I went through hundreds of women, maybe even thousands, believing that." Devil shook his head. "Then, one fucking whore got pregnant by me, and I follow her to a small little backward town of Piston County. There I saw a stripper who was not only the whore's sister, but she was stripping to feed *my son*. That's right. Lexie has a heart of gold, and she took her clothes off for my little boy. She didn't know anything about him, other than her sister dumped him on her. You tell me how someone could walk away from that?"

"It helps that we all settled down there," Dick said, coming to take a seat.

"Even Dick has found his old lady."

"Look at all of us. Ripper, Curse, Pussy, Death, Snake, and now Spider," Dick said.

"We've got to get Paris back," Devil said.

"We will." This came from Dick.

"You know, while you're all saying how good it

is to have settled down, what about me? Huh?" Sinner asked. "Then there's Slash, Dime, Butler, Reese, Sexy, Guts, and Charlie, Smithy as well. There's plenty of us that haven't settled down."

"I'm an ex-addict," Butler said.

"So am I," Dick said. "I've settled down. Martha's everything."

"Yeah, well, tell me how you get a girl to see that you want them," Baker said, coming to take a seat.

Stink smirked. "Millie still giving you a hard time?"

"She's not giving me any time. I thought after the shooting I'd get some reprieve. Other than talking to me when she has to, she hasn't said two words to me."

"Millie, she's that sexy toy shop owner, right?" Sinner asked. "Got nice curves on her, and a fine ass."

Baker stood, his hands going to fists as he stared at Sinner. "You'll stay away from her."

Sinner held his hands up. "Just making an appreciative observation. That woman has a smoking hot body, and any man would want to hold her curves as they rode her sweet pussy."

Baker lunged, but the club was ready. Stink got to his feet, wrestling him back.

"You go near Millie, and I'll fucking kill you," Baker said.

Stink was surprised by the strength of Baker. So much so that he was struggling to hold him back. Fucker was tough.

"What the fuck is going on here?" Lash asked, coming toward them, and gripping Baker by the collar. With a tug he'd separated them.

"Ask your boy here," Sinner said.

Lash glared at Devil. "Get your fucking boy under control."

Devil was laughing as he held his hands up in surrender.

"As for you, Baker, your problem with Millie is your own. Another guy can look at her all he wants. You haven't claimed her, and if you ask me, keep manhandling her, you're not going to. Millie doesn't like that. Any of us fuckers can see that," Lash said.

"And you handled Angel so damn well?" Baker asked.

Lash held up his hand with his wedding ring on. "Look at that fucker! I handled my woman because I know Angel. What do you know about Millie?"

"She owns a toy shop."

"Yeah? I knew that Angel was a damn good cook, a sweetheart, with a quiet loving to her. She wasn't going to love brazen, or loud. Find out what she likes, and then work to be what she likes." Lash shook his head. "We came here to conduct business. You need to get your shit together. They were fucking with you."

Sinner nodded, giggling. "Dude, you've got it bad. I'd sort it out before you get an anger management problem."

"I'm sorry."

Lash went to open his mouth, but just then ringing started. They all turned toward Whizz. He'd installed top of the art technology that also included a large television for them to watch any game they wanted while they were there. It was where they had brought Nash to do a radical detox.

"What the fuck?" Whizz picked up the phone, and the computer came to life. With everything connected to the internet including the television, it was a quick way to access it.

"Hello, gentlemen," Andrew said, coming into view.

Stink tensed up, recognizing the son of a bitch from many years ago. Back then he didn't like the fucker, and he still didn't. This man had killed their own, and enjoyed it. He'd taken kids and women as well. No one brought women and kids into a problem. This man, as far as Stink was concerned, had to go.

"Ah, I see my brother Gash is there. Hey, brother."

"How's the arm?" Gash asked.

The change on Andrew was instant, the anger, the rage showing across his face. Angel had gotten to him. "What can I say? It's not the first time a little whore was about to betray me. How's Charlotte? Can she have your kids yet? The last one I took from her would be perfect bait right now, wouldn't it? Maybe I'll take the next one, and the next."

Gash smirked. "I'd like to see you try."

"Oh, so now you've got balls?" Andrew asked.

"Funny thing about you, Andrew, you were only ever scary when you pretended to be someone else. This, knowing it's you, I'm not fazed by you. I don't care," Gash said. He chuckled. "In fact, I should have seen the whole gang taking out a hit. Three mil, that's pretty steep for you."

"What can I say, old chicks dig me."

"Angel says hey," Lash said.

Once again the anger was back.

"You know, Andrew, all of your money is down to old chicks that die quite quickly after meeting you. I'd say there's something seriously messed up about you," Whizz said.

"What I find really funny is you think this is a game."

"We took out your little gang," Lash said.

"Oh, and we have the three mil. We're

considering it compensation for our fallen ones. The first round of drinks is on you," Whizz said.

Stink watched. He saw how flummoxed Andrew was becoming. This was not a side that Stink had ever thought Andrew possessed.

"Do you really think this is a game?" Andrew asked.

"You set the rules."

"How about these rules?" There was a feminine scream, and suddenly they were staring at Andrew he moved the woman he was holding as if she was rag doll.

"Paris," Spider said.

"Ah, I've got your attention now." Andrew gripped her bruised face, squeezing it. "Tell them, Paris, tell them how I took your fucking virginity." He laughed cruelly. "Little Spider didn't even get a look in. Her cunt was nice and warm."

"You let her fucking go, you piece of shit!" Spider moved forward.

"Let her go? Okay, fine." Andrew dropped her and kicked her three times afterward. "Do you want to play this game, Spider? You're on—"

"No!" Whizz yelled the word, stepping in front of all of them. "Let's play *this* game. Find out what I've done, and then come and get me!"

The screen went dark as Whizz cut him off.

"What the fuck are you doing?" Spider asked. "He was beating Paris, and now he's going to kill her."

"What did you do?" Devil asked.

"That's one of ours there," Dick said.

"Enough!" Lash turned all the attention back to him. "Whizz, what did you do?"

"As of right now, all of Andrew's wealth ceases to exist. I cleared his accounts. He's worth nothing. I've also initiated the correct documents to go to Alex's friends in law enforcement. His days of hiding are outnumbered. Andrew thought he was smart. He left a trail that he got people to cover up. I've found those people, and now they're being hunted."

"How the fuck does that help my girl?" Spider asked. "She's black and blue. He's raped her. You tell me how the fuck is that supposed to help?"

"What about this?" Whizz asked. The screen lit up with a message that was highlighted. To Stink, it looked like weird ass code. "'Come and get me from Beauty caught in a web'?"

"I don't—"

"Tell me this message is from your woman?" Whizz asked.

"Beauty was her stage name," Spider said.

"Then someone on her side sent a message. Whoever just did that also left everything they could for me to locate them. Their computer coordinates. This was a message, and we know where Andrew is."

"This is dangerous, right?" Spider asked.

"If Andrew finds out she or he sent this, they could kill her." Whizz did some more tapping, and a map was brought up. "That's where he is, right there." Some more tapping, and the screen seemed to zoom in.

"Will you slow fucking down?" Lash asked.

"Sorry. This was his first wife's property. It's an hour's drive from Fort Wills. It's secluded and has three different security codes to access the main gate. Hopefully, if the person who sent the message is smart, we could access this shit, and we could finally have Andrew."

"If he knows we're coming?" Stink asked.

"This is our one chance to take him out. He could leave before we get there," Whizz said. "It's a shot. If he's not there for whatever reason, it doesn't matter.

We'll get to the girls without a problem. Andrew's out of options. He has no money. The cops are raiding his homes as we speak. He dug in deep with Gonzalez, but that kind of mud, it sticks."

Stink glanced at Lash, wondering what decision he'd come to.

"We go tonight."

****

They had removed the tube from her throat, and she was being monitored every hour by the doctors. Sasha touched her cheeks and held her hands out. Her wedding band was gone, but the mark from wearing the ring was still there.

She could see.

"Where's my wedding ring?" she asked, looking at Pussy. He was more handsome than she had ever imagined.

"You had to go have a CAT scan, and an MRI, and a few others." He pulled a necklace out of his shirt, and she saw the single gold band. "You weren't allowed to wear any jewelry, and I wasn't about to let it disappear."

"Thank you," she said.

She held out her hand, not knowing why he hadn't touched her yet. Since waking him, everything had seemed different.

Pussy stared at her hand, and stepped closer. Her heart was hurting with the distance that had been between us.

"Do you hate me?" she asked.

"What?"

"You won't touch me, or come near me."

He took hold of her hand, kissing her knuckles. "I love you."

"If you're going to stop being the way you were

then I'll ask the doctors to take back my sight."

"You screamed at me, princess. I'm scared, okay? You were in the dark, and now you see what an asshole you fell in love with."

She stopped him with a kiss.

Leaning up, she pressed her lips against his.

"You shouldn't be doing any sudden movements," he said.

"I don't care. They can fuck off for all I care. I love you."

He gripped the back of her neck, kissing her once again.

"Who did this to me?" she asked.

"Andrew."

"Master?"

"Yeah. He sent a fucking gang to off us all for three mil."

"Pretty big sum."

"Yeah, well, last I heard shit was going down."

"Why aren't you with them?" she asked.

"Why would I be with them when my woman wouldn't wake up for me?" He took her hand and slid the ring on her finger. "I made you a promise to always be here, and I intended to keep it, now and always." He kissed her cheek. "You mean the world to me."

"You always did know what to say."

"You're my woman, Sasha."

"I can't deal if anything was to happen to you." She gripped the back of his head, and kissed him again. "I love you."

"I love you more than anything."

"I can see."

"What do you see when you look at me?" he asked.

"I see a man I fell in love with. My imagination

145

didn't do you much justice."

"I'm an ugly fucker."

She laughed. The future now looked a little different. Sasha couldn't look away, nor did she try. Instead, she stared at the man she called her husband, and fell in love with him all over again.

****

"So you're heading straight out?" Sandy asked.

"We've got a chance of saving this girl, baby. I've got to go with them," Stink said.

"It's okay. I get it. Maybe we'll both be lucky and Andrew will be there." Sandy hoped so. She just wanted this mess to be all over. The only downfall to this plan was the fact she wasn't going to get a front row seat to witness Andrew's death.

"Here's hoping. I miss you."

"I'm going to stay at the hospital. I'll talk to Berman about making my position here permanent. What do you think?"

"I think that's good."

Sandy was worried. What if something went wrong?

"I can feel your worrying, Sand, talk to me."

"Part of me doesn't want you to go."

"And the other part?" he asked.

"The other part hates me for even thinking it. I'm sorry. It's your life as much as mine."

"Sandy, baby, if you don't want me to go then ask me not to."

She closed her eyes. "I promised myself I wouldn't be that woman, so I'm not going to be."

"Do you know how hot that makes me?"

"What? Me being a crybaby?"

"Nah, you caring about me like that."

"Of course I do. I wouldn't marry you for your

good looks alone. Hello, they fade." She couldn't help but smile as he laughed.

"I'll pick you up at the hospital when it's all over."

She sighed. "Okay. I'll keep busy until then."

"Love you."

"Love you too." She hung up her cell phone and blew out a breath.

"They're going after them, aren't they?" Alex asked.

His sudden appearance made her jump, and she gripped her chest. "You scared me."

"Sorry. I remember a time when you were ready for anything."

"Yeah, I know it. God, I hate this. I hate this fucker." She leaned against the wall, resting her head back, and taking a deep breath. "How are Sunshine and the baby?"

"They're doing good."

"Don't you think everything is moving so fast, all the time?" she asked.

"When it comes to this business with Andrew, yes. He attacked us, and now we're trying to fight him. It's the Skull way."

"Is it, really?"

"Think about our other enemies. We didn't stay and wait for them to fight us. We took the fight to them." Alex sighed. "What a fight it has all been."

"Do you ever just hope that one day, it's all going to be over, and we're all going to be sane once again? Maybe just maybe, sleep in our own beds?" she asked.

"It'll happen. These moments will soon be just another memory. Something we can all smile, and laugh about."

She sighed. "It was easier when I wasn't in love."

"It was all easy when you didn't love anyone. I never had that luxury. I stayed away as I had many of my own enemies. Still, they always catch up to us, don't they?"

"Yep, they do."

"What are you doing now?"

"I'm going to see Sally."

"Yes, poor girl. What will happen?"

"Her leg needs time to heal. They'll be therapy, and physiotherapy to help her adapt. Once her leg has healed, a prosthetic will be made to fit her, and she'll have more therapy, and more physio. She'll be doing a lot of her schooling at home for a while. I imagine Whizz and Lacey are already dealing with that."

"I'm heading to the children's ward to see my niece. I promised Tabitha a chocolate, and I have to be careful. Make sure I don't get caught."

"You're a bad influence for all kids, you know that?"

"Yep, I do."

She walked beside Alex trying her hardest to forget about Stink, and the danger he was about to get himself into. When they got the children's ward, she squirted anti-bacterial gel onto her hands, and let Alex in with her. She left him to Tabitha, and made her way toward Sally's room. She saw Steven standing outside, staring in.

Going to his side, she saw Lacey, Daisy, and Ned in the room. "Why are you out here?" she asked.

"Sally doesn't say anything when I'm in the room. I make her uncomfortable."

"Why are you here, and not helping the others?" she asked.

"Whizz asked me to keep an eye on the girls. I'm not needed."

"You're distracted, which is why you're not needed. The club doesn't need a guy who isn't thinking straight." She folded her arms, staring at the man. He was once a prospect, and he'd put his life on the line to protect Angel and Tate. Steven had done what he needed to protect the club, and for that, he'd earned his right to be a full-fledged member.

Ha, Andrew, fucker can't do that right.

It was petty, and completely lame of her, but it made her feel better to think of him like that.

"Yeah, I am."

He stepped away from the window, and leaned forward. She listened as he took some deep breaths, and stood. "Fuck. I don't know what it is about this girl. One minute she's just a girl, and now it kills me to see her in any kind of pain."

"She's underage."

"I know that!" Steven glared at her. "I'm not going to go do something stupid. I want to protect her. I want her to know that she doesn't have to be afraid anymore." He ran fingers through his hair, and she saw how troubled he was. "She doesn't even have a crush on me. I thought she did, but I was fucking wrong."

Sandy didn't tell him otherwise. Every woman had a reason for not letting their man know that they had feelings for them, even Sally.

"She's been through so much," he said.

"Sally is older than her years."

He nodded. "It doesn't matter. I'm only going to be there to support her, okay? You don't have to worry about any bad shit from me. I only want to help."

"Why don't you go and get some coffee?"

"Yeah, that's a good idea." She watched him walk away before heading into the room. Daisy was reading to the room. She was sitting on Ned's knee, and

Sally was smiling. She looked pale, and a little withdrawn.

They stopped as she entered.

"Please, don't stop for me. I've just come to spend some time. That's all."

Taking a seat, she listened to Daisy's reading. As she stared at the little girl, Sandy started to wonder if she wanted kids.

Kids had always seemed like a foreign concept to her. They were adorable, but you had to devote all of your life to them. She didn't know if she was ready for that or not. It was a great deal of commitment.

"I'm going to get some coffee, and food. Do you want anything?" Lacey asked.

"I'll take a piece of chocolate cake," Sally said. Daisy agreed, as did Ned.

"Take a break, Lacey. I've got this."

Getting to her feet, Sandy followed her out. "I'll come with you."

"Thanks. It has been a long day."

"Have you heard what is going on?"

"Whizz told me. He told me shit was going to hit the fan in a big way." Lacey groaned, gripping the back of her neck, and stretching. "I hope they find him, and kill him."

"I'm a doctor, and I hope they find a way to torture him, and feed him his own dick," Sandy said. She pushed her hands into her white jacket. Her hands were so cold. She smiled at the passing people, and blew out a breath.

"Do you ever wonder what the hell we're doing wrong?" Lacey asked.

"With all the drama?"

"Yeah. I mean, come on. There's no way a club has this much drama for fun. It's exhausting."

"That I do agree. It sucks."

"Congratulations by the way. Was it a nice wedding?" Lacey asked.

"It wasn't like yours. Whizz planning for everything with the club around you. It was good. I liked it. When all of this crap is over, we're going to have another ceremony with the club."

"It makes sense. I'd love to be there, and I'd make one hell of a bridesmaid."

"I'll remember that."

They got to the hospital café, and they took their own orders first. Lacey ordered for Sally, Ned, and Daisy so that she could pick it up on the way out of the café.

Taking a seat, Sandy opened up her bagel and took a bite. It was nice, but not as good as Angel made them. That woman could make anything taste a great deal better.

"So, the white jacket, the wedding, are you going back to being a doctor?"

"Yeah. I'm talking to Berman about taking my position again. I love being a doctor. It's all I've ever wanted to do." She took another bite before sipping at her coffee.

"Do you think it's possible for us to go one year without any of us being here?" Lacey asked. "The food is actually starting to taste good."

"That's because your food is awful."

"Sally has taken over from cooking. I'm so awful they think it will be safe if I don't have anything to do with that."

Sandy laughed. "Now that I could see."

"Some have talent in the kitchen, others don't."

"Stink is talented."

"He can't smell."

"Yeah, I know. It's such a shame really. He'd

make one hell of a chef." Sandy finished off her bagel and the last of her coffee. Lacey was moving around a salad on her plate. "How is it going with Sally?"

"Until Ned came, it was hard. She was crying, and she wouldn't talk to anyone but Daisy. I've been through a lot of awful shit to get to this moment, but seeing Sally like that, I was petrified." Lacey licked her lips, putting her fork down. "I, um, what do you say? What do you do? I've lost my ability to have kids, but I've never lost anything." She shoved her cardigan up her arms, showing off the tats. "I dye my hair, I ink my body. I don't know how to handle this."

"You haven't run away, nor have you dumped her back in foster care. That's a good thing."

"I'd never do that. Dumping her in foster care never entered my head. She may not be my blood, but she's my girl." Tears filled Lacey's eyes, and she took a breath, staring down at her plate.

Sandy paused. Out of all of the women in the clubhouse she'd never seen Lacey cry. Lacey covered her face and shook her head. "I promised myself that I wouldn't cry, that I'd never cry again."

"That's silly to say." Out of all of the words she could use, silly?

"I'm really sorry. Sally will get there, and all of this will be a faded memory."

Lacey nodded. "I get it, I do. It's just, I want to hurt him for hurting my daughter. I could have lost Sally, and I love her. I don't care what others say. I love her. She's mine, and I love and care about her. I don't want anything to happen to her."

Getting up from her chair, Sandy gave Lacey a hug. It started out tense at first, but slowly, the other woman accepted the hug. It wasn't much, but it was something, and that was all that counted.

****

Paris coughed.

She saw the ceiling of her cage and wondered if she would ever get out. Andrew had gone into a fit of rage, and her arms were broken. She couldn't move. The door to the basement opened, and she didn't even have the energy to see who it was.

Whimpering, followed by a string of curses. Paris heard Russell open one of the cages and throw Lola inside.

With the pain she was in, she couldn't even roll over, which was pitiful.

The sound of retreating footsteps allowed Paris to sigh. He was going, and maybe she'd be lucky enough to die tonight, and she'd never have to look at his big face again. When Spider got a hold of him, she hoped he'd tear his cock off with a blunt knife, fry it, and feed it to him.

That was a wish, and sometimes it gave her hope that one day soon, she was going to get out of here.

"Did you send the message?" Paris asked. It hurt to talk. Her lip was cut, but she needed to know the answer.

"Yes."

"Good."

"If they know who it's from, they'll be able to track it as well."

"Huh?"

"Every computer has an IP address. If you're smart, you can make sure not to leave a trace of yourself. I decided to play dumb. If one of them is computer smart, they'll know where to find us, and they'll also discover that I infiltrated the security codes. Soon, this place is going to be more open than a whore's thighs."

Even though it wasn't supposed to be funny, Paris

couldn't help but laugh. "Thank you, Lola."

"Don't thank me yet. Let's hope your friends come otherwise we'll be dead soon."

It was a sobering thought yet a hopeful one.

Spider had promised to take care of her, to protect her. He hadn't seen this coming, and ever after everything she'd been through, she still believed he was coming to get her. He didn't give her a reason to doubt him.

Chapter Ten

"You can't do this without me, Devil. That's my girl in there," Spider said.

They had all ridden back to the clubhouse to get their supplies. Spider had ridden at Devil's back, much to his annoyance. "Spider, man, we're going to go and get her for you. I don't know how many times I need to make this clear to you."

"I'm capable of riding."

Devil pressed his foot against the wound in Spider's leg. Spider grunted and went down, the crutches falling to the ground as he gasped at the pain. "I've barely touched you, and you're down. You're a liability. We don't know what we're going in to, and if you think I'm going to risk any of my men, you're wrong!"

"She's mine. I have a right to be there for her." Spider didn't want to let it go. Paris was his. She belonged to him, and he wasn't about to let her go. Staring at his leader, Spider took several deep breaths.

"You really want to come?" Devil asked.

"Yes."

Everything went dark.

****

"You hit him?" Lash asked. "That's how you solve that problem?"

"Any of us in his situation would be exactly like him. We've got loved ones to protect. Right now, I can't have him coming with us. He's not up to his full health, and I'm not willing to risk it because he wants to come," Devil said, tucking a gun into his jeans pocket.

Stink shook his head. "Still seemed a bit harsh."

"When he wakes up, he'll get it."

"What am I supposed to do with him until he wakes up?" Jessica asked. "I've only got one arm."

"I'm going to chain him to the bed. I hit him pretty hard. He should be out cold for a few hours," Devil said. "Come on, someone help me lift him."

Sinner grabbed Spider's legs, and they carried him upstairs to a room.

"Is it bad that we have cuffs?" Dick asked.

Stink laughed. Even though they were about to go into something that was uncertain, Chaos Bleeds were still cracking jokes.

"If any of you for a second think knocking me out will be okay—" Lash said.

"Come on, brother, everyone knows I throw people around like a rag doll," Killer said.

Stink shook his head. This was why he loved The Skulls. They were a family to the core. It was what built them up.

Tiny came into the room. They were all wearing their leather cuts, each one of them about to meet their maker if they had to. Prior to getting married to Sandy, Stink had made sure to have a will that meant Sandy was taken care of. She was his number one priority outside of the club. The Skulls would look after her, keep her safe.

When Devil returned Lash stood in front of the group. "We hit hard, and we hit fast. We have a small window here. Whizz has shut down Andrew's funds, but we don't know where loyalties lie. We get in, we get shit solved, we get the girl."

"Hey, if luck is on our side, we get Andrew tonight, and party by the weekend," Whizz said.

They all cheered, and even Stink held his hand up going along with it. It would be a mighty end to a fucking horrible week.

"Do you have any questions?" Lash asked.

No one raised their hands.

"Let's ride, boys."

****

Angel stood at her bedroom window and took a deep breath. The men filed out of the clubhouse, all of them ready to do war. Holding little Chloe against her chest, she held in the tears. Lash paused at his bike, and he turned toward her. He placed his fingers to his lips, and held them out to her.

"I love you."

He mouthed the words, but she didn't need to hear them out loud. "Come back to me."

She spoke them aloud even though he couldn't hear.

One simple nod was all she got.

Her heart started to race, and she let out a breath, looking at her little darling.

"Hey, Mommy," Anthony said, surprising her.

"What are you doing up, sweetheart? You should be in bed." She turned from the window to move toward her son.

"I couldn't sleep."

Anthony was advanced for his years.

"What's bothering you?" she asked.

"Everything. I don't want to go to school when bad stuff is happening."

"Would you like some hot chocolate?" Angel asked.

"Please."

"Come on." When she held out her hand, Anthony took it, and she walked down the stairs of the clubhouse toward the kitchen. In the days she was first taken by The Skulls for her father's debt, she'd been scared of this clubhouse. Now, it was a safe haven for her. She relished the days of big cookouts, barbeques, and fun. The Skulls had taken her in, become her family, and she had devoted her life to them.

She found Jessica, Brianna, Kelsey, Prue, Emily, Rose, and Martha at the table. They were all nursing drinks. Some of them looked like whiskey, others coffee.

"Take a seat, darling."

Kelsey held her hands out, and Angel placed Chloe in her arms. "She's so beautiful."

"Yeah, she really is." Heading to the fridge, Angel pulled out some milk, and headed toward the stove. "Does anyone want some hot chocolate? I know it's late, and you're all stressed."

"I'll take hot chocolate," Brianna said.

The rest of the girls murmured their agreement.

"Fuck, don't forget about me," Adam said.

Angel screamed, gripping her chest. She hadn't seen Adam sitting in the corner. "Jeez, you don't have to go around scaring people."

"It seems I do to get noticed. I can't even fucking repay the bastard for taking out my friend. I've got to settle for sitting out of it."

"Weren't you in the Nomad chapter? Don't you like not get involved in any of this?" Jessica asked.

"Yeah, I was in Nomad, but I came back to see if this settling down business is all it's cracked up to be."

"Settling down business?" Brianna asked.

Out of all of the women, she was the shy one.

"Yeah, testing it out."

Angel frowned as she looked toward Adam. "Why are you testing it out?"

"A woman," Rose said. They all turned toward her. "I'm right, aren't I? Every guy's weakness is another woman, unless of course it's a man."

Adam sighed. "Fuck me."

"Hey, language," Angel said. "My son is there."

"Dad says worse, Mom."

"Not in front of me he doesn't." Angel smiled at

her son. Lash did have a problem with his language. All he seemed to know was cussing words, and he knew it drove her crazy when he used them in front of their son. Anyway, that was a problem for another day.

"Your mom's right. Curse when she's not in hearing distance."

"Adam!"

Anthony chuckled. "Good one."

"So, this woman, who is she?" Angel asked.

"She's a woman I've met on the road. Well, I passed through this town several times, and she works at a mechanic's shop. She's handled several repairs to my bike."

"Wow, Adam has the hots for a woman," Rose said. "Why didn't you say anything? We'd have invited her around. Believe it or not, us women can be very inviting."

Angel chuckled. Baker had tried to get them to help. Millie was proving difficult though, but Angel didn't blame her. Baker hadn't exactly made it easy for her to fall in love with him.

Adding some chocolate chips to the bowl, she splashed in some vanilla. When the milk was scalding, she poured it over the chocolate, and waited a second.

"What would be the point? She's settled, and I'm not. It doesn't exactly bode well."

"So all of this time you've been experimenting?" Kelsey asked.

"You got it."

"I feel used," Prue said.

Angel whisked the chocolate and milk, and then when it was smooth and lovely, she poured it into cups, before carrying them toward the table. "I think it's sweet what you're doing." She handed him a cup and went back for more. When everyone had a cup, she stood, facing the table, sipping on her hot chocolate. "I don't think it would be fair for you to pursue a woman that you wouldn't know if you were going to be with from one day to the next. I get it."

"Thank you."

Movement outside of the kitchen caught her eye, and she saw Millie. "I'll be back in a moment."

Pouring some hot chocolate into a cup, Angel made her way outside.

Millie was sitting on the swing staring up at the night's sky.

"It's dangerous to be out here on your own."

"I know, but it helps me to think. I'm not used to being kept under lock and key."

"It does take some getting used to." Taking a seat beside her, Angel sighed. "It really is beautiful out."

"Yeah, it is. Baker's gone."

"He's gone to try to get rid of the threat. Let's hope you can open your shop soon."

"I hope so." Millie took a sip of her hot chocolate.

"Can I ask you a question?" Angel asked.

"Yes."

"Why don't you want to be with Baker? He's a sweet guy, and loving."

Millie sighed. "Every time I look at him I feel like a bad person. I know he's sweet, and he's loving." Millie stopped, licking her lips. "I am an awful person."

"No, you're not."

"He lost his wife and his kid. The blow hit him so hard that he stopped baking, stopped with his own business, and became part of an MC. Baker hasn't accepted what happened to him. He's not gotten over what happened. How can I love a man who is always going to be in love with his former wife?"

"You don't know that." Angel's throat felt thick with tears.

"Yeah, I'm probably wrong." Millie sighed. "I'll just have to wait and see."

****

Paris jumped as alarms started to blaze. There had only been silence since Lola had returned.

"They've come," Lola said.

"What?"

"Your friends. The ones that you said would help. They have come."

Staring up at the ceiling, Paris smiled as best she could. They had come for her.

****

The house was clear. Stink walked from room to room, looking for any sign of Andrew. Entering a room toward the back, he saw a bunch of computers. The screens showed the security footage of the hospital. They were connected in.

"Score," Whizz said, coming into the room. He did some typing, and he chuckled. "Oh, he found out what I did, all right. There's no way this man is leaving the country."

"How do you figure?" Stink asked.

He saw the droplets of blood on the floor. There wasn't a lot, and it was smeared. Pulling out his torch, which happened to be a gift one year from Sandy, he followed the direction of the smears.

"I sent customs the relevant documents. His face is going to be everywhere."

"Why didn't we do this before?" Stink asked.

"We didn't know who he was, and I didn't have an updated picture. Andrew is a connection to Gonzalez."

"Yeah, and if the authorities get him, it's prison.

He can make friends with people in prison. We need this fucker dead, Whizz," Stink said.

He stormed out of the room, following the blood, and came to a door. Gritting his teeth, he opened the door, and pointed his flashlight into the darkness. He didn't see any signs of anyone. Reaching around, he found the light switch, and flicked it on.

"Help!" It was a single feminine cry.

"Someone's here," Stink said, calling out.

He made his way downstairs to the basement, to find the dungeon. There, in two cages, he saw two women. One was curled up in a ball, the other on the floor. Both were naked.

"Paris, which one is Paris?" Stink asked.

"She is. She stopped talking. I think she lost a lot of blood."

"Who are you?" Stink glanced toward her.

"Lola. I sent the message."

The cages were locked. Several men made their way downstairs, including Whizz, Lash, Devil, and Sinner.

"Paris is unconscious."

"This is a job for me," Sinner said, going to his knees. He pulled out some wire and set to breaking the locks.

"Where did Andrew go?" Lash asked.

"Don't know. He dumped us in these cages, and we haven't heard anything."

"Did you hear them leave?" Devil asked.

"No."

"Call Ned. Warn him that Andrew got away."

"He has a sidekick as well, Russell."

"Spider did mention a 'Sir'."

Stink kept his gun aimed at the door, and something glinted, catching his eye.

"We're in," Sinner said. Two men went in, helping Paris. The woman was completely unconscious.

"Sinner," Stink said.

"What?"

"Hurry up."

"I'm working fast."

"Yeah well, so did Andrew. He's rigged the house with explosives. We've got to get out of here."

"Fuck it. Step back." Sinner fired his gun, and the cage popped open. "Let's go, princess."

Lola tried to cover herself, but it was hard. In the end, Sinner removed his jacket, draping it over her shoulders.

"Go, go, go, go," Stink said.

They ran out of the house, and kept on running, all of them heading toward the gate. Lola was too slow. Bending down, Stink shoved his elbow against her stomach, and lifted her up. She wasn't small, but he carried her, running.

They made it to the gate just as the explosion ripped through the house.

****

"Reduced to filth," Andrew said.

"You told me there was no way they could get to you. No way they could find anything on you."

"Well, I was wrong."

The man Russell had once known as Master, who had seemed so strong, so resilient, was falling apart before his eyes. What was worse, he was part of it, and he couldn't just walk away. Andrew had saved him, nurtured him, provided for him. The Skulls and Chaos Bleeds had taken that all away.

If you don't leave, you're going to die.

He didn't want to die, but he was not a coward. He wouldn't go down without a fight, not now, not ever.

"All the money is gone," Russell said.

"Yes."

"Your houses. Even your lawyer has been arrested." Russell had gotten the call an hour after Andrew had talked to The Skulls. The cops were after his ass. Their informants, their allies had all scattered, terrified of being branded.

"Did I tell you The Skulls have a reputation for killing their enemies? No one survives. Not one single person. Creepy, isn't it?"

"What the fuck is going on, Andrew?"

Andrew burst out laughing, sipping at the scotch he'd purchased. They had limited funds, and Andrew was drinking away the money they had.

"What is going on? I'll tell you what is going on. We're going to drink this scotch, and as we do, we're going to come up with a plan to save us. It's all we can do."

"Fuck's sake!" Russell growled the words out, getting to his feet. "That's it? You're going to give up."

"I've got to wait for this to die down."

Russell wasn't going to roll over. There had to be a way, and he wasn't letting his friend down.

****

The following day Spider stared into the hospital room that now held Paris. Lola was in another ward, a less critical one. Paris's broken bones and lacerations had become infected. They'd had to reset her bones, and healing up the cuts. She was in isolation, and in a sterile environment. The doctors had also placed her in a medically induced coma to deal with the pain, and to allow her body time to heal.

"You got her," Spider said. "You knocked me out."

"Yeah, I did, and I'd do it again," Devil said.

"She could die."

"Yeah, she could."

"He blew up his house." The more Spider heard, the more he realized that Devil had been right to knock him out. He would have put the whole club in danger, and it would have in turn hurt his woman.

"Yeah. If it wasn't for Stink finding it, we'd have all been dead."

"Andrew was gone. That little prick working for him was gone as well."

Devil nodded. "Whizz said it's only a matter of time. He's doing that facial recognition thing."

"I want a piece of him when they find him."

"We all do, Spider. Don't worry. You'll get your time with him."

"Good. I'm going to go and see that other girl. What do you know about her?"

"Lola Sparks. She's eighteen years old, and finished high school top of her class. From what Whizz told me, she's almost as good as he is on the computer. He seemed impressed. Andrew took her from the streets, beat and raped her to do what he wanted. She's terrified. Doesn't want any computer or technology in her room." Devil shook his head. "Whatever that bastard did to her, it has changed her."

Spider nodded.

"I'll walk with you," Devil said.

They made their way down the long corridor of the busy hospital. Spider was exhausted, and even though Paris was safe, he wasn't going to rest easy until Andrew was put in the ground.

Devil paused outside of the room. "Her family is being contacted."

Spider knocked on the door, and opened it. "Hey, Lola, is it okay if I come in?"

Her room was bare. There wasn't even a television screen in the room. "You're Spider, right?"

"Paris tell you about me?"

"Yeah, she talked about you. She always said that you'd save her."

Spider moved into the room, keeping a careful distance. He lowered himself into a chair. "I couldn't be there last night."

"He hurt you?"

"His little minion did."

"Russell?"

"Huh?"

"The guy who was with Andrew. His name is Russell."

"So that's the little shit's name. I've got to find him at some point, and repay him for the damage he did to my girl."

"Repay him?"

"When we find Russell and Andrew, it will be the last moments they take breath."

"You're going to kill them?" Lola asked.

"We're going to kill them, and you'll never have to worry again."

Tears spilled from Lola's eyes. "I like that."

"It's our promise to you, Lola. What you did, it was brave, and incredibly stupid. He could have killed you."

"I deserve it. I did what he asked by hacking into the security feed. I helped him get in the hospital." She tried to wipe away her tears, but more kept on spilling down her cheeks.

Spider couldn't be angry with her. Everything she had done, she'd done out of fear. Andrew had the control—not Lola, not Paris, not any of them.

"Don't cry. You've got nothing to cry about, or to

be sad about. The fucker that hurt you, he's the one that needs to suffer. If you ever need anything, come to me, and I'll do what I can to repay you."

****

"You're really distracted today. Do you want to talk about it?" Sally asked.

Whizz shook his head, pulling out of his thoughts. "What?"

She smiled, tapping her head. "What has you staring into space?"

"Fuck, sorry. We were talking about your problem." He leaned forward, resting his hands on the bed, and when he looked down, he noticed that where he was leaning was where her leg would have rested.

"Fuck, I'm sorry."

"Don't worry about it. I've got to get used to it. It's not exactly going to grow back."

"You're too strong for your own good," Whizz said, running fingers through his hair.

"Mom told me what was going on. She was scared. Worried about you."

"She didn't need to be worried about me."

"I bet the cops are having a field day. A mass shooting, a blown up building. Are you sure your name is Whizz for the right reason?"

He leaned back, folded his arms, and chuckled. "You, young lady, are getting very sassy."

She took another bite of her breakfast, chewing. "When can I come home?" she asked.

"Soon, honey, soon."

"I hate it here. I hate the nurses who come in, and stare at me as if it's the end of the world. I don't want or need pity. They can't change what happened to me. Please, I'm begging you." She placed her fork down, and he leaned forward, taking her hand.

"They're here to help you."

"Why can't they look at me like you, or like Sandy, and Ned?"

"How do we look at you?" he asked.

"Like normal. Like I haven't just lost my leg. Like my life isn't going to be changed forever. They see a young girl who lost her leg, and I don't want to see that. Yes, I've lost my leg, and so have a lot of people. They don't cry about it. I want to be strong, like them."

"Sweetie, your life is going to be changed forever. We've spoken to the doctor about this. Your prosthetic will need to be updated throughout the years. Not to mention you're going to struggle to disassociate with your limb."

"I know. Sandy told me that some people struggle. They imagine an itch, and it's killing them, and they can't scratch it, or something like that."

He held her hand tightly. "Sandy's a doctor. She has seen so many people go through what you're going through. Me, I know what a strong and capable woman you are. You went through shit, and instead of it making you weak, you became tough. You're a fighter, Sally. My fighter, okay? We're going to get through this together, as a family, and as the club. Ned, well, he's become the voice of reason, which is what I've heard older people are."

Sally chuckled. "I wouldn't let him hear you say that. He'd wipe the floor with you. He told me yesterday that the problem with people today is they don't know any respect. If you want to get up in this world, show some fucking respect." Sally imitated his voice, which made Whizz laugh. "I like him."

"That's good to know," Ned said. "I take it you don't want these cookies?"

"Yes, yes, I do."

Whizz got to his feet. "I've got to go and talk some business. Will you stay out of trouble?"

"Always."

Shaking Ned's hand, Whizz left the room, and made his way toward Lola's room. The girl they had saved last night, he had some questions for. Standing outside of her room, he saw Spider talking to her.

Folding his arms, he leaned against the wall, and waited.

Sandy was rushing past when she noticed him. "Hey, have you seen Stink?"

"He's waiting for you in the waiting room."

"Thank God, we had a big road accident last night, and I didn't want to be home alone."

"You stayed?"

"Yeah. It's shocking, but home without Stink isn't home anymore." Sandy patted his arm. "I've got to run. I haven't seen him, and I really want to."

Whizz watched her leave.

"You here to talk to her?" Spider asked.

"Yeah, she know anything?"

"No. He did a number on her."

"How so?"

"No technology in her room." Spider started back toward Paris's room. "Thank you."

"No problem. We've always got your back, remember that."

Entering the room, Whizz held his hands up, showing he was no threat. "I'm the one you sent the message to."

She was tense as he took a seat.

"I'm not going to hurt you."

"I'm sorry. I'm not usually like this. Everything has changed, and it's hard to think of life before him."

"Bastard did a number on you, didn't he?"

She shrugged. "No different than other women. Paris, she was really hurt. I hope she makes it through."

"As you can see, I know what I've been through." He pointed to his face. "More than you know. I've been taken against my will."

"Have you been threatened to be fucked until you bleed until you do something bad for them?" Lola asked.

Whizz got up and closed the door. "I don't make a habit of saying this. People know what went on, but I don't take my time to actually relive it."

"What?"

"I'm with The Skulls. We had a particularly nasty guy, and he did fuck me until I bled. These cuts, bruises, I begged for death, and it never came."

"Yet you're here talking to me."

"The club, my wife, they are what drive me."

Tears were falling from Lola's face, and he didn't even think she realized she was crying.

"I've only ever been good at one thing. From the moment I was handed a computer, they've been easy for me to work with. They don't require me to be nice, or to talk. I just have to type."

"How old were you when you did your first hack?" Whizz asked.

"I was ten. I hacked into the school's files. I actually discovered there was a perv working at the school. I made sure people avoided him." She smiled, and even as she was smiling, she was crying.

"It'll get easier."

"My family is going to be here soon I was told. They're going to be different. I don't know if I can look at them the same. I'm me, but I'm different. I'm not the same person as I was."

"This world is a fucked up place. I can't tell you that it's going to get easy. When you're alone, you'll start to relive it, and as you relive it, you'll remember, taking you back to the point you were most afraid. I've been there, and I know it's going to suck you down hard."

"There's no cure for that?"

"There's no cure, Lola. Time as with all things, it's supposed to cure you, make you feel better."

"This doesn't help me. I don't feel help." Lola stared down at her hands. "I was just walking home. I'd been such a good girl. I know I hacked. A lot of people do it, it doesn't make me a bad person."

"You're not a bad person. The Skulls will always be open to you. If you need any help, give us a call. We'll be there. I'll be here."

She offered him a quivering smile.

"You did good hacking into the security footage here," Whizz said.

The tears fell harder. "He was going to kill that nice woman with the blonde hair. I didn't want to. You know I watched hacking movies where people are forced to do bad shit, and I always thought I'd be different, that I wouldn't fall for the lies, the bullies. I'd be strong. I wasn't strong."

"We never know what will happen until we're put in that position. You were very brave, and I don't think you should be beating yourself up. You're young, and I bet he made you suffer long before he forced you to do anything."

"I just wanted to be better than that."

"I know, honey. Don't think about it. Just rest. None of us blame you for what happened."

"It doesn't make it easier. I can't rest. I'm scared."

"I'll be right here. I'm an immovable force against everyone, and everything that tries to move toward you."

"You'd do that for me?"

"Of course."

"Thank you."

"Don't mention it."

Whizz had been in her position. He knew what it was like to be vulnerable.

Chapter Eleven

"Stink!" Sandy ran out of the doors, and he held open his arms, picking her up. He breathed in the scent of his woman, his wife, holding her close. Stink had gone home, and saw their bed hadn't been slept in, nor had the clubhouse's bed that they shared.

"I went home, and you weren't there."

"I couldn't go home without you. I stayed at the hospital, worked, and there was an accident that needed me."

Pushing her hair out of the way, he stared into her eyes. "It has been too long since I've been inside you."

The wicked smile he loved so much played on her lips. "I can rectify that." She took hold of his hand, and they walked toward the ladies' bathroom. Sandy pulled him into a private stall, and with it being early morning, it was silent. She pushed him down onto the toilet seat, straddling his hips. "I've missed you," she said.

Sinking his fingers into her hair, Stink pulled her down to claim her full lips. His cock thickened, and he ran his down her back, holding her close. Her tits pressed against his chest, and he moaned. She ran her hands down his chest, going down to his dick.

"You're so nice and big. I want you inside me."

Sandy wore a skirt, and he pulled it up to her hips. "I can't wait. Baby, we're going to need to figure out if you want kids. I've got no rubbers on me."

"I don't care. Just fuck me."

She tugged at the belt holding his jeans up. Together they fought to get naked. She pulled his cock out, and with her ass near the door, she bent over, and took the tip into her mouth. He cursed, loving the feel of her warm mouth wrapped around his dick. He closed his eyes, groaning as she went right down to his balls.

"Fuck, baby, one night away from you and I felt like I was dying."

"Me, too. We better not fight again, don't you think?" She ran her hand up and down his shaft, staring up into his eyes.

He was captivated by her. She called to him in a way that no woman ever had before, or ever would. Cupping her cheek, he leaned back and thrust into her mouth. There was no longer any need to close his eyes, and imagine. Simply staring at her was all the imagination that he needed.

She moaned, sucking on him.

After a few more hard sucks, she climbed up his lap to straddle his waist. The sight of her bare pussy was the prettiest he'd ever seen. Gripping his cock, he held himself poised at her entrance, and she gasped as she slowly took him.

Her hot cunt enveloped him, and when his cock was deep enough inside her, he took hold of her hips, and forced her down his length. They both cried out together.

To Stink it felt like they had been apart a lot longer than a few hours. Lifting her up, he started to fuck her onto his length. Her cream coated his dick, and he couldn't help but watch how slick he got with taking her. Sitting up, he took her lips by holding the back of her head, and together they fucked. Sandy bounced on his cock, lifting up and sinking down. He ravished her lips.

"I can't wait until I get you home."

If women entered the stall, he didn't know. His only focus was on the woman on his cock. Reaching between them, he teased her clit, stroking over the nub. Each time he did, her pussy tightened around him.

"You're driving me crazy, woman!"

He groaned out. When she came all over his cock, it was almost his undoing, and seconds later, his orgasm washed over him. Sandy got off his cock, and before the first spurt of his cum came out, her lips were over his cock, swallowing it.

Stink watched her throat milk his cum, such a sexy, dirty sight to see. It was sheer perfection. When it was all over, he pulled her onto his lap. "Do you have to stay here?"

"Not today. I've been here for over twenty-four hours, and I haven't even signed a working contract yet. I can go."

"Let's go, then. I need to sleep. I'm exhausted."

They put their clothing into place, and left the cubicle. There was a middle-aged woman washing her hands, cheeks flaming.

Stink held up his ring with his wedding finger on. "Newlyweds."

They walked outside, laughing.

"I can't believe you said that," Sandy said.

"I didn't even hear her come in. Your pussy puts everything on mute."

"So I have a magical pussy?"

"You bet your ass you do." He climbed on his bike, and handed her the helmet, pleased that she didn't argue with him. She wrapped her arms around his waist, snuggling against him.

"Where are we going?"

He wished he could say home, but that wasn't going to happen, not today. "We're going to the clubhouse."

"I'm tired."

"Me too."

****

Angel dropped the kids off, giving them a wave as they made their way into school. Anthony held Daisy's hand, and she watched her son take the lead with

Miles. Both of them walked on, and the others followed. She hated seeing the kids like this, dejected.

Turning the car around, she drove back home. In the past couple of months, she had learned to drive and gotten her license. She'd had to convince Lash to let her do it. It wasn't that he didn't trust her. He worried, constantly, about her, which was romantic, nice, and sometimes a real big pain in the ass.

She down the street, waving at several of the locals as she passed, thankful they still waved back. Normally, she'd have stopped off to get groceries, but she wasn't going to risk it, not with Chloe in the car. Pulling into the parking lot, she saw Gash sitting on the wall, nursing a coffee. She hoped it was a coffee. Ever since he'd gotten back with Charlotte, he'd been different.

Climbing out of the car, Angel smiled at him.

"Hey, darling," he said, moving toward the car.

Before she could stop him, he was helping Chloe's carry car seat out.

"Hey."

"Kids get off to school okay?"

"Yeah, no problems. Where's Lash?"

"You haven't seen him?"

"No." She rubbed at her temple.

"He went to the hospital last night." Since he'd become the President of The Skulls, he'd taken over the jobs that Tiny would do. She didn't mind, for the most part. Last night after spending some time with the girls, and putting Anthony to bed, she'd crashed. "Are you okay?"

"Yeah, I'm fine. Just a little tired."

"You've just had a baby. Rest. I would have taken the kids in this morning."

"No one else was awake, and besides, lots of

women have done what I've done. It's nothing great."

She made to take Chloe, but Gash wouldn't have any of it. "No, you need to rest before you put yourself in an early grave."

"Don't be silly."

"Tough. I'm being silly. You do know that behind Lash's niceness is a monster, right? If anything happens to you who do you think is going to be able to control him? Me, Killer? We're no match for Lash when he goes crazy."

"Lash wouldn't do that."

"No?"

"No."

"Don't be too sure about that. Please, do this for me. Charlotte and I, we can take care of Chloe. You never know, it could be practice for if we ever have one." Sadness shone in his eyes, and Angel couldn't hurt him. She couldn't hurt anyone.

Even though she had plunged a blade into Andrew, she'd been so upset with herself. Violence never solved anything.

Making her way toward the clubhouse, she didn't even bother going into the kitchen, and went upstairs. Entering the room she shared with Lash, she paused as she saw him sitting on the edge of the bed. He looked … rough.

"Hey, baby," he said.

She didn't run into his arms. Wrapping them around her, she stared at him. "You finally came home."

"Of course I came home. Why wouldn't I come home?" Lash asked, getting to his feet.

"I don't know. It's the first time you haven't called, or come straight home. What's going on, Lash?"

"Nothing, baby." He took a step toward her and held open his arms. "I love you."

Angel stared at his open arms. She wanted to run to them, but last night, he hadn't come home. He'd changed how he kept in touch with her, by not actually keeping in touch, and she didn't like it. She liked the way they were, and if this was going to be their future, she wanted no part of it.

Some of the women might think she was overreacting, but this was only the beginning. Lash wasn't Tiny. She didn't know how Eva and Tiny worked, nor did she care to know.

When he came close to her, she held out her hand and stopped him.

"Baby, what is this?"

She took a deep breath.

"I didn't call for one night."

"It's one night now. You don't think I've seen how destructive couples can be together, and with each other? It's one night now, but what happens in a week, a month, or a few years? You've just had a little girl, Lash, a baby girl."

"The club has just been fucked over, Angel." His arms were still open.

"And what makes a club strong are the people who stick together, who remain devoted to each other, and to the club. Deep down, you know I'm right. Last night, you should have called me. You didn't. What if it was the other way around?"

****

Lash would have gone hunting for her. He'd have dumped their kids on the first person he saw, and gone out to get her. Angel was his entire world. He loved his kids, and the club, and over the years she'd become his main focus. In the beginning, he'd said the club would always come first, but that was a lie. Angel came first, and would always come first, apart from last night.

He had planned to come home, scoop her into his arms, and take her back to their place because he'd made the world safe. He hadn't. Lash had failed to protect his family and his club. For the first time in his life, he'd been angry, ashamed, and hadn't wanted to face Angel with his failure.

"He's still alive," he said. His throat was tight, and he felt like he couldn't breathe.

"What?"

"Andrew. He's still roaming free out there, and I saw the look on his face. He wants to hurt you."

"So, what does that have to do with not coming home last night?"

"I failed you. I failed this club."

She frowned. He saw it, and he hated it.

"Wait, you saved two women last night."

"So?"

"So? Seriously, Lash, you're going to see last night as a failure when I see it as a win." He looked at her, and there was a smile on her face. She stepped toward him. "You didn't come home because you thought you failed me? Lash, by not coming home, *that's* the failure. I was so worried, so scared. Even Anthony talked about you this morning. This is the first time our son had to leave for school without hearing or seeing his father. Imagine how he must have felt. We all love you." She wrapped her arms around him. "You'll get Andrew."

"How do you know?"

She smiled up at him. "You're not a failure."

He stroked her cheek. Tears filled his eyes as he stared down into hers. "I'm so sorry."

"You're the leader, the Prez of The Skulls, but you're my husband. You're the father to our two beautiful kids. Don't make me hurt you. You've taught me how to take men down, don't forget."

He started to laugh. "If you took me down, I'd deserve it."

Lash pulled her into his arms, holding her close. Her soft body melded against his. He couldn't make it up to her with sex. She wasn't allowed to be intimate for a couple of weeks more.

"I'm sorry."

"I know."

Pulling away, he saw she was tired. "I fucked up. Come on."

"What are you doing?"

"I'm going to hold you while you fall asleep."

"You don't have to do that. I bet you've got the whole club waiting for you."

"I don't care if they're waiting. My only focus is you. Come on, I'm going to hold you, and we're going to get the rest we both deserve."

She walked over to the bed, and he wrapped his arms around her, holding her close as she settled against him. "Did the kids get to school okay?"

"Yeah. Anthony and Miles took them in. They're growing up so fast."

"Yeah, they are. How was Chloe last night?"

"After her three o'clock feeding, she went back to sleep without a fuss."

He saw she was still so tired. Kissing her neck, he closed his eyes.

"Where do you think he could be?" Angel asked.

"He's got to lay low. Whizz made sure that his face was sent to law enforcement along with the whole documentation of his crimes."

"He's going to get mad about that," Angel said.

"Yeah, so we're going out later on. The club's going to go hunting for him. We're not going to give him a chance to retaliate."

"You don't know where he could be."

"We've limited our search to motels, hotels, and abandoned apartment buildings. We'll find him, Angel."

He locked their fingers together, and she sighed. Within seconds she had fallen asleep.

Sleep was the last thing on his mind. There was no way he'd be able to find peace until he'd put Andrew in the ground. Even though he wanted to rush out, and start hunting, their men needed time to regroup, as did he.

Inhaling his wife's scent, everything within Lash calmed. Even though he didn't feel sleepy, his eyes started to droop, and everything went dark.

****

Devil made his way into his son's hospital room. Both Tabitha and Simon were sitting on the same bed, eating, and watching television.

"They've been like that all morning," Lexie said.

He turned to find the woman who had claimed his heart and soul. Wrapping his arm around her, he drew her close. "I'm sorry I didn't get back last night."

"I heard what happened with Paris. Is she going to be okay?"

"I guess time will tell with this one. I don't know." Devil sank his fingers into her luscious locks and stared into her eyes. "I love you."

She smiled. "What's the matter?"

"It's nothing. I'm just tired of all this fighting and shit. It makes a man sick to his stomach."

She nodded. "I get that. Are you going to go and say hi to Sasha?"

"I heard the little tank can see now."

"Tank? Devil, I mean it—"

"I'm not being mean. After everything she's been through, she's still fighting. She's like a little tank, don't you think?"

"There you go saying all nice words, and making me fall for you all over again."

"That's me." He kissed the top of her head. "So, I was thinking after all this shit is over, and the kids are off school, we all go out. Family holiday. Hell, we'll even take Ripper and Judi, and Paul."

"A family holiday? Are you sure you can cope with that?"

"It's not about coping. It's about needing it. I need this, and I need you."

She rested her head against his chest.

"Yes, of course yes."

"It'll also work for us to have Ripper and Judi. We can dump the kids on them, and I can have my way with you, that doesn't require a PG-13 rating."

"Shut up." Lexie's gaze gave her away.

She was as hot for him as he was for her.

"You can count on it."

"Hey, Dad, did you catch the bad guys?" Simon asked.

"Showtime."

Devil entered the hospital room, and pointed at his son. "Why are you in Tab's bed?"

"She has bad dreams."

"Oh, you do know that it stops when you get out of the hospital?" Devil asked.

"You sleep with Mom all the time."

"That's because your mom and I are married."

"Then I'll marry Tabitha. She's going to be my girl, anyway. It'll be cool."

"Son, you're not marrying. You're not even ten."

"That's not fair."

"Lucky for me, it doesn't have to be fair." For the first time in his life Devil was thankful for government rules.

"I'm sorry, Devil, the nightmares were bad. I dreamt of bullets and stuff. It was scary."

Why did Tabitha have to be so sweet? She was Tiny's daughter, for Christ's sake. She should be a bitch, a horrible little brat, like Tate. No, Tiny had to have a sweet daughter.

"It's okay, sweetie, I hope he chased the demons away."

"He did, and he told Gavin what for as well, which was really funny."

His son was going to get himself hurt one of these days.

Eva and Tiny came in ten minutes later, carrying a bag full of goodies. Devil watched as they handed Tabitha a bear, and then an action doll to Simon. His son was very sweet.

Kiss-ass.

Devil could see his son as a teenager right now, worming his way into Tiny and Eva's good graces.

The doctor came into the room, and let them know that tomorrow Simon and Tabitha could be discharged. They were healthy, and providing they rested at home, they were good to leave.

Tiny and Devil followed the doctor out of the room.

"We want them to stay here," Tiny said.

"I can't authorize that."

"You've said providing the kids rest. They're kids, and resting at home isn't an option," Devil said.

They were not going to have their kids at home while the threat outside was still apparent, especially ones who needed to rest. Simon and Tabitha were injured, the others were in school, and those who weren't didn't have an old injury.

After convincing the doctor, he made sure that Tabitha and Simon could stay in another week.

The Skulls and Chaos Bleeds crew were slowly being discharged. Sally because of her leg, was staying in the hospital, as was Sophia, and Sasha. Murphy, Phoebe, Fighter, Alex, Sunshine, and Mia were being discharged within the next twenty-four hours. The brothers who were injured were staying at The Skulls' clubhouse. Those that weren't, were going on a hunting party.

"We're going to be heading out soon," Tiny said. "Are you coming?"

"Yeah, I've got to go and see Pussy and Sasha."

"Send her my love," Tiny said.

Lexie waved at him.

Holding his hand up, Devil made his way back toward Sasha's ward. He left the children's ward and made his way toward Sasha's room. Standing at the doorway once again, he looked inside.

Just once he wanted to go an entire year without visiting a fucking hospital. The fact he could go from one end of the hospital to another without checking the signs of where he was going pissed him off.

Sasha looked toward him and frowned. Pussy, following her gaze, stood. "Devil."

"Sorry I didn't get the chance to be here earlier. Business to attend to." Turning his attention to Sasha, he nodded. "Hello, Sasha."

"Hello, Devil. It's nice to see you."

"I bet you wished you held out for me, don't you?" He held his arms out giving her a little turn. "I'm hot stuff."

She chuckled. "Nah, I like my man just fine."

"I'm sorry for what happened."

"I'm … not. Does that make me weird? I can see, and I'm actually happy about that. It makes me weird, doesn't it?"

Devil held his thumb and finger together. "A little bit."

He took a seat in the spare chair on the opposite side of her. "So, every time you hit your head you're going to suffer like this?"

"You'd think that. I don't know. The doctor has said I'm a unique case. I'm happy. I won't be a liability anymore. I hated that for you, for all of you."

Devil gritted his teeth. Seeing Sasha like this, even with her eyesight, hurt him. He liked the young woman. Hell, she'd made Pussy settle down, and anyone who could do that was a stellar woman in his book. "Sasha, it wasn't just about the club that I said that. Your … condition, it scared me. If you couldn't help us, what if we couldn't help you?" he asked.

"You cared?"

"Of course I cared. You were part of my club the moment Pussy claimed you. You've been my concern, for a long time, Sasha." Tears filled her eyes. Devil leaned forward and took her hand. "I care about everyone in my club. I may not show it. I may be an insufferable ass, who acts like a selfish prick, but I'm not. Every single man, woman, and child in that club belongs to me, and I make sure I protect them. No matter the cost."

****

Lacey entered the basement of the clubhouse. Ned was visiting Sally, and Lacey was about to head on over there. First, she wanted to see how her man was doing. He tried to hide it, but she knew he got hit hard when they were defeated.

"I thought I'd find you down here," she said.

Whizz was hard at work typing on three different keyboards. The pictures on the boards were moving faster than she had ever seen.

"What's going on?" she asked.

"Nothing. I don't want us to waste our time with nonsense. We've got to find him now while he's retreating. We can't let him get strong again. What if he has a stash of cash I don't know about? What if he's been storing it in a safety deposit box, or some shit like that?"

Lacey moved up behind him and stroked his neck. She had to touch him. With all the crap going on, it had been a while since they had been close. "You're putting a lot of pressure on yourself."

"I'm not. I'm putting the right amount of pressure. Fuck, this man killed Happy, injured our club, and Chaos Bleeds. He also took our daughter's leg, Lacey. I'm not going to sit back, and watch him get happy. I can't do it. We're ending him now."

"Sally's going to get better."

"Every time I look at her, I'm going to see my failing as a father."

"How?" she asked. "How did you fail?"

"I didn't hunt hard enough, fast enough."

"Whizz, you've been at this nonstop. The only reason you've been able to make a breakthrough is because of Gash. You know who Andrew is. You were chasing a fucking ghost. Do not beat yourself up about this. The whole of the club would tell you exactly the same thing, and you know it."

Whizz paused, and the basement went silent. Lacey stared at the man who had proven to her that love really could conquer everything. She loved him more than anything in the world. He was her sole reason for surviving. If it wasn't for Whizz, she wouldn't be part of The Skulls, nor would she have two wonderful children. They were adopted, but they were there. No one else wanted them, but she and Whizz did. She had a home, a family.

Cupping his face, she forced him to look at her. "You've done everything, Whizz. There's no blame here. Not from you, or anyone else. One man ordered that attack. That's where the blame lies."

"She's so scared," Whizz said. "She doesn't want pity from anyone."

"Sally's strong. We'll get through this."

She rested her head against his.

"Love you, Lacey."

"Of course you do. I take your code, and actually make sense of you. Who wouldn't love me?" She tried to make a joke. "When was the last time you slept?"

"I can't sleep right now. I'm too wired."

"If you keep on going without any sleep, you'll make a mistake, Whizz. Don't make mistakes. Rest."

"I can't, right now."

"You will." Lacey kissed his lips. "I'm going to the hospital."

"I might not be here when you get back," he said.

"I'll always be here, and you better come back to me."

"I will."

****

Death made his way toward the swings where his woman, Brianna, sat. She looked so beautiful, staring up at the sky. When he opened the gate, she turned those pretty eyes toward him.

"I thought I'd find you out here," he said.

"It's so peaceful. It's hard to believe that just a few days ago, there were guns going off, and people dying, people hurting."

He took a seat beside her, reaching out to take her hand. "With all the crazy shit going on, I haven't come to talk to you, or to see how you were feeling."

"I don't know what you mean? We sleep together

every night."

"You were taken by Andrew. You've got the brand on your skin, the one that has been covered by ink."

She averted her gaze, staring at the ground. "There hasn't been a lot to say."

"He hurt you. Is this hurting you?" he asked.

Brianna bit her lip. "It's not hurting me. This is … I think it's closure. He's been part of my life for so long, even after Gonzalez, and everything. It'll be nice to walk down the street, and not wonder if he's there, watching, and waiting for me. Does that make sense?" she asked.

"Perfect sense."

She shrugged. "How is Jessica?" Brianna asked. "I'm not the only one he tried to ruin."

"She belongs to Snake. I'll talk to him about it soon. I wanted to come and see you. See how you're handling everything."

"I'll be happier when he's dead and gone. That man has destroyed many women, and I'm tired of him being there in the recess of my mind."

****

"What are you thinking about?" Snake asked.

Jessica was standing outside of the hospital, staring up at it. Her arm was still in a bandage. She glanced behind her and smiled. "Hey."

"I've been looking for you."

"I caught a ride here. Sorry."

"What's going on in that head of yours?"

"Not a lot. I'm just thinking about the unfairness of it all. You know?"

"Andrew?"

"Yeah. The brand, the pain, he's hurt so many people, and has gotten away with it."

"Not for much longer."

"How do we know that?" she asked. "I should be in there helping, and I can't because of this stupid arm."

"Jessica, you're injured." He wrapped his arms around her, kissing her temple. "You've got to learn to rest."

"I don't know how to rest." She rubbed at her temple, sighing. "I'm not used to being like this."

Snake held her tightly against him, and she gave herself up to the pleasure of being in his arms. "You've been strong a long time. It's time you let me be the strong one."

"But I'm much better at it," she said.

He laughed. "That you are. I prefer being a goofball."

She leaned back and stared up at him. "I missed you last night. You didn't stay after you came for Spider."

"Paris is in there. She's hurt pretty bad. The doctors have her in a medically induced coma to help her deal with the pain." Snake kissed her shoulder. "I miss home."

"Yeah, Fort Wills is great, but most of the time we visit, we're either in the hospital or in the clubhouse. It would be nice to actually see what the town has to offer."

"It would." He kissed her cheek, and she just knew he wanted to ask her something. "Jess, baby," he said.

"What?"

"How are you holding up?"

"I'm pissed. Not only did the son of a bitch brand me, he's now shooting at us. Then he has the fucking audacity to come to the hospital to try to hurt us?" Jessica shook her head. "I tell you, if I ever get my hands on him. He's going to die a very slow, a very painful death, and while it's happening, I'm going to laugh. We should probably film it as well so we get more pleasure out of it."

"Bloodthirsty."

"Too damn right, I am. Fucker deserves to pay for what he's done. His death can't come too soon as far as I'm concerned."

Chapter Twelve

One week after the shooting

The funeral had been a sad affair. The Skulls' Nomad Chapter had turned up in town, and now the clubhouse was so full people were camping on the back lawn. There were several who hadn't been able to make it. Sasha and Pussy were still in the hospital, but the good news was the doctors believed Sasha could be released in a couple of weeks. Sally was being discharged in a couple of days. Her leg needed time to heal, but she didn't want to stay in the hospital all day. The club would be taking turns to take her to the hospital for her appointments.

Sandy stood outside with the club, drinking some beer as she listened to tales that were told by the Nomads, Adam, and Twisted.

Happy had been well loved, and he'd be missed.

Stink walked up behind her, gripping her hip. "You okay, baby?"

"Yeah, I will be. I hope so. I don't know. After a funeral, and with the guys here, it all makes it real. Any news from Whizz?" she asked.

"Andrew is keeping a low profile."

"What about his little sidekick? Spider mentioned he had one, as did that girl. Russell, they said."

"It's hard to go on one name. Whizz has run his name through several databases. A lot of names have come up, but it's about going through each profile to try to find the right person."

"Sounds like a cop problem."

"Lucky for us, we have Whizz and Lacey. She can't cook, but she seems to be able to find people. Whizz has her reading through the profiles while he monitors security footage in a twenty-mile radius of the house that went bang."

"Why doesn't he do it on a twenty-mile radius of the clubhouse or the hospital?" she asked.

"Why would he do that?"

"He's after the two clubs. It would make more sense of him being close to us."

"Andrew also needs to be secluded. His face has been posted up."

"So we find the sidekick, and we find Andrew."

"Needle in a haystack."

"Yeah, his sidekick could be anyone." She took a sip of her beer, and when there was a cheer for their fallen, she raised her bottle.

Stink did the same.

After her first one, Sandy went to juice. It wasn't the time nor was it the place to get drunk.

Music started to play, and she wrapped her arms around his neck. "Hello, husband."

Stink wrapped his arms around her waist, drawing her close. "Hello, wife."

"This has been a rather interesting courtship, don't you think? she asked.

"It has certainly been long for the two of us." He took possession of her lips.

With Stink's arms surrounding her, all of her worries fell away. "Thank you," she said.

"What are you thanking me for?" he asked.

"For not giving up on me. I imagine it would have been really easy to do. You waited for me, and I think that has to be the nicest thing that anyone has ever done." He leaned forward, taking possession of her lips.

"You can count on it always."

"Now, I know we're honoring the dead, but I knew Happy for a while, and I know he'd be upset if we didn't raise our drinks in another kind of toast," Lash said.

He stood up on the wall, staring down at them all. Stink pulled her into his arms, wrapping them around her, and holding her close.

"We have all come together for something bad. Andrew. He took Happy from us, and we will make him pay. First, I want to offer up a huge congratulations to Stink and Sandy. Guys, you've made us wait fucking years for this moment. You deserve each other. I don't know what took you so long, but it's a good job that you both finally found the will to actually be with each other. Love you both."

Sandy chuckled, accepting kisses from those closest to them.

"To Alex and Sunshine for their baby girl. We can see her right now."

She looked behind her to see the happy couple together, with Sunshine holding the little bundle.

"Welcome to fatherhood, Alex. Trust me, you're going to love it, and possibly hate it. I think we're all looking forward to what the future can hold. Also, to my little baby girl, Chloe. She's going to be spoiled rotten, I can feel it. Angel, you're mine, and if I don't get into heaven when I'm dead, it's because I'm living it now."

There was a round of applause at his speech.

"I also want to say a special call out to Sophia and Sasha. Both are strong women, and knowing we didn't lose them, makes me a better person."

Another round of cheers.

"I always want to thank Whizz. Where is he?"

"I'm here."

Sandy saw he was standing by the door, and Lacey was holding his arm.

"Out of all of us here, you've done the best. The

fight with Andrew is not a fight just with our fists. If it was, we'd have gotten him weeks ago. This fight needed you, and we're a lucky bunch of men to have you with us."

"Thank you."

"To all of our clubs, whether it be Skulls, Nomad, or Chaos, we're going to win this thing."

Another round of cheers erupted.

The music was turned up, and Sandy turned around in Stink's arms. "So, Stink, what do you say to carrying me over the threshold, taking me to your room, and having your wicked way with me? Do you think you can handle that?" she asked.

Stink bent down, picking her up in his arms, and holding her close.

"That's one order I'm more than happy to oblige."

There were catcalls and some dirty words spoken as Stink carried her toward the threshold of the clubhouse. He didn't drop her, and he took her to their room, where he placed her on the bed. Stink left to go and shut the door, returning to her.

"I want you to make love to me, Stink."

She never had to ask her man twice.

****

Spider rubbed his head as he stared into Paris's sterile room. He couldn't just walk in and see her. The doctors wore protective equipment, and they demanded he suit up before going inside. He was limited to how much time he could spend with her. It fucking sucked, and it pissed him off.

Pussy was walking down the long corridor returning to his woman. He held a cup of coffee in his hand, and he paused to take a seat.

"How are you holding in there, brother?"

"I'm sick and tired of the fucking crutches. I want to get out, and pummel the shit out of the fucker who thought they could put a hand on my woman. Look at her, Pussy. Look at how fucking weak she looks. He beat her, raped her, tortured her, and now I've got to find a way to make it all fucking better for her. How the fuck do I do that, huh? How do I make shit like that better?"

Pussy gripped his shoulder. "First, you start by realizing that you can do that."

"What?"

"I'm not saying this shit will be easy. In fact, I bet with you and with Paris, shit is about to get really fucking complicated. She's been hurt in ways that are going to require patience. You've never been known for your patience before."

"I have to do this for her."

"And you will. I have every faith in you. You've got to realize you can do it. Paris, she got that girl to send a message to you, didn't she? She helped to fight this. Paris called out to you. On some level, you've got to see that it means something." Pussy took a sip of his coffee, sitting back.

"Doesn't Sasha want you?" Spider asked.

"Not right now. She's sleeping."

"I heard she can go home soon. That's good."

"Yeah, home. We're living in Fort fucking Wills. With the Nomad Chapter turning up, people are sleeping on the fucking ground. You've got more chance of her resting here." Pussy shook his head. "I just want this shit to be over. I want Andrew dead, and whoever he's working with to be gone so we can head home. I'm missing Piston County."

Spider chuckled. "I never thought I'd hear it or be feeling the loss of my own town. It's not right, is it?"

"We'll be there soon, and this will be a passing

memory."

Staring into Paris's room, Spider wondered how she would feel waking up after everything that happened. Andrew was a sick fucker, and his poison was trying to spread to those that they loved. He was an animal.

"I need a smoke." Spider got to his feet.

"I thought you were giving up smoking?"

"I will, when I'm no longer hanging out in a hospital. Until then, my only comfort is this." Grabbing his crutches, he gave a nod at Pussy. "Chat soon."

"Look forward to it."

Spider went to the elevator. It was pointless taking the stairs. He couldn't navigate stairs with his leg. Pressing the button, he leaned against the wall, rubbing at his eyes as he did. So much had happened in such a short period of time. Spider was tired, he was exhausted, and he wanted it to all be over. The doors opened, and he walked out, leaving the main entrance, and someone bumped into him. Spider paused, and stared up at the man.

"You're right. I work for Master, and you can call me 'Sir'."

He had spent many days remembering this fucking man, hating him, loathing him. Even as his leg killed him, Spider gripped the bastard's jacket.

"Hello, Russell. Do you remember me?"

Spider somehow managed to get them both out of sight. Slamming his fist against Russell's face, he landed blow after blow. Seeing Paris's wounds play in his mind, he gripped the back of Russell's head, and slammed it against the brick wall. With all of Spider's rage, Russell was no match for him. Like a spider, he had locked Russell close, and now there was no mercy. Over and over, he fought Russell, beating the shit out of him, until finally, Spider couldn't do anything more. He sat on the floor with Russell's still body beside him. Pulling out his cell phone, he dialed Devil's number. His hands were shaking.

"What's going on?" Devil asked.

"I've just killed the man who put me in crutches. I'm outside of the hospital."

"Fuck!"

The call was disconnected. Resting his head against the wall, Spider wasn't surprised when he heard the hospital doors. Opening his eyes, he saw Pussy standing over him. "What the fuck? You went out for a smoke."

"Yeah, and this fucker who took me down, fucking *Sir*, bumped into me. I tell you, it was the wrong fucking thing to do today. My head, it's fucking ready for them, Pussy." He put the smoke to his lips, and lit it. "This man was not innocent."

His hands were shaking as he took a deep draw. He needed to calm himself. His heart was racing, and he was covered in blood.

"I've got to go and see Paris."

"Dude, you're covered in blood. The only place you're going to is the clubhouse and getting cleaned up. Damn, is that brain on the wall?"

"Don't know."

Minutes later a large truck was pulling up outside of the hospital, carrying Devil, Lash, Tiny, Sinner, and Snake.

"What the fuck did you do?" Devil asked.

"Told you on the phone. I exacted a little payback from this son of a bitch." Spider slapped Russell's ass. "It's about time really. I was owed some." He started laughing.

"Has he gone crazy?" Tiny asked.

"Don't know. Load him up in the truck. We've

got to do this quickly."

"Whizz already has access to the hospital footage. He's going to erase all trace of Spider."

Spider sat in the truck, smoking a cigarette as he listened to the guys clean away Russell.

I knew I was going to have you, you little punk ass prick.

He hummed to himself, giddy at what he'd achieved. Time passed, and finally, the guys were climbing back in the truck.

"Let's get out of here."

"Come on, you're not mad at me, are you?" Spider asked. "I simply saw an opportunity and took it."

"You took an opportunity. You fuck! Why didn't you knock him out, huh?" Devil asked. "We're still hunting for Andrew, and you're killing off people who knew how to find him. Russell shot you. Andrew gave that order. What you did was kill a nobody with a shit ton of information," Devil said, climbing behind the wheel.

The buzz Spider had been having started to die. The danger was still out there. Andrew was the danger.

Throwing his cigarette out of the window, Spider sat back. "Sorry."

"Yeah, you should be fucking sorry. Your leg was hurt, but your girl back there, she's been fucking tortured. She has a right to feel safe, and with Andrew still out there, we can't give that to her. You're the reason for that."

Spider glanced in the back of the truck, and he saw the same look on everyone's face, including Pussy's.

"Shit, I'm sorry. We're going to get Andrew."

"You better hope so," Lash said. "Andrew has proven himself to be an expert in *not* getting caught. You had a perfect opportunity here. A perfect one, and what did you do? You beat the shit out of him. Did you even ask him where Andrew was? Bargain?"

Spider stayed silent. He hadn't thought. He had reacted.

"Sorry."

"Take your sorry, and shove it up your ass. We know you've got fucking issues," Lash said. His voice suddenly went high-pitched. "Oh, my leg. Someone help me, I want to kill the fucker who shot me." His voice went deep again, normal. "News flash, this was just fucking bait to a larger fucking fish. Men and women have fucking died! Men and women, even fucking kids are in the hospital because of these two fuckers." Lash hit the roof of the car. Spider was under no illusions that given the choice, Lash would rather be pummeling him.

Once they got back to the clubhouse, they parked toward the back, and Spider climbed out, watching as they carried the body to the back. He lost sight of them, but he heard Lash ranting and raving.

"I'm sorry, man, I didn't think," Spider said. Pussy was leaning against the side of the van.

"No, you didn't. The club is about more than you, and you failed it tonight, Spider."

"But—"

"You don't need to explain why you did it. I get it. We all get it. We're just seeing the bigger picture. That guy could have led us to Andrew. It could have been over tonight. Instead, it's going to keep on going on now."

Spider watched as Pussy walked away. He'd fucked up, in a big way. This was not going to be easily solved.

****

Andrew paced up and down the length of the small room. Russell had gone out to do some recon on the hospital. No one but Spider knew what he looked like, and Russell could see what was going on with The Skulls. Going to the clubhouse was too much risk. Besides, Andrew wanted Lola and Paris taken care of. No loose ends. Maybe Russell was right. He should have left The Skulls alone. Russell had been gone for well over an hour. Andrew had not heard from him, and he didn't like that. Yes, he had fucked up, and Whizz had taken him by surprise. Both clubs had been more than he could handle. Instead of leaving them alone, he hadn't, and now, he was fucked. There was no doubt that The Skulls and Chaos Bleeds were going to win, but even as he thought it, he couldn't believe it. Andrew was not one to be beat down. He always found an out. Now, he was trapped, and relying solely on what little money he had on him and on Russell. He'd been stupid not to find some way to pay Russell. Instead, he'd always paid the kid in cash.

Being locked in a motel for the past couple of days was driving him crazy. Especially as the money he'd spent taking the room was running out. Russell had to go and get them food, pay for housekeeping, and all that shit. His face was on the news, every fucking day. If he was playing a game of chess, he'd be in check.

Not checkmate. Not yet.

Andrew still had a few contacts. It all depended on how loyal they were to him. Once the money was gone, he didn't have anything else. Whizz had royally fucked him.

I'll get him back.

Even as he thought it, he had to wonder how.

He'd built himself up because people had forgotten who he was. No one had cared about Gash's brother, or what had become of him. Over the years, he'd appealed to lonely old women. He'd fucked them, married them, gotten them to change their wills, killed them, and gotten rich. Andrew had a knack for acting like a victim.

Sometimes the police had asked him about his previous wives, and he'd sob, asking why it was always him? Why did he lose the women he loved?

If they suspected anything, they could never prove it. His money, his wealth, his power had only grown until he was able to do it without diving into some wrinkled old pussy. There he'd found Gonzalez, and he was granted access to as many women and girls he wanted. Master was born, and the power had been all his.

Sitting on the edge of the bed, he thought about all the women over the years he had begging at his feet. They had wanted to leave, but he wouldn't let them. No, he'd held their freedom in his palm, and each day he gave a little ray of hope, only to squash it into the dirt. He loved doing that. Andrew loved to break them down until they were empty shells. Only then would he finally give them peace, killing them.

It wasn't over. He didn't accept that it was over, not now, not ever.

Grabbing his cell phone, he put a call through to Russell's phone. They would get out of this, he was sure of it.

****

"The fucking corpse is ringing!" Lash said, stepping back.

They all glanced down at the remains of Andrew's little sidekick, the sound of a ringing telephone seeming so loud in the quiet of the fields outside the back of the clubhouse. Lash had stored many dead bodies out here. Sometimes he'd left them for the wild animals to come and take. He'd never let his kids or his woman wander around here.

Devil stepped toward the man, touching his

pockets.

They found a cell phone. The name of the caller was Andrew. "He's fucking calling," Devil said.

"Answer it," Tiny said.

"Wait." Sinner held his hand up. "What if Whizz can trace the call?"

"Do we even know what Russell sounds like?" Lash asked.

The call went to answer phone. Lash stared at the phone, and seconds later it started ringing again.

"If we don't answer this soon, he's going to stop calling," Devil said.

"Answer it," Death said.

Devil slid his thumb across the green phone sign, and clicked it on speaker.

"Russell, where the fuck are you?"

"Busy," Lash said, speaking up.

Glancing up he saw the men looking at him. Holding his hands up, he shrugged. He was taking a fucking gamble.

"What's it look like at the hospital? We good to leave?" Andrew asked.

"What?" Lash kept it to one word answers. A weird-sounding person was hard to detect with one-word answers.

"Are we good to go? You were going to pay Paris a visit, right? I told you I didn't want any loose ends. She's got to go, and so does Lola."

Lash looked at Devil. The leader of the Chaos Bleeds crew was struggling to keep it together.

"Yeah, clear," Lash said.

"Clear? What the fuck does that mean? Did you kill her or not? Have you killed Lola?"

"She's dead. They're dead."

There was another pause on the phone. The sound

of Andrew's heavy breathing was easily detected.

"This isn't Russell, is it?"

"Long time, no see," Tiny said, speaking up. "Surely you remember me?"

Another short pause where none of them spoke.

"Tiny, leader of The Skulls."

"Former leader."

"Ah, how is Lash handling The Skulls? Personally I think you need a change of leadership. He's not doing well at all. Then again, you did send a baby to do a man's job. No wonder he's not holding up to it."

"Send a baby to do a man's job. Isn't that what you're doing with Russell?" Devil asked. "Not even man enough to finish the girls off yourself. You're nothing but a coward."

"Ah, Devil. How is your son? Does he know Lexie's not his real momma yet? You see, nothing gets past me."

"Apart from money. Tell me, Andrew, what's it like to live in a little box, and never be allowed to go anywhere? Your face looks really beautiful on the news. Cops are raiding your places. I have to say, it sucks to be you right about now," Lash said.

"You think you're so fucking smart. I'm going to kill Angel, but first I'm going to take my time with her, get her used to the feel of my dick as I tear her apart. After I'm done, I'll give her to Russell—"

"Russell's dead, asshole," Lash said.

Andrew was beaten, and he heard it. Looking at the men beside him, his brothers during this war, he saw the same on their faces. Andrew had lost, and there wasn't a thing he could do about it.

"No!"

"Wrong. Spider beat him to death. He's got no brain left," Devil said. "Why don't you just hand yourself over, and we end this? Clearly, you're not a very good enemy if we're having to do the damage for you."

"You made a big mistake."

The call ended, and Lash looked around at the men. "Does anyone care?" he asked.

"No," Devil said. "He was bluffing. I heard it in his voice. He doesn't have anything to go on." Devil sighed. "You know, this has actually been interesting."

"Interesting?" Lash continued to dig down. He was tired, and he wanted to curl up with his woman, and instead, he was digging a fucking grave, for a bastard who didn't deserve it. "I'd call this fucked up, not interesting."

"It brought us all together. We're out digging a grave. I'd say that's pretty fucking great," Sinner said.

Lash shook his head. "Remind me to never get on your guys' bad side. Tiny, I thought our club was badass."

"Our club *is* badass."

Laughing, Lash climbed out of the pit that he'd dug, and they shoved Russell into it.

"Does anyone want to say anything?" Lash asked.

None of them did.

"What can I say, buddy, next time, pick your friends wisely." Lash started to scatter the dirt over the body.

Before he let his woman kiss him, he was going to take a shower, and scrub his skin. He was fucking filthy.

"So, when is the wedding going to be?" Lash asked.

"Wedding?" Devil spoke up.

"Yeah, Simon and Tabitha. It's going to happen. Will you make them do it in secret, or after he's gotten her pregnant?"

"Lash, I love you like a son, but if you don't shut your fucking mouth, I swear I'm going to hurt you," Tiny said.

Lash laughed, putting the finishing dirt on the grave. "Done."

Heading back toward the clubhouse, they were just about to enter when Whizz came out. "I've got him."

Chapter Thirteen

"When I'm grown up I'm going to be part of a gang," Gash said.

"No, you're not." Andrew giggled.

"Am too. I'm going to be big and strong."

"Whatever. Gangs are stupid. I'm going to be the most powerful warrior in all the world, and I'm going to hurt you." Andrew's voice grew dark as he picked up his imaginary sword. *"No one can defeat me."*

"My fists are made of pure steel. No one can harm me."

Gash woke up with a gasp.

"Are you okay?" Charlotte asked. She was shaking him, and he nodded.

"Of course."

"You were shouting. Fists of pure steel or something."

Gash sat up, reaching over to turn the light on.

"Is everything okay?"

He nodded, rubbing at his eyes. "Yeah, it's fine."

"It doesn't sound like you're fine."

He glanced over at her, his woman, and took a deep breath. "I was dreaming about Andrew."

"What about him?"

"About when we were kids, and he wasn't so much a monster, but a little brother."

"I guess you would. I take it he wasn't always a monster?" she asked.

Gash licked his dry lips, needing a drink. Grabbing his empty glass, he got his feet, and made his way into the bathroom. Pouring himself some water, he took a large drink, and entered the bathroom.

Charlotte glanced down his body, and he smirked.

"You just can't help but admire the goods."

"They're damn good goods." She winked at him, dropping the blanket so he got to see her full tits.

His cock started to swell.

"Tell me about this dream of yours."

Running fingers through his hair, he blew out a breath. "I don't know. I was remembering when we were kids, and we used to play around. It was a long time ago."

"Are you having regrets about killing him?"

"No, I'm not. I'm just, I'm trying to figure out what went wrong, you know? He was a good kid for a little while, and then he started doing all this bad shit." He shrugged.

"I don't know what it takes to make a man like Andrew. He's pretty sick and twisted."

"Yeah, and I'm not. That's what I'm saying. What if somewhere down the road, there's a switch?"

"That doesn't happen in real life. What you're saying happens in movies."

He opened his mouth to talk, but someone knocked. "Who is it?"

"It's Stink. It's time. Whizz found him."

Gash tensed up and looked toward Charlotte. "I'll be there."

He went to his jeans and tugged them up his thighs.

"If you don't want to do this, you don't have to," she said.

Gash went to the bed, and held her face, staring into her eyes.

"He locked you in a building, trapped you, and set the building on fire."

"Gash? He was your brother."

"He framed me for rape and murder, and I got sent to prison. The boy I was remembering in my dream, that's not the man he is now. He's not even worth thinking about, and I'm angry at myself for not seeing it before." He pressed his lips against hers. "I love you, Charlotte. I'm going to get our life back, one way or the other."

He kissed her again, and grabbed his shirt, followed by his leather jacket. "I'll call you as soon as I know more."

****

Charlotte pulled a shirt over her head and moved toward the window. Once again she watched as Gash rode away, outside of the clubhouse grounds. Would this be the last time she saw him? Would she see him again? She didn't know the answer to that question, and it scared her.

Leaving the bedroom, she made her way downstairs, and wasn't surprised when she saw most of the women there. Angel was once again making hot chocolate. Lexie and Eva were there this time. Jessica, Sandy, all of the women, apart from the ones who were still in the hospital.

"What's going to happen with Lola?" Lacey asked.

"We don't know. Her parents are due tomorrow. They got waylaid due to traffic. Whizz wants to be there with Lash, doesn't he?" Angel asked.

"Yeah. Whizz is rather protective of her," Lacey said.

"I'm not surprised. Lola was very brave to do what she did," Charlotte said, entering the room. She was one of the latest women to be part of The Skulls. She didn't feel like she belonged. Angel was the most accepting. The other women seemed to stare at her.

Rose pulled out a chair, smiling.

Or maybe Charlotte wasn't used to being part of

large crowds of women.

"Thank you."

"It's a big night. Stressful. Hardy's gone. The twins are resting," Rose said.

"It was nice having Butch back," Tate said. "I've missed him."

Several women agreed.

"I know Alex misses his son," Eva said. "It's sad that he doesn't see him more often."

"It's nothing we can do. It's between Cheryl and Alex," Rose said.

"I always thought he'd make a good dad," Angel said. "He's good to Tabitha and the kids. I don't see why he wouldn't be with his own."

Charlotte accepted the cup of hot chocolate.

The tension in the room mounted as they all waited for their men to get back home. Charlotte wanted Andrew dead, and with Gash's sudden conscience, she hoped he was able to do it, for all of their sakes.

****

Riding toward the motel where Whizz said Andrew was staying, Stink's heart raced with anticipation. He wanted this to be over. He wanted Andrew to be dead, and for them all to be getting on with their lives.

Lash and Devil drove the truck that they intended to transport him on. They were not going to kill him at a motel. This kind of business was for them to take back to the warehouse.

To Stink, it seemed surreal that they were riding toward this moment. For so long they had all been suffering at Andrew's hands, his actions having hurt them all. Some of them would be remembering Andrew's actions for the rest of their lives, like Sally.

With the motel in sight, Stink fell behind Tiny as

they approached. All three clubs heading toward one man, one man who had killed, tortured, and raped. After tonight, Andrew wouldn't be a problem anymore.

Parking his bike, Stink sat, waiting.

They had all agreed Gash was to be the one to bring him out. Devil reversed the van, and both leaders climbed out, opening the back.

Gash made his way toward the motel room door, Whizz by his side.

The door was kicked in, and it was time for the show to begin.

"Not a lot of this happens in Vegas," Butch said.

"Fighting?"

"No, riding. I don't get riding all that much. Vegas is a busy fucking place. I'd probably get run over."

"It's good to have you back."

"It's good to be back. At least, it's good to be helping you guys again. I fucked up in the past, and I'm hoping to right that wrong."

****

"Are you ready for this?" Whizz asked.

"Why are you asking me that?"

"He's your brother. I'd understand if this is hard for you."

Gash glanced over at Whizz, and shook his head. "He stopped being my brother a long time ago."

Raising his foot, he kicked the door in. Andrew was sitting on the bed, staring at his cell phone.

"Well, I'd say this was a surprise, but then we both know different," Andrew said, looking up at them.

The anger on his face was plain to see.

"Hello, brother," Gash said.

"Hello, Gash. Long time no see. Charlotte still alive?"

He stared at his brother.

"Yeah, she is. You got her out of that burning building, and I royally fucked up." Andrew pointed at his cell phone, blowing out a breath. "Whizz, you beat me at my own game."

"I wasn't playing a game."

"No? Didn't anything of what we've been doing get you all excited?" Andrew asked.

Whizz simply stared back, bored.

"Wow, you're no fun. How does Lacey put up with you? She looks like a girl who knows how to party. Maybe she can have her fun with the one legged daughter, Sally."

Whizz's hands tightened into fists, which was the only sign he was pissed.

"You knew this moment was going to come," Gash said.

Andrew laughed. "You know what? I didn't. I really didn't anticipate this." He turned to look back at Whizz. "Tell me where I fucked up?"

"You told us who you were. The moment you did that, I could go back, and track your movements to this moment. Every single marriage, will, deed, you name it. I found it."

"Russell told me my ego was going to be my undoing." Andrew shook his head. "I didn't think it was going to be his."

"Did you actually like Russell?" Gash asked.

"Yeah, I did. He was … special. Like a nice little pet. He thought the world of me, and in this shitty little world, you've got to find the people that mean something to you."

Gash stared at his brother, and for a split second back with Charlotte, he had felt guilty of what he had to do. Knowing what Andrew had done, every sick, twisted thing, he felt nothing.

Stepping forward, Gash grabbed him. Andrew fought, brandishing a weapon, but Andrew was no match for him. Easily, Gash got the knife from him, and tossed it away. Securing Andrew's wrists, Gash started to drag him out of the hotel room. Staring at his brothers, The Skulls, Chaos Bleeds, and the Nomads, Gash gripped Andrew's hair, and forced his blood brother to look. "You got off on making them hurt. Now look at them."

"Do you think this scares me? This is nothing," Andrew said.

Holding him tightly, Gash felt Andrew shaking, which was the truth. The words coming from his mouth were a lie.

"So this is it. So brave of you all to take down one man."

It wasn't just one man.

Andrew had proven that he had the power, and the manipulation to drive others. This was more than one man. It was about what he was also capable of doing.

"I wonder if I should feel proud of this moment," Andrew said. "None of you thought I was worth being part of your club. Now, I have all of your attention."

"Is this what it was all about? Wanting to belong to a club?" Gash asked.

"Pathetic. No, it was about power. I was happy. I had a regular supply of girls, and I didn't cause any problems."

"You killed people," Tiny said. "Women and girls, even men. You spread their bodies in your wake, and you don't think that was a problem?"

"Come on, they were all whores. No one really missed them." Andrew scoffed at him.

Gash stared at his brother, and knew if he didn't kill him, if the club didn't kill him, this was only going to come and bite them in the ass.

"I'm going to ride in the back with him."

"Are you ready for that?" Lash asked.

"Yeah, I am."

"Oh, big brother is going to spank me. I've been a very naughty boy."

Gash secured Andrew's wrists with the metal cuffs and climbed in the back of the truck. Devil, Spider, and Lash would all hear whatever Andrew had to say. Spider wasn't in any position to keep Devil and Lash safe, and Gash wouldn't risk Andrew getting away.

Shoving into a seat, Gash kept his gaze on him.

"Well, this is cozy. It's not the high life I'm used—"

"So you got rich by vulnerable older women falling for you?"

"Vulnerable. That's a big word for you, big brother."

"Cut the crap."

"All right. I have a stellar tongue, absolutely wicked, and most of the women I teased loved it." Andrew shrugged. "You see, lonely women are so easy to take down because they've been used in the past. I find women who are divorced, or a little ugly. They couldn't refuse when a guy like me came along, ready and willing to take them."

"You gave them a good time, made them fall in love with you, and then what?"

"I got in their will, and after that, they met a horrible end. It was ever that came first. One was a suicide. Very sad. Another was tripping on heels falling down the stairs. What can I say? I improvise a lot." Andrew sighed. "I had some good times. Look at all of you, settling down. Lash has his little Angel now. What will you do with him when Angel dies? Guy can't even function without her. It's sad, pathetic, and to be honest not really worth my time."

"You could have been an uncle by now."

"I could have been a father. I did kill one of my favorite girls because she got pregnant." Andrew shook his head. "What a waste. She even fell in love with me, was willing to do everything I asked. It was such a shame to waste her, but I don't do kids. Speaking of, how is little Simon doing? You do realize one day he's going to figure out Lexie's not his momma, right?"

Devil didn't respond.

"You're not going to be around to see it," Spider said.

"I know. Such a shame. So, I'm going to die tonight. I'm going to miss out on a great deal, but I've had a good life. Not many men can say they bagged a virgin. Apart from you, Gash, you got one with Charlotte. I got mine in Paris. Her pussy was so damn tight." Andrew groaned. "I've never had a pussy so good."

When Spider lunged, Gash held him back.

Andrew burst out laughing.

"All of you are pathetic when it comes to women. They will drag you down, and you'll be a pathetic excuse for a man," Andrew said. "All of you. Do you really think I give a fuck?"

Over and over Andrew ranted. He raved about how annoying women were, and how irritated he was.

Gash listened, and with each passing second, a safe kind of peace settled over him. These were his brother's last moments. For his club, for his woman, and for himself, Andrew would die.

Chapter Fourteen

Andrew was dead.

Stink stood with the men in the warehouse as they surrounded the man who had caused them so much trouble.

Gash was covered in blood as he'd been the one to finally end Andrew. They hadn't tied Andrew down. Only a select few men had been given the chance to take a swipe at him. Pussy for Sasha, Whizz and Nash for Sally and Sophia. Devil for Simon and for Tabitha. Spider was supposed to be there, but he'd decided that his revenge was taken out with beating Russell. He hadn't wanted to leave Paris's side. No matter what anyone said, he just wouldn't do it. Tiny had stepped out. The only one who was allowed to kill Andrew was the one who had the most taken from him. Gash had not only gone to prison for a rape and murder he didn't commit, he'd lost a child, and Charlotte had almost taken her life. It was only fair for the brother to end the life of a brother.

Stepping away, Gash held the knife in his hand, droplets of blood falling to the floor as Andrew lay lifeless.

Silence fell on the warehouse as they all looked at one another, and then at the body.

"He doesn't deserve a burial," Gash said.

"We can burn him," Tiny said. "There's a guy who'll make the body disappear for a price."

"Do it," Gash said. He dropped the knife and wiped his hands down his pants.

Taking a step back, he kept taking deep breaths, and Stink saw that he was losing it.

"Gash, you okay?" Lash asked.

"I'm fine."

"You're not fine. Gash, talk to us. We know he

was your brother."

He shook his head, holding up his hand. "I'm fine."

"Dude, he just had to kill his brother. For any of us, that's got to hurt," Nash said. "As fucked up as Andrew was, for a long time they grew up together. I imagine it's hard to push that aside."

Stink looked at Gash as he crouched down on the floor, gripping his head. "I know that he needed to go down. He's a fucking monster, but he was still my brother." Gash snorted. "God, I was told to look after him, and I fucking failed. It's right that I be the one to stop him. It's my fault he's the way he is."

"Don't do that, Gash." Nash took a step toward him.

"Andrew did this to himself," Lash said, taking a step toward him.

Gash nodded. "Yep, he did. I get it, okay. I get it all. I just … I need to have a minute."

Stink helped to clean up the body as Gash simply watched. None of the brothers blamed him. This was what was supposed to happen all along. They cleaned him away, and as the first waves of morning sunshine started to come, Stink made his way toward the clubhouse.

It was over.

There wasn't any celebration or euphoria, only regret.

Their women were waiting for them. Sandy rushed toward him, and he held her. Picking her up, he carried her toward their private room.

"What's going on?" Sandy asked.

Kicking the door shut, Stink held her close, breathing her in.

"Stink, you're scaring me."

"I'm sorry."

"Is Andrew dead?"

"Yeah, Gash was the one to deliver the final blow."

"Fuck, is he okay?"

"As okay as anyone who has just killed their brother."

"Wow," Sandy said. "I thought someone else would do that."

Stink shook his head. "He's hurting."

"I'm not surprised. It's over?"

"Yeah, it's over. It's all over."

Sandy caught his face in her palms, and pressed her forehead against his. "We can go back to normal now."

"You're not divorcing me."

She chuckled. "Not a chance. You're stuck with me now. You'll wish you hadn't given yourself to me."

"That would never happen." He kissed her lips. "I'll take you on that honeymoon soon."

"We can't go yet. Not until everyone is back home."

"I can wait. So long as I've got you to come home to, I can wait for anything."

****

Charlotte ran a bath and started to remove the clothing that Nash was waiting for. It was covered in blood, and it had to go. Gash was just stood there, completely silent. Every man who touched Andrew was having their clothing disposed of. Charlotte eased Gash's jacket off, and then the rest of his clothing. When he was naked, she left him in the bathroom, and rushed toward the door.

"How is he?" Nash asked.

"I don't know. He's not really talking. He should

be fine. I'll take care of him."

"Okay. Give us a shout if you need us. The whole club is looking out for him."

"I will."

When Nash turned away to start downstairs, she closed the door, and made her way back toward the bathroom.

Gash hadn't moved from where he stood in the center.

Holding him, she urged him toward the bath, and she reached for the soap. She didn't force him to say anything. Charlotte waited, soaping her hands, and grabbing a sponge to soap the rest of his body.

Sometimes, silence was much more fun. She washed his body, focusing on him, nothing else.

"The water is the color of blood," Gash said.

"So it is."

"Time for a shower."

He stood up, and she pulled the plug. The shower was in built with the bath tub. Gash turned it on, and she closed the curtain so no water would come.

"Get in the tub with me," Gash said.

Leaning around the shower curtain, Charlotte gave a little scream as he hauled her into the tub.

"I wasn't going to climb in."

"I know. It's why I made you."

"What's the matter?" she asked.

"Nothing. I just want to look at you, and hold you."

"What's going on, Gash?" she asked. "Everyone is worried about you."

"They don't need to be."

"They love you. Everyone loves and cares about you."

"It doesn't matter."

She growled, glaring at him. "It does. Today you killed your brother. Don't pretend that doesn't mean something because we both know it does."

"It shouldn't though."

"Gash—"

"No, hear me out. He was a monster, Charlotte. Growing up he used to hurt animals, girls—he was a cruel boy. Then he got older, and his sickness only got worse. He took our baby from us, our future."

"We're together. Be upset that you had to hurt your brother. I get it. All of us do. It would be stupid not to. Don't let it ruin you, or us. We're together, and nothing is going to tear us apart, nothing."

He cupped her cheek. "What would I do without you?"

"Probably be drinking yourself into oblivion."

"Don't you think I deserve it?"

"Oh, you deserve it all right. Just not tonight. Give yourself time to heal, and if you still want to go around shooting things, we'll talk."

"I love you."

Charlotte smiled. "It's never going to get old hearing you say that."

"I'm never going to stop."

He started to remove her clothing, and rather than complain, she just let him lead. Lifting her arms above her head, he took off her shirt, followed by her pants. She gave a wiggle to help him remove them.

"What happens now?"

"Now? I'm going to hold you against this wall, and fuck you hard."

"After all of this? What do we do?"

"Honeymoon, living life, maybe kids. Things return to normal."

"Normal would be nice," she said.

"You know what, with all the shit that has happened, I agree. Normal would be fucking good right about now."

****

Sitting in The Skulls' office, Tiny, Devil, Lash, and Ripper all shared a drink. They had dropped Spider off at the hospital to continue his vigil on Paris.

"Can't believe it's all over," Ripper said.

"It is all over, and we're all living life now, and that fucker is burning in hell," Devil said, swinging back a shot.

It was early morning, but he needed a drink. Lexie had the kids, and they were all heading toward the hospital to see Simon. Eva was going with her while they all had a drink, and acknowledged what had happened.

"You started without me, boys," Ned asked, coming into the office.

"Seat right here for you," Tiny said.

"Thought I'd come to have a drink for what we've achieved today."

"What we've achieved?" Lash asked. "I didn't see you there, old man?"

Ned started laughing. "I may be old, but I can still put you in your place."

"Fair enough." Lash tipped back another shot.

Devil placed his glass on the table, waiting for a refill. "If it's okay with you, we're going to stick around for a little bit. Spider's not coming home without that girl, and that girl's not coming home just yet."

"It's fine with me. Lockdown is over. We can go back to finishing what we're doing," Lash said.

"What are you doing?" Ripper asked.

"We've got a bakery in town, opening up. That'll be a hoot. A gym, and something else, which right now, I can't think about. It'll come to me. It always does."

Lash poured another round of drinks, and they all raised their glasses, taking another shot.

Devil licked his lips, holding his glass so it didn't get another refill. "It has been a long couple of years."

"Yeah, it has. That's it though. No more shit to come from us," Lash said.

"Families are growing," Tiny said.

"We've got to keep an eye on family. We don't want anything bad to happen," Lash said.

"Amen." Ripper spoke up this time.

Devil placed his glass on the table, ready for another refill.

"What about you, Devil, what are your plans?"

"When Paris is all fixed and well, head on back to Piston County. Help that girl and her sister. Neither of them deserved the hell that Andrew put them through. We're out of the drug and gun runs," Devil said. "Since Gonzalez hit, and Jerry was killed, it doesn't hold its appeal."

"All of the guys are clean and sober. None of them are going back to that life," Ripper said.

"Look at Dick now. Who knew that son of a bitch would ever settle down? Martha's good for him though. She makes him fight, and that's what he needs, a woman who'll make him beg. It's what Lexie does to me. She keeps me on my toes, and I'm grateful for having her near. Love her."

"Speaking of drug and gun runs, The Skulls are out of that trade," Lash said. "I've thought about it long and hard. We're all settling down, we've got families to support. If the past couple years have taught us anything, it's that life is so fucking short."

Ned agreed. "It's fine. I'm getting old, and I don't want to be dealing with punk ass kids anymore. Times are changing. There's no respect anymore. I see it on every single fighter that walks through that fucking door of my gym. They think the world owes them something, that they're the next best thing."

"What happens?" Lash asked.

"The first fight they're down within seconds, every time." Ned laughed. "It's funny to watch, but I don't have time for the bad attitude that comes my way. You want to fight, put your fists up, and fight. Don't give me mouth. Mouthing only gets you hit. Your fists, that's what gets people to listen."

"I don't know. Eva can scream some, and when she does, I pay attention," Tiny said.

"That's the exception to the rule. Women make the rules. Men follow them, and uphold them."

"I can see why you're such a hit with the ladies," Devil said.

"Years of practice."

"What was it like raising a girl?" Lash asked.

"Hell."

"Be serious."

"Why didn't you ask me?" Tiny asked. "I raised Tate."

"Eva raised Tate. You just spoilt her. Ned, he raised Eva. She was around fighters growing up, and she didn't turn out too bad."

"I was being serious. Having a girl is a fucking nightmare," Ned said, taking another shot.

"How so?"

"Well, first, I had to deal with the fact that Eva was a girl. She was a sweet girl, and she liked being around the gym, which worked for me. Growing up, she gave me several heart attacks. She used to love climbing up everything, and over everything. Then, she goes from this sweet, cute phase, to this attitude phase, and let's not forget puberty. She's got lady parts, and once puberty starts, they do lady things. Do you know what it's like for a man to discuss menstrual cycles?"

Devil smirked as he saw Lash go pale.

"Yeah, boy, you're about to figure it out, aren't you? Once menstrual drama hits, then it's boys. You're a guy. All you wanted when you were growing up was sex. Well, now all those punk-ass bastards want your precious, angelic little girl. Yeah, not on my watch."

"Fucking hell. No, Chloe's going to become a nun. She's not allowed a boyfriend until I'm dead."

"All the things I said, and I still have to deal with this fucker every time I come to visit."

"I'm a good guy."

"You're still an asshole. Another thing, no man will ever be good enough for your little girl, nobody."

"I've got all of this to come with Elizabeth," Devil said. "At the moment, she's my adorable little girl, and that's how I'm happy for her to stay."

"It won't happen. Don't be fooled. They all grow up, and I wonder if that hurts us more than them. They've got to grow up, and realize the world is full of bad people. They stop believing in fairytales, and all too soon, all the magic is gone," Ned said.

"This is a fucking bummer," Ripper said. "I'm not getting Judi pregnant again. The last one nearly killed her."

"She wants another," Devil said. "I heard her talking with Lex about it."

"Not happening."

"I wonder how Whizz is going to get on with Sally and Daisy," Lash said.

"He might not have to worry about Sally all that much. That girl is one hard cookie. She'd got a lot of other challenges to deal with."

"Her loss of a leg it hitting her hard," Tiny said.

"The Skulls are behind her," Lash said.

"Andrew's memory will live a lot longer than it ever should," Devil said. "It's not something we should worry about. Just deal with whatever shit falls our way when it does."

Another round of drinks was poured, and they raised their glasses, saluting their fallen men and women.

****

Millie sat on Baker's bed waiting for him to finally make his way upstairs. She had heard the news of what was going on, and knew she had to talk to him before she left. Ever since he'd taken her from her toy shop, she'd been giving him a hard time, but it wasn't on purpose, not really. Maybe it was a little, but it was hard for her when it came to Baker. He'd forced her to be at the clubhouse, and now that she was, part of her didn't want to leave.

Baker was a nice man, sweet, and charming in his own kind of way. The biggest problem was the feelings he had for his deceased wife. Baker's wife had been taken from him. Neither of them had walked away from a bad relationship.

There was no way she could ever compete with that.

She had thought about it. What it would be like to be with Baker. Her thoughts were not good. Throughout her life Millie had always been passed over. She wasn't a beautiful woman, or someone people remembered. Her sister, Bethany, was the dashing beauty. All of her life she had been pushed aside, and laughed at because of her sister.

She hated that, being laughed at, ridiculed. Her sister had honey blonde hair, blue eyes, and a slender body. Bethany also was a fine actress who had many people believing she was a good person, a nice person.

It wasn't true. Bethany was evil, vindictive, and cruel.

The door to Baker's room opened, and she looked up to see the man himself.

"Hi, I was looking for you."

"Yeah, I came looking for you. Last night was a success." She stood up, pushing her shirt down.

"Yeah, it was."

"So it's safe for me to return to my shop, and to return to normal life."

Baker hesitated.

"You don't have to lie. I already know."

"I don't want you to go."

"That's not a decision you get to make." She tucked some hair behind her ear. "I want to thank you for everything you've done. You protected me when you didn't have to. You could have just forgotten about me, but you didn't," she said.

"Millie, I don't want you to go."

She stared at his chest, and for the first time in a long time, tears filled her eyes. "Baker, you and I, it's never going to happen. I'm not the woman for you, and you're not the right man for me."

"I'm a good person." He took hold of her hands, pressing them to his chest.

"You are a good person. If your wife was to be here, you wouldn't even be looking at me."

"Don't do that. Don't make her part of this."

She bit her lip trying to keep the tears inside but it was growing hard with every passing second. "I care about you. You're a sweet man. I have lived all my life never knowing a man like you, and I bet if you were to give your whole heart to something, you'd be the best damn husband in the world."

"Give me a chance."

"You see, I've spent a lot of my time being second best. Being the girl that is always chosen last. I'm even the daughter my parents didn't want. I'm fat, and I'm not pretty enough. I don't make enough money, and I have no dreams to be a rich millionaire, not that I could ever snag a man of wealth, of course." Tears started to fall, recalling every single nasty word that had ever been said to her. "You love your wife. I'm second best, Baker. I'm sorry."

"I want to take you out on a date."

"No."

"Millie, please," he said.

"Don't."

"I lost my wife, and yes, it killed me. I love her, I'll always love her. She was taken from me, but you've come along, and *you* take every part of me, Millie. Every part. I think about you constantly. I worry about you. I want a chance."

She shook her head. "I'm going home now. The threat is gone, and I need my space." Millie pulled her hands away, and made her way toward the door. There was nothing else to be said.

****

Baker followed her downstairs, and even watched her leave the clubhouse parking lot. He couldn't make her stay, and right now, he didn't know what to say to keep her. Words failed him when it came to Millie. Everything failed him. Watching her walk away once again was just another failure.

"Are you okay?" Rose asked, coming out of the house, carrying a child carryall.

"Yeah, I'm fine."

"You don't look fine." Rose placed one of her twin girls in the back of the car.

He kept staring at the gate willing Millie to come

back, but of course, she didn't.

"Millie left, and told me there was no way we could be together." The words spilled out, and he had no power over them.

"Oh, I can see why that was painful." Rose stood, folding her arms. "Why don't you win her over?"

"She's convinced that I would always pick my wife over her. My wife is never going to be an option, never."

"I know what you're saying, but I also see what Millie is saying."

"What?"

"She's not your number one choice."

"I don't get it." Was he just too thick to get it?

"You love your wife, and that's never going to change. You're wanting to move on, but for Millie, she hasn't been married. You'd be her number one, and for you, she wouldn't be yours."

Baker sighed. "I don't know how to answer that."

"Hardy would always be my number one. What you've got to figure out, is do you love her enough for her to become a number one?"

"I won't know that until I get to know her a bit more. She's not even accepting one date."

"Be patient, and if you like her enough, it doesn't matter. You'll constantly ask her out until you what you want."

"Is that what happened with you and Hardy?"

"Hardy and I are a little different."

"You've got that right," Hardy said, carrying out the second baby carryall. "You've got to make a choice, Baker. If you ask me Millie isn't the kind of girl you fuck and forget. She's the keeping and loving forever kind. Don't break her heart."

Baker had no intention of breaking anyone's

heart, least of all Millie's.

Chapter Fifteen

Three weeks later

Sasha got out of the hospital first much to everyone's surprise. Her eyesight was back, but she wouldn't get rid of her dog. Everything was all new to her, and she had to learn people's faces, not just their voices. Next, Simon and Tabitha got free of the hospital. The doctors were sure of their speedy recovery, and while Paris was in the hospital, they got to stay together.

The clubhouse wasn't bombarded.

The Nomads went back on the road. Andrew was gone, their fallen respected, and the itch to move on was once again calling to them. Devil, Lexie, and the kids moved in with Tiny and Eva. Ripper and Judi shared with Lash and Angel, and several couples took some of the Chaos Bleeds couples in.

Alex, Sunshine, and their baby girl Candice stayed at the clubhouse for Alex to help his leg heal.

Spider spent his time at the clubhouse and at the hospital. The only one left in the hospital was Paris. Sally got out, and she was going to regular therapy and physio sessions. Sophia was also out, and taking care of her and Nash's two kids, Rachel and Bruce.

Eating breakfast, Spider stared at The Skulls and Chaos Bleeds that were still there. Sandy was finishing up her breakfast, and she'd be taking him to the hospital, like she did every morning. Well, Stink took them both, and he crashed their ride. It was a thing between them.

"What's the news on Paris?" Adam asked.

Adam had fully recovered. Three weeks of doing nothing had healed him up, and now he was back to full strength.

"She's over the infection, and her breaks are now

healing fine."

"Have they pulled her out of the medically induced coma yet?"

"Today, they're going to do it today. They didn't think she was strong enough to handle that kind of pain. They're hoping she'll be ready."

"Fuck, do you want me to come with you?"

Spider shook his head. "It's fine. I'm not exactly good company right now." His own injuries had healed up, and he was able to come and go as he pleased. Still, it was easier accepting a ride from Sandy and Stink. He got the excuse of being at the hospital all day until his ride showed up.

"It's not like I'm doing much."

"Are you finding the quiet life a bore?" Sandy asked.

"Not at all. I'm just wanting to be of help," Adam said.

Sandy finished off her toast, and stood. "I'm heading out."

He finished his coffee and got to his feet.

Spider took his empty cup to the kitchen, and made his way outside. Sandy and Stink didn't keep him waiting long. Climbing into the back, Spider rested his head.

"I'm thinking the Caribbean, what about you?" Sandy asked.

"I like it. Three or four weeks?"

"There's a cruise. We could go on that?"

"No. I'm not spending my honeymoon on a boat. I'd be too scared in case any waves came, and tipped the boat upside down."

"Seriously, movie references?"

"No cruises."

Sandy sighed. "Okay. How about resorts? Can I

book a resort?"

"I like the sound of a resort."

"Good. We'll go over the details. There has to be a spa. Also, I was talking with Charlotte, and she and Gash are looking at a honeymoon."

Stink turned his head. "You want to go on honeymoon with our friends?"

"Why not? It could be fun. I'd have Charlotte to go get manicures and pedicures, my hair done, luxury so I'm waxed, crimped, and buffed up. You and Gash can do whatever it is guys do. We meet up, have dinner, go back to our respective rooms, and fuck like rabbits. That actually sounds like it would be a lot of fun. I want to do that."

"Let me talk to Gash about this. I don't want him to think we're invading on his honeymoon."

"Why not? He thinks it would be a great idea."

"So you've talked to Charlotte and Gash about this?"

"It was more like I was looking through the brochure, Charlotte was there, we got talking, and ta-da. Come on, you don't think it will be fun?"

Stink sighed. "I thought the point of a honeymoon was that you spent time with the person you married."

"To a point, you're married to The Skulls. I'm just deepening that marriage."

Spider laughed. "I wouldn't mind if I spent time on a honeymoon with a brother."

"See, it's totally normal," Sandy said.

"Seriously?" Stink asked. "You'd spend your honeymoon with Devil, Ripper, Sinner, all of the guys."

"Yep. They're my brothers. They have my back. Sandy hasn't said that at night you're going to be swapping bedrooms. It's logical, and it sounds like fun."

"Put like that, I do agree. Okay, book it, and

that's what we're doing." Stink pulled into the parking lot, and Spider climbed out.

"See you guys later."

Heading into the hospital, he smiled at the women on the front desk, and made his way up toward Paris's floor. Spider noticed a couple of nurses leaving the room, and he rushed toward the door to find Paris ... awake.

She was sitting up in bed, and the doctor was talking to her.

"What's going on?" he asked.

Paris turned toward him. "Spider?"

"Do you want me to get rid of him?"

"What? No. He's a ... friend."

"Okay. I'll leave you alone."

"What happened? I don't understand." Spider took a seat in the chair, amazed that she was actually up.

"They pulled me out of the medical coma early. The doctor was just explaining it all. He was using rather big words, so I hope I understood it all."

"You're awake."

"Hey, Spider."

"You have all your memories?"

Paris paused. "Yeah, I have all of them. None of them disappeared." One of her arms was still bandaged up, and she had the other wrapped in a binding. "I'm hungry."

"Crap. I'll feed you." He reached out, taking the bowl of cereal that had been left there. "It's soggy."

"I like soggy cereal. I know, it's bad, but it's something I did as a little girl."

"Celia is living at The Skulls' clubhouse. I've been taking care of her, and if I haven't, one of the old ladies has. She's in good hands."

She took a deep breath, and she seemed to breathe easier. "Thank you."

"I'm so sorry about what happened."

"Is he still—"

"He's gone. You don't have to ever worry about him again."

"That's a relief." She took a deep breath, and slowly exhaled. "I must look a mess."

The bruising had started to fade, but it was still apparent that she was used as a human punching bag.

"You look beautiful to me."

"I can't wait to have a shower, or a bath. I want to scrub my body clean."

"You can as soon as we get home."

"We're not in Piston County, right?"

"No. We're actually in Fort Wills. It's where The Skulls live."

"What happened to Lola? Please tell me she made it?"

"Of course she made it. She went back to her family."

"Oh, right."

Spider reached into his pocket and took out her number. "She gave me this. Told me to give it to you, and for you to call her when you're ready."

"That's nice." He placed the card in front of her.

He continued to feed her in silence.

When all the cereal was gone, he held a straw to her lips, waiting for her to suck her milk.

"Thank you."

He put her glass down and stared at the bed. What the fuck was wrong with him?

"You can't treat me the same, can you?"

He looked up. "What?"

"You know what he did to me, and now you can't even make small talk."

"You've been through a lot."

"Bullshit, Spider." She rested her arm across her stomach, and he saw some of the burn marks on her arm that wasn't in a bandage.

"You weren't ever supposed to get hurt."

"I get that, but guess what? I was. Is that it? Paris is too damn broken now to have a proper conversation with, or did you just want to fuck me?"

"I know he was your first." Spider forced himself to look at her.

"Did you want to be?" Tears filled her eyes.

"Fuck, I'm doing this all wrong."

"I can't believe this. Get out," she said.

"Paris?"

"I was the one that was taken. I was the one that was hurt, not you. I want to just talk to a guy who not only got my sister to safety but also helped me get out. You can't even look at me. I'm sorry I wasn't strong enough to fight him off. Get out. Get out. Get out." With her bandaged hand, she tipped her tray. The noise brought the nurses, and they advised him to step out of the room.

Not knowing what else to say, he left, reeling from what had happened.

Spider walked down the long corridor in a daze.

****

Paris stared at the number that the nurse had placed on the tray in front of her. They had cleared up the mess she'd created, which she had apologized for. Using the tips of her fingers, she wiped away her tears. Spider hadn't come back, and she had spent the rest of the morning and early afternoon staring at the number.

Looking up, she saw a doctor standing in the doorway.

"Hello, you don't know me. I'm Sandy."

Frowning, Paris stared at her.

"I'm one of The Skulls' old ladies. Stink, I'm recently married." Sandy held out her hand, which bore an engagement ring, and a wedding band.

"Hello," she said.

"I know this is kind of weird right now," Sandy said. "I heard through the wards that you had a bit of a breakdown with Spider."

"Do you know Spider?"

"Not really. I've been part of The Skulls for a lot longer than I've known Chaos Bleeds. Spider is kind of new to me. From what I've seen, he can be a bit of jerk. His heart's in the right place."

"He couldn't even look at me," Paris said.

"What?"

"I don't know if you knew this, but I worked for them in that strip club, Naked Fantasies. My stage name was Beauty. The other strippers called me the fat one. I knew it." Paris licked her lips.

"I didn't know you were a stripper. Lex, Devil's old lady, she used to be a stripper. A hot one as well."

Paris smiled. "I didn't know that. I haven't met Lex."

"Lexie. You're going to meet the whole gang. They adore you. With your help they were able to locate Andrew, and take him down."

"At least I did something right," she said.

"Anyway, you were telling me about yourself," Sandy said.

"Spider would always come to see me dance. It was like I'd feel his eyes on me. He didn't like it when I got naked. After some time, he finally met me around the back of the strip club. Scared me half to death, and wanted to give me a ride home. At first I thought he was only interested in sex."

"Then what?"

"He seemed interested in helping me. Now, I'm not so sure."

"How do you mean?"

"I just wanted to talk to him. After everything that has happened, I wanted a friend to talk to, and he couldn't even look at me. It made me wonder if he didn't want me because I'm no longer a virgin. Did he only want a virgin, and I'm not good enough for him?" Tears started to fall once again. "Sorry. I can't seem to stop crying just lately."

"You deserve to cry. After everything you've been through, you deserve it."

She wiped the tears away even as more started to fall.

"I'd say that Spider is feeling guilty. He showed an interest in you, and because of that, you got taken, then you got hurt. No matter how much you say otherwise, he blames himself. Spider saw what had happened to you. Your bruises are starting to fade, and your bones are healing. Spider saw you at your worst, and it scared him."

Paris stared at the other woman. "What do you think I should do?"

"Give it time. You're hurting, but so is Spider. He shouldn't be worrying so much. His ass needs to learn to put you first. Just think of how you'd feel if your sister was here right now." Sandy got to her feet. "I've got to get back to work."

"Um, could you do me a favor?"

"Sure."

"Would you type this number into the phone, and hand it to me? I have one good hand, but I can't dial the numbers and hold the phone."

Sandy grabbed the phone beside her bed, and typed in the numbers.

"Thank you."

"No problem."

Putting the phone to her ear, she listened to the number ring.

After several rings, someone finally picked up.

"I'd like to talk to Lola, please," she said.

"Who's speaking?"

"It's Paris. She should know who I am."

There was shuffling and mumbling over the line.

"Hello."

"Hey, Lola, it's me. I'm finally awake."

"Paris, thank God. I wanted to stay until you finally woke up. My parents wouldn't let me."

"They were worried about you. How have you been?"

"I'm ... okay."

Paris stared across the room. "Okay?"

"It has been ... hard. I-I got rid of my computer, my e-reader, and my cell phone. I don't want anything to do with technology. The scholarship I was going to have, dead. If I'm not willing to handle computers, then my education doesn't come free."

"I'm so sorry."

"Yeah, me too. I just can't do it, you know? I find it too scary."

"He's not coming back, Lola."

"There are plenty of bad people in the world. It has been over three weeks, and you're only just calling me. That tells me what was wrong with you was serious."

"How about when I get out of the hospital, and back to Piston County, you come and visit me?"

Lola paused. "Do you promise?"

"I have your number now. I can call you whenever I want, and we can talk. It would be nice to talk to you outside of a cage."

Lola laughed. "I really shouldn't laugh. I just think it would be nice to talk to you in a coffee shop. That would be nice. No cage, our freedom still part of us."

"He's not going to control us forever."

"Speak for yourself. I feel controlled, even now."

"You've got to get on a computer, or something."

"I'm not ready yet."

"One day you will be, maybe."

Silence fell between them.

"What are you doing, then?" Paris asked.

"I'm trying to look for a job. I think that would be good for me, you know? Concentrate on something else. The biggest problem is everyone near where I live knows what happened, and they keep on asking me. I don't get that. Why do they keep on asking me about what happened? I don't want to keep reliving it. They'll see me for an interview, but when I tell them hell no, I get told I'm not what they're looking for."

"I'm sorry."

"We're saying sorry a lot, and we didn't do anything wrong. It's hard to get your head around."

"Yeah, it is." All she had wanted to say to Lola was how sorry she was that she didn't fight, that she got hurt, that she had to look after her sister. Life wasn't fair, and she hated that Andrew had done this to her, to them.

"I've got to go, Paris. My mother is looking at me as if I'm going to slit my wrists any second, and it's freaking me out."

"Please don't do that," Paris said.

"I'm not going to let him win. I do that, and he won, Paris. Don't do it either. We're stronger than this, and we're going to prove that to ourselves, and to him."

"You're right. We can do this."

"I'm going to cut the call now. It was lovely talking to you, and to be able to look at something more than bars."

Paris smiled. "Talk soon."

****

"You're leaving soon," Tabitha said.

"I know." Simon looked up from coloring to stare at Tabitha. They were both sitting at the table in the front room. Tiny, Eva, Mom, and Dad were in the kitchen talking, making arrangements. They were both better now, and the girl in the hospital was making a full recovery.

"I'll miss you," Tabitha said.

"I'll always miss you."

Tabitha smiled. "I wish you didn't have to leave. You could be my friend all day. Daisy likes you as well. She's always scared around new people. I think Anthony likes her. He likes her to read. She does read stories really well."

"We can call though. Dad will let me. He's told me so."

"Do you think it's ever going to be fun?"

"One day." Simon reached over the table and held her hand. "I know we were in the hospital, but I liked it. I'd spend any time with you, wherever we have to."

"Even if we were in the snow freezing?"

"Yep."

"What about horse poo?"

Simon laughed. "Yeah, even in horse poo."

"Wow."

"That's love, and I've heard my Dad tell my mom that he loves her so much that he'd rather his dick rot off than stick it in another pussy."

"What does that mean?"

"I don't know," Simon said, frowning. "Dad

239

always says weird things. They make no sense, but then Mom blushes, and she seems happy with them."

"I think I like you standing with me in horse poop. That's nice."

"Yeah, it is."

****

Sally nibbled on her finger as she stared at the calculation in front of her. None of it was making sense, but she needed to finish her math homework so that she could get back to that good book she was reading. She didn't care what anyone said, vampires were still in.

"What are you doing?" Steven asked, making her jump.

Looking up from her book, she stared at the handsome club member who had been trying to spend a great deal of time with her. "I'm doing my homework." She went to scratch her leg, and paused just as she was about to reach down. It was her left leg, but there was nothing there. Closing her eyes, she counted to ten, and opened them again. Steven had pulled out a chair, and sat opposite her.

"Leg giving you trouble?" he asked.

"It's fine." Her cheeks started to heat, and she hated that. She hated that she was embarrassed by what was happening. Gritting her teeth, she ignored it, and carried on staring at the calculus question that wasn't working itself out.

"Whizz said you'd be studying from home," Steven said.

"I didn't want to be home alone right now. Lacey's going to beauty college at night. I've heard they're planning on opening their own salon in town," Sally said. It would have been nice to work there, but right now, she had other focuses. Between talking about her fucking feelings, and learning to move around on crutches, she was going stir-crazy. She couldn't wait to have a prosthetic so she could wear pants, and pretend that she was normal again. Walking down the street on crutches made her aware of people staring, gawking at her as she went by. Whizz was working at the gym, and rather than be alone, she'd come to the clubhouse. Since Lacey and Whizz had adopted her, they had said the clubhouse would be open to her as well.

Fortunately, they weren't making her go to school. That would have sucked.

No one had stopped by to see her though. She wasn't completely without friends, or maybe she was, and this was the way people were saying she wasn't part of their group.

Staring at her book, she looked over the numbers again even as her heart started to break. Sometimes she forgot about how much people seemed to naturally dislike her. She had to wonder if she wore a neon sign that said, "vermin passing through".

Don't do that.

"Do you want some help?" Steven asked.

"You don't need to keep me company or worry about me. I'm fine. I can do my homework on my own." She forced herself to look at him again.

"I want to keep you company."

"Why?"

"You went through something awful, and I want to be here to help."

She put down her pen. "I don't need pity, Steven. I just want to be left alone."

There was a knock at the door, and Sally turned, and was surprised to see Drew on her doorstep.

"I hope I'm not intruding?" Drew asked.

"Who the fuck are you, punk?" Steven asked, getting to his feet.

There was no way she was going to stand up. Drew was the star at her high school, and usually he hung around with a lot of cheerleaders, and had a bit of a reputation. Sally hadn't been watching where she was going in the school library, and had bumped into him. Rather than yell at her or taunt her, he'd helped her.

It was the only time they had ever spoken.

Most of the time she ignored him, and he ignored her.

"I, um, I came to see Sally, and I knew her parents were part of The Skulls. You weren't at home," Drew said, staring at her.

"I'm not at home."

Baker, Fighter, Ink, Twisted, Curse, Lash, and Pussy got to their feet. This had to be embarrassing. They were standing up to a teenage boy. Okay, that teenage boy looked like he was in his early twenties, and he didn't look scared of them. Why were they getting all defensive? Drew wasn't interested in her.

"I've been away the past month. I had surgery on my knee, and I had to go out of state. I was at school, and I heard what happened. You're being taught from home?"

"I lost my leg, Drew," Sally said.

Grabbing her crutches, she held them straight, and lifted herself up. Making sure she was balanced, she gripped them tightly, and moved out of the way of the tables. She was wearing shorts, so her lack of a leg was easy to see.

"I'm not coming back to school. I'm hoping never." Her cheeks were on fire, but she forced herself to face her peer.

"Wow, here I was thinking I'd have a tale to tell about my busted knee. You win, that is fucking hard," Drew said.

"Busted knee?"

"Played a game about five weeks ago. I was running, and I turned, knee went pop, I went down. My career is officially over."

"You're talking like people care," Steven said.

"Don't be rude." Sally glared at him. "I had an, um, accident."

"I can see. I wanted to come and offer you friendship."

"Thanks, Drew, I appreciate it." She didn't know what else to say, and instead offered him a smile. "It was nice of you to come by."

Drew smiled. "Any time."

She watched him head back toward the door, then stop.

"I don't suppose you'd like to go out some time? Catch a movie?"

"Really?" she asked.

"Yeah."

"I'd love to."

"Great."

"I don't think you should be going on dates without Whizz and Lacey knowing about it," Steven said.

Glaring at him, she turned her attention back to Drew. "I'll call you."

Drew had his phone. "Give me your number, and we can set it up later."

Sally told him her number, and then he was gone. She smiled as she thought about the prospect of a date. Not once had she been on a date. Maybe, just maybe, this could be something … nice.

Chapter Sixteen

One month later
Piston County

Spider sat at the clubhouse drinking a coffee. They had been back home for over a week, and nothing had changed. Well, apart from the fact none of them were under threat. Chaos Bleeds had pulled away from drug and gun runs months ago. Now they were handling legit businesses. They already owned the strip club, and they were hoping to invest in several buildings within the town that had been left derelict after years of neglect.

Devil was looking into them with Vincent.

Spider already had the memo that they had church at the end of the day. Until then, he didn't have a clue what to do.

"What's got you looking all sad in your coffee?" Sinner asked, taking a seat beside him.

"Nothing."

"Does this have to do with that sweet girl that came home with us?"

Paris and Celia had come home with Chaos Bleeds. Devil had promised Paris that she wouldn't have to work for them again. They were going to be taken care of. All she had to do was ask, and they'd be there. There was also an allowance, and every member had agreed that Paris deserved it.

She had been discharged from the hospital after making a full recovery. They were also paying for therapy. Lexie had been insistent that she have someone to talk to. Her first session was yesterday. Spider had kept his distance, though.

"Why would she bother me?"

"Don't play fucking dumb. You clearly had a

thing for her. Why don't you just admit it?" Sinner tapped his knuckles on the counter and raised his hand. "Coffee, Lydia."

Jessica's friend was still hanging around the clubhouse, but Lydia had become more subdued in recent months. She placed a coffee in front of Sinner.

"You know, I think I preferred her when she thought she'd become an old lady," Sinner said, taking a sip of his drink. "Bitch makes disgusting coffee. Now, back to your problem."

"I don't have a problem."

"You're sitting alone in the clubhouse. Why don't you go to Naked Fantasies, or tag along with Devil and Vincent?"

"Why the fuck would I do that?"

"Before you became a club member, you worked in construction."

"So?"

"So, you could help them invest properly."

"That was a long time ago. Nearly twenty years."

"I imagine seeing a good building from a bad one isn't forgotten."

"I'm drinking my coffee."

"We've been back for a week, and you're moping. Dick's not even here to rib you about it. That fuck is on his honeymoon. Devil's making arrangements to take the whole family away, including Ripper and Judi. We're all moving on, and you're moping like a little bitch just got her period."

"Fuck off, Sinner. I don't have to listen to you."

"Actually, you really do. I don't see you going anywhere else."

He closed his eyes, rubbing at his temples.

"Why don't you go and see Paris? She took a lot of shit because of your interest in her. The least you could do is be nice."

"I am being nice. Don't you think I don't know what kind of shit she has been through?" Spider slammed his cup down, and glared at him. "Fuck! Every time I look at her, I see what happened. Don't you get that? All of her problems, all of her issues are because of me. She was the most beautiful woman I'd ever seen, and instead of staying away, I was insistent that she be mine." Spider got to his feet. "Don't go telling me what I should and shouldn't do."

He grabbed his leather jacket, and made his way toward the door.

"Where are you going?"

"To check on Devil and Vincent."

"That a boy."

Spider raised his middle finger.

"Love you, Spider."

"Fuck off!"

Straddling his bike, Spider turned the ignition over, and listened to his baby purr. Nothing was going according to his own plans. Back at Fort Wills, he'd promised himself that he'd be different with Paris, that he'd make her see he didn't think any less of her. Instead, he spent all of his time staring at a fucking coffee cup, or a shot glass.

Coward.

Yeah, he hated to admit it, even to himself, but he was being a fucking coward. Paris deserved better than him. She should be happy with a man who would enjoy a nine to five desk job, being bound inside. Spider was never going to be the kind of guy to get a steady job. He loved Chaos Bleeds, the open road, and he loved being part of the club. His job was to be whatever his Prez needed him to be. If Devil wanted him going over the club's books, that's what he did. If he was required to be a guard for Naked Fantasies, he did it. No job was too hard.

Taking care of Paris, that was one job he hadn't taken. Since they had returned Devil had assigned different brothers to check on Paris and Celia. Sinner had been the one to take her shopping. Ripper and Dick had gone around to her house to help clean up. They had been away some time, and her house had been dusty, not to mention trashed from Andrew and Russell taking her and Celia.

Devil had offered for him to be the one to care for her, but he'd said no.

Riding toward town, Spider couldn't bring himself to find a single reason as to why he should be the one to help Paris.

He was the reason they were taken.

She was beaten, raped, and tortured.

Even as he thought about the reasons why he was staying away, he couldn't help but think about how strong Paris was as a person.

When he saw the abandoned building near the library, along with Devil's car, he parked his bike, climbed off, and headed on inside.

"This building has seen several generations of staff manning it," the real estate agent said. "According to records this was once a settlement building. The first built in Piston County."

Spider heard the doubt in her voice. Rounding the corner, he found Vincent and Devil knocking on walls. They were hollow sounding.

"Excuse me, I have this room booked," the woman said.

"I'm with them, Miss ...."

"Hargrove. Laura Hargrove." She shook his hand.

"Spider."

"Oh, is that your real name?" Laura asked.

"Yep. The only name I go by." His real name was Stuart Cox. Yeah, he was going by Spider.

"What do you think of this place?" Devil asked.

"Yeah, we're doing the usual knocking on walls, but I don't know. Is it good?" Vincent asked.

Spider looked around the room. There was plaster coming off the walls, and the ceiling also had holes as well. It wasn't about the interior of the room. The building depended on a structure being sound. Interior decorating was easily fixed, and often what a lot of people walked away from.

Spider knocked on the walls, to find the supporting wall. The wall that Devil and Vincent had been trying it out was hollow. Moving from one room to the other, Spider wasn't happy.

"How long has this place been empty?" Spider asked.

Laura looked at her paper work. "Ten years. I really don't know much about this building. My boss told me to take you guys out to see it. I usually deal in homes, housing, apartments, things like that. This is a little out of my area."

Spider saw her wrinkle her nose.

"What happened to the previous owners?"

"I don't know. This was some kind of artisanal department store, an incident went wrong with the insurance, and they had to sell up short."

"That's because they knocked out a supporting wall, and built this up instead. The ceiling needs support, and those holes are not very comforting." Spider looked toward his Prez, and the Vice Prez. Vincent may not have been on the road with them all that much just lately, but he'd found love in Piston County, and so that was why they had come back here. "You could take this place, but you're looking at taking it down to the ground, and building it back up. I'd say even the foundations didn't look right."

"You sure?" Vincent asked.

"Positive. People can knock down walls providing they don't support the structure. Each building has a point of strength, and provides the foundation for the next level. This wall runs directly through the beginning to the end of the building. With no actual activity in here for ten years, it doesn't look bad. You can go and check it out, but I don't even want to go on the next floor. It's not safe, and I'm not comfortable being here."

Spider didn't wait around. He left the building, and walked toward his bike. Laura followed him second.

"Wow, I had no idea about that. I'm so sorry."

"Who is your boss?" Spider asked.

"Earl Mill."

"Isn't he on the Piston County committee?" Devil asked, finally coming out of the building with Vincent.

"I don't know. I think so."

"Yeah, fucker has been trying to shut us down, and send us out of town," Vincent said. "He's got a problem in front of a bunch of churchgoers, but he's all right watching women at our club shake their tits at him."

"You own Naked Fantasies?" Laura asked.

He saw her cheeks darken.

"You know it?"

"Yeah, I do, actually. It's a pretty cool place." Her cheeks went a deeper shade of red. "Anyway, I had no idea about this building, and structural problems. I wouldn't have shown you. I know you're serious about creating work in Piston County, and with the latest recessions, jobs in this place are pretty scarce."

"You probably find Earl wanted us to invest in a

money pit, and drive us out of town. The moment we bought that place, we'd have all kinds of checks that we'd likely fail," Devil said.

"Do you actually have something decent in there?" Spider asked.

"I don't know. Like I said, I'm in housing, apartments and stuff. There's usually a guy who deals with buildings, but he's out today." She handed Spider the paperwork. "Would you like to have a look, and tell me the places you'd like to see?"

Spider took the folders and glanced through. He looked at the details and tossed the ones that even in the pictures showed signs of being a money pit. Chaos Bleeds were not strapped for cash, but they weren't fools who spent it on investments that would ultimately suck.

"Nope, nope, nope, maybe," Spider said, handing Laura back the yes files. "Those look pretty good."

"Excellent. Would you like to follow me to the locations? I've got all the keys for them in my car."

Spider agreed and went to his bike. He may as well do something constructive with his time. He'd turned down taking care of Paris. That job now fell to another brother. He just couldn't do it, and at least here, he could do something useful with his time.

****

Paris smiled at the Chaos Bleeds man who was sitting with Celia, coloring. Her sister had gotten a hell of a lot better since they had returned home, and even Paris felt much better. She hated being away. Piston County was her home, and even though she had enjoyed being near The Skulls, Fort Wills would never be her home. She liked to think that she'd made some friends in the women. Angel was so lovely, and she liked Prue, Emily, Sophia, and Rose. Tate wasn't the easiest person to like.

"You don't have to do this, you know?" She

picked up her used cup and made her way into the kitchen.

"It's okay. I like it," Sinner's voice said, carrying toward her. Cleaning the coffee cup, Paris looked out toward the back yard to see that it needed to be mowed. She'd do that once Celia had settled down for the day. Her sister was a good kid. They were the same age, but her sister had the mental capacity of a child. Running fingers through her hair, she let out a sigh.

"What's up?" Sinner asked.

"Where's Celia?"

Sinner held his hands up. "The television caught her attention. Don't worry, she's settled watching whatever shit is on it."

"Oh, right. It's probably cartoons. She likes them." She nodded. They had been back a week, and still Spider hadn't visited her. Tears filled her eyes, and she turned back to look at the window. "I've got to do some gardening."

"Spider's hurting. He's being a complete dick about it."

"Yeah, a super sized dick that thinks it's okay for himself to have problems," Paris said. She wiped the tears away.

"He's not being fair, making it about him."

She spun around to face the man who had put himself in charge of her care. "What is this?"

He shrugged. "This is me telling you that Spider is being a dick, but soon, he's going to wake up."

"So?"

"Look, Spider rarely acts like this."

"He walked away because he wanted my virginity and some fucking asshole took that pleasure from him." She covered her mouth, hoping she hadn't upset her sister. Sinner turned, to go and check on her.

251

"She's fine."

"See, I'm even shouting now."

"Spider doesn't give a fuck about your virginity."

"You could have fooled me."

"He showed an interest in you. Out of all of the women on stage, you were the one that caught his eye. You were the one he wanted to help more than anyone, and now look where we're at. Because of his interest in you, you got taken. Not only did you get taken, you got fucking hurt in a really bad way. You got hurt so bad that you were in the hospital, having to reset bones. Yet, to me, you look like you can handle it."

She had been to see a therapist, and even though it was one visit, it had helped Paris to put things into perspective. "Everyone deals with life's troubles differently."

"You're just going to say that? Life's troubles?"

"What do you want me to say? I can sit here, and cry over the fact my first experience was by a man I couldn't stand. I was beaten to the point that I begged for death. I was broken, I was hurting, and throughout it all, I was still fighting. I got Lola to send that message. I had every faith that you, Spider, and the Chaos Bleeds MC would save me. You wouldn't see me dead by that fucker, and I was right. I wasn't saved right away, but you saved my sister. That bad shit is gone, and maybe I'm lucky because I know he's never coming back. I can sleep knowing that he's not laughing anywhere. I'm laughing because I survived. Life goes on. I have to get up in the morning, and if it wasn't for the club, I'd be working. I get up, I take care of my sister, I do the chores, and we go out. I have no choice. I have to keep on moving, keep on living. Life doesn't just stop because of what happened."

Paris had always been able to put her life into a

bunch of boxes, and to deal with life's troubles. Her parents' deaths, check. She'd arranged the funeral, and dealt with everything on her own. Growing up, she handled the bullies who tried to make fun of her sister. Paris had fought all of her life, and she would keep on fighting.

"You don't have to be alone to deal with this crap anymore."

"Are you telling me to have a breakdown?"

He shook his head. "I'm telling you to lean on us a little bit."

"I think not going to work covers that. I'm not a lazy person. I like to do things, everything myself."

"I've come to see that."

"Would you like some coffee?"

"I'd love some. Tomorrow Butler is coming over."

"Will you all be taking turns?"

"Most of the time. You may even get Devil and Lexie on a few visits. Lexie likes to get involved with the club, and not leave it to run itself."

"Good to know."

Sinner left the kitchen, and she took a deep breath. It would be a lot easier to just sink down, and let everything build upon her, until she feared going outside that front door.

Andrew, wherever you are, asshole, I'm not going to let you win. You took me, and hurt me in ways no one should ever hurt. I'm done being your bitch. I'm my own person.

Her hands were shaking.

Opening the back door, she inhaled the fresh air, and closed her eyes, facing the sky. "I can do this."

She stayed at the door for several minutes, basking in the peace. Turning around, she jumped as she saw Celia in the kitchen, staring at her. It was spooky some days staring at herself. She and Celia were twins. They shared the same face, but nothing else. There were times she wished they had that twin connection she had read about so much.

"I'm hungry, Paris," Celia said. "Can we have some food?"

"Sure, how about I make Nanna's meatballs? You like them."

Celia clapped and ran off to tell Sinner all about Nanna's meatballs. The recipe had been passed down each generation of women, and now she made them for Celia.

"Apparently I'm in for a treat. I get to eat Nanna's meatballs, but when I ask about Nanna, I'm told she's in heaven. I'm worried."

Paris chuckled. "Nanna died a few years ago. It's a special family recipe that combines ground meats, parmesan, some nuts, and other secret ingredients." She tapped her nose. "Those are for me to know, and you to never know."

Sinner laughed. "Fair enough. I have to say if you're going to start feeding me then I'm more than happy to come here, and enjoy the fruits of your labor."

Paris grabbed the meat out of the fridge while thinking about Spider. He wouldn't be enjoying the fruits of her labor because he never came to see her.

"You were the first woman Spider ever really cared about."

She looked up to find Sinner sat at the table. "You're going to watch me cook?"

"Why not? Are you going to keep avoiding the obvious?"

She tilted her head to the side, staring at him. "Spider has been avoiding me, Sinner. Not the other way around."

"Why don't you go to the club?" he asked.

She stared down at the ground beef and shook her head. "You don't get it. He chased me, and he was the one to walk away. I'm not going to hunt for him. I need him to be ready to deal when the time comes."

"Spider's a stubborn ass."

"So am I. This is not my problem."

Sinner sighed. "Do me this one favor, and I'll never bring it up again, call him. Keep it on speaker phone so I can hear what he says, and what goes on."

"If I do this, you'll stop?"

"Yeah, I'll stop."

She blew out a breath and took the phone from him. "This is a waste of time. Let's see."

"Why don't you try and invite him to dinner or something. Spider never says no to dinner."

Grabbing his cell phone, she found Spider's name, and after a brief hesitation, she clicked on his name. Her heart was racing once again, which seemed to be the way her body reacted in these events.

You can do this.

"Sinner, what's up?" Spider asked.

"It's not Sinner, it's me, Paris," she said.

There was a second's pause. "Hey, Paris … is something wrong?"

She didn't look at Sinner, hating how guarded Spider sounded.

"Nothing's wrong. It has been some time since I last saw you, and I wanted to see how you were doing."

Biting her lip, she waited for a response.

"I'm doing good. You?"

"I'm doing great." She glanced up to see Sinner shaking his head. "So, I was wondering if you'd like to come to my place, and we can have some dinner?"

"I can't right now."

"Maybe in the future? Tomorrow?"

She heard him curse, and that was when she struggled to contain her sadness. The tears that she'd been fighting to keep at bay came forward, and started to fill her eyes. Sinner reached over, taking hold of her hand. It was too much, and it was the wrong man.

"Look, I'm busy right now."

"Call me when you're not so busy."

"Bye."

He hung up.

"Will you let it go now?" she asked.

"Shit, Paris, I'm so sorry," Sinner said.

"Whatever Spider and I were going to have, it has gone. Andrew took it."

She stared down at the meat once again, took several deep breaths, and went to grab the other ingredients. Never was she going to put so much hope into a guy. Never again. Being alone was a lot easier than trusting another person.

****

"Are you fucking stupid?" Sinner asked, walking into the main clubhouse.

Several of the guys who weren't attached to old ladies, turned to look at him. Devil was still there with Vincent, and they were going over some paperwork.

"What the fuck?" Spider asked.

Sinner shoved him hard. "You went chasing after that girl, watching every single one of her strip shows, and now, you're what? Running away."

"What is going on between Paris and me is none of your fucking business."

"None of my business? I made her call you today. I thought if you heard her voice you'd at least see that she's waiting for you. Instead, I was fucking embarrassed with the way you acted. You're breaking that girl apart."

"Andrew fucking broke her, and it's all my fault."

Sinner shook his head. "He hurt her, and she's healing." Pointing his finger at Spider, he couldn't believe the asshole. "You're the one that is going to break her."

"You don't know what you're talking about."

"I've spent time with her. Fuck, even Butler has spent time with her. You just don't see it, do you? You don't see what you've got, and you're going to let it slip through your fingers, for what? For guilt?"

"I made her suffer."

"This is not about you! This is about Paris, and you're being too damn selfish to see what is right in front of you." Sinner threw his hands up in the air. "You know what, I'm done. If you can't get your head out of your ass, then if she moves on, it's your own fault."

****

Paris rushed toward the phone as it started to ring. She didn't want it to wake Celia up, and after her conversation with Lexie, Paris just wanted to relax. Lexie wanted her to go see a therapist to talk through her troubles.

"Hello," she said.

"Hello, Paris, did I get you at a bad time?"

She frowned, not recognizing the voice. "Who is this?"

"Oh, I'm so sorry, it's Angel. I should have told it was me, silly, I'm so sorry."

"What's wrong? Is everything okay? Has something bad happened?" Paris wondered if Andrew had gotten someone somewhere to take over from what he'd done. Crap, she'd promised herself that she would never think about him, and yet here he was, invading her thoughts. She didn't want to think of him. This was where she struggled with getting over the past. Andrew had invaded her thoughts too often since she'd woken up in the hospital. He was dead, and he was never coming back.

"No, everything is fine. I just wanted to call, to talk. I thought that would be okay for me to do. If you don't, I can hang up, I'm so sorry."

Feeling like a real bitch, Paris shook her head, hating her response. "It's okay. It's me, and I was the one that fucked up. I'm so sorry. I thought something had happened."

"I should have warned you that I get quite close to people. I like to call, talk, and just get to know one another."

Taking a seat, Paris held the phone to her ear, slowly calming down. She didn't like how tense she'd become at the mere thought of Andrew.

"How're the kids?" Paris asked.

"They're beautiful. Anthony is doing really well in school. Chloe, she's a darling like always. She's got her father wrapped around her little finger. It's so adorable to watch. I worry when she gets older, he's going to be a sucker."

"You'll always be number one to Lash."

"How is Celia?"

"She's doing really well. I'm so pleased there is no lasting damage of what Andrew did to her."

"What about you?" Angel asked.

"I'm doing ... fine."

"If you ever need to talk, we're all here."

"Who is that?" Paris heard someone shout in the background.

"Hey," Angel said. "I was talking."

"Put it on speaker. Hey, Paris, it's Lacey here. How are you doing?"

"Angel has Paris on the phone. Hey, Paris, this is Rose. How are you holding up?"

"I'm sorry, Paris, you're on speaker. Nearly all the ladies are here."

Paris chuckled. "I'm doing well."

"I bet you're feeling much better hearing from us, aren't you?" Tate asked. "We are awesome."

"Correction, *we're* awesome. You, Tate, are a pain in the ass," Prue said.

Paris giggled, listening to them. She stayed on the phone for well over an hour, and at the end of it, she was happier for it. They had all told her that if she needed to talk to anyone, she only had to call.

"Paris," Celia said, drawing her attention to her sister.

"Hey, what are you doing out of bed?"

"I couldn't sleep. I dreamed of the bad man. The man who made you scream."

Once again, her stomach turned as she recalled the same memories that Celia spoke about. Andrew had left a mark with her, a constant reminder of what he did. "Well, that bad man is never going to hurt you, or me." She got to her feet, pulling her twin into a hug. She closed her eyes as Celia stroked her hair.

"I missed you, Paris."

"I missed you, too. Come on, time to go to bed." She took her sister's hand, and took her to the bedroom. Paris waited for Celia to get under the covers. Sitting on the edge of the bed, she pushed some of Celia's hair out of the way.

"I'm scared."

"There's no need to be afraid. I'm here, and I'll always be here with you."

Slowly, Celia started to close her eyes. Even when her sister was fast asleep, Paris didn't move. She stayed staring at her sister for as long as she could. She couldn't live without her, and she never wanted to. Glancing over at the time, she saw it was getting late, so she got to her feet, letting out a breath. Closing Celia's door, Paris made her way toward her own room, and paused in front of her full length mirror. There were dark shadows underneath her eyes, and she looked a little poorly. Considering everything she'd gone through, she didn't look too bad.

"I'm going to get through this. You're not going to control me. You're dead, I'm alive. You don't control me anymore."

Chapter Seventeen

Three months later

"How are you feeling today, Paris?" Annie, the therapist, asked. Paris hated going to the therapist more than anything else. Always the same questions, the mindless repetition of life.

"I'm doing good. Um, Devil got Celia into a good school, which means during the day throughout the week I can do some college work." Paris tucked her hair behind her ear. Lacey had been visiting from Fort Wills last week and had given her a trim. Well, it was more than a trim but not a full-fledged cut. She ran her fingers through it, loving how it shaped her face, and made her look and feel older. It was nice to have something different to do. Lacey was a lovely woman, and Paris adored her. She loved her conversations with The Skulls women. They were all so amazing, and boisterous. She found their love of life intoxicating.

"How many times have we shared?"

"About eight, I think."

"I've been trying to increase the number of times you visit," Annie said. "Why won't you see me more?"

"I don't need to. I'm here as an advisory from Lexie. I wouldn't be here otherwise."

"It has been nearly four months since you were saved, and three months out of the hospital."

"Yep." She said the p with a pop to it. This hour she spent with Annie was the longest of her life. She sat on a comfy sofa, and stared at woman dressed in a smart business suit, as she made notes on her pad. Every now and then, Paris looked out of the window to see what was happening. It was fall once again. Leaves were falling off the trees, and it had started to get cold.

"Where do you see yourself in a year from now? Two years from now?"

"I imagine one year from now I'm still coming to see you, and a second year, I don't know. I don't have to come and see you anymore, and I can just get stuck in my work without ever having to worry about seeing you again." The thought of another year sitting with Annie actually made her feel sad. It wasn't that she didn't like the woman. Paris was never the kind of person to talk about her feelings. Not when her parents died, not when she took over caring for her sister, and certainly not now. By not thinking about it, and just getting on with her life, that was how she was healing.

Just last week when she, Sinner, and Celia went shopping, she was able to go to the bathroom all by herself without fear. For Paris, that was a win for her.

"I know you don't want to come and see me, Paris. What I want is for you to talk to me."

"You want me to talk about what happened, and then you want me to cry, and then focus on ways to mend."

"See, you understand. This is all in your control."

Paris shook her head. "I understand what *you* want me to do. You refuse to accept how I want to do this. Talking about it, will what? Make me cry?"

"It will allow you to deal with what happened."

She snorted. "Annie, I'm dealing with what happened. He's no longer around to hurt me. He's never going to hurt me again. This isn't where he goes to prison, and he could be released on parole for good behavior. This man is dead. D-E-A-D. That's how I'm dealing with it. I come here, to sit and do as I've been asked to." Tears once again filled her eyes. "You want to really know what happened? Andrew came to my house, and because I was doing the fucking dishes, Celia opened the door. As I was about to see who it was, I saw him with a gun pressed to her head, and his little sidekick, Russell standing there. I wanted to fight, and they shoved a few things around, made it look like we fought. Russell then hit me, and made sure I left a little blood at the scene. When I finally came to after being knocked unconscious, I was beaten, raped, beaten some more. He made me watch as he hit my sister Celia, and I begged him to hurt me. To never hurt my sister. I would die for her. When Spider made it out of his injuries alive, I watched them take her, and I was happy about that. I was happy for her because I knew they'd keep her safe. The beatings kept happening, but I think he lost his appeal with a bruised body. After a while he was no longer interested in me. Then, Lola came. She was this amazing tech buff. He's destroyed her love of technology. She's terrified every single day. Last I heard, she won't even hold a cell phone. This the kind of stuff you want me to talk about? Express my feelings to show you that I'm growing?" Folding her arms, she kept her gaze on Annie.

"You've been in a lot of pain."

"No different from everyone else."

"We all deal differently."

"Exactly," Paris said. "This is how I deal. This is how I make sure I keep on going. I'm moving on, Annie."

Her therapist glanced at the clock. It was the first time she had ever done that. Usually Paris was the one to look at the clock. The silence hung heavy in the air between them, and all the time, she kept on staring at her.

"What are you thinking?" Paris asked, unable to handle not knowing.

Annie looked a little uncomfortable. "To be honest, I don't know how to help you. I help by having people talk about their situation, and then move on."

"You want to talk about a situation, prior to being taken, Spider showed a great deal of interest in me. He wanted to fuck me, and guess what? I was a virgin. Since I've been taken, I haven't seen him. Do you have a reason for that?" Many nights she woke in a cold sweat from the nightmares of what Andrew did. She felt sick to her stomach that even with him dead, Andrew was still there, taunting her. He resided in her head all the time, and Paris had to deal with that herself.

Annie's cheeks went a deeper shade of red. "When something like this happens, people struggle to deal with the consequences."

"Spider's guilty?"

"He's feeling guilty, and that's what is eating away at him."

"How do you know that?" Paris asked.

"From what you've told me, he's suffering."

"Tell me—"

The buzzer went off signaling their time had come to an end, which only pissed her off. The one time she was willing to talk, and the session hadn't lasted long enough for her. *Whatever!* She didn't need a therapist. She was handling everything on her own anyway.

"I'll see you in two weeks, Paris."

Grabbing her gloves, Paris left the room, not looking back. Sinner was in the waiting room, playing on his cell phone as she approached.

"How did it go?"

"I don't know. Do you have any reason to think why my therapist would know that Spider is feeling guilty and he's hurting?" Paris asked.

Sinner cursed and pocketed his cell phone. Together they walked toward the car, and she linked her arm through his. "Are you going to tell me?"

She got into the car, snuggling into her jumper,

and fighting against the chill.

"Spider has been going to see Annie."

"What?" Paris asked.

"You heard me. She's been helping him to deal with his own problems."

"Spider's in therapy? He's having therapy? Why?"

Sinner stared straight ahead outside of the windscreen. "The guilt, it's eating away at him, and he's even tried to come and see you several times, but he can't do it."

"He's tried to see me?" Her heart started to race. She'd thought Spider had lost all attraction for her.

"He has, and I've seen him standing there, staring at your house."

"When?"

"I've been drawing the curtains, and there he has been sitting, straddling his bike, guarding you. He'll be gone in the morning, but he's struggling, Paris."

"Why didn't you tell me?" she asked.

"Because you're already hurting, and there's not a lot you can do to help him." Sinner reached over, and patted her knee. "He'll be okay."

"I had no idea that he was seeing a therapist."

"It's something he needed to do. It has helped him to deal with some of the effects of what has happened."

"Has anyone else?" she asked. "I know Lola talks to one."

"No one else. We all handle things in our own way."

"I get that. It still sucks."

"There's nothing you can do about it. Can I ask you for a favor?" Sinner asked.

"Sure. Ask away."

"Don't give up on Spider. He's getting there, and this hit him harder than any of us could have ever anticipated."

Licking her dry lips, she nodded. "Sure, I don't mind waiting." There wasn't anyone else she wanted to spend time with.

"Thank you. So we don't need to pick Celia up until around four. I was thinking we could get some groceries, what do you think?"

"I'd like that."

"Also, we're planning a Thanksgiving visit with The Skulls. Would you like to come?"

Paris nodded. "Hell yeah. Angel, Sandy, and Tate used to visit me in the hospital, and we talk on the phone. How have they been? I haven't heard from them in a couple of days."

"They're doing good. Babies are all growing up, and Prue is pregnant with her and Zero's first baby."

"Oh, my God, how awesome is that? Do they know the sex yet?"

"Not yet. Also, Kelsey gave birth to another boy. They've called him David."

"I can't wait to see them. I'm invited, right?"

"Paris, you and Celia are invited to all of the Chaos Bleeds events. It was you that didn't come to the barbeques that were organized, or the picnics. We worry about you."

"I only worked for you. There's nothing important about me."

"That's where you're wrong. You've been really important to all of us, and we all know how Spider feels about you."

"I do enjoy your company. Butler's funny as well. Reese is nice, too. I'm not too sure on Slash. I think I saw him sniffing my knife set, which was just weird."

"Slash likes his knives, and he's a good expert on them."

"I bet." She ran fingers through her hair, and sat back. "Do you think the only way to get over what happened is to talk about it?"

Sinner groaned. "Don't ask me that."

"Why not?"

"I'm not a therapist, or a doctor. I don't know what makes people tick, or their heads. Some people handle things differently."

"Would you want to talk about it?"

"Me, no. I'm more of a hands-on kind of guy. I wouldn't talk, I'd just carry on."

"I thought so."

"The thing is … I'm not you, Paris. I haven't gone through what you had to go through, and what you had to go through was some really serious shit."

Paris took a deep breath, hearing the concern in his voice. "Annie wants to talk about it. That's what therapists do, they talk."

"Why don't you set the pace for when you're ready? This happened to you, no one else. Only you can decide what you do or not. No one else."

Sitting back, Paris thought about what Sinner said. He made a valid point. This was her life, and her body. There were times in the middle of the night where she'd wake up from a nightmare. She'd get out of bed, and go check on her sister. One of the Chaos Bleeds' boys stayed with her at night. They took turns, and it was nice to have the change of company. She'd watch her sister sleep, and then go down stairs to have a drink of water, and stare outside. In those moments she'd think about Spider, and how nice it would be to have him standing with her, his arms wrapped around her body, helping her to deal with the dreams.

She hoped that Spider got to deal with whatever had been plaguing him. She missed him, and wished this void between them could be closed. A couple of times she had seen him, but Spider had found all kinds of excuses to leave.

Watching him leave, to her were the hardest moments of her life.

Maybe one day, he'd stop running away, and talk to her.

****

Millie stared out of the shop window into the street. People were going about their daily business as if it was a regular day, which it was, to most. It was the same day to her as well. She watched people come and go, wondering what was going on in their lives, and as she did, she couldn't stop thinking about Baker.

He hadn't tried to see her, and she didn't know if she should be sad about that or not. Ever since lockdown had been lifted, and she'd been able to go home, nothing was the same with her. She went through the motions of her life, going to work, going home, cooking, eating, reading, and nothing happened.

Stepping away from the window, she rounded the desk, and stared at the day's worth of deliveries that she had prepped.

The same old boring routine.

Why did he have to ask her out?

Why did he have to forcibly take her to the clubhouse?

The person who had changed her life was the same person she wanted to keep at arm's length. Baker. He was dangerous, and she hadn't been lying to him either. Millie didn't want to be second best, not to his first wife, and she just knew he'd make comparisons.

The doorbell rang, and she glanced over to see

Eva entering the shop. "How come your signs aren't out?"

"I didn't feel like putting them out today. Most of the time people ignore them." She opened a magazine that advertised toys, hoping it would inspire her.

The bubble that had been around her had been popped, and she didn't know how to get it back.

"What's going on?" Eva asked.

"Nothing."

"I don't know. Something is going on with you, Millie. What's the matter? You're usually in your fantasy world."

Millie sighed. Most of the old ladies at The Skulls visited her, and tried to get her to go out with Baker. He was an amazing guy, sweet, charming, wonderful … and taken. His wife might be dead, but in his heart, he'd always be with his wife, and she didn't want that, not for herself.

"I'm not always in a fantasy world. I'm sometimes just happy."

"Sometimes happy but not right now?" Eva asked.

Millie bit her lip, staring up at the woman. Lacey had dyed her hair, and it looked a deep blue, almost black, color. "I like your hair."

"Answer me, Millie."

"I don't know what to say. No, I'm not always happy."

"What did Baker do?"

"He didn't do anything. I did everything. He wanted to go on a date, and I don't want to date a man who's hung up on his ex-wife."

"One day he'll get over her."

"Really? Do you think people really get over that? If ever given the choice, he'd have her. I've talked about this." She held her hands out, took a deep breath, and forced a smile. "Eva, what would you like today?"

"I'd like for you to come out with me and the girls. Just us girls?"

"Some fun?"

"Fun, wine, food, what do you think?"

"I like that."

"Good." Eva smiled at her. "It'll get better, Millie, I promise it will get better."

****

"Do you ever think of talking to her?" Annie asked.

Spider stared at his therapist, and wondered why she was asking him that. He spoke all the time about how he felt when it came to Paris. The only reason he was here was because of Devil and Lexie. He'd gone to them to ask for advice.

Devil had told him to get his head out of his ass, to which Lexie slapped him around the back of the head. She'd then turned to Spider, and suggested therapy. This was the same therapist that Paris was seeing. He wondered if she was getting a better result from Paris.

All of his life he'd accomplished shit by doing, not by sitting around, talking about his feelings.

"I try."

"Tell me what happens."

"Do you even listen to me?"

Annie held her pen poised over her notes. "I listen to what you tell me. Now I'm asking you as a question."

"You want me to tell you how I talk to Paris?"

"Yes, it might help if I hear your process, step by step."

He rolled his eyes, and rubbed his hands together, sitting forward. "I get on my bike determined to talk to her. There's a lot of stuff that needs to be said, and I know she thinks bad of me. She thinks I don't want her. I do. I fucking crave her, and being apart from her, it kills me. Knowing my brothers are taking care of her, sickens me. She's mine, and I should be there for her." He stopped to take a deep breath. "Then I get to her house, and I see the front door. Only in my head I step back to visiting her once before."

"The night she was taken?"

"Yeah, the night she was taken, and I freeze up. I look at her house, and I see that I failed her. She was lying on that hospital bed with broken bones, bleeding, infected, and I was scared that I was going to lose her."

"You love her very much?" Annie asked.

"Yes."

"Why don't you call her?"

"What?"

"You've got a lot to say. You can't say it to her face, so why don't you try calling her?" Annie asked. "It could be a step in the right direction for you?"

"A phone call wouldn't work," he said.

"Why not? It's a start."

"What I've got to say has to be said in person. As far as I'm concerned nothing else will work."

"Nothing?"

He shook his head.

"The more time that passes, the longer it's going to take you to build that trust again," she said.

"Then I'll wait to build that trust. Annie, I love Paris."

"If you love her, why are you doing this?" Annie asked.

"Because I need to be the man she deserves more than anything else."

The rest of the appointment went by in a little

haze, and when Spider came out of the building, he grabbed a cigarette, and lit it.

"You've started smoking again?" Devil asked.

"No, I'm lap dancing."

"You're not doing a lot of that either. Heard you weren't around Naked Fantasies, and you'd taken yourself off the roster for managing it."

"Vincent does a better job of it." They had purchased two of the five buildings that Laura had shown them around. The first one was a rundown, derelict apartment building, and the plan was to build it from the ground up for some luxury apartments. That was the first plan for that building. The second building they had found outside of town was similar to an old warehouse, something like what The Skulls owned. Instead of using it as a training facility or a gym, they were going to use it for storage. Lexie had been looking at a vacant shop within the town. Of course the guys had instantly wanted a sex shop, but Lexie was thinking fashion, or maybe food.

Either one worked for Spider. The clothing stores were at the local mall, which was over thirty minutes away. Piston County needed a clothing store, not just for women but for men as well. He believed it could be a good investment.

Lexie had put the word out, and they even had a local by the name of Natalie Pritchard who had offered up some modern designs. Natalie had graduated from college with a fashion degree. However, demands on her parents' ranch meant she had to come home and help rather than go and explore her dreams in the big city. Spider had looked over her designs, and they were awesome.

Several of the guys hadn't wanted to invest in fashion. So, the old ladies banded together and said it would be theirs.

Spider was happy enough with his masculine side that he didn't need to worry about what it would do owning a fashion shop. He wondered if Paris would like to get involved, and of course, he'd never been able to ask her.

"What are you doing here?" he asked.

"How was therapy?"

"I don't think it's working."

"Why not?"

"I'm no closer to being with Paris than I when I started. When she was gone, I thought of everything I wanted to do with her when I finally got her back. Now, I spend more time worried in case she's going to appear where I am, and that's not me."

"We're all having to make changes here," Devil said.

"What changes are you making?"

"For one, have you noticed that Sasha keeps pranking me? She rested a bucket of water on top of a stick yesterday, and when I opened it, all of it came tumbling down on me. Pussy even got it on his phone so that he could remember it. I tell you, Pussy was bad enough on his own, but now that he has an accomplice, it has gotten a whole lot worse." Devil shook his head as he rested his hands on his lips.

"You were the one that called her a liability. She's just getting her own back."

"She called me old man the other day. The sass of it. Old man."

Spider laughed. "You're loving it."

"I'm loving that I'm getting to see a different side to Sasha. She was always a worry of mine. The club's protection including that of the old ladies falls to me, and it will always fall to me."

He was aware that Devil took his job seriously.

"So why are you waiting outside for me?" Spider asked.

"I wanted to talk to you about heading up the rebuilding of the apartment buildings. You were in construction. You know what needs to be done."

"We're heading into winter. Not a lot can be done unless they get the main walls, and the roof on. This project is going to be a lengthy one, and I did warn you about that."

"I get it. What else are you doing, Spider?"

"What do you mean?"

"To some, therapy is the answer, and I get it, I do. To some, they just need to focus on something else to clear their head. You're the best one for this job."

Spider took a moment to think about it. The money was the club's, and if someone did it wrong, it would fall to them to fix it. The guys all had their many talents, but building wasn't one of them.

"I'll do it."

"Good."

Spider went to leave, but Devil called him back. "We're having a big dinner on Sunday. Everyone is going to be there. Are you coming?"

"A big dinner? You know me, I wouldn't miss something like that."

"Good."

Devil drove away, and Spider went to the parking lot behind the therapist's building, and unhooked his bike.

Four months without Andrew, and life had gotten back to normal. The Skulls were growing, and from what he heard Sally had even been fitted with a prosthetic leg. She was in physio, but her life was back on track. She didn't go to school yet. Whizz and Lacey had her studying from home.

Straddling his bike, Spider rode out of the therapist's parking lot, and made his way toward Paris's home. He saw Sinner's car was parked out front, and Spider parked several feet away. Paris came out of the house, laughing at something Sinner said, as she grabbed a bag from the back of the car. Sinner leaned over, talking to her, and Paris burst out laughing, hitting his shoulder as she did.

The club adored her. He heard several of the brothers talking about her spirit, her fire, and he wished more than anything that it could be him making her smile.

Lexie loved her as well. The old ladies all did, and so did some of the club whores.

Paris made her way back inside, but Sinner had spotted him.

Spider watched as he locked up his car, and made his way toward him.

"What's up, man?"

"Nothing. I'm just watching, you know?"

"She would love for you to come inside. We've got thirty minutes until we go for Celia."

The temptation was strong, and as he looked at the door, he saw that night where the door was open. "I can't."

"Spider, she's waiting for you."

"Take care of her for me." Spider didn't wait around. He revved his engine and shot off down the street, leaving Sinner and Paris behind.

He had to get his shit together soon. There was no way he could live like this.

Twenty minutes later, after failing to clear his head, he entered the clubhouse. He found Jessica heading out with Snake behind her.

"What's going on?"

"Snake's taking me to work. I've got the evening shift. I'll be back by two in the morning."

Snake fist bumped his hand as they passed.

Entering the clubhouse, he saw Lydia behind the bar. The woman hadn't left yet, but she'd changed. She wasn't the same loud mouth that she once was. "I'll take a shot of whiskey," he said.

"It's a little early to be on the hard stuff, right?"

"I've never been an addict. I'm fine."

Lydia handed him a glass and drizzled in some whiskey.

"I'll take some ice as well."

She poured in the ice, and he stared at the glass. Lydia didn't stick around. She moved down to another brother. Butler came to take a seat beside him.

Spider looked around the clubhouse. Death and Brianna were playing a fucking board game. Reese, Slash, and Dime were playing pool. Charlie, Smithy, Prospect, Guts, and Sexy were playing cards. Several of the club whores were dancing. He also saw Pussy and Sasha dancing together.

"What has you drinking from the bottle as this time of day?" Butler asked.

"Where's the rest of the guys?"

"Mia and Curse haven't been around for a couple of days. They're trying to pick out a new kitchen from what I've heard. I'm sure we'll hear from them when they want help fitting it. Dick and Martha have gone back to their house for a few days to have some alone time. Ripper and Judi are at home with baby Paul. Lexie and Devil are probably at home. The other guys are looking at the two buildings. Did Devil talk to you?"

"Yeah, I'm heading up the apartment block."

"Thank fuck for that. I didn't have a clue what the

hell was going on." Butler held his finger up to the new girl. Mandy her name was, and she was a sweetheart. Spider didn't think she was a club whore. She was dressed in a pair of jeans that hugged her curves, and a shirt.

"What can I get you?" Mandy asked.

"A strong black coffee."

"Coming right up." She disappeared from behind the bar, and he noticed the cloth sticking out of her back pocket.

"Who is she?" Spider asked.

"She's the new cleaner. She cleans up the clubhouse, and comes recommended by Mia."

Spider smiled as he saw the interest in Butler.

Usually the brother's response was, "how the fuck should I know?"

Interesting.

****

"I wonder what they're thinking right now?" Tate asked.

"I don't know, probably working out how they got to babysit, and we got to check out this latest nightclub in the city. We're so bad," Lacey said, raising her glass in the air.

"Excuse me, but I thought we were celebrating my upcoming kid?" Prue asked, touching her rounded stomach.

Tate shook her head. "We'll celebrate that when you have it. Believe me, when you realize what came out of your vagina, you're going to be needing a drink."

All of The Skulls women who had given birth cheered loudly, even Angel.

"I was worried it would spoil, you know, sex," Angel said.

"Wow, is anyone else seriously shocked right

now?" Sophia asked. "Angel talking about sex."

"Shut up. I can talk about sex. I've had two kids. I'm not some stranger to it."

"Ha, two kids. I'm surprised Lash even gave you one," Tate said. "He's so damn possessive of you."

"He loves me."

Millie smiled, watching all of the ladies talking about their men. She wasn't sad, and there was no point her joining in. There was no tale for her to tell.

"I'm going dancing," Lacey said, grabbing Sandy's hand, and making her way onto the dance floor.

Millie sipped at her wine and watched the girls dance.

"Come on, Millie, it's not just about them," Angel said, grabbing her hand. "Our drinks are safe. Prue can't drive, nor can she drink."

"Hey, so not fair," Prue said, yelling to be heard over the music.

Running onto the dance floor, Millie at first felt a little embarrassed. Being around Angel, she had a way about her that made you want to join in and have fun. Abandoning all of her thoughts, Millie threw her arms in the air and let the music take her. She had no cares on the dance floor. No concerns, and she didn't have to worry about Baker, or what she felt for him.

"Tonight, just relax. Nothing is going to hurt you here," Angel said.

Millie took her advice and danced with the girls. She ignored the men, not interested in them. When she needed a drink, she went back to the table, and chatted some more, drinking, and even eating some tacos, which were delicious.

As the night wore on, she noticed a group of men entering the nightclub, and smiled as she caught sight of Lash, Nash, Zero, Tony, and Baker. There were several more men, but the moment she saw Baker, she lost all focus.

Sipping on her wine, Millie listened to the women as they all complained about their husbands being there.

"This was supposed to be a fun night out away from you guys," Prue said.

"We're fun. Besides, it's nine o'clock. We gave you plenty of time to get your girly shit out of the way. Now, it's our time to show you what real fun is all about." Zero took his woman onto the dance floor, pulling her into his arms.

Millie tried not to be envious of the couple. It was hard not to be.

"How have you been?" Baker asked.

While she'd been watching Prue and Zero, Baker had taken a seat next to her.

"I'm doing good. You?"

"I miss you."

Millie stared down at her hands, not knowing how to answer that.

"Come on. Dance with me," he said. He offered his hand, and she stared at it.

What do you have to lose?

Go for it.

Dance with him.

Placing her hand within his, she followed him onto the dance floor. He pulled her into his arms, and the music changed to a slow one.

"I miss you, Millie."

"You've said that already. I haven't been anywhere."

"I didn't think you'd want me to visit you after everything."

She sighed. "I don't know. You have to see things from my side."

"I do. I'm so sorry, Millie."

Looking up at him, she saw the contrition in his eyes. "I believe you."

"I don't want to lose you."

"Baker, you never really had me. I thought we were friends, and you tell me that you want me. You don't want me, not really."

He held her a little tighter. "I do want you. I'll hold off, and I'll prove it to you."

"I don't need to have it proven, Baker. I just, I'd rather not compete with a dead woman. I know that sounds awful."

"It doesn't."

She looked around the whole of the dance floor, wishing there was something else she could say.

"Friends. Let's be friends, go to the movies, have fun, maybe go dancing—what do you say?"

At first she wanted to say no, and then she decided against that. Instead, she agreed, even though she was terrified of how much Baker could hurt her. He was a good man. She only hoped he was considerate to her feelings.

Chapter Eighteen

Paris had baked a Key lime pie. She'd baked three Key lime pies so that no one went without. Angel had given her a recipe, which was pretty foolproof, and she loved it. With Celia strapped in the back, resting one in her lap, Paris sat in the front of the car, holding the other two.

"I don't know if I should go," Paris said.

"Lexie came and gave you a personal invite to dinner today. You're going." This was not the get-together with The Skulls. That was being organized for another time. This was just for Chaos Bleeds. Lexie had been very sweet to invite her, and her sister.

"The whole club is going to be there."

"Yes, including Spider."

"I don't know if I'm ready for him to just walk out again. I don't know if you noticed, but he seems to enjoy doing that."

"He's just being an asshole. Don't think about it, and if you don't think about him, he'll leave you alone."

"I wish that was true."

"Do you trust me?" Sinner asked.

"Yes."

"Do you trust the club?"

"Yes."

"Then stop worrying about it. We'll take care of you, and Spider won't hurt you."

She sighed. "I wasn't thinking of the physical kind of hurt." Every time he walked away, that hurt.

"I'm sorry. We can't stop him from walking away."

"You're right. Don't worry, I'm not going to pressure him. In fact, I'll ignore him, and pretend he's not here."

"Pie's good," Celia said. "I like pie. I want to eat it."

"After dinner. Remember Lexie is going to be feeding us today. We've got to eat her food first."

"I like Lexie. She smells nice."

Paris smiled. Lexie was a sweetheart. Even after four kids, she was still so patient with Celia.

She had really come to love that woman, and her patience. It was becoming a rare quality to find in a person nowadays.

They pulled up into the Chaos Bleeds clubhouse, and Sinner got out, helping Celia out. Paris eased out, holding the two pies.

I can do this.

Don't pay Spider attention.

Wait for him to come to you.

Walking beside Sinner and Celia, Paris walked up to the front door. The moment the door opened, she heard the welcoming sounds of conversation, and laughter.

Celia was in, and dumped a pie at the nearest man, which happened to be Slash.

"Why did she give me pie? Is it all mine?" Slash asked.

"No, it's for dessert. I hope that is okay?"

"Lexie's in the kitchen. Come on, I'll take you."

She smiled at Sinner, letting him know she was okay to follow Slash. Lexie was in the kitchen, basting three large chickens.

"Guess who has brought dessert," Slash said.

Lexie turned around, and smiled. "Let me get these back in the oven."

"It's Angel's recipe. I'm pleased I got it. All my Key lime pies curdle."

"Angel does know how to cook."

The chickens disappeared into the oven, and she wiped her hands on the towel, moving toward them. "I'm so pleased you came." She held her arms out, and Paris went into them.

"It's a pleasure. Celia's gone to play. I hope that is okay?"

"Sure, the guys and girls will keep an eye on her. Don't worry about it."

This was where Celia could be herself. Most of the time she either read, watched television, or built with blocks. Celia wasn't a difficult child, not at all.

"Mom, is this mixed enough?" Simon said.

Paris hadn't seen Simon standing there. He looked so adorable wearing a pink apron, and mixing. The arms on his shirt were folded back, and Paris smiled as she spotted a rub-on tattoo. It would fade as he washed.

"You're the one that wants to learn to bake chocolate chip cookies, you tell me?" Lexie raised her brow, put her hand on her hip, and stared.

"It needs more chocolate chips."

"Simon Dawes, I put three cups of chocolate chips out for you to add to that batter. Where are they?"

At the corner of his mouth were the obvious signs of chocolate chips.

"I ate them."

"If you keep eating all the candy, you're going to get sick."

"I'm sorry, Mom."

Lexie grabbed the chocolate chips, and weighed out another cup. "Stir that in, and then we can scoop them out, and get on baking." She turned toward Paris. "We're baking plenty for after dinner. Key lime?"

"Yes. I have three. I hope that's enough."

"I hope so as well, but you never know with this

hungry lot. They'll complain either way." Lexie chuckled. "Simon has been practicing to bake."

"Do you like baking?" Paris asked.

"Tabitha likes eating. I only want her to eat what I've cooked, or what she cooks."

Tabitha was the young girl from The Skulls.

"Right, you want to be super smart so that she doesn't find a boy better than you?" Paris asked.

"Or man. I'm not going to be a boy forever."

"That's … really sweet."

"Sweet? The boy is in a frilly pink apron," Devil said, entering the kitchen. He carried a little boy that couldn't be more than a year old. He was squirming in his arms, looking ready to explode.

"It doesn't matter what I wear, Dad. I'm still me."

"Baking cookies."

"You love my cookies. I'll be the best baker an MC has ever known," Simon said. "Tabitha's going to love me forever. Can I mail her some? She'll love them."

"They'll taste nasty, honey. When she comes to visit we can bake her some more," Lexie said. She walked up to Devil, taking the squirming baby from him. Devil wouldn't let her get away that easily, and wrapped his arms around her, kissing her neck. The baby soon settled down once he was in his mother's arms.

"He missed you, and so did I," Devil said.

"Ew, Mom and Dad are going to get gross again," Simon said, looking at her. "If you don't want to vomit I'd leave."

Devil smiled toward her. "It's good to see you coming to join us for dinner."

"It's a pleasure."

"Brianna, Jessica, and a couple of the others are out there looking over Natalie's designs," Devil said.

"Designs?" Paris asked.

"Remember I told you that we're opening up a fashion boutique? Well Natalie has already started some designs. We can get them manufactured locally as well. Natalie knows how to do that part, and we'll be selling them at the store."

"What about online?" Paris asked. "That's a big market now."

"Online, that's amazing. We could do that, and get the orders to the factory," Paris said.

Instantly Paris thought of Lola. "Crap."

"What is it?"

"Lola would have been perfect at this."

"Shit," Devil said.

"Bad words, both of you need to put a dollar in the swear jar," Simon said.

"We're not at home, and rules say it's when the jar is present."

Simon pointed at a shell. "It is."

"When did that get fucking here?"

"Two dollars, Dad."

Paris pulled out a dollar, and placed it in the swear jar. "I'll watch my language from now on. I'll call Lola and see if there's any way I can convince her to give it a try."

"That would be great," Lexie said.

Leaving the kitchen, Paris found the group of women huddled over a table. She moved toward them, and Jessica saw her first, pulling out a chair. "It's great to see you here."

Paris had already seen her sister watching the television. She was holding a teddy bear, and Butler was near her.

The club would never harm her sister, and she trusted them implicitly. Also, after the days Celia had spent with them while Paris had been captured, her sister knew them better than she did.

"Paris, this is Natalie. Natalie, this is Paris."

She shook hands with the woman, who was a few years older than she was. "Pritchard, you own the ranch with the cattle, right?"

"We're a cattle ranch. I was a few years ahead of you in high school. Sorry to hear what happened to you, but I'm not going to say anything more."

Paris watched as Natalie smiled at her before going back to looking at the book.

Natalie had always been a sweet girl. Paris remembered her being by herself at school, always drawing in a notebook.

Staring at the designs, some of them for dresses, and others for shirts, skirts, and other kinds of clothing, Paris saw that she had a great deal of talent, and was more than impressed by what she was seeing.

"These are amazing. You did graduate from school?"

"Yep, top of my class. I was head hunted, but my folks needed me, so I turned them down."

She saw the sadness in her friend's eyes. "I'm so sorry."

"It's family, and they always come first."

Glancing over at Celia, she nodded. Her sister would always come first, before school or work. She had stripped for a living just to have a comfortable lifestyle for her sister.

"I get it."

"So, did you two go to school together?" Judi asked.

"No. I'm four years older. So I was in my last year as she entered her first year," Natalie said.

"This shop is going to rock," Jessica said. "I haven't told anyone at the hospital, but I know some of the nurses there would love a place to shop for in town. The mall is thirty minutes away, and some of their prices are just scary."

Paris pointed at several designs she liked.

"We could do our own fashion shoot for the opening," Brianna said.

"Fashion shoot?" Jessica asked.

"You know, we have a grand opening, and as part of it, we can have select models, local gals of course, show off the clothes that will be on offer," Brianna said.

"You know what, that sounds like a fantastic idea," Judi said. "Let's go and tell Lexie."

With two girls gone, Paris looked toward the front of the design book, and sighed. She wished she had this amount of talent. Natalie was amazing.

"Spider's here," Martha said.

"I know. I saw him the moment I entered the room."

"I thought it would be more tense, but you're behaving like you don't see him."

She looked up from the book to see the rest of the women staring at her.

"Spider has chosen every means of avoiding me when I try to talk to him. Now, I'm going to wait for him to come to me."

"I heard you're going back to college," Natalie said.

"I'm doing online courses. I study when Celia's at school."

"What are you studying?"

"I'm just doing some English classes. It's hard to determine what kind of future to have, when I don't really see much of one. I take care of my sister, but that's really all I see."

"I always wanted to be a designer so it was easy

for me to just go to that field," Natalia said.

"You're going to make one hell of a designer. Once the big leagues see this, you're going to be snatched away from us. We must exploit you now."

"Nah, I believe in loyalty. It means a lot to me that you asked the locals, and I wouldn't have known about it, if my mom hadn't seen the advertisement in the paper. She encouraged me to approach you guys. I was so scared. You're an MC, and I had heard a lot of bad stuff. I'm pleased I ignored it all. This place is amazing." Natalie took a sip of her soda, and Paris could completely relate with her.

Chaos Bleeds was supposed to be one badass group that you should avoid, and yet to her, they had been nothing but kind and caring. Celia adored them, as did she.

****

"She didn't want to come because of you being here. She worried that you'd consider this your turf, and her trespassing over it," Sinner said.

Spider frowned. "She didn't, did she?"

"Paris did. She doesn't want to do anything to hurt you. She's a keeper, Spider. I keep telling you this, and she only has eyes for one, and that is you."

She looked beautiful. He watched as she talked with the old ladies over the designs that Natalie had brought to them. They were damn good, and they all knew it. This fashion shop was going to be huge.

Drinking his coffee, he watched as Paris every now and again looked toward Celia, checking to make sure her sister was okay. She loved her sister more than anything. Celia fit right into the club. She was sitting with Butler, watching the television. The scent of the chicken was making his mouth water.

Go over there, and talk to her.

He kept holding himself back, not going toward her, and it pissed him off. Paris got out of her seat, and headed toward the back, near the bathrooms. Ever since Mandy had been part of the club, the bathrooms had been spotless, but then, so had all of the club.

Putting his cup down, he followed Paris, waiting outside of the bathroom doors for her to leave.

It's just talking.

Nothing else.

Tapping his fingers on his leg, he waited for her to exit the bathroom. No one else had come back this way, and he wondered if the club was giving them both the space they needed.

What do I say?

Spider ran his fingers through his hair, and tried to figure out what else he could, or couldn't say. She looked pretty. Could he say that? This was so fucking hard.

Suddenly, the door to the bathroom opened, and he didn't have much of a choice anymore.

Paris paused when she saw him.

"Hey," he said.

"Hey."

He noticed her hands went into tiny fists. Her tongue peeked out as she licked her lips.

"You look really beautiful today," he said.

She glanced down at the simple blue dress. It was rather conservative, but the material looked thick.

"I didn't know what the occasion was, and so I picked this. It used to belong to my mom. I guess you can call it vintage now."

He smiled.

"You look good, too," she said.

"I look the same as I always do. Scruffy biker."

"You carry the look well."

He pursed his lips, and then smiled. "I'm sorry," he said.

"Me too."

"You don't have anything to be sorry about. I'm the one that is sorry. You think I don't want you over what happened, but it's not that at all."

"It's not?"

"No." He took a step toward her and reached out. After three months, Spider finally touched her, placing his palm against her cheek. Her skin was so smooth, and perfect. That one touch, reminded him so much of the attraction he held for her. "I've tried, Paris. I've tried to come and see you, but it's so hard. I've failed you, and I can't take any of it back." He ran the tip of his thumb across her quivering lip, and he hated himself for making her cry. "You didn't see the damage of what he did."

"I lived it, Spider."

"I can't get it out of my head, and it's all my fault." He pressed his head against hers, regretting touching her, and yet not being able to let go.

She cupped his face, holding him close. He didn't pull away. Spider didn't want to let go of her, not now, not ever.

"I've been in a really fucked up place," he said.

"I heard you had to go to therapy."

Someone cleared their throat, and he turned to see Slash there. "Sorry, you're in front of the men's bathroom, and I've gotta go."

"Let's go out and talk."

Spider took her hand, and they made their way down toward the kitchen. He grabbed an extra jacket for her, and they left. With the cold coming in, everyone was inside, so the whole of the outside was free and clear for them to talk. Taking out a cigarette, he lit it up, and blew a puff of smoke into the air.

"I didn't know you smoked," she said.

"I don't. Not really." He took hold of her hand, locking their fingers together, and never wanting to let go of her. Spider had missed this, and now that he was doing it, he had to wonder why the fuck he hadn't been doing it in the first place.

"You're smoking right now." She chuckled.

"Yeah, I guess I do."

"So, therapy, you see Annie?"

"Yeah, I do."

"Does she help you?"

"You know, I'm not sure if she helps, or if I help myself by having a few hours of talking about shit," he said.

"Be careful. I had to pay a dollar into the swear jar," Paris said.

"Yeah, Simon's a stickler for that jar." They held hands, and made their way out toward the park. It was a little like The Skulls. With the kids being born, they had to make it more kid-friendly at the club. Spider loved the way the clubhouse was developing. It was great to be part of.

"I'm not doing well with Annie," Paris said.

"You're not?"

"I can't talk about my feelings all the time. It's exhausting." Paris stopped, and he watched as she tried to find the right words to talk to him. "I'm not saying that I don't struggle. I do. I struggle all the time, and it's so hard to be not afraid. The thing is, he's done, and he's never coming back. I can live with that."

"Why don't you stop seeing her?" Spider asked.

"I don't know. Lexie suggested it, and I don't want to let her, or you, down. It's kind of hard. I feel like I have to go and see Annie."

"I'm going to stop."

"You are?"

"My biggest struggle was this. Talking with you. For some reason I was struggling to do it, and I couldn't get past it."

"And now?"

"I'd say I'm doing pretty well right now, considering that I'm talking to you."

Paris smiled. "I've been hoping you'd talk to me, or at least say something. I'd even take you screaming just to get you to talk to me."

Spider threw his cigarette to the ground, and stubbed it out. He tugged her closer to him, and sank his fingers into her hair. "I like this cut on you. It looks sexy."

"Thank you."

"The shit I was going through in my head, it had nothing to do with you, or your virginity or anything else. I want you, Paris. I want you more than anything, but I want us both to be fixed before we move on."

"How can we be fixed if you keep on running?"

"I'm not going to keep on running. I'm staying right here, and I'm not going to disappear again." He leaned in close, and gently placed his lips against hers.

It was a chaste kiss, but it was a start.

"Wow," she said, sighing. "I got a kiss."

"I want to start visiting you. Taking you out. Do you think that would be okay?"

"I'd love to."

Locking their fingers together, they made their way back inside, where he saw commotion had kicked up. Everyone was rushing to fix the table ready for dinner.

"I'm going to help Lexie." Paris released his hand, and he watched her go, wishing he could pull her back to him.

"You took the leap," Sinner said.

"I had no choice. I didn't want to lose her, and I was ready."

"Or, Paris was ignoring you, and you didn't like it."

"Either way, I got to talk with her, and for me, that's what I wanted."

The table was set, and Lexie, Simon, and Paris brought out food. Paris sat beside her sister, and Spider took the other side of Celia. The entire clubhouse was full, with the kids on a smaller table. Even the club whores were sitting there as they enjoyed their Sunday lunch.

Devil said a quick prayer, offering thanks to the food, and to the men who had gone from their club. They all shared an amen, and then started to serve out dinner. Paris placed food on Celia's plate before doing her own.

"Can I have everyone's attention?" Death said, standing up. "I know we're all serving up, but I just wanted to say something."

Brianna's cheeks were a bright red as she smiled up at Death.

"We're going to have a baby."

There were hoots of laughter and joy as Death told them the news. It meant a lot as Brianna had been through hell. Spider leaned over, shaking Death's hand.

"Seeing as we all had something to share, Judi and I are expecting again," Ripper said. "We're nervous about it, you know, with what happened with the first, but the doctors are going to take every precaution."

Judi had suffered with pre-eclampsia during the birth of Paul and nearly died. For several weeks, everyone had been tense, scared for Judi and Paul.

"So are we," Mia said. "I found out in Fort Wills three months ago. I'm not getting fat. I'm going to have a little girl." Curse gripped the back of her neck, and Spider watched as the brother kissed Mia so passionately that even he blushed.

"Well, seeing as I was the one who organized the dinner, I'm pregnant again," Lexie said, leaning back, and touching her stomach.

"What the fuck?" Devil said.

"Dad, a dollar," Simon said.

"Shut up, son. You're pregnant?"

Lexie nodded, tears filling her eyes. "Two months."

"Do we know what it is?"

"No. The doctor will be doing an ultrasound in a couple of weeks to determine sex. We're going to be parents again."

"Woohoo, another brother or sister. I've got to tell Tabitha," Simon said.

"You're going to eat your food. I told you, no talking to Tabitha until you eat all your vegetables," Lexie said.

Simon saluted his mother, and sat down, ready to start eating.

The club was growing, and the next generation was growing.

Spider leaned behind Celia's chair and stroked Paris's arm. She took hold of his hand, and gave his a gentle squeeze.

It was small step, but a big one to them.

He refused to let Andrew win for another second.

****

"How did Devil handle the news?" Eva asked. She held the phone to her ear, as she put away sauces from dinner.

"He's happy. He's always happy. How is life with you and the kids?"

"It's peaceful. Can you believe that? Life is actually peaceful, and I never for a second believed that it could be like that." Eva giggled. "What about you?"

"No threat. Devil's actually relaxed. I've never known him to be so relaxed."

Eva heard Lexie chuckle. They had both been through so much, and with Simon and Tabitha, they knew it was never going to stop.

"How is Paris?"

Lexie sighed. "I don't know. She's gone to the therapist like I asked her, but I think she's only done it for me. I won't want to pry too much, but it's hard to do. I care, you know?"

"Of course I know. She went through hell."

Eva poured herself a large glass of orange juice, taking a seat. Tiny walked in carrying some paperwork, and she smiled at him. He moved behind her, kissing the back of her neck.

"Do you think I should try and draw her into conversation, talk about it?"

"I don't know. How was Brianna?" Eva asked.

"I don't know. They're both quiet women. I just want Paris to know if she needs me, she can talk to me."

"Then tell her. I'm sure she'd understand."

"Oh, Simon's looking pissed, and I hear Devil shouting. Got to go."

Lexie hung up before she could say goodbye.

"Trouble in Piston?" Tiny asked.

"No. Lexie's pregnant again."

"Another of Devil's brood to contend with."

She chuckled. "Tab's only interested in Simon. You don't have to worry."

Tiny had put on a pair of glasses to read, and she loved it when he did. He looked so … serious and educated. It was a huge turn-on.

"I always imagined my kids being close to me, Eva. Simon's going to take over from Devil, which will mean my kid won't be near me. I don't like that."

Eva shrugged. "You can't come between love."

"You're incorrigible."

"And you don't see what my father has to go through."

"Please, Ned's fine."

"His daughter is miles away. He has to get here by a car or by plane. Plane is quicker. You don't think that upsets him? Yet I'm here."

Tiny tilted his head to the side. "You always have the means of making me feel guilty."

She chuckled, moving behind him. "It's a gift, baby." She kissed his neck. "All the kids are asleep."

"They are."

She ran her hand down his chest, moving toward his cock. It had been a long time since they'd been together. Eva didn't want to wait any longer. "I've got some quiet time with your name all over it."

The glasses were gone, papers forgotten as he grabbed her, picking her up, and carrying her toward their bedroom.

****

Lash climbed into bed and snuggled up against his wife. They were in their own home, and they had just had a Sunday lunch. He kissed her neck, breathing in her scent.

"Is Chloe down?"

"Yeah, she's fine. Just wanted a hug off Daddy."

"What about Anthony?"

"He's okay. Sleeping like a log."

"Can you believe Zero and Prue are going to have a baby?" she asked.

"I know. It's pretty something, isn't it?"

Angel rolled over and smiled at him. "I'd like to have another baby."

"We've just had Chloe."

"Not now, but I'd like another one. I always wanted a big family."

"I don't want to share you, and with two kids, you get tired."

"Please, Lash. I thought you wanted a big family as well."

"I do. I want a big family with you. I just can't stand the thought of never seeing you again."

"You'll always see me. I'll carve out a minute of every single day to see you." Angel wrapped her arms around him.

"Very funny. A minute is never going to be enough, and you know it." He ran his hand down her hips, feeling her womanly curves. Lash had never been able to get enough of her. His cock pressed up, demanding attention. "Do you see what you do to me, woman?"

"I feel it, but, Lash, how can we do anything about that when using it makes babies?" She winked at him, and he couldn't help but chuckle.

"You, Angel, are a little vixen."

Turning her over, he took possession of her mouth, and started to slide up her dress. She released a moan, and then they both paused as they heard Chloe whimper. They held their breath, hoping she'd settle, but no. The whimper turned into a full blown scream. "I'm going," Angel said.

He groaned, having to release his woman as she went to deal with their girl.

His own daughter was being a cock-block, and he was so going to pay her back when she was older.

****

Sandy groaned as Stink sank further into her ass. She was on her back and he held her legs apart, staring into her eyes as he claimed her anus. He loved fucking her ass, and she was sure he was addicted to it. With him above her, he teased her clit, heightening the pleasure.

In the last few months, they had had a whirlwind romance. At first, they had waited until the club had settled down after the attack from Andrew. Also, Sandy wouldn't leave until everyone was out of the hospital, and that included Paris. She really liked that woman. Then, only when there were no other signs of danger, she and Stink had taken a month-long honeymoon in the Caribbean with Gash and Charlotte. Even though Stink hadn't wanted the other couple with them at first, she knew without a doubt he had fun. She wouldn't have suggested it otherwise. Many nights they had taken drinks down to the beach, and sat watching the waves, talking and giggling.

It was nice to see Gash and Charlotte having a good time. The couple deserved their happiness after being so long apart. When they had gotten back, Sandy had been worried that her feelings for Stink would slowly fade, but they hadn't. They had gotten stronger.

"I love you, baby," he said.

"I love you, too."

Falling for Stink had been the best thing she ever did. She had never known another man like him, and she was never going to find anyone else. He owned her heart, and she'd given it to him willingly.

The future was theirs to do with as they wished, and she intended to never lose sight of what she had.

Chapter Nineteen

Paris stood at the sink clearing away the breakfast dishes. Celia had gone to school with Butler, and Paris had opted to clean up and then start her school work. She'd been talking with Natalie on the phone about the choices she could make for the future. Paris really didn't know what she wanted to be. Growing up she'd wanted to be a variety of things: a vet, a hairdresser, a nurse, author, and even someone who just ate food all day. That would be a pretty awesome job, and even now she thought so.

Taking care of her sister in the past couple of years was all she'd ever known, so she hadn't yet experienced the luxury of thinking of a career outside of taking her clothes off.

Andrew entered her mind. She'd been stripping and then he'd come into her life, ruining her. Gripping the edge of the sink, she closed her eyes, trying to forget about him.

"You're not important to me. You're dead, and you're gone."

She took several deep breaths, and started to focus on the now, not the past. Annie had told her that memories and fears would sometimes bleed into one another. Paris liked to think they were few and far between now. Andrew didn't control her. There were only moments when he seemed to invade her thoughts, and scare her. All she had to do was remember that he was dead and gone.

Once she finished with the dishes, she sat down at the laptop, and started to go through the lists of different careers available to her. A therapist was the last thing she wanted to be. She could only just about abide her trips with Annie, and they were annoying to her at times.

An author would be kind of cool. She used to write stories growing up about princesses and monsters. Then as she grew older, the more cliché of the not-so-hot girl getting the guy. Maybe she should do something like that? She was taking English, and she could try writing a few words down, see how she felt.

Opening up a fresh document, she started with chapter one, and stared at her screen wondering if this was complete and utterly stupid. After another ten minutes of nothing, she headed upstairs to her closet where she pulled out a large box filled with her old notebooks and journals. When her parents died she'd stashed them all together, and decided against doing anything with them.

Taking the lid off, she saw at least twelve different kinds, and picked out the last one, opening it up. She started to read through the last page of her journal that told of the funeral of her parents, and the pain of seeing the pity in their closest friends. No one had come by in the last few months to help.

Pushing the journals aside, she grabbed one of her notebooks, and took out the story "Princess". She was very original at the grand old age of thirteen, and yes the story was just as lame.

She loved reading, though, and had even bought herself an e-reader in the last couple of months to read some stories.

The sound of her doorbell being rung made her put them all away, and head downstairs once again. She never expected Spider to be on the other side, nor did she expect him to be holding a large bouquet of red roses.

"Spider?"

"In case you didn't know, I'm Stuart Cox, and I have been a total asshole to you. I haven't given you what you deserve. I was hoping that we could start over.

Instead of me lurking outside a strip club like a creeper, or me showing up where you work, I think we could do this the good old-fashioned way."

She leaned against the doorframe, not caring about the chill or anything else.

"I'm listening."

"So, I think you're the most beautiful woman on the planet, and being away from you is the worst thing in the world. I want to change that, and the only way to do that, is to move forward. Paris, will you go out with me? It's just a date. Nothing scary or overly new."

"A date?"

"Yes. I'd like to take you to dinner, or to a movie."

"I can do a dinner."

"I can talk to one of the guys about watching Celia."

"Lexie has said she'd take her." She looked at the roses, then back at him. "Are those for me?"

"I guess seeing as you said yes, they're for you. I was going to give them to the next woman I asked out on a date."

"You better not. I said yes." Biting her lip, Paris couldn't help but smile. "Would you like to come inside?"

"I'd love to."

Moving out of the way, she watched him cross the threshold, and in her heart she knew they had finally crossed that final step. "Would you like anything to eat?" She'd done the dishes, but she'd gladly do them again for him.

"Celia's gone."

"I know, but I make a large batch of pancake batter, and store it in the fridge. It's awesome like that." She went to the fridge pulling out the batter she'd made that morning. This would last for at least another day. "I've got nuts, chocolate, or I can flavor it with whatever you like."

"Blueberries?"

"You like blueberries?"

"In pancakes, I think they're the best."

Looking into her fridge, she did see a small box of them leftover. She'd made some lemon and blueberry muffins the other day, her favorite. Putting the ingredients on the counter, she grabbed a spare bowl, and dolloped out several spoonfuls before adding in a large handful of blueberries. Stirring them together, she put a non-stick skillet on the stove, and heated it up, adding a little bit of butter.

"I like watching you in the kitchen."

She smiled at him. "Thank you. I like being in the kitchen. Even when my mom was alive, I'd always be in here."

"Lexie's a damn good cook."

"Tell me about it. Did you taste her Sunday lunch? One word … amazing."

"Yeah, Devil's been complaining that he's piling on the pounds. Lexie bakes enough that she has to bring the excess to the club. There's always a pile of brownies or a chocolate fudge cake."

"Sounds like heaven. She brought me a chocolate pie the other day. Between me, Celia, and Sinner, we ate all of it."

"You and Sinner have gotten quite close?"

"It's not like that. He's a friend. I promise."

"It would serve me right if you ended up with someone else."

"Why are you speaking like that? I finally got your attention, and you're making out that I want something different. I don't." She looked over at him.

"I'm happy that you finally came to your senses."

"I am, too. I'm really sorry."

"It's okay. At first I thought you were being really selfish, and then I had it explained to me. I imagine I looked really rough."

"I hated that I couldn't save you. I'll never be able to take away what happened to you, but I want you to know I'm not going anywhere. Never again."

"You're here to stay?"

"I'm here to stay."

Turning back to the stove, Paris smiled, dolloping out pancakes as she did.

"What are you doing here? Chapter one? Are you going to write a story?"

"Ugh, I don't know. To be honest, I haven't got a clue what I'm going to do with the rest of my life. On the one hand, I used to love to write. I've got an entire box of a lifetime of journals. Then I think about that kind of commitment, and writing is hard."

"It is, but you don't have to worry about money or anything like that. We've got you covered."

"Then there's Celia. I'm not ever going to allow her to go in a special facility. She's all the family I have."

"I don't expect you to. I already figured out that you and Celia were a package deal."

Paris smiled, and looked toward him. "And you're still here?"

"I told you, I'm done walking away from this. I'm going to be the man you deserve, and there's no getting away from that."

Looking back at the pancakes, Paris couldn't stop the little flutter from occurring.

The sound of the door opening and closing let her know that Sinner had arrived. "Fuck me, it's fucking cold. My balls have frozen solid."

"We're in here, Sinner."

"We? Who is we? Do you have a hot chick in there with you?" he asked.

His footsteps getting louder allowed her to hear him getting closer.

"Spider, you finally got your head out of your ass."

"Yes."

Putting the cooked pancakes onto a plate, she handed them to Spider. "He's even asked me on a date."

"Yeah, I got a call from Lexie. She told me not to worry about sitting for you tomorrow. She's more than happy to have Celia."

"Did you talk to Lexie before coming over here?" Paris asked.

"Yep, I wanted to make sure that we'd be able to go out together. I know Celia's care means a lot to you."

She couldn't fault him on that. "So you assumed I'd say yes?"

"I hoped that you'd say yes, and then I prayed a little."

"Will you be wearing a tux?" Sinner asked.

"Maybe."

"He's going all out for you, Paris."

"Leave him alone, Sinner."

"Oh, Lexie wanted to know if you'd gotten in touch with Lola."

"Not yet. She works at her local library during the day. She packs the shelves. She doesn't deal with the computer." The staff knew about Lola's aversion to technology, and were helping her to grow accustomed to working there.

Paris had gotten quite close with the woman, and they talked regularly on the phone. It was one of the reasons why she didn't believe she needed to talk about what happened with a stranger. She talked about it with Lola, a woman who went through the same ordeal. They helped each other.

"What's this about?" Spider asked.

"The building you bought, we're going to turn it into a clothing store."

"I know that."

"Oh, well, most businesses are more successful if you take your work to the internet, and that's what we're hoping to do. Expand it onto the internet, and of course, Lola is perfect for that."

"She can't touch computers," Spider said.

"Well, the grand opening isn't for a few months. We're hoping to have some time to convince her. It'll be good to get her back into technology. She had a bright future ahead of her."

"Let us know if she needs anything," Sinner asked.

Paris would, but she doubted Lola would. Her friend had become very reserved in the last few months.

****

"You're going out with him tonight?" Lacey asked.

Paris nodded, and then remembered she was on speakerphone. "Yes. I'm going out with him tonight. Was I wrong to have caved so quickly?"

"I'm not the expert on making a man wait. I went hunting for Whizz, not the other way around."

"Ugh, this is so frustrating. I'm nervous, and I'm excited. Is that even normal."

"Sweetie, I don't know what normal is. I spent a great deal of my time on the run, remember?"

Paris did remember. Lacey had confided the truth of her life before The Skulls, and before Whizz. Even thinking about it, Paris's heart went out to her. She understood the pain that Lacey had gone through, or at least part of the pain.

"I want to look pretty."

"You'll be pretty. I'm sure of it."

Paris looked in the mirror and twirled. "How's Sally doing?"

"She's doing much better. She worries me all the time." Lacey did some moving around. "She's made a friend in Drew. He was some kind of jock that blew out his knee. It's interesting watching Steven."

"He still got feelings for her?"

"Yeah. He doesn't like Drew, and he worries about Sally. It's cute."

"I bet."

"Whizz also likes to let him know that no man is going to be taking advantage of Sally. He really does care about her, and he's worried about her."

"He takes his fatherly role seriously," Paris said.

"Yep. I'm the cool mom. I'm awesome."

Paris giggled. "I bet you are. How is everyone?"

"Everyone is doing great. Lash is proving to be a pretty rock on leader. We've got a couple of Prospects that are looking, um, challenging."

"Challenging how?"

"They're weak. I think they want the title of MC Prospect. They won't last two minutes with the boys. How about you?"

"I'm doing good. Date, remember?"

"Oh yes, date. Sorry, we were talking about me that I totally forgot about you."

Paris laughed. "Ha, it's always about you."

"The sooner everyone realizes it, the better they will be."

Glancing at the time, Paris saw she didn't have

much time, and said her goodbyes. Lacey promised to talk to her soon. She'd grown close to The Skulls women, and talked to them all regularly. They were good women, strong.

Paris paused as she recalled why *she* didn't feel so strong.

Andrew once again invaded her thoughts, and she sat down on the edge of the bed, gathering her thoughts. Twice in one day. It wasn't good, and she wasn't going to allow Andrew's memory to come between her and Spider. He'd already taken too much from them. She had to fight a little harder.

****

The following night Spider stared at his reflection, and winced. He hated wearing formal wear, and a tuxedo was too fucking tight. Spider had already booked a seat at the French restaurant in the city, and they had told him there was a dress code. He'd even gone to find Paris an appropriate dress for the night. It was a long black evening gown that molded to her curves, and he'd even gone the extra bit and given her some jewelry.

"Wow," Butler said, leaning against his doorframe.

"If you're only going to say some wise-ass shit, I suggest you fucking leave," he said.

Butler held his hands up. "You look dashing. Paris is a lucky woman."

Staring at his brother, Spider finished his tie, and sighed, taking a step back. "I look like a fucking penguin."

"A dashing penguin. You really did go the extra mile."

"I wanted Paris to have an experience she'd never forget. The first time I spoke to her, I scared her."

"How did you scare her?"

307

"I was hanging around the back of the club, and I talked, she didn't know I was there. I looked like a creepy stalker."

He fisted his hands and turned to look at Butler.

"You look a lot better than some kind of stalker."

"I don't want to show her up tonight."

"You're nervous?"

"I'm fucking terrified. I've fucked up every single way imaginable with this woman. I don't want to do that again."

"Then relax. Take a deep breath, and just chill," Butler said. "Paris is a good woman. You'll do right by her."

"You think so? I think I've been fucking up at every turn."

"We all fuck up in our lives, and you're being given a second chance to turn all of this around."

Spider nodded. "I'm not expecting sex either. It's too soon."

"Then beat off in your own hand when you get home. None of us are going to hold this against you. You and Paris, it's a special circumstance."

"You're not going to rib me for being pussy-whipped."

Butler shook his head. "The club is in agreement about this. You and Paris have been through so much. None of us are going to pressure you into taking the next step."

"Wow, you guys are being mature?"

"Blame Devil. I think Lexie had a talk with him. No, we're to be nice, and considerate to you, and to Paris's feelings. It helps that we all like her. She's a keeper, Spider, and she'll be one hell of an old lady."

Spider took a deep breath. "I'm fucking nervous."

"Don't be a pussy."

"I thought I was going to get special treatment."

"You will, but not for being a pussy. Our girl is waiting for you." Jessica, Brianna, Mia, and Judi had offered to stay with Paris to help get her ready.

"Okay, I'm going to go and get her."

Grabbing his keys and wallet, he saw a condom wrapper peeking out, and he threw it into the trash can. He didn't need a condom tonight. He was going to enjoy this date with her, and not even worry about later tonight.

Spider intended to be a gentleman for a long time yet.

Leaving his room, he walked down the long staircase, and paused as he saw Mandy making her way up them. She was wearing latex gloves and an apron.

"Spider, you look rather dashing tonight."

"Thank you. Where are you going?"

"Devil asked me to clean out the loft space. They're thinking of building up with the club getting bigger, and he interviewed a couple of guys as a prospects. There's some junk, and he's given me the job of going through it. Hey, Butler."

"Hey."

Mandy passed them, humming as she did. Spider saw Butler staring at her ass. He waited for Mandy to be out of earshot before he said anything. "Why don't you tap that?"

"She doesn't even know I exist."

"So, make her see you exist."

"Devil has a ban on fucking the cleaners. Mia also asked that none of us harass Mandy."

"Harassing and taking an interest are two different things."

"Tell that to Mia, and to Devil. Besides, I'm an ex-addict. I don't have much to offer her."

"Stop that shit about being an addict. Look at

Dick, and he's a fucking prick when he starts. If he can find love, then why not you?"

"Hey, I heard that, and I have a lovely personality," Dick said, coming downstairs.

"Where's Martha?"

"Having drinks with her friend, Lynne. I'm going to go and pick her up. It has been a while since they had a chance to chat. See, I have a personality of a saint," Dick said.

"Yeah, that's because you're in a good mood, and constantly getting your dick sucked."

"There's nothing wrong with enjoying getting your dick sucked."

"Being an ex-addict, did it hold you back from Martha?" Spider asked.

"It didn't hold me back. She knew about it already. Be open about it, and don't try to hide shit. What I've come to see with Martha, I keep secrets, she gets pissed. I don't, I get my dick sucked."

"So charming," Spider said.

"No problems. Enjoy your date tonight, and give Paris a hug from me." Dick left them alone, and he was humming as he went past as well.

"I don't think I like this relaxed attitude that everyone seems to have."

"You and me both," Butler said. "I don't want to deal with another enemy though. Another one pops up, and I'm on the road with the Nomads. People can fuck off if they think for a second that I'm going to allow that kind of shit."

Spider wasn't afraid of dealing with the enemy, but he'd rather not have to. He rather looked forward to the coming years of being able to relax, and enjoy the carefree attitude of going all legit. He was tired of being on the road during the long drives of transporting coke or guns. Being out of that business was more than good for him.

Several brothers stopped him on the way out, to wish him luck.

He accepted their lucks, and hoped he could give Paris a good night. It would be the first time they were together, alone, on a date. A lot of pressure but he was more than happy to deal with it.

Shaking Butler's hand, he made his way out into the freezing cold, and started up his car. It was cold, but not snowing, not yet. Once snow hit, getting out was going to be tough.

Driving toward Paris, he kept consoling himself that he was doing the right thing. That he was good enough for Paris, and Andrew wasn't going to take any more time away from them.

Parking outside her house, he turned the ignition off, and climbed out.

Going to her front door, he knocked, and waited.

Paris opened the front door, and words left him. Her hair was bound in a loose, looped braid at the back of her head. The black gown molded to her curves in ways that he hadn't imagined correctly. Her tits were pushed up, showing the mounding tops, and large cleavage. She looked … stunning. The diamond earrings and necklace only added to her class.

"Hey," she said. "Is it too much?"

"It's perfect. You look like a dream. A vision."

She reached out, grabbing her jacket. "Are we ready to go?" she asked.

Jessica, Mia, Brianna, and Judi came into view behind her. They were smiling at him, looking a little scary as they did.

"Yes, I'm ready to go. I'll have her back before midnight."

"Okay. We look forward to it."

Paris put on a jacket and followed him out. "Do I need to get my purse?" she asked.

"Not a chance. Tonight is all on me."

"It doesn't have to be."

"I want it to be. Please, let me do this one romantic thing for you."

"Okay." He helped her toward the passenger side of the car, and opened the door, letting her inside. "I'm really nervous, and a little excited."

"Me too. My hands are sweating." He held them out for her to touch. "It's cold out, and I'm sweating."

"We can make this good for both of us."

"Yes, we can."

Closing the door, he rounded the car.

You can do this, Spider.

You love her, and you want to be everything for her.

Climbing behind the wheel, he started the car up, and pulled away from the curb.

"The dress is really beautiful. Thank you."

"You look amazing in it."

"Thank you. I was worried it might not fit, but it did, perfectly."

She rested her hands on her knees, and Spider took one, locking their fingers together. "So, any thoughts on what you want to be?"

"When I grow up?"

"I'd say you're already a grown up, but what do I know?"

She chuckled. "Thank you. I don't know. I was talking to Natalie, but it's kind of hard to get her advice. She knew from a young age she wanted to be a designer. She's amazing, too. I don't know what I want to be."

"You like writing, though."

"Yeah, I did like writing, and it kind of disappeared with looking after Celia, and then with work. It's not really inspiring taking your clothes off for a room full of men you don't know."

Spider smiled. "You captivated me."

"As much as I hated it, I'm pleased I did it."

"Why?"

"It got me to you, and for me, that is better than anything else. If I hadn't been stripping, you wouldn't have known I existed."

"And now we're here, heading toward our first official date."

"Where are we going?"

"You'll soon see."

The drive to the restaurant was fun, and he listened to her talk about college, and the future. Once they were outside the restaurant Paris paused. "Wow."

"Come on."

"This is really fancy."

"I know, and it's all for you." He got out of the car, and rounded to her side, taking hold of her hand. Spider handed the valet the keys, and he escorted her toward the maître d', who seated them in quick time.

He caught the arm of the maître d' as he was about to pull Paris's seat out for her. "I'll do that, thank you."

Paris smirked, and he smiled with her as he held her seat. She lowered herself down, and he helped her under the table. Kissing her shoulder, he rounded and thanked the man. They were handed some menus, and Spider ordered some water for himself, as did Paris. He had called ahead to make sure they were both allowed to order non-alcoholic drinks. When they were alone, he reached across the table to take her hand. "This is really fancy."

"I know. Do you think we stick out like sore thumbs?"

She looked around the room, and turned her attention back to him. "Nah, I think we blend in. How did you find this place?"

"Snake told me about it. He brings Jessica here on really special dates. He told me the food was delicious, which for Snake is saying something. He's not into French food."

"Well, I can't wait to try it. So tell me, Spider, what's new with you?"

"You want me to talk about me?"

"Yeah, I want to know what you've been doing."

"Did you know we bought a derelict old apartment building?"

"Yeah, Lexie was telling me about you refurbishing it or something."

"We're working from the ground up. The structure is still intact, and the foundations. It needs some love and care."

"That love and care falls to you?"

"Before becoming a Chaos Bleed, I was in construction. I know what to do, and this week I'm looking for a group of builders who are not only good, but are reliable, and ones that I can trust without fear of them ruining the building."

"Putting more work into Piston County?"

"We're not going anywhere, and the club intends to invest its future there as well."

"I'd like to see these apartments, if that's okay."

"I'll take you soon."

Their drinks arrived, and he watched as Paris took a sip of hers. "How did it go with Lola?"

She scrunched up her nose. "Not good. She's keeping a wide berth with technology. Her mother

wondered if I would be willing to have her come stay
with me for a few weeks. Lola had a bit of a breakdown.
One of the kids in the library handed Lola a cell phone
they had found, and it scared her. It sent her into a panic
attack so bad that they had to call the doctors to sedate
her. Lola called me not long after her mother, and asked
if she could come and stay with me."

"She okay?"

"She will be. I talked to her about it, and she
seemed kind of excited, and said she could talk to
someone else about how to set it up. I don't know. I think
if we got her involved in the clothing, trying stuff on, it
might inspire her a little more. What do you think?"

"I think that anything that allows Lola to heal will
be a good thing, and I'm standing beside you a hundred
percent to help you."

She gave him a full beaming smile. "Thank you."

"Anytime."

The date went without a hitch. They enjoyed
some wonderful steak with some creamy potatoes that
Spider couldn't remember the name of, nor pronounce.
The dessert was a chocolate mousse, which was divine.

At the end of the date, Spider took her to the
construction site for the apartments. There was a metal
cage around it, and several dump trucks, and equipment.

"Wow, that is huge," she said.

"There're over thirty floors, and each floor will
have a minimum of three apartments."

"Just three?"

"We're trying to decide if we should do smaller
one bed apartments, or two beds allowing for a start to a
family. You know, the luxury of space."

"I can see that. I've always lived in a house so I
haven't had to worry too much about space." They
leaned on the hood of his car, and he wrapped his arms

around her shoulders. "I love this, being with you."

"Great, does that mean I can take you out to the movies Friday night?"

"Yes, I've love that."

He cupped her cheek, stroking her soft, supple skin. Leaning in close, he pressed his lips to hers. That touch was enough, and Spider pulled back, staring into her eyes. "Let's get you home before you catch a cold."

****

Charlotte leaned against the wall as she listened to Gash play the piano. They had gotten their own place within Fort Wills, and he'd organized a piano. At first she had thought he was going a little crazy, but then she heard him play.

The song was a sad one yet filled with passion. Folding her arms, she listened to him, closing her eyes as the notes filled the room. They didn't have any neighbors close so neither of them had to worry about complaints.

"I didn't mean to wake you," Gash said when he stopped playing.

"It was beautiful. Did you dream about him again?"

Ever since he'd taken Andrew's life, Gash had been struggling with the guilt.

"No. I just wanted to play. I dreamed about you, about us."

"Gash, do you regret us being together?"

He glared toward her. "What?"

"I just, I was wondering if you blamed me, or if you wished you and I were not together anymore."

Gash left the piano and advanced toward her. He cupped her face, pulling her toward him. "The only thing I regret is not killing him sooner."

She licked her lips, holding onto his arms. "You've been so different."

"I'm relieved, Charlotte. We've shared our honeymoon with Sandy and Stink. I loved every second of it. I love being with you. You're my girl, always. I want us to have a baby."

"You're ready for that?"

"Aren't you?" he asked. "Charlotte, I love you, and that's never going to change. I want us both to move on. Do you regret being with me?"

"No, of course not."

"What do you say?"

"A baby?"

"Yeah, do you think you could handle us having a baby?"

Charlotte smiled at her man. A baby. One baby had been taken from them by Andrew, and with him gone, they'd be able to have another. A family, the start to a family. She was never told that she wouldn't be able to have another.

"Yes, I want a baby. I want us to be a family."

Gash leaned down, picking her up. Charlotte squealed, wrapping her arms around his neck, not wanting to let go. He always picked her up, and because she wasn't a slender woman, she worried that he was going to drop her.

"I love you playing the piano."

"You do?"

"Yeah, it makes me hot. My little musician. When did you learn?"

"A long time ago when I was a boy. Never cared for it but I find I enjoy it a lot more now."

She liked watching him play, and listening to him. A family, a future, she couldn't wait.

Chapter Twenty

In the weeks that followed, Lola came to stay with her, and it was nice to see her friend getting along so well with Celia. Paris continued to study, and she also started to write. It was just a random collection of words without any real thought to it, but she enjoyed it. Late at night when her sister was in bed, Lola had gone to sleep, and one of the brothers was playing on a video game, she'd sit on the sofa, eating ice cream, and writing.

Spider didn't take over from the guys in taking care of her. He had become her boyfriend, taking her dates, several times a week. She didn't pressure him, nor did she rush him to take the next step. They had gone to several good movies, enjoyed lots of dinners, and they always hung out when Lexie threw a large dinner for the whole of the Chaos Bleeds club. Spider was giving her a romance that she never thought she'd have. He took his time, and he came to see her often. Celia adored him as they shared breakfast plenty of times.

Memories of Andrew invaded her when she least expected it, but she found that his hold on her mind was starting to fade. There had been more time away from him now. She was a stronger woman now, and Andrew, he'd failed.

With Lola visiting, she had to get used to being around Spider, and a few of the Chaos Bleeds men.

At first Lola was a little skittish around him, but then she was skittish around the whole of the club. Not really knowing what to do with her, Mia got her a job at the diner in town where there was no risk of her ever having to deal with modern technology.

Lola was a complete technology buff, and that had been taken from her.

She still refused to do the online thing, and so far,

her being able to talk them through setting one up had been a complete failure.

Natalie, three weeks before Christmas, hoped to have several of the outfits ready to show to Lola. Paris had told Lexie and the girls her plan of getting Lola involved. This wasn't just about getting them on the internet. Yes, if they could get Lola past her fear, it benefited them, but Paris wanted her friend to be happy in life. If she was constantly hiding, then she wasn't living her life.

The colleges that Lola had once been planning to attend had withdrawn their scholarship. She was working as a waitress, refusing to take a chance at a future. Spider believed her plan could work, and he understood why she needed to do it.

"How are my two favorite girls?" Sinner asked, coming into the kitchen. Lola was looking through a Christmas recipe book, and Paris was finishing her latest batch of cookies.

Lola's cheeks went a deeper shade of red, and she mumbled a response, ducking her head into her book. *Weird*.

Paris smiled. "Are The Skulls visiting for Christmas?"

"Some of them are. Stink, Sandy, Gash, and Charlotte are taking a Christmas vacation somewhere. Apparently they all had such a good time that they're going off to do it again. Lash and Angel are having a private affair this year."

"Who's coming?" Paris asked.

"Tiny and his lot. Whizz and his lot. He wanted to come and see you, Lola."

"Why?"

"I don't know. He had a gift for you. I don't know what that is. Steven is coming as well. Everyone else is staying at home or something like that. It has been a long year for us all. I don't know about you ladies, but I'm looking forward to the next year. I'm fucking exhausted."

"Remember, if Simon's around, that swear jar will be there as well," Paris said.

"Not a chance. The swear jar only comes out when it's him. Tabitha coming to visit, kid won't even be thinking straight. Last I checked, he's getting Lex to teach him to bake. It's fucking funny watching that kid fall head over heels."

Paris had witnessed firsthand that kid's love over Tabitha. The Skulls were going to come during Thanksgiving, but with Tabitha being sick, The Skulls had decided to stay at home for Thanksgiving. Simon had been in a mood all day, not talking to anyone. She'd felt bad for the little boy.

"How are we on Christmas presents?" Paris asked.

"I spoke to my parents. They're going on a cruise so I'll be staying here. I hope that is okay."

"More the merrier," Sinner said. "There's usually several large turkeys cooked up. A ham, it's going to be a tasty Christmas. I can already feeling the pounds adding to my ass."

Paris smiled as she saw Lola blush. Yeah, Lola had a little crush.

"I'm going shopping later with Spider. I want to get the last few bits for my Christmas shopping," Paris said.

"Excellent, I've gotten everything," Sinner said, looking at Lola. "And I got something for you so I expect a gift in return. I do give to receive."

"I have brought you something. I just need to finish it off."

"I'm free tomorrow afternoon. Do you want to do that?" Sinner asked.

"Sure."

"Right, I'm going to head on over to the clubhouse for a little bit. You two good?"

"Yeah, more than good."

It had been over six months since Andrew's death, and life had gotten so damn good. Paris found herself smiling more than ever now. Once the last of the cookies was done, she made her and Lola a drink, and together they headed into the sitting room. Celia was at school, and her sister was flourishing being around others.

"So, do you have a little crush on Sinner?" Paris asked.

"God, is it so easy to see that?"

"It's not easy. Nah, that's a lie. You blush every time he looks at you."

"I don't mean it. It's not like he'd ever look at a girl like me."

"Girl like you?"

"I'm not exactly beautiful, and I'm a nerd."

"Can't be a nerd unless you touch a computer."

"And I can't do that, so I guess I'm just miserable and ugly."

"Hey!" Paris glared at her friend. "You're not ugly. Stop calling yourself that, and what's with all the negativity?"

"I'm sorry. I'm just having a bad day."

"Why?"

"I know what you guys are hoping for with me trying on those clothes, and it's not going to happen."

Paris ate her cookie and licked her lips of the few remaining crumbs. "Look, we want you to have a good time. You love technology. You spent your whole life perfecting what you do, and all of a sudden you're going to stop doing what you love for one stupid guy."

"I have the same talk with myself over and over. I just, I can't do it."

"Then don't worry about it. I'm not going to lie to you pretend we're not hoping it will inspire you. We are hoping that. You deserve to be happy, and being a computer nerd makes you happy. However, if that doesn't happen, then boo on us. We still want you to have fun, trying on new clothes. You can't deny that Natalie is the bomb of new clothes."

"I do. Do you think she and Sinner have something going on? I have noticed him talking to her a lot."

Paris thought about it and cringed. Shit, she had seen something between the two. "I don't know."

"You do know. It's okay. I can understand."

Blowing out a breath, Paris turned to her friend. "I know they're friends, and that they get along. There's more men out there, you know. You know you don't have to go for the first man that looks at you."

"I'm not. It's okay."

"I think Natalie is friends with everyone."

"It's okay, Paris. Don't worry about it."

Still, later that night hanging out with Spider going through the mall, she couldn't get it off her mind.

"What's troubling you?"

"Do you think Natalie and Sinner have a thing going on?"

"No. They're friends. Natalie is the same with everyone, even Slash, Dick, and Reese. Why?"

"Lola has a crush on Sinner."

"He knows."

"What?" Paris asked, holding onto Spider's arm. "How does he know?"

"When a girl blushes and struggles to talk to you, you kind of know. Sinner has already spoken to me about it. He thinks it's cute, and sweet."

"He doesn't like her?"

"I didn't say that. Lola is still … damaged by what happened. She's also young. She turns nineteen after Christmas."

"I hadn't thought about that."

"I've seen Natalie with the guys. She's nice, but again, she's not overly nice to them."

Thinking about it, Paris did see that. Natalie was nice to everyone.

"I don't know why I was worrying."

"You care, and that's a good thing. It's good to care."

****

Paris sipped her orange juice as she watched Natalie organizing the dresses. Lola was relaxing as all the girls drank and had some fun. Lexie came to sit with her. She was only just starting to show a little bump, as were the other women.

"How is the dating going with Spider?"

"It's slow, but I'm loving it."

"You're taking it slow, and that is a good thing."

Paris didn't feel under any kind of pressure, and her time with Lola, Spider, working, and being part of Chaos Bleeds, were healing a wound she thought was never there. Annie hadn't helped, not at all. She'd stopped visiting her therapist over a month ago as it was a waste of both of their time.

"Lola's flourishing while she's living with you."

"We're not coddling her, and I think that is good. She can even sit with me when I'm on the laptop. It's good." The first night she'd had the laptop, Lola had disappeared to the other side of the room. It made for a

323

really uncomfortable experience, and not one Paris hoped to ever repeat.

"Whizz wants to spend a little time with her. He's got something he hopes will help."

"Good. I can't wait to see what it is."

Lola came out, and the little fashion show for themselves was startling. Natalie fitted the clothes to each woman, making careful adjustments to make sure they fit just right. Paris noticed several bruises along Natalie's arm, and started to worry about her.

When Natalie made her way toward the bathroom, Paris followed her in.

"It's going great, don't you think? The clothes have come out really good."

"They're amazing. I'll be trying a few on myself. Where did you get your bruises from?"

Natalie looked straight at the bruises. "Ranching. Got caught by a damn calf who went all skittish on me today. Damn things hurt. I tell you, ranching is not the same as designing. However, you still get injuries from that." She held her fingers up, which showed a little blood from the pins she'd been putting into the clothes. "Ouch."

"You'd tell us if something bad was going on, right?"

"Paris, not everything is bad in the world that is going on. Ranching is hard work. It's labor intensive, and it can leave a lot of bruises. Honestly, I wouldn't allow anything bad to happen to me. My parents are the best."

She watched Natalie leave to join the others, and she cursed her own stupidity. Since the crap that went down with Andrew, she'd been seeing the bad side to everything. Staring in the mirror at her reflection, she had to wonder if she would ever be normal. Not only that, would there ever be a time when she'd be able to accept

Spider into her bed? They were taking it slow, and when the time came for more, she hoped she was there, right there with him.

****

Stink waited outside of the hospital for Sandy. She had returned to work part time, and he always made sure that he was there to pick her up. Staring at his wedding band, Stink smiled, recalling married life with his woman. She had been so skittish, almost afraid to commit to him. In a couple of weeks, they would be heading to Piston County for Christmas. Several of the guys were going, and Stink had decided to go with Sandy.

This was their first real Christmas together as a couple, and he wanted it to be a memorable experience. He'd purchased a bracelet for her, and some matching earrings. He'd already wrapped them up. If he didn't wrap them he'd be tempted to give them to her.

Sandy came out of the main doors, and the moment she saw him, she smiled, rushing toward him. Holding out his arms, he caught her up in them.

"I missed you," she said.

"I missed you, too." He kissed her neck, pulled away, and stared into her eyes.

"What are you thinking?" she asked.

"I'm thinking I'm the luckiest man in the world."

Sandy bit her lip. "I always know what to give my man."

He wrapped his arms around her, and together they walked out toward his car. It was already freezing cold, and the moment they hit the cold air, Sandy shivered.

"I love Christmas," she said.

"You do?"

"Yeah. When I was a kid my parents used to find

ways of hiding my presents so that the whole day of Christmas was spent with me hunting for them." Sandy smiled. "I'll never forget how happy I was."

"Well, we're heading to Piston County this year, and we're going to have a lot of fun."

"Whizz has a surprise for Lola, doesn't he?"

"Yeah, he wants to help the poor girl." Stink turned over the engine in the car, and made his way back toward their house. Whenever he thought about Lola, he always found himself feeling sad.

"I can't imagine being so totally affected by something that I just stop touching stuff. She has nothing to do with technology. Nothing."

Stink had heard about the damage that Andrew had done. Even now, months after Andrew's death, he still affected them in different ways. They were slowly getting over it, evolving, but there were moments where he invaded. Those moments for Stink, were the worst. Only the person who was thinking about him, could fight those memories.

"Whizz will help her. If anyone can, it's him."

****

Christmas was a loud, and yet very quiet affair at the Chaos Bleeds clubhouse. There was enough space for the visiting families, and Spider was happy to see Sally slowly healing. She was wearing a prosthetic and using crutches at the same time. He'd heard Lacey telling Lexie that this was the second prosthetic as the other hurt her too much. Still, Sally looked a lot better than the last time he saw her. He couldn't say the same about Steven, who looked fucking angry. Spider had to wonder why Steven had even turned up, but hearing him talk about a certain male friend called Drew, he'd already figured it out.

Steven had a thing for Sally, he cared about her,

and she had a thing for Drew, or at least, that was what he summed it up to.

When Lola, Paris, and Celia joined them all, it was complete for Spider. He placed his arm across Paris's shoulders, chatting with the club. In the corner there was a large tree, with what looked like hundreds of presents beneath it. Tabitha and Simon were dancing to a Christmas song. There was music and laughter, and peace. Yeah, peace was a big one for him, and for the whole of the club. It wasn't something he'd known all that much, yet in recent months, it had happened. Lola was talking with Sinner, and he watched as the brother placed his arm around her shoulders, kissing her temple. It was a sweet movement. Whizz moved up to talk to Lola, and Spider made his way over as well. Sinner was holding her still, and he was curious to know what the gift was that Whizz wanted to give her.

"How have you been, Lola?" Whizz asked.

"I'm doing okay."

"Any computer work?"

Lola glanced at the floor, shaking her head. "Not yet. I don't really need it. I work at the diner, and I'm getting by."

From what Paris told him, Lola hated working at the diner. She hated lecherous drunks with their suggestive comments, kids who vomited everywhere, cleaning, and serving rude customers. She hated being a waitress.

"I think you're missing your calling," Whizz said. "Now, I don't want to pressure you into anything, but I want you to look through this when you have a chance." Whizz handed her a neatly wrapped package.

"What is it?"

"That's for you to know when you're ready to open it. I think you have a right to see what's inside."

Lola licked her lips and stared at the present. "I'll take it upstairs."

She turned toward the main stairs. With Christmas being at the clubhouse, they all had their rooms there. Spider doubted they'd get much sleep, but it would be worth it. He liked watching the kids open their presents.

"I've gotten you a few presents. They're underneath the tree."

"Let's hope Santa doesn't take them then. That's where presents always come from, Santa."

"Does Celia believe that?"

"Yeah, and it seems wrong to change her views. She's going to be forever the same age. Why should I ruin her magic?"

"We're not going to." He kissed her temple, and enjoyed having her in his arms. In the last few months they had made real progress. There might even be a time soon where they could take their relationship to the next level. He wasn't going to force her though. The last thing he ever wanted to do was force her to do something she didn't want to do.

****

Sitting on the bed in the clubhouse, Lola stared down at the wrapped package. She didn't know exactly what it was, but knowing Whizz it was something to do with computers. Her hands were sweaty, and her stomach tightened as she stared at it. Life had been a lot easier when she didn't have to deal with technology. Sitting beside Paris as she typed was more than enough for her. Yes, it wasn't the life she had planned. She'd wanted to be a code breaker, or a designer, or something to do with software that put the years of her understanding code, into use.

Andrew had taken that away from her, and now

she served food to crappy customers. She had to wonder if Paris had put the customers up to treating her bad, just to try to help her. Then she'd felt stupid. People were crappy because they wanted to be crappy, and it didn't matter what she did or said. They'd find fault with whatever she did.

There was a knock on her door, and she called for them to come in. Sinner's head came around the door.

"It's Christmas, and you're invited to join."

"I'll be down in a minute." She smiled. It was easier to talk to him now. She didn't know why. He was always nice to her, but at least she didn't suffer with constantly getting a red face.

"Do you want to talk about it?" he asked.

"It's just a gift."

"From a fellow computer genius like you."

He took a seat with the wrapped present between them.

"I never thought this would be so hard."

"How about we make a deal," he said.

"A deal?"

"You open your present for me, and when you're ready, I'll kiss you."

She looked into his eyes to see if he was joking. "Kiss me?"

"Yes."

"You don't have to kiss me. I don't need something like that."

"Lola, open the present. Stop letting him win."

She picked up the present and slowly started to remove the wrapping. It was a box, and lifting up the box, she found a folder. Opening it up, Lola saw pictures of herself. Her very first computer, to Christmases of where her parents had bought her books on computers, exactly what she asked for. Flicking through the pages, she saw the awards she had for work that had come from her skills. It went all the way up including her scholarship letter, and then the coded message she had sent to Whizz for Paris.

At the end was a little message.

Computers are used for many things. You have a gift, Lola. Use that gift to help others just like I do. Whizz.

Tears filled her eyes, and she closed the folder, holding it close. "My parents helped him with this."

"It was a good present."

She nodded. "Very good."

Lola knew in that moment, she would try. It wasn't much, but she'd try to gain what had been lost to her. "I'm ready to go down now." Leaving the folder on the bed, she got to her feet, and made her way toward the door.

Sinner grabbed her arm, stopping her, and spinning her around.

"What's the matt—"

His lips silenced her, and all protest died as he pressed her up against the door. He sank his hand into her hair, and held her tightly as he claimed her lips. Lola melted against him, loving the feel of him against her, surrounding her.

When it was over, he rested his head against hers.

"You didn't have to do that."

"I wanted to."

Chapter Twenty-One

It had been a year since she was taken, and Paris was stronger than ever. She had finished her first year of English, and had decided that becoming an author was indeed something she wanted to pursue. She loved writing stories, but she didn't know if she was any good at it. Lola had decided to stay with her, and in the past few months, had gone from simply touching a computer to working on it.

She hadn't gone for her scholarship. Instead, Lola was studying at an online course. They both were. There was something going on between Lola and Sinner, but Paris wasn't sure exactly what it was. She did think they were sleeping together, but she couldn't be sure as they both played it cool around her. Andrew's hold over her had started to decline. His place in her thoughts grew less and less with every single passing day.

Talking with Lola, The Skulls old ladies, and Chaos Bleeds she felt so much more in control of her own path, her own destiny.

The dates with Spider were amazing, and she loved hanging out with him. It was the height of summer, and Celia was with Lexie and Devil for the day. The whole club had taken her in and treated her like part of the family.

Getting the lawnmower out, Paris stood outside of her backyard, and whimpered as she saw the overgrown grass, weeds, and bushes that were invading. She had been putting it off because she hated gardening more than anything else in the world.

What she hated more than gardening was being left alone with her thoughts, and right now, Spider was plaguing her.

Starting up the mower, she began to cut the grass.

It didn't take long for the compartment thingy to fill up, which meant she had to empty it.

Trying to run from her thoughts with Spider didn't help, nor did mowing. At Christmas she'd been worried about not being ready to take the relationship to the next level. Now, she was wondering if they were ever going to do anything more. He didn't even kiss her, not passionately. The sweet brush of the lips was actually annoying the hell out of her. Overnight it seemed her body had woken up to needs, and now demanded to be sated. Only there was no sating going on, nothing. Lola looked like she was getting more satisfaction than her, which made her pause. Sinner was fucking Lola? It was all so confusing to her. She preferred her life when she didn't have to worry about anyone or anything, apart from her sister.

At this rate, Simon was going to get more than she was.

Spider might not be ready. Hell, *she* might not be ready, but she wanted something more than a chaste kiss every night.

Replacing the compartment thingy, she got to work mowing the lawn, which was fucking tiring.

"I hate fucking gardening. Useless excuse for land. I hate you. Why can't you just mow yourself," she said.

"Wow, you really have it in for that garden," Spider said.

Oh, don't even start on me, Spider. I will tear you to shreds.

Pausing, she glanced over at him, only to get angry. He wasn't wearing his leather jacket, and the shirt he had on highlighted how thick and defined his muscles were.

Not fair. Even his shirts get more action than I

do.

I'm cursed to be a lonely person.

"Have I done something to upset you?" Spider asked.

Taking a deep breath, and hoping she didn't lose it at him, Paris turned to look at him. "Why would you think that?"

"You haven't spoken to me."

"I just talked to you. Maybe you need to clean your ears out." Turning on the mower once again, she started cutting the grass. Only she had to stop, to empty the stupid compartment thingy again. Lifting up while holding the grass smelling thingy, she was stopped by Spider suddenly being in front of her. "What the hell are you doing? Are you just trying to irritate me?"

"I'm not doing anything, but I'm curious what has you in this attitude."

"Attitude. I don't have any attitude. You're in my way, and I'm trying to mow my lawn. It's what people do."

"Then what's with the attitude?"

"I don't have an attitude!" She yelled the words.

"You know what, I think your problem is the fact I haven't touched you."

"Touched me? That would be a laugh. At best I get a little feel of your lips every now and again. I'm surprised if you even know what a damn kiss is."

Spider laughed. "My brothers warned me about this. They said if I wasn't careful I was going to send you into a fucking meltdown, and it has happened."

"It doesn't matter. You don't want me."

He took another step toward her, and she craned her neck to look into his eyes. "Wanting you has never been the problem."

"You have a funny way of showing it."

"You want to me to fuck you, is that it?"

"Yeah, I do, but it doesn't matter because you're not man en—"

Spider lifted her up, making her drop the basket full of grass.

"What are you doing? Put me down right now. I mean it, Spider. You had your chance every single time we've been on date night."

He entered the house, without saying a word, locking the door, and then moving her up toward her bedroom.

"Damn it, Spider. You're so annoying. Now you think you can do what you want, and I'm just going to accept that?"

"Nothing about accepting it."

He carried her upstairs, and even through her anger, she was excited. This side of Spider was what she'd been hoping for. She'd been watching love stories with really hot sex scenes, even that one with the billionaire boss who was into BDSM. That man could do her any day. Of course, every time she played with herself, she thought about Spider. He was the only one she wanted, the only one that ever brought her to orgasm.

Yes, she had been so desperate for Spider, she'd started to touch herself on a nightly basis.

She wanted him so much.

It was time.

He kicked open her door, and even that gave her a thrill to witness. Her body was on fire, and when he closed the door, pressing her up against it, Paris gasped.

"What are you doing?" she asked.

"I'm taking what belongs to me." He took hold of her arms, pressing them above her head.

"Why? You haven't done it yet."

"I've been waiting for this moment. I bet your

pussy is like fire, isn't it? You want me, baby?"

"Yes, please, Spider, I want you so much."

He slammed his lips down on hers, silencing her. It was everything she thought it would be, maddening, passionate, and full of love. Spider pressed her hands above her head, holding both of hers in one of his. He caressed down her arms, and she moaned as his hand hovered above her breast.

"Do you want me to touch you, or are you still mad?"

He was becoming less annoying as he kissed and touched her.

"I want your hands on me, please, Spider, don't stop."

Spider had pulled away from her long enough to talk. His lips crashed back down on hers at the same time his hand cupped her breast through her shirt. His thumb ran across her nipple.

She was so sensitive, and she wanted more. Pushing herself against him, she tried to get closer to him. Spider wouldn't have any of it. He pressed his body flush against her so that she felt every single inch of him against her.

"Do you think it has been easy for me?" he asked, breaking the kiss, to trail his lips down to her ear.

Closing her eyes, Paris bit her lip, loving every part of him surrounding her.

"Yes, you haven't touched me."

"You haven't been ready for me to touch you. What kind of a man would I be if I forced myself on you?"

"I wanted you, Spider."

"Not enough to tell me what you want. I've waited so long for you." He bit her neck, making her gasp once again.

Her body woke up for his touch, and she didn't want it to stop.

Suddenly, he stepped back. "Show me you want it," he said.

"How?"

She wasn't sure how she was supposed to show him.

"Take my clothes off, and then strip for me."

Once again he was making himself vulnerable in order to make her relax.

She stepped toward him. He wasn't wearing his leather cut, but then, it was hot outside. Tugging his shirt up, he held his arms up so that she could remove it with ease. His arms, chest, and as she circled his back, she saw that it was covered in ink as well. Each of his muscles bulged, and he was defined. Once she was in front of him, Spider took her hand and placed it against his stomach. "Touch me. I belong to you."

Stepping close, she put both of her hands on him, and glided them up, staring at each of his tattoos before staring him in the eye. "You're beautiful."

"No, babe, I'm sexy as fuck. You're beautiful."

She chuckled. "I want you."

"Baby, I've been desperate for you, but for reasons you know, and why I'm not bringing them up, I had to wait for you."

"You care about me so much."

"No, I don't care about you. That's not a strong enough word for what I feel for you. I love you. I love you so fucking much, and I can't bear for anything bad to happen to you."

"You love me?"

"Yeah, I love you, more than anything, I love you." He cupped her cheek, tilting her head back, and kissing her lips. "So I was waiting for you to be ready."

"I love you, too, Spider. Every single day from the moment you first creeped me out behind the strip club. I love you, and I want to spend the rest of my life with you."

"What about the club life?" he asked.

"What about it?"

"Not every woman loves the club life."

"It's a good job I'm not most women. Chaos Bleeds, they're my family, and I love them, just as I love you." She rested her head against his. "They're part of my life as well, and I'm happy about that. There's no one else that I want in my life."

Reaching down, she took hold of his belt, and started to open it.

"You have a one track mind."

"You're in my bedroom. Nothing else is going to happen for me. I want you naked with me, inside me, and making me scream and beg for more."

"Well, baby, your wish is more than my command."

She pulled the belt from his jeans and opened the button, sliding down the zipper. Going to her knees, she pulled his jeans down. Through his boxer briefs, she saw the outline of his rock hard cock. Damn, he was huge. She didn't doubt for a second he would be, but even hiding he was pretty impressive.

"Do you like what you see?"

"Hell, yeah. I can't wait until I get you naked."

He kicked off his shoes and pushed his jeans aside. When she made to take his boxer briefs, he stopped her, lifting her to her feet.

"I was hoping to get my mouth on you."

"That will come, baby. First, I want my mouth on you."

Before he had even finished she started to tug her

shirt over her head. He gave a little chuckle. "I haven't been doing well with my duties."

Paris didn't speak. She couldn't find the words, and her hands were shaking. Removing her shorts, she stood before him in her underwear alone. Spider didn't keep her waiting. He banded his arm around her waist and pulled her close.

"Do you have any idea how sexy, hot you look?"

"No, I don't. You're going to have to keep on telling me."

"I will. You've got nothing to worry about there. I'm going to tell you every single day, how hot you look, how beautiful. You're all mine." He sank his fingers into her hair, slamming his lips down on hers.

She opened her mouth, sliding her tongue against his lips, hoping he'd get the hint that she wanted him to open up, to take what he wanted.

Spider plunged his tongue into her mouth, and she followed his direction, kissing him back.

His hands glided down her throat, then to her shoulders where he fingered the strap of her bra.

Achingly slowly, he started to move the straps down her shoulders until they fell to the elbows. Still kissing her, he reached behind her, flicking the catch. Her tits sprang free, and Spider pulled away, removing her bra as he did.

"So fucking perfect." He swiped his thumb across an erect peak, and she shivered from the touch.

"Is it too much?"

She shook her head. "Please don't stop. I never want you to stop."

"I'm not going to stop. Not now, not ever. This is for the rest of our lives, Paris."

His words meant everything to her. Spider kissed her lips, and then leaned down, capturing one of her nipples. She cried out as he sucked hard, and then eased out the pain with a flick of his tongue. The pleasure went straight to her clit. She closed her legs tightly, hoping to keep the pleasure up.

Spider gripped her hips, and turned her so that her back was to her bed. He moved her back, and she fell down.

"Lie back."

Lowering herself to the bed, she kept her gaze on him. The fire in his eyes made her tingle all over.

"There's no way I could ever walk away from you, Paris. I've wanted you from the first moment I saw you, and that's never going to stop. All that keeps happening is the way I feel about you deepens."

He knelt on the floor and spread her legs. With one yank, he tore her panties from her body, leaving her bare, exposed, and wet.

****

The dusting of hair on her pussy was slick with her arousal. Spreading open Paris's lips, he saw the swollen nub of her clit and her slicked entrance. The scent of her only further aroused him.

Sliding his tongue through her cream, he moaned. She tasted so good, better than he imagined, and he'd been doing a lot of imagining. Ever since they started going out, he had made her wait, not allowing her to have more. He wanted her to be ready, and the only way to be sure of that was by waiting for her to take the next step. Spider was ready, but he wasn't going to force her, or pressure her to take things to the next level.

One of the last conversations he'd had with Annie was about taking his time, and making sure that Paris was ready.

She was part of his life, and even if she was never ready for sex, he'd be fine with that. He loved her, and being part of her life was enough for him.

To him, knowing she was now ready to the point she was frustrated was just a bonus. Now, he was going to make sure that this first time with her, was going to be the best time that anyone could have. He was going to wipe all memory of Andrew from her mind.

He'd seen the change in her, the development. She was a lot happier, and there was no darkness in her eyes, only happiness. Her part in the club was easy to see. The women loved having her, and especially now that they were all due to drop any minute.

Sucking her clit, he moaned as the taste of her cream filled his mouth. She was so wet, musky, and perfect. Sliding his tongue down, he fucked it inside her, watching as she gripped the sheets beneath her. He checked to make sure she wasn't having any doubts.

She started to thrust her pelvis up against his mouth, moaning his name as she did.

"Do you like that, baby?" he asked.

"Please, don't stop. It's perfect, please."

"Don't worry. I have no intention of stopping." Releasing the lips of her pussy, he coated two fingers in her wetness, and teased one finger inside her. She moaned, trying to thrust down on his digit. Taking her clit, he caused a little pain, which stopped her from moving anymore. "I'm the one in charge."

"It feels so good."

"I know it does. It's going to feel even better before I'm done." Soothing out the pain with his tongue, he teased her clit with light strokes. At the same time, he plunged one finger inside her, finding her so incredibly tight. Pumping in and out of her, he slowly started to add a second finger but being careful the whole time not to hurt her.

She kept on thrusting on his fingers, trying to get

him to go deeper.

"I need more."

With two fingers, he twisted them around until he found the beautiful G-spot, and started to stroke. He tongued her clit, flicking his tongue across, around, and over. When that wasn't enough, he sucked it into his mouth, loving the way her pussy tightened around his finger as he did.

Glancing up, he saw her looking down. Her eyes were dilated, and her chest flushed with her arousal.

"Do you like what I'm doing?" he asked.

"Yes, much better than myself."

"Have you tried to finger this pussy?"

She nodded. "I needed to. It was hard being with you, and you'd only touch me. I had to do something."

"You come to me. That's what you do. Every time you want something, sex, my mouth, my fingers, you come to me, no one else, not even yourself. Is that clear?"

"Yes, Spider. So clear."

"Good."

"What if you're busy?"

"Paris, I'll always make time for you. There won't be a time for me to be too busy for you."

He saw that smile, and it lit up his whole world. She was worth it, and he needed for her to see that, to understand that she was his entire world.

When he'd teased her enough, and knew she needed that blessed release, he sucked her clit, fucking her pussy with his fingers. He felt the change inside her, the way her body tightened around his digits, squeezing him tightly. Her cream soaked his hand, and he teased her clit.

She started to pant, and he had her at the mountain of pleasure. Instead of holding her there, balanced and poised, he flung her over the edge.

Paris came, screaming his name, flooding his fingers with her release so that some of her cream leaked down the crack of her ass.

Spider wasn't done though. This was about her, so even as she was panting from her first release, he didn't stop. Driving her toward a second orgasm, Spider flicked her clit lightly, knowing that she'd be sensitive but also wanting her to plunge into another orgasm just as quickly.

"What are you doing?" she asked. "Oh, wow, there's no way I can have another one."

Each word she was breathless as he drove her toward that second orgasm. He didn't stop, and she crashed over, screaming his name, and rising up to hold his head against her clit.

In that moment, Spider knew that Andrew's hold on them had ceased. Paris was his woman once again, and no one was going to hold them back.

It was a joyous occasion, and he wasn't going to spoil it by pointing out the obvious.

Standing up, he removed his boxer briefs, allowing his cock to spring forward, to show how happy he was to see everyone.

"Wow," she said. "I knew you were big."

"You haven't seen anything yet, baby."

Crawling up her body, he stopped at her breasts, sucking them into his mouth.

"That was amazing."

"Ah, you're finally going to compliment me."

"Do you need compliments?" she asked, giggling.

"They go a long way in helping a guy see what he's done right."

"Why didn't you stop?"

Spider didn't answer until he took her other

nipple into his mouth, sucking it hard. "I wanted you to be so totally wet, and to blow your whole world."

"You blew my world."

He reached down grabbing his cock.

"Can I touch you?" she asked.

Taking hold of her hand, he wrapped her fingers around his length.

"It's so soft, and hard. Kind of weird."

He laughed. "Don't go telling guys their dicks are weird."

"It's not a bad-weird, just different." She ran her hand up and down his shaft, and he watched her gaze on him, turning him on even more.

Out of the tip a little pearl of pre-cum escaped, and she swiped it with her thumb, rubbing it into the head.

His balls were incredibly tight, and even with her hand on him, he was struggling to keep it together.

"Paris, from the first moment I saw you, there hasn't been another woman."

"No woman, not even when I was stripping?"

"Like I said. You've been the only woman I've wanted."

"Thank you."

He chuckled. "There's a reason I'm telling you this."

"What's the reason?"

"When I start, I may not last all that long."

This time, she chuckled. "You have no control?"

"I have control, and our second time together will be a lot better. This first time, you've got no chance."

"I won't judge no matter how long you last," she said.

"That's good. I want you to have a very high opinion of me. So wait until after this first time to judge me."

He'd never spoken so much during sex.

She caught his face, holding on to him, and kissed his lips. "Spider, make love to me."

Spider moved her up the bed so that her head was amongst the pillows. He didn't miss her long locks of hair. The short cut did it for him.

"What are you thinking?" she asked.

"I don't miss your hair."

"My hair?"

"I did once think about it fanned out across the pillows, but now, I like this cut. It's sexy, and totally you."

Taking possession of her lips, he slid his tongue into her mouth. Reaching between them, he gripped his cock, and worked the tip, sliding it between the lips of her pussy. He bumped her clit, causing her to moan with each touch. She held onto his waist, and he looked down between them to see his cock resting between her slit, the tip leaking a trail of pre-cum.

Unable to hold back any longer, he gripped the base, and found her pussy. Sliding the tip in, Spider returned his gaze to her.

"Make me yours," she said.

He was so hard that with the tip inside her, he didn't need to guide himself into her anymore. Holding her hands, locking them together, he slowly penetrated her, inch by glorious inch.

She gasped. Her mouth opened just a little, and he kissed her. When only a few inches remained, he slammed inside her, hearing her cry out his name, which was muffled by his lips.

"You own me now," he said.

"You own me as well. I'm yours."

Her pussy tightened around him, fluttering from

his penetration. He waited until she was ready, and then he withdrew a little, and started to thrust.

"Look down at us."

He followed her gaze, seeing his slick cock entering her pussy.

"We look good together."

Taking her lips, he fucked her harder. He knew he wasn't going to last, and was thankful that he'd made her come twice before being inside her.

"I'm so sorry," he said.

"It's okay."

He slammed within her, twice more, and groaned, holding her tightly as he filled her with his cum. Burying his head against her shoulder, he couldn't look at her.

"I'm a failure to all men." The orgasm had made his head thick. His entire body was tense.

Paris wrapped her arms around him, stroking his body.

He felt the tremors of her body, showing him that she was indeed laughing at the fact he'd come quickly.

"That was a, um, quick one."

Spider pulled back to look into her eyes. He saw the laughter in them, but also the love.

"You're going to tease me about this for a long time, aren't you?"

"A little bit. Yeah. Thank you for allowing me to have two orgasms."

"You're ahead of me. The next time, I'm going to be the one having you come again, and again, and again."

"Don't you need to pull out, have a rest?" she asked.

Spider shook his head. "I'm happy being inside you. I'm in no rush to leave you, and you'll know when I start to get ready again."

She raised her brow. "In that case, what would

you like to talk about?"

"Anything."

"I like you being inside me. I also thought your cock was very pretty."

"My cock is pretty?"

"Yep, one day I'm hoping to return the favor and put my mouth on you."

"I'd like that. I love your pussy. It's tight, sexy, and you taste amazing."

Her cheeks heated. "I do, do I?"

"Hell yeah, get ready because I'm going to be doing a lot of licking down there."

She started chuckling.

"I've missed this, us, talking."

"We never got to this point before. I kind of hate that it was taken from us."

"Yeah, we've got it back now, and we're closer than ever before." She stroked his cheek, and he watched her eyes go wide. "It doesn't take you long to start back up, does it?"

"Nope. I just needed to get that first one out of the way. It helps that you keep tightening around me. It feels so damn good."

She laughed, and Spider the proceeded to spend the next three hours bringing her to multiple orgasm as she screamed his name, begging for him to follow her into bliss.

He did, only when he couldn't hold it back any longer.

****

"We took it to the next level," Paris said, whispering into the phone. Spider was downstairs, getting them something to eat. She had quickly grabbed her cell phone, so excited about what had happened, and she put a call through to Lacey.

"You both had sex?"

"Total sex. Complete, and utter rapturous sex," Paris said. "It was amazing."

"Wow, I never for a second thought he'd give in to you."

"I know. I can't believe it. My body is just humming."

Lacey chuckled. "That means you've been well and truly fucked."

Paris ran a hand down her face. "I want to do it again. Is that wrong?"

"You're going to have to give Spider some time to get ready, but I don't see why he wouldn't want to. You're right there with him, and he's hot stuff, all right."

"Is it weird I wanted to tell you?"

"Honey, I'm pleased you did. After everything you've been through, I was worried about you."

"Why?"

Lacey paused. "I know what it's like to have your choices taken away. I understood what you went through, Paris. Coming back from what Andrew did to you, it takes time. Sometimes, it takes even longer than you can imagine."

"I was scared that I wouldn't be able to move on. That I wouldn't know how to love," she said.

"And now?" Lacey asked.

"Now, I'm tired of the moments when he still comes and visits me inside my head. It doesn't happen as often but it is still there, and it's hard."

"Paris, there will come a time when he almost disappears. There will be days, weeks, and months where you don't even give him a thought. Your life will move on. When he does appear, and he will, just remember, you're the strong one. You survived, and you're living to tell the tale again. No one else. This is all on you, and no one can take that away from you. Trust in Spider, and talk to him about how you feel."

"Do you talk with Whizz?"

"All the time. He's my rock, Paris."

She looked up to see Spider there carrying a plate.

"I've got to go."

"Have fun, have lots of sex."

Paris chuckled, hanging up the phone. "That was Lacey. She's a bit weird."

Spider chuckled. "You still have thoughts of Andrew?"

"Sometimes. They are fleeting, but they're there."

"What did Lacey say?"

"Talk to you about them. Don't hide them, and don't let them make you afraid. She talks to Whizz all the time about hers."

"I want you to share yours with me, Paris. I don't want you to hide them."

"I won't. I promise. My thoughts, and my fears, I'll share all of them with you."

Chapter Twenty-Two

Life got even more perfect for Paris. Spider moved in with her, and even though he stayed at the clubhouse from time to time, she loved him being there. Celia loved his company as well. What Paris loved even more was being his old lady. The girls had promised that after they gave birth, they were going to throw her a welcome party.

With all the chaos, and the enemies that they had to face, none of them had been given an old ladies' party. Lexie was determined to do one, even though it meant finding a competent babysitter for all of them.

Lola hadn't left either. In fact, she was seeing about either renting or buying one of the apartments that Spider was building. Paris had been to the construction site, and since they had some glorious sunshine, they were making excellent progress. In a month's time, after all kids were born, the clothing store, named Old Ladies MC, had hit a bit of a snag when Natalie had to take time off with her mother having a heart attack. The club was there, and even some of the guys had gone over to the ranch to help her father out. Arnold Pritchard had been more than thankful for their help. The club had helped him at a time when he was close to losing everything.

It made a lot of people in Piston County look bad when word got out that Chaos Bleeds helped to keep him afloat. Paris didn't do much. She cooked for the men, delivering them food, and making sure that Arnold and Natalie had enough so they didn't have to worry. She also made a point of going to the hospital to visit Natalie's mother, who was making steady progress.

The Skulls kept in touch. Paris had spoken to Sandy many times over the past few months, and discovered that she and Stink were expecting their first baby. The news had been a shock, a welcome shock, and they were preparing their house.

Paris had also decided to pursue English at her online college, also with the hope of one day becoming an author. She still wrote something every single day, and even though writing a full story was a long way off, it gave her hope.

Death and Brianna were the first to go into labor. Spider was deep inside Paris in the middle of the night when the call came through. Both of them had been worried, but Paris had made Spider go to the hospital. She couldn't leave Celia alone, and she didn't want to.

They had cut their lovemaking short, and Paris had been sitting at home, writing her story, and waiting for the news.

She snuggled up on the sofa, and was startled when Celia rounded the corner. "What's wrong, honey?"

"Can't sleep."

"Come on, come and cuddle up with me."

"Why are you awake?"

"I'm waiting on some news about a friend."

Celia lay down beside her, and Paris stroked her fingers through her sister's hair. Grabbing the remote, she turned on the television and put some cartoons on, enjoying the closeness with her sister.

It was toward six o'clock when Spider called.

"What's wrong?" Paris asked, the moment she picked up the phone.

"It's nothing to worry about. Brianna just had a long labor, and she wasn't fully dilated so they had to wait."

"Is she okay?"

"More than okay. They had a little girl, over nine pounds."

"Wow."

"Yeah, Death is beside himself, and so damn proud. I've been to see her, and she's beautiful. When Celia's at school tomorrow, I'll bring you to see her."

"Did they have a name for her?"

"Elisha."

"It's a perfect name."

"Yep. They're happy parents."

The following day, Paris was at the hospital seeing Brianna and Elisha when they heard that Judi had also fallen into labor. Paris stayed at the hospital, and went to see Judi afterward. She was told this pregnancy went a lot smoother than baby Paul.

Judi had a little boy, Channing. Paris was so happy. She was the first person after Mom and Dad to hold him. He was a strong boy.

A week later, she was picking Celia up from school when Spider called to say that Mia had given birth at her own home. There hadn't been enough time to get to the hospital. With Curse, the ambulance crew, and a great deal of improvisation, their baby, Ashley was born.

The last person to give birth was Lexie. She gave birth to Laurell at the clubhouse, one night. She'd been having contractions all through the night, and hadn't bothered to wake Devil up. When Lexie was close to giving birth, Spider had told her that she stayed at the clubhouse so that everyone could keep an eye on her. It was something that Devil demanded.

So, for everyone to see, in the main room of the clubhouse where they had Christmas dinner, Lexie had Devil helping her as she gave birth to a little girl. Four new babies to the fold, and a party was organized. Some of The Skulls came, including Whizz, who was happy to see that Lola was working on computers once again.

Paris stood outside near the barbeque as she watched the club mingle with The Skulls. They were both so fierce, and so loyal. She had to wonder why they had never joined the two clubs, and made a note to ask Spider about it one day.

Lola was chatting with Whizz, laughing at something he said, when Sinner came out of the club and stood close behind her. If Paris hadn't been watching them, she'd have missed it. Sinner caught Lola's hand, giving it a squeeze, before moving away.

He came toward her, and she sipped at her drink, smiling.

"Where's Celia?" he asked.

"She's over there, reading a book." Celia was on a bench, reading. The school she'd been going to had encouraged more learning skills, and because of it, Celia was able to learn new things. It was nice to see, and Paris was more than proud of her sister. "What's with the secret?" Paris said.

"What secret?"

"You and Lola. I don't see why you're not shouting about your relationship from the rooftops."

Sinner sighed. "She doesn't want to shout about it."

"Why not?"

"She's worried that I'm only interested her because she's new, and exciting."

"Wow, that's kind of harsh," she said.

"Also, I think she's planning to go to college later this year."

"Really?"

"I've seen her looking at applications, and when I bring it up, she changed the subject."

"That shouldn't be too hard."

"Do you know what I think?" Sinner asked.

"No, what do you think?"

"That I'm just for her to play with while she's

here, and now that she's had it, she's going back home."

"How can that be? Last time I heard, she was hoping to have one of those apartments that Spider is working on."

"You tell me. Spider even told me that he's given her a reservation form, and he hasn't got it back yet. He gave it to her over a month ago."

"Oh."

"Yeah, oh. Anyway, this reality sucks. I'm going to go and get another drink."

Paris watched him walk away, just as Lola came toward her. "Hey."

"Hey."

"It's nice to see everyone having a good time, don't you think?" Lola asked.

Staring at Sinner's retreating back, Paris turned to Lola, frowning. Sinner was hurting, and that was just hard to deal with. He'd been a real sweetheart to her. She couldn't allow him to go on hurting.

"What's happening with you and Sinner?"

"I don't know what you're talking about."

"Please, don't treat me like a fool. I've been here the whole time, and seen the little interaction between the two of you. What the hell is going on?"

Lola's cheeks were on fire. "We've been seeing each other."

"Newsflash, I already figured out that part. What I want to know is why he thinks you're using him? Are you?"

"No."

"Then what is it?"

"I don't know. I'm scared."

"What are you afraid of?"

"What if he doesn't like me?"

Paris shook her head, confounded by that.

"What?"

"I've been struggling, and what if he's only been sleeping with me out of pity?"

"Okay, you do know I'm talking about the same person here, right?"

Lola licked her lips. "He's sweet, kind, and caring. I get all of that, but, I don't know. He's different with me. Also, I got a letter a few weeks ago from the university that turned me down. They've seen some of the work I've been doing, and they'd like for me to have a chance at studying with them."

"What do you want to do?"

"I don't know. I've never had to make this decision before."

"I can't make this decision for you, Lola, nor can Sinner. This is something you've got to do all on your own."

Spider came up behind her, kissing her neck, and wrapping his arms around her waist.

"Hello, ladies."

"Hey, Spider," Lola said. "I've got to get a drink."

Paris sighed, watching her friend disappear inside. "What was all that about?"

"She's struggling to make a decision with the rest of her life, and it's hurting her and Sinner's relationship."

"Damn, I hope they can figure it out."

"You know?"

"Of course I know. Every brother knows what is going on. It explains why Sinner has been really crabby lately. He's got a woman, and he can't show her off, oh well." Spider turned her around. "How about you dance with me, woman?"

"Woman?"

"My woman. You do have my name on your

body."

Right above her heart, she'd gotten his name inked on her skin. She had enjoyed the experience so much that she already planned to get another one soon. "I'll dance with you."

"Good."

****

Lola didn't see Sinner in the kitchen, so she made her way up the back stairs toward his room. She knew where he slept as she had been there many times. He'd shattered her world in this clubhouse, taking her, and making her belong to him.

Knocking on the door, she gasped out as it flung up, and Sinner caught her, and pulled her in. He pressed her up against the door, caging her in.

"What the fuck is going on?" he asked.

"I don't know what you're talking about."

"Don't lie to me, Lola. A month ago Spider gave you the reservation papers, and you've done nothing with them. You haven't given them back to him, or anything. I know about the letter from the university. Is this it? Are you done with me? Bored?"

Each of his words cut her to the core.

"No, you're scaring me."

Instantly, he stepped back, giving her space. "I want to know what the fuck is going on, and I want to know now."

"I have the reservation letter because I wanted to talk to you about it first. Every time we're together you distract me."

"What do you need to talk to me about?" he asked.

"If you want me to think of moving to Piston County. I buy an apartment here, or rent, that's a great deal of commitment. I need to know that you want me here as much as I want to be here. If this is just some fun to you, then I don't want to be just that. I want to be something more."

"What makes you think you're just a bit of fun?" he asked.

"I heard a couple of women in town talking. I didn't know who they were, and I didn't stay around to ask them who they were either. They seemed to know a great deal about you."

"For fuck's sake, Lola, before you came along I was fucking every pussy that came my way. That's what I did. I fucked them, and forgot them. I haven't had a single pussy but yours since you came along. There is no one else. You call, and I come to you. Doesn't that tell you anything?" he asked.

"What?"

"I've fucking fallen for you, okay? Christ, Lola, you're nearly twenty, and I'm thirty-fucking-six. I'm older than you, and this wasn't supposed to be like this, okay? You need a man your own age, and I thought to myself, I can let her go, but you know what? I fucking can't. I don't want another man touching you. Just the thought alone makes me so fucking mad."

Tears filled her eyes, and Lola launched herself into his arms. "I'll sign the paperwork today, and I'll turn down the university."

"You will?"

"Yes. I don't need anyone else, just you."

He wrapped his arms around her, holding her close. "Don't ever fucking do that to me again, woman."

****

Spider sat in his trailer going over the recent reports. They had just passed the first initial inspection, and could now go toward completing the walls. The electrics had passed, and the gas had passed. Spider was more than happy with the progress of the apartments. Providing he could keep up the production of the team, this was looking like it could be completed within the next three months, fully. He liked those figures.

There was a knock on his trailer, and he called for them to enter. He was due to go out and check on all the recent work, but having them come to him would work as well. When heels clicked, he knew it wasn't one of the guys, and he looked up to see Paris. She wore a long coat that was tied at the front. Ever since their relationship had become physical, she'd gotten more adventurous. He enjoyed this side of her. The heels did wonders for her calves. She flicked the catch on the trailer's lock, and his cock thickened.

"What do I owe the pleasure to?" he asked, sitting back.

"You went to work early today."

"I had to drop some paperwork to Devil's house." Since Laurell had been born, Devil had spent more time at his home helping out Lexie with the kids. They had been on summer vacation, and soon Simon and Elizabeth would be returning to school. Josh would also be going to nursery.

"I see. Well, Celia had a play date with Beatrice."

Beatrice was one of the girls in the school that Celia attended.

Paris loosened the belt around her waist, and he watched as the jacket fell open. *Fucking hell.* She wore a bra that only held up her tits, and as she moved they bounced. When she took a seat on the table, and lifted first one heeled foot to his knee, then the other, he saw that she was also wearing panties that had a nice slit down the center, showing off her pretty cunt. He also saw that his little adventurer was wet.

Looking up into her eyes, he saw that she looked

a little nervous.

"Don't worry, baby, you're owning this."

"Good." She moved her legs and got off the desk to straddle his thighs. She wrapped her arms around his neck, and kissed his neck. "I was thinking about you, and about all the things we could get up to."

"Oh, yeah, and what were you thinking?" he asked.

"I was thinking that I'd like to suck your cock while your men are out working."

Damn, this woman was going to be the death of him.

Her hand moved between them, stroking his dick, which had only gotten hard from her whispering the sweet words into his ear.

"How would you like that?"

Wrapping his arms around her, he cupped her ass, drawing her in close.

"I'm wondering why you're not doing it already."

Paris sank to her knees, and he watched, holding onto his chair as she peeled away his jeans, and pulled out his long, thick, cock. She licked the tip, which was already leaking pre-cum. She moaned, licking the tip again, then sliding her tongue down the side where the thick vein pulsed. "Do you like that?" she asked.

"Fuck, yeah."

She covered the head and sucked him deep into her mouth. Spider tried hard to keep his eyes open so that he could watch her at all times. Every now and then, he closed his eyes, basking in the heat of her mouth as she sucked him in deep and hard.

Opening his eyes, he reached out, holding the back of her head. Her hair was still short so he didn't have the pleasure of wrapping it around his fist, and holding her.

She looked up at him, sucking him hard into her mouth, taking him until the tip of him hit the back of her throat. She pulled off until only the head was in her mouth. Using her hands, she worked the rest of him that she wasn't sucking.

He loved the moans she made as she sucked his cock, the pleasure humming all the way through his body. Spider loved everything about this woman. She was his fucking soul. His very reason for breathing at times. In the middle of the night, he'd wake up, and have to reach out to convince himself that she was indeed still there. He couldn't let anything happen to her.

"Fuck, baby, I'm going to come."

She didn't pull away, and kept on sucking him.

With the sounds of his men shouting backward and forward instructions, Spider came, filling her mouth with his cum. She swallowed him down, milking every single drop until there was nothing left.

She stopped when he was shuddering and couldn't take another second worth of torture.

Paris rested her cheek against his leg, and he stroked her hair.

"I love you," he said.

"I just wanted you to know that I love and miss you." She got to her feet, but Spider wasn't going to allow her to disappear like that. He got to his feet, putting his cock back into his pants, and buttoning up his jeans. He lifted her up, and placed her on top of his desk, urging her back. The coat lay open, and he cupped her large tits, fingering her nipples. "When did you get this outfit?"

"Yesterday. I went shopping with Lexie. She wanted to get a special something for Devil so that he knew she appreciated all of his help. I saw this, and thought it would be nice to surprise you."

"You did surprise me."

"Good surprise?"

"You've just milked my cock of all my cum, what do you think?"

She chuckled. "I think I did a damn good job."

Sliding his hands down her body, he slid his fingers between the slit of her pussy, finding her wet. Pushing two fingers inside her, he sank down to his knees this time and flicked her pretty clit with his tongue. She cried out, and he made her put her heeled feet on his shoulders, and pulled her a little closer to the edge of the desk. Sucking her clit, he teased her cunt, and drew her juices from her pussy back to her ass.

Paris tensed up, but she didn't stop him. He circled that tight ring, pressing inside her. Caressing her clit, he glided down to fuck inside her pussy, going deep, but not as deep as his cock would go.

Fucking her pussy, he teased her ass, and alternated between her cunt and her clit. Spider got her off on his desk, having her scream his name as she reached her climax, and as she did, he smiled.

"Wow," she said. "I hope no one heard you."

"If they did, they won't say anything. They'd know I'll kill them first."

"You'll be my hero?"

"Always." She cupped his face, kissing his lips. "Now, forgive me, but I did dream of this moment, and I have these waiting for you." He reached into a cabinet, and pulled out a skirt, shirt, and some underwear.

"You planned for this to happen?"

"Planned, hoped, prayed, you name it, I did it."

Paris took the clothes off him and quickly dressed. Spider even had a pair of sneakers for her to wear. There was nothing like being prepared.

Placing her seduction clothes into a bag, he

pressed her up against the wall. "I don't mind you wearing stuff like that, and giving me nice surprises, but no one gets to see what belongs to me."

"I gave that up a long time ago," she said. "You've got nothing to worry about. I'm all yours now."

"Good, would you like to see some of what we have going on here?"

"I'd love to."

Taking hold of her hand, he led her out toward the construction. None of the men showed any signs of hearing her, and treated her with politeness.

"Lola signed the paperwork, and gave it to me finally."

"Good, I'm glad. I really thought Sinner was going to lose her," Paris said.

Sinner was a goner, that was for sure. Lola and Sinner were two unlikely people who'd been able to find something together. He was rooting for them both.

****

Around Thanksgiving, the apartments were done, and the holiday season was in full swing, Devil had decided to take a visit to Fort Wills, and allow The Skulls to host a dinner. Christmas neither of the club was visiting the other, so Thanksgiving was the event. The Skulls and Chaos Bleeds had both decided at least twice a year, they were going to visit. One event would be in the summer for a picnic or barbeque where they caught up. The second would be either Thanksgiving or Christmas. Spider liked the tradition, and he also liked the relationship between the two clubs. It had been on the rocks a few years ago, and now it was back with full force, and nothing was going to stop that. Prue had given birth since the last time they had visited, and he got to see Killer and Kelsey's latest, David. Sandy was showing with her pregnancy, and Stink had become even more protective of her, if that was even possible.

Tate's little girl, Isabella was grown, and he was shocked to see Tabitha, Miles, and the others had all grown up as well. The clubs were changing, and without having to do the rides for drugs and guns, they were all flourishing. There was no fear of having to go to prison, which he liked.

Sally's latest prosthetic was turning out to be more successful than anyone could have hoped. She was still using crutches to help her, but with the fit, they had been able to strap it to her body, and she was practicing without the crutches.

"She's doing well," he said, talking to Steven.

The brother looked pissed.

"Yeah, she's doing good. She'll be graduating next year, and then off to college."

"What's up?" Spider asked.

"Nothing. I'm fine."

There was a knock, and then a guy Spider didn't recognize came in.

"Wrong, that's my problem."

"I'm sorry I'm late," the man said.

"It's okay, Drew, I saved you a seat."

Spider looked at Steven, and then at Drew, and back again. "You've got feelings for Sally."

"Ever since her accident, that little fucker has been sniffing around her. I don't get what his deal is, but I will." Steven looked ready to explode.

"Okay, does Sally know?"

Steven snorted. "I need some air."

Food wasn't ready, so Spider followed him out, curious to know what was going on. He found Steven lighting up a cigarette. Since staying with Paris and Celia, he hadn't touched them.

His woman didn't like kissing him with smoker's

breath.

"Do you know what's funny?" Steven asked.

"That you're hung up over a girl you could have."

"You see, she did have a big crush on me, and then she went and told me she didn't care. You know what, fine, you don't have a crush, I can deal with that, and now…" Steven took a long pull on his cigarette. "I care about her. I don't even know what I'm fucking feeling half the time. When I'm around her, she puts up with me. Yet that little shit who lost his fucking future, he's here, and now everything is fine, and I have to watch him fuck with her."

Spider listened to his rant. "Have you talked to her?"

Steven laughed. "I'm thirty-one years old, Spider. How the fuck can I talk to her about it? I'm not going to do anything about it."

"What about Whizz and Lacey? You talked to them."

"They like Drew. They think he's a good choice for her, and you know what? Any other time, I'd agree. He's a nice guy. Even I like him, which pisses me off. He's nice. Guys like him are supposed to be assholes, and do you know why I know that? Because I was like that. I was the asshole. I was the jerk in high school. I could bag any chick I wanted without any hassle. Just looking at him makes me so damn mad." Steven ran a hand down his face. "I'm sorry. It's Thanksgiving. I really shouldn't be unloading all this crap on you."

"There's nothing I can do to help you. Sally is too young."

"And I'm too old to tell other guys to back off. God, when did I get so old?"

"Thirty-one is not old."

"Speak for yourself. At least your girl is in love

with you."

"I'm going to propose to her."

"What?" Steven asked.

"I've got the ring picked out, and I even know when I'm going to do it."

"When?"

"Christmas morning."

"Dude, that's next month."

Spider shrugged. "It's time, and I want her to remember it."

"She's already head over for you."

"So? When it comes to Paris, I want her to remember everything, and to smile, and every little thing she sees, for her to remember why she fell in love with me."

There were a few seconds of silence, and then Steven groaned. "Fuck man, I'm in love with you." Steven threw his arms around him, hugging him.

Pulling away from him, Spider laughed, shaking his head. "You need to get a life."

"Nah, I'm happy with my life. For the most part." Steven looked behind his shoulder, and Spider turned to see Sally coming out, holding her crutches.

"I'm going to head on inside."

"It's okay. You can stay," Steven said.

"I'll give you a chance to make a better impression with the lady."

Spider smiled at Sally as he passed her, and made his way inside to his woman. He found her holding Prue's baby girl, Willow. Prue was sitting beside her.

"She's gorgeous," Spider said, moving to stand beside Paris.

"I won't lie, she was a handful, and giving birth wasn't exactly a picnic either. It was damn hard, but every second of pain was worth it."

"Didn't you have anything for the pain?" Paris asked.

"I didn't have time. She came, and she wasn't waiting for anyone." Prue smiled. "She's so spoiled. All she has to do is make a noise and Zero's there, picking her up, cuddling her."

Paris smiled and glanced up at him. "One day, I'd like for us to have a child."

Imagining her swelling with his kid had his dick hardening. Quickly pushing the image aside, he kissed the top of head. "Soon."

First, he was going to get his ring on her finger.

****

Steven watched as Sally made her way toward the swings. He saw the pain on her face, and he wished there was something he could do to take the pain away. She sat down, and he watched as she closed her eyes.

He, Whizz, and Lacey all knew the pressure she had put herself under to get this prosthetic leg. She trained with the physio every week, and she pushed her body to the breaking point.

"Are you okay?" he asked, moving up toward her.

She opened her eyes, and he saw the tears shining inside them. Sally blinked several time, and wiped underneath her nose. "I'm not okay."

"Tell me what to do."

"There's nothing you can do. I just need, I just need to feel the cold, and hopefully, everything will be better."

She was massaging her knee, and he frowned. "What's going on?"

"My leg, it's burning, like it was—"

"When you were at the hospital, just before they took it?"

She nodded. "Yes."

Kneeling down before her, Steven threw his cigarette to the ground, grinding it under his foot, and started to massage her leg. The moment he touched it, she cried out as if she was in actual physical pain.

"It's not there, Sally." He knocked on the prosthetic.

"Nothing is there."

Lifting up her pant leg so that her prosthetic and her real leg were showing, he made her see that she wasn't in pain. The pain was not there.

She started to take deep, controlled breaths like he'd seen her take in the hospital.

"Thank you."

"It's fine. How often do you get it?"

"Not often. Usually when I get distracted, and I forget. It's phantom limb or something. The doctor said that it's my memory believing the limb is still alive, and feeling. It's trying to cut the feelings off."

She rested her hand on his shoulder, gripping his jacket as he rubbed her leg.

"I get it." He'd talked to the doctor extensively about her leg.

"I never thanked you for all the time you spent in the hospital."

"Don't worry about it."

"It meant a lot, and even though I was a bitch, I appreciated you spending time with me."

"You had a good reason to be a bitch."

She snorted. "Not really. I shouldn't have been mean to you, and I'm really sorry."

"Don't worry about it." He kept on rubbing her knee, and stared up into her eyes. The fear that had once haunted her eyes in past years had gone. "What's with the doofus?"

"Drew?"

"You know it's him."

Sally smiled, even though she had pain. "I tried to tell you many times before. Drew is a friend. We share a common problem."

"He looks more than fine to me."

"He's in pain. His injury causes him problems, and when it seizes up, he struggles to walk. Drew's nice, and if you stopped being an asshole, you'd see that."

"It's hard not to be," he said.

"Why?"

"He gets to have a reason to be close to you."

"What?"

"You know what, Sally. I'm fifteen years older than you, but it doesn't stop the jealousy."

"Oh."

"Yeah, oh. Don't worry about it. I'll try." Steven knew that he had to stop being a miserable bastard otherwise he'd lose time to be with her. "Come on, I'll go and make it up to your friend."

Sally stared at his hand, and she took it. It was the start of a future, one that Steven hoped that he came out the victor.

Chapter Twenty-Three

Spider was acting weird, and Paris was finding his behavior a little scary. He was withdrawing from her, no, he wasn't. The man had her so confused. When she thought he was hiding something, he'd wrap his arms around her, and she truly believed she was imagining it. There was nothing wrong between them.

"Here, more tinsel," Lexie said.

"We're already decorated the main room."

"I know, and now we have some more."

Paris chuckled. "You really do love Christmas." This was her second Christmas with Chaos Bleeds, and she had already gotten her shopping done. It was Christmas Eve, and everyone was at the clubhouse, enjoying food, music, and laughter. Celia was dancing with Simon and Elizabeth on the dance floor. Her sister was so much better since being around the clubhouse. She was loved and cared for by them all.

Sasha took the tinsel from her hand, and climbed onto a chair.

"You shouldn't be doing that," Pussy said, coming to hold his wife by her waist.

"Shut up."

"Hold on!" Lexie held up her hand. "Why shouldn't she be doing that?"

Lexie's raised voice had caught everyone's attention, and seeing the warning in Sasha's hand, Paris was struggling to hold in the laughter.

"We're having a baby!" Pussy yelled the words, and the whole room erupted in a series of congratulations.

Paris hugged Pussy, and then Sasha.

"Congratulations to you both." She stepped out of the way to watch the happy couple who had only grown from strength to strength.

Rubbing her arms, she felt Spider come up behind her, and she melted against him. "Merry Christmas, Paris," he said.

"Merry Christmas, Spider."

He kissed her neck, and she felt so happy, so loved. "I'm really happy for them."

"Me too." She turned around, wrapping her arms around his neck. "Maybe one day that will be us?"

"Maybe one day that will be."

"Paris, honey, will you go into the kitchen and grab the champagne?" Lexie asked.

"Sure."

She pulled away from Spider and made her way into the kitchen, looking for the bottle of bubbly. Going to the fridge she saw it was full with champagne. Grabbing out two bottles as she knew everyone would want a drink, she turned around to pause. Simon was standing by the door staring at her.

"What's wrong?" she asked.

"It's a nice day, don't you think?"

"Yeah," she said, drawing out the word.

"Well, I thought it would be nice to say hello."

"What's going on?" she asked, moving toward him.

"No, stop, stay there."

"Simon, what's going on?"

"I can't stand for you to come closer. You're too beautiful."

She frowned now. Simon had only ever said that to Tabitha, and she doubted he was meaning it.

"I was thinking you could date me instead of Spider."

Paris smiled. "That is really sweet, but I'm in love with Spider."

"And I love Tabitha. Shoot, that was a bad improv."

"Improv? You mean improvisation?"

"Yep, learned about it at school, and I promised that I could do this, that I could keep you talking, and you wouldn't have a clue what was going on."

Staring at the door, she had seen he was guarding it. "Simon, what's going on?" she asked.

"Nothing."

"That's not nothing. You're hiding something."

"She's on to me," Simon said, yelling.

"This is silly," she said, stepping closer.

Simon disappeared, yelling as he did. "She's coming. I can't hold her back."

Opening the door, Paris came to a stop as the entire main room was dark, with the only light coming from candles. Wow, there were so many that the moment she left they must have started lighting them.

"What's going on?" she asked. As she stepped out of the kitchen, the doors closed with a bang, making her jump.

There was a small walkway, and she followed the tinsel. Chaos Bleeds stood on either side, and she looked at each of them as she passed, a little creeped out.

There, near the Christmas tree, down on one knee was Spider. He held a velvet box in his hands, and she paused.

"Paris," he said.

"Spider." She walked up to him, and as she did, her heart raced. "What is this?"

"I want you to be my wife, and this is me trying to make it the best moment in the world, only Pussy ruined it with his news. Not cool, man, this is my moment, and I told you to wait."

"Sorry, I couldn't help it."

Spider shook his head, turning back to her. "Paris, I'm in love with you. From the first moment I saw you stripping I knew I had to have you—"

"Keep it PG. I have kids here," Devil said.

Paris laughed, thinking about his words. Yes, they didn't exactly meet in the most conventional of places, but she still loved it.

"I had to have you, and then I lost you." Her throat thickened as she saw his anguish. "I was never going to stop until I had you back, until you were safe. I'll never fail you again. I will protect you. You're my other half, and even though men probably say the same old shit in these kinds of speeches, please know that this is spoken from the heart. I love you. You own me, Paris. I want to be the man you deserve. You want me to get you pregnant, well, I want you to make an honest man out of me, and marry me."

Tears filled her eyes, and she didn't stop them from spilling over.

"What do you say?" he asked.

She couldn't speak. Her throat was thick, so she nodded.

"I can't hear you."

"Yes, totally yes. It's about time you asked me. What took you so damn long?"

He stood up, and she threw herself into his arms, holding him tightly.

He pulled her away, long enough to put the engagement ring on her finger. She couldn't stop smiling as she took in the ring.

"You really mean this?" she asked.

"I was going to do it tomorrow, during presents. I had it all planned with everyone staring."

"Then he changed it to tonight with candles," Lexie said.

"He's been changing his mind for week," Sasha said.

"So, I figured I'd share our news, and that way, you'll get to bask in your own happiness as well."

"I love it, I really do."

He tilted her head back and kissed her.

"I can't believe you did this," she said.

"I'll do anything for you, Paris. Anything."

"You wouldn't even die. You kept on fighting." It was the first mention of Andrew for her in a long time. Whenever he did invade her thoughts, she always made sure to tell Spider about it. They never had any secrets from one another, and she hoped they never did. They had even talked about Andrew and Russell, Spider explaining to her his fear, and what it was like waking up in the hospital. Their memories, for Paris, had brought them closer together.

"Well, I had to protect the woman I loved, and the only way to do that was to be a stubborn asshole."

"You're the best stubborn asshole I ever know, and I love you for it."

"You better. I'm about to marry you because of it."

"Can I have everyone's attention?" Devil said.

Paris turned in Spider's arms. He held her tightly and kissed her neck.

"When I first started Chaos Bleeds, I didn't know the first thing about heading a club, or leading it. I'd left Fort Wills, without much to my name. I traveled, and I knew what I didn't want in my life. Along the way, I found you guys. Not all of you were in your best shape, but with the club you've found your reason to keep on living. We've been a club for over twenty years. Riding beside you has been one of my greatest pleasures."

"And mine," Pussy said.

All the men raised their hands in agreement, including Spider.

"Settling down in Piston County was a risk. None of you anticipated us staying here long, and then Lexie, you—fuck, babe, you took me and turned me into a fucking pussy. You had Simon, and then I just couldn't be without you." Lexie moved to his side, hugging him tight.

"We have faced many enemies, and not all of us have survived. Ashley, she didn't wear our jacket, but we all know she was one of us."

Paris saw Mia crying as she held her baby. Spider had told her the past of Chaos Bleeds. Simon was Lexie's sister's baby. Mia had been best friends with Ashley who ended up getting killed. So much death, and yet here they all were.

"I want to say it hasn't been an easy twenty years, but you know what, I wouldn't do anything different. We have what I thought a club never should be. We're a family, to the core of us. To family."

They all raised their glasses in the toast.

It was a fucked up family, but it was their family. Andrew had tried to come between them, but he had failed. They were stronger, and his memory would fade, until there was nothing left.

Epilogue One

The Skulls

One year later

Stink sat in the school's football yard, holding his baby boy, Philip. Sandy had gone to get them both some drinks as they waited for the ceremony to begin. Sally was graduating from high school and was moving away to college. Whizz and Lacey were freaking out about that, but they had also been the ones to encourage her to go.

It had been just three years since Sally had lost her leg, and Andrew's attack on the club. They had found a great deal of peace in recent years, and Stink loved it. There had been no more drama, no more past enemy waiting to take them all down, just living. With everything that had been happening in the club, he was more than happy for the break. He didn't want to worry about attacks, or his woman and kid getting hurt.

Philip clapped his hands together and started to blow raspberries. Stink chuckled, wiping away the spittle.

"He's always doing that," Sandy said, handing him a drink, and taking their son from him.

She had become a wonderful mother. In the early days of her pregnancy she had panicked about being awful, and Stink spent a great deal of time convincing her she'd be amazing.

Of course, he was right, and they now had a little family of their own.

"I bet she's nervous." He looked toward the school thinking about Sally.

"She has Drew to help her up, and she's earned

this. Anyone tries to ruin it for her, will face the wrath of the club," Sandy said.

They were all here. Some of the families were keeping a wide berth of them, and he didn't give a fuck. Sally was one of them, and no one was going to let her graduate without being here.

Stink watched as Millie arrived. She was by herself, wearing a pink summer dress. Baker was instantly there, and even though they weren't together, Millie had accepted his friendship.

"Do you think she'll ever trust him?"

"Only if he shows signs of getting over his wife. He doesn't even work in the bakery we have set up," Sandy said.

The Skulls now owned a gym, a bakery, and a beauty salon in town.

Sandy took a seat next to him, just as Steven joined them. Whizz and Lacey were in front with Daisy. The whole of The Skulls were there to watch as Sally walked out. She smiled over toward them, and Steven whistled, making her blush.

Drew was there, helping her. The principal got up, and started to talk.

"How are things with you and Sally?" Stink asked, whispering.

"We're doing good."

"How are you going to handle her going away to college?" Stink was curious. Steven had confided in him about his feelings for Sally.

"I'll do whatever makes her happy, Stink. You don't have to worry."

When it was Sally's turn to get her graduation certificate, she nearly stumbled on stage. The whole of The Skulls got out of their seat ready to help her. Drew took her on stage, where she made a quick joke, and accepted her certificate.

"One day Philip will be up there," Sandy said.

Stink kissed his wife's lips.

They had a future. Their life was filled with one more day, and Stink was going to love, support, and grasp this chance with every fiber of his being.

Epilogue Two

Chaos Bleeds

Paris and Spider got married three months after Christmas in a spring wedding, in a church. She didn't have to fight him to wear a tuxedo, but they all had to bargain for the rest of the club to wear them. For the next year after her wedding, they had babysitting duty, which neither of them minded.

They stayed in the house her parents once shared, but instead of leaving it as Paris parents' house, Spider made them put their stamp on the place. They redecorated with the club's help. Spider took over everything, getting the materials, and making sure she wasn't screwed over with the pricing. No one would mess with him.

Sinner and Lola moved in together. Their relationship was tense at times, but neither of them was hiding it from the club anymore.

There was no point in hiding it.

Sasha had given birth to a little girl, Shay, in the past few weeks, and the whole club was helping with the nursery. Pussy wouldn't let her put a nursery in their home before then as he believed it was bad luck for them.

When she was in the hospital, they all had to quickly strip a room, wallpaper, paint, and allow the fumes to dissipate before bringing in furniture. It was a mad rush, but Paris had found it funny watching nearly ten men try to squeeze into a room. She had the whole thing on camera, and every time she watched it, it made her laugh.

Paris was making a batch of cookies when Spider came home. Chaos Bleeds had bought another derelict apartment building, and Spider was managing the team to make sure they were getting the best out of their staff.

"Hey, Celia, did you have a good day today?"

Celia lived with them, and Paris was so grateful for their friendship. Her sister launched herself on Spider, and he carried her through to the kitchen, setting her down. Celia quickly grabbed a book, and started to read through it.

"How are my other two girls?" Spider asked, coming toward her.

"We're good. Your little girl likes me to know that she's still there, and waiting to come out."

He placed his hand on her stomach. She saw the wonder in his eyes as he touched her. "She kicked. My girl is going to kick ass."

"Yeah, she is. Did you get everything done at the construction site?" she asked.

"I wasn't there, baby. I went to Arnold Pritchard's ranch. He's not been doing so good, and Natalie is struggling."

The clothing store in town was doing better than ever. Paris worked there three days a week, and it was hugely successful helped by Lola's expertise with the online store. Natalie continued to design clothes, even though she had been approached by bigger companies. After Natalie's mother had her first heart attack, everyone had thought she was picking up, getting healthy. That hadn't been the case, and within three months she had suffered a second heart attack, and had not made it through the night.

The whole of Chaos Bleeds had been there at the funeral to pay their respects to a woman who had been kind her whole life.

Natalie had stayed at home more, trying to help out. The club did what they could, but now Arnold was looking ill, and the stress was taking its toll on Natalie.

"How are they?"

"Arnold wants to sell."

"What?"

"Yeah, he wants to sell. There's no boys to pass the ranch on to, and he doesn't want to burden Natalie with it. Natalie doesn't want him to sell. It's the only home she has ever known. It's tough. She can't handle the cattle, and the men are walking all over her."

"That's hard."

"It is. Arnold told me he had to get her to make a decision soon. He spoke to his doctor the other day, and it's not good."

"Oh, no, what?"

"Cancer. He's got a year tops, and he doesn't want to spend the last year of his life manning the ranch. He wants to spend it with his daughter. Slash thinks he has an idea, but I don't know if it will work." The baby kicked, and Paris held her stomach. "She wants to come out, doesn't she?"

"Yep, another month, and she can come out."

"Don't worry about Natalie and Arnold. Slash will think of something, and if not, Devil."

"I won't worry."

"Good." He tilted her head back and claimed her lips.

She'd worry about the rest of her friends tomorrow. For now, she had her husband, her sister, and her daughter, and in that moment everything was perfect.

The End

www.samcrescent.com

EVERNIGHT PUBLISHING ®

www.evernightpublishing.com

www.ingramcontent.com/pod-product-compliance
Lightning Source LLC
Chambersburg PA
CBHW031422240626
47154CB00001B/155